THE ASSASSIN'S BETRAYAL

AUSTON KING

CONTENTS

SIGN UP TO THE MAILING LIST

To sign up for my mailing list, please visit: www.creatorcontact.com/
auston-king/
The mailing list will only be used to update you about upcoming
releases.
NO SPAM.
I promise.

Thank you for purchasing this book. A lot of time and work has gone
into it and I truly hope you enjoy it.

If you spot any errors, typos with this copy, or would just like to
say hi, please let me know by emailing:
austonking@creatorcontact.com

I am always interested in hearing what people think about my
work.

Thank you and enjoy the read,
God Speed,
Auston King

PROLOGUE

Jason Drake ran down a side street off Pennsylvania Avenue in Washington, DC. He did his best to avoid making it obvious that he'd been shot in his lower back. Luckily, the bullet had missed his vital organs. His kidneys and the main aorta to his legs were fine—if they weren't, he would have been either dead or paralyzed. His only concern now was bleeding out. He figured he had less than thirty minutes before he was dead.

He compressed the wound with his hands and took a heavy and slow breath.

He'd have to keep his blood pressure low.

Droplets of blood stained the concrete.

If he turned around now, it would all be for nothing.

He had to keep going. He had to push through the pain. He'd gone through too much to get here.

Sirens echoed throughout the dark of the city. Police cruisers responding to the smashed-up SUV Drake had abandoned a quarter mile back. Inside, the CIA director's assistant. She was injured, but she'd make it. Surrounding the SUV were six bodies. The men who'd tried to stop Drake. They'd failed, but not before putting a bullet in his body.

Drake winced. He felt weak. He'd lost too much blood. He

leaned up against a brick wall to catch his breath. Then he saw it. He was close. Almost there. The glow from an art exhibit's spotlights danced across the clouds. That was the target. That was where it would end.

Wealthy elites in expensive tuxedos and flashy, sequined dresses walked by Drake, ignoring him. They were too lost in their own world of privilege and power to realize the puddles of blood on the street were staining their thousand-dollar shoes.

Drake chuckled at the thought.

As the moment of pain passed, Drake pushed himself from the wall and continued. He knew what the elites thought of him. They figured him drunk, what with the way he was awkwardly resting up against the wall. To them, men like Drake were blemishes, inconvenient truths, nothing to be concerned with—he was the help. Nothing more.

The rich assholes were all coming from or going to the art exhibit. The one put on by a Russian art dealer as an olive branch to help ease relations between the two countries.

Drake knew the real purpose of the exhibit, though. It had nothing to do with peace. Only war. And if he didn't get inside, six blocks of the US capital would go up in flames.

Covered in a thick sweat and feeling a bit better, he pushed on. He stumbled toward the entrance of the brick warehouse where the exhibit was taking place. Two bouncers stood on either side of the door. In his periphery, he spotted the black silhouettes of security personnel patrolling the rooftops with sniper rifles. They were watching him. Making sure he wasn't a threat.

The bouncers had eyes on him, too. Drake stood out like a sore thumb. His dirty leather jacket and hobbled steps didn't help. Neither did the fact that he was tall. He stood a full three inches over the next tallest man on the street. It was hard to blend in when you were six-foot-five.

Drake walked up to the bouncers and then stopped.

"Move along, pal," one of them said. "This is for invited guests only."

"Yeah, move it, buddy!" the other chimed in.

Their accents were Russian.

Drake pulled a pair of keys out of his jacket pocket. He dropped them and then bent down to pick them up.

"What the hell are you doing?" a bouncer said. "Are you deaf?"

Drake winced in pain as his knee hit the concrete. It felt like his abs were being torn apart. Blood pooled below him, staining his leather boots.

The bouncers' eyes widened. "What is wrong with you? Get out of here. You are not our problem! If you're injured, go to the hospital."

Drake grunted. "Do you think one of you could call an ambulance?" More blood pooled on the ground. "I've been shot. I need assistance."

The bouncers looked at each other and nodded.

"No," one of the bouncers said. "We're going to bring you out back and put you in the trash. That is where you belong."

It was precisely what Drake thought they would say. He was testing them. He didn't want to kill any civilians. He only wanted the crooks. He only wanted the criminals.

A bouncer approached him. The bastard looked tough, ex-military. Whatever Drake did, he'd have to be quick, and he'd have to play dirty.

With the speed of a lightning strike, he elbowed the bouncer in the crotch, grabbed hold of the guy's weapon from its holster, stood up, and kicked the other bouncer in the face. He turned around and kicked the first bouncer, the one who was nursing his genitals, in the temple. Both men dropped to the ground at the same time. It took two seconds.

The snipers on the rooftops were too slow to respond. They scrambled and radioed for help, but Drake was already inside the exhibit.

He cautiously opened the exhibit doors taking it slow so as not to attract any more attention. He made his way to the coat check, rendered the young man working there unconscious, and grabbed an expensive-looking blazer from the rack. He took off his leather jacket, buttoned up the blazer, and made his way back into the lobby. The blazer made him fit in better and would throw off the security personnel just long enough to buy him a few precious seconds.

The place was so packed, hardly anybody noticed. Like the rich snobs on the street who didn't notice the blood on their shoes, they were all too busy laughing at their boring jokes and wallowing in their wealth.

Drake walked into a large, open room. Each one of his steps sent tremors of pain through his body. He couldn't even feel his feet. He then stopped. He saw his target.

He clenched his jaw and pulled out the gun he'd stolen from the bouncer. He fired three shots into the ceiling. It was time to stop the spark that would start a world war.

PART 1 - THE BETRAYAL

ONE

Three months earlier

Andrei Zadorov was dying. Brain cancer. His own body had turned on him. It was inoperable, according to the doctor. Andrei would have to live with it, suffer through it, and die from it. A former spy, he thought it a fitting way to go out. An invisible enemy, cutting him down from the inside, only making itself known when it was too late. How many men had he killed the same way, he often wondered. Born in Sochi, Russia, he was born into immense wealth and power in the late seventies. Up until the diagnosis, he'd believed the world was his oyster.

His father was a wealthy oligarch with connections to the Russian president and military, a proud man who wanted nothing more than to see Russia return to its former glory and to see America burn. His mother was a celebrated painter. Educated and intelligent, she was as loyal to the motherland as his father.

Because of his father's influence in Russia and his mother's international art connections, Andrei entered the Foreign Intelligence Service of the Russian Federation, or the SVR, when he was in his early twenties. The SVR was the heir to the KGB after the collapse of the Soviet Union.

The SVR was also known as the Foreign Intelligence Service of the Russian Federation. It was Russia's equivalent to the CIA. Brutal, efficient, and above all else, dedicated to upholding Russian power and hegemony. Espionage, assassinations, disinformation—they got deep within the mud of international conflict, and they never shied away from taking the gloves off.

The top brass at the SVR figured Andrei was an ideal candidate for undercover operations, so Andrei was sent to Washington, DC, where he worked as a spy under a new identity. His alias, Dimitri Nabakov, was an art dealer.

He'd spent years in America. He found allies, uncovered secrets, and grew close to those with power. He was good at his job. No one in Washington suspected a thing. But then he collapsed while on a morning jog along the Potomac River. His head smacked against the pavement running path. Blood spurted out from the cut on his head. He felt nauseous. His hands shook with a violent tremor. The doctor found the tumor. Andrei went back to Russia for treatment.

His days as a spy were over.

As he lay on the hospital bed in Moscow, holding his mother's hand, the doctor told him he had three to five years at best. His father, a stout man with a mustache like Stalin, was shaken. Andrei was his only heir.

"My boy," he said. "This world is so cruel and unfair. I hate it."

"I thought I was going to change the world," Andrei said to his father. "I thought I was going to make Russia proud of our name."

"If things were different... if life were different, if this sickness hadn't burrowed its way into your head, you would have returned Russia to its former glory," his father said.

Shortly after the prognosis, his father began to drink, and his mother grew frail. They were both dead by the winter, taken by their sadness and perhaps their unwillingness to see their son buried before them.

Andrei inherited his father's wealth.

He could have spent the last few years of his life in luxury, but he didn't see the point of that. He wanted to honor his father. He made it his life's mission.

Russia was all that mattered.

He met with generals who had been friends with his father and some of the Russian president's advisors. They agreed to visit the young, dying former spy out of respect. Andrei told them that Russia couldn't idly sit by if it wanted to be great again. It needed to stop meddling in foreign wars. For too long, Russia and the United States had been fighting proxy battles. Wars of attrition where nothing was lost or gained. Abstract conflicts that benefitted the military-industrial complex only.

It was time to make America pay for its ignorance.

It was time to take the fight to them directly.

The generals and advisors laughed at him, thought him crazed. Andrei didn't see what was so funny, and he left the Kremlin more determined than ever, angry and bitter at his own country and the men who ran it.

If they weren't going to do what needed to be done, then he was going to use every last bit of the breath he had to make it happen. He used his father's money and traveled the world. He put in motion a plan knowing he might not live to see its fruition, recruiting people as desperate, as distraught, and as fatalist as he was.

That was why he was back in Washington, DC. Where it all started, where it all would end. He had re-assumed the identity of Dimitry Nabakov and once again ingratiated himself among the Washington elite. He began making plans to put on an art exhibit in honor of his mother, naming it after her. He called it: Natalay's Wish.

Of course, Andrei wasn't hosting an art exhibit.

He was going to force the Kremlin's hand.

He was going to start a war.

The newly risen sun was bright. Andrei was dressed in an expensive but minimalist-style suit. It was white with dashes of black—the cufflinks, the buttons. He stepped out of his BMW sedan and adjusted his tie. He looked up at the brick warehouse he'd rented for Natalay's Wish. It was two miles northeast from the White House. He'd hosted art events there in the past.

He walked up to the shipping doors, entered a passcode into the keypad, and waited.

The eighteen-wheeler truck that had followed him from New Jersey backed up toward the warehouse's shipping doors. The truck beeped as it reversed. Once inside, the driver turned the engine off and hopped out.

Andrei lit up a cigarette and watched as the driver got to work.

"Those things will kill you," the driver said in a jovial manner. He had a thick New York accent, and his white t-shirt had mustard stains on it.

Andrei shook his head and sighed. He didn't respond to the man who he knew was below him in almost every way.

The driver sensed Andrei's disdain. He shrugged. "Where do you want the boxes?"

"With the others. Along the wall," Andrei replied, happy that the driver had gotten the message. "I'll have my men take it all to the basement tomorrow."

The driver grabbed a jack and began moving the massive six-by-six wooden boxes out of the truck's trailer. There were thirty in total. They were nailed shut, and each one was marked with a black stamp that read: 'FRAGILE'.

Andrei didn't lift a finger while the driver unloaded the crates. He didn't want his manicured nails to get scratched, nor his suit to get dirty, but he also didn't have the physical strength. Each day was becoming a struggle. The cancer was winning.

It took twenty minutes for the driver to unload all the boxes. His shirt was damp with sweat. His thinning hair stuck to his plump face.

"What the hell is in those things?" he said. "They're all as. heavy as a damn piano!"

"Artwork," Andrei said.

"That's some heavy art you got there."

"They're sculptures from Russia. I'm celebrating history."

The driver shook his head and said, "Whatever, man. Well, have a good day, Mr. Nabakov. Nice doing business with you."

Andrei nodded and waved the driver away. But as the driver closed the door to his truck, a panel on one of the boxes fell loose. The contents inside were exposed and rolled out onto the floor. The driver saw what had fallen out from his truck's side-view mirror.

"Holy hell," he muttered to himself. "That's no art!" He stepped out of the truck and walked back into the warehouse. He approached Andrei. "Hey, what the hell is that?"

Andrei rubbed his brow and sighed. How many times had he told his people to make sure they used more than two nails per panel? Those boxes needed to be treated with more respect. He gritted his teeth, walked up to the driver, and said, "How much will it cost you to be quiet?"

"Two thousand."

"Of course, of course."

"No, wait... three!"

Andrei smiled. "Greedy man. Just wait here."

He walked to his sedan, opened up the passenger side door, and opened the glove box. He grabbed what he needed, walked back to the warehouse, and found the truck driver kneeling on the ground, inspecting the contents that had fallen out.

"You some kind of farmer?"

Andrei smiled. "It's like I said. It's a celebration of Russian history."

He walked up to the driver and pulled out a 9mm Makarov pistol. The driver froze when he felt something at the back of his head. Andrei pulled the trigger.

A spray of blood and brain matter splattered out from the open hole and mixed with the dirt and dust on the warehouse floor. The barrel of the Makarov still smoking, Andrei grabbed his cellphone with his free hand and dialed his assistant. He'd need someone to come in and clean up the mess.

After making the arrangements, he walked back to the box that had opened up and pushed the contents back inside. He broke out in a sweat in the process, which made him very frustrated. He hated feeling weak, but it needed to be done. The cancer in him felt like it was everywhere—all around him. It was in people like the truck driver, greedy assholes who stood in his way, or in the Russian politicians and generals who had refused to help and snorted in his face with pathetic smiles.

When he was done, he left the warehouse and drove back to

Dulles International Airport. He had to fly to Sochi that evening. He had a chemotherapy appointment that he couldn't miss, and he had to pick up the final piece of his puzzle, the weapon which he'd use to spark the war.

TWO

The ocean was dark and calm. Thunderclouds hung low in the sky, and the wind bellowed. Even inside the Goat's Grin pub, there was a chill. The windows rattled with the patter of heavy rain.

"I bloody hate this country," Clyde Colt said.

He looked out the pub's window and grimaced. He thought a vacation down to Brighton's beaches would be nice. He should have gone somewhere warm, somewhere where there were palm trees and pretty girls in bikinis that he could look at while he drank sugary drinks and pissed the days away.

The pub was mostly empty, save for the bartender and two overweight blokes who had round tummies, no chins, and exposed ass cracks.

I'm an idiot, he thought.

He finished his pint and turned his attention back to the soccer match. Manchester United were playing in the Champions League. The team they were playing, Barcelona, had just scored, and the player who'd potted the goal was parading around the pitch in celebration, rubbing it in.

"Pansy," Colt muttered under his breath. He tapped his fingers on the bar to get the bartender's attention. "Another pilsner," he barked.

The bartender, an older man with skin more weathered than the wood on the Brighton piers, nodded and got to work. He placed the pint in front of Colt and went back to his daily routine, washing the dishes, cleaning up the vomit that some drunk arsehole had left in one of the bathroom stalls the night before, and sweeping the floors.

Colt took a large swig of the beer and closed his eyes. He'd be drunk by four p.m. Again. But what else was a fifty-six-year-old SAS captain supposed to do on his four-week *mandatory* vacation? His superiors in London had forced him to take it. If he didn't, they said they'd retire him. Bunch of wankers, the lot of them. Tight arsed bureaucrats more worried about the results from Colt's last psychological and physical assessment than they were about actually getting shit done. Who cared if he had an irregular heartbeat, high blood pressure, and was prone to angry outbursts? He was in charge of one of the best troops in the SAS, and he always got the job done.

All Colt wanted to do was work, but they said that was the problem. For too many years, he'd been pushing himself too hard, and now it was time to take a break.

They didn't know that Colt had no choice. He had to work. If he didn't, his mind would wander back to the past, back to everything he'd lost. If he couldn't work, the only way he could escape those memories was by drinking. It was as simple as that.

He picked up the pint and chugged it back until it was all gone and then wiped the beer suds from his thick mustache. He was about to order another one when he felt a buzzing in his pocket. London was calling.

"Well, I'll be damned," he said. He tapped on the bar for another beer, let his cell ring a couple more times to piss off whoever was calling, and then answered. "What do you arseholes want?"

"How's your vacation, Captain Colt?" the voice on the other end said. It was his commanding officer, Graham Howe. His accent was upper-class, BBC broadcaster worthy, and he bothered Colt more than a kick to the balls.

"You're interrupting my third pint of the day. I need about six more before I can handle your voice."

Howe was an old vet who'd served as a helicopter pilot during the

Falklands War in the early eighties for the British Air Service. In the nineties, he'd worked as a helicopter pilot instructor with Colt. When he moved to the SAS, he'd brought Colt along with him. He put up with Colt's crude insults because Colt was good at what he did and because, deep down, he knew they were friends.

"You might want to wrap it up at two pints, old chap," Howe said. "Your vacation is ending early. I've got an assignment."

Colt's eyebrow perked up. "What?"

"According to intel from one of our assets in the Middle East, two thousand tonnes of ammonium nitrate fertilizer went missing from the Beirut port one week ago."

"How do two thousand tonnes of ammonium nitrate go missing? That's enough to blow up a small city."

"I know. That's why we're concerned. It was being held in a storage house close to the port, but when Lebanese officials went to transport it to a safer location, they were ambushed, and the ammonium nitrate disappeared into the desert."

"Why do you need me?"

"Why do you think?"

"My troops refused to do the mission without me?" Colt said, chuckling.

"No," Howe said with no enthusiasm behind his voice. "We couldn't give a damn about what your men want. We need you because the Beirut port master, the man who oversaw the shipment of the nitrate, has been spotted in Edinburgh. He fled Lebanon shortly after the ambush. If anyone knows where the missing fertilizer is, it's him. We need you to bring him in. And you know Edinburgh better than anyone else. It is your hometown, after all."

"Aye."

"Your troops are already in Scotland. They're waiting for you there. They've been rehearsing a house raid for a couple of days now. I need you to look over what they're planning, see if they have any blind spots. See if they've missed something."

"When's my flight?"

"Tomorrow. We've secured a runway at Gatwick. You'll fly in a private jet to Edinburgh. Can you be in London by the morning?"

"I'll be there."

"Good," Howe said. "I'll send you the rest of the details tomorrow. You can look them over during the flight. Oh, and Colt? Before I go, I want to make sure that you feel healthy enough to complete this assignment—"

Colt hung up before Howe could continue. He grabbed the pint the bartender had just placed in front of him and downed it in one swig. He slammed the glass down on the bar and took a deep breath. It was a good thing he was going back to work. He was getting tired of the drinking.

He went to leave a twenty-pound note on the bar, but when he opened his wallet, he saw the past he was running from—a small photograph behind a plastic sleeve. The photo had been taken years prior. Happier times. The happiest of his life.

His boy died after the photo was taken. He and his wife separated shortly after that.

He pulled out a twenty-pound note, closed his wallet, and put it back in his pocket.

He left the pub and went to the bed and breakfast he was staying at, gathered his things, and took a short nap to sober up. Once he felt better, he left the town and made his way to London.

As he sped down the motorway, the BBC sports anchor read the Champions League game results. Manchester United had won. A miracle comeback, they said. Colt smiled. He felt good. He knew he'd feel even better when he was back with his troops.

THREE

The flight from London to Edinburgh gave Colt time to run over the operational details. From the looks of it, it was simple stuff. Raid the house, bring the port master in alive for questioning, and leave without waking the neighbors.

The sixty-two-year-old Beirut port master was believed to be alone in the house, and was unarmed. In other words, he wasn't a threat. But London was worried he was going to run. They wanted him quickly and cleanly. That was why they weren't sending the police.

Colt took a cab from the airport and was dropped off at the warehouse where his troops were rehearsing the operation. He stepped out of the cab, pulled out a pack of cigars, and lit one up. As he walked inside, a brisk wallop of cold Edinburgh air followed, and he was met with a big, loud, "Hurrah!" from his troops.

He smiled. Cheeky bastards. All of them.

His troops were getting their gear ready. Their faces were painted in camouflage, shades of green, brown and black. They had their combat gear on, too.

Gaz, the troop's frontman, walked up to Colt. He was holding an AC900 Kevlar helmet, wore suede abseil gloves, a Nomex III assault suit, an assault vest, and GSG9 army boots. In terms of weapons, he was carrying an H&K MP5A5 assault rifle, and as a sidearm, a Browning L9A1 pistol. His vest was strapped with extra magazines and clips for both weapons. Three flashbang grenades were strapped to his vest, too, along with a pair of night-vision goggles, just for good measure. He was ready.

"How was your holiday?" Gaz asked Colt.

Colt shook his head. "Don't be a smartarse, mate."

Gaz laughed. "When I heard they put you on mandatory leave, I burst out laughing. I'm surprised you didn't put Howe in a headlock and render him unconscious."

"Who says I didn't?"

"I'm glad you're here."

"Me too." Colt gestured to Gaz's gear. "Let's get down to business."

"Alright," Gaz said. "Did you notice any blind spots in our operation?"

"Just one."

Gaz shook his head. Colt always found something. "What did we miss?"

"You're going through the front door?"

"The backyard is fenced off. The guy inside is in his sixties. I figured we'd all go in through the front. Rush him. Take him head-on. Grab the bull by the horns, y'know? He won't get far if he runs."

"You're thinking with your dick, mate," Colt said. "You need to split up in the front garden. Slow and steady. Don't tempt fate. A man in his sixties might still be in good shape. After all, he got out of Beirut quickly enough. You should go through the back of the house first, let three of your mates monitor the front. If he runs, they'll grab him."

"Got it, sir."

"I know you do," Colt said. "When do we leave?"

"One hour."

Colt smiled. "Damn, it feels good to be back."

FOUR

There was a gentle rain. The street lights looked like orange globes floating in the dark, and save for the sound of an ambulance siren three miles west and the rattle of an approaching train, it was quiet. Another gloomy night on a suburban street in the southwestern end of Edinburgh.

In the shadows, across the street from a three-floored, redbrick townhouse, Colt's six SAS troops waited for direction from their captain. The men were hidden within the shadow of an old willow tree.

Colt was a block away, in the back of a white Mercedes-Benz Sprinter. He listened via headphones and watched a video display from a camera Gaz had set up a day earlier on a hydro pole across the street from the house.

For the past few days, the troops had been watching the house, paying attention to even the smallest detail; when lights turned on and off, when the bins would get taken out, when curtains would close. Everything.

"Easy, boys," Colt said into his mic while taking a long drag from his cigar. He exhaled and filled the back of the van with a thick plume of white smoke.

"Final light is out, sir," Gaz said. "We're good to move."

"Stay frosty," Colt said.

Gaz looked at the house from his position of cover and gripped his assault rifle. He nodded at his team. "Let's go," he said.

The troops nodded back and followed Gaz toward the house. Every step and action was set to a timer. It was clockwork. It had to be.

Gaz leaped over a pile of dead leaves clumped together at the street's curb and rested up against a stone wall that shielded the house's front yard. He counted to three, which gave the rest of the troops enough time to catch up and mimic his position. "About to split up," he said to Colt via his mic. "As you requested."

"Atta boy," Colt said.

Gaz maneuvered out of the cover. Two others in the troop followed him. The remaining three waited behind. He guided the two men following him down a small alley that led to the backyard, where they found a swing set, a sandpit, and some children's toys. It looked suburban. Innocent. Gaz shook his head. In the days that the SAS had been watching the house, they'd never seen a child come in or out. The toys were just a ruse to keep the neighbors' suspicions at bay.

Once the backyard was secure, Gaz pulled out a small, foldable titanium ladder from his backpack. It was no larger than a computer monitor, and it weighed less than three pounds. He hit a switch on the ladder's rail, which made it sprout upward and downward at the same time. It was ten feet tall by the time it was fully lengthened and strong enough to hold the weight of one four-hundred-pound man. He placed the ladder up against the house, resting the top rung below the lip of a second-floor window. He lowered his night vision goggles on his helmet and grabbed hold of the first rung, then waited for the train to approach.

He climbed up the ladder as the train tracks that ran behind the backyard began to rattle. Once at the top, Gaz checked his watch. Fifteen seconds. He pulled out a small pressurized explosive device and stuck it to the second-floor window. As the train passed, he ignited the device with a trigger attached to his vest. The sound of the passing train concealed the pop of the explosion. The device shattered the window's glass, making it easy for Gaz to stick his hand through and unlock it. He pushed the window frame up and climbed inside.

The two SAS officers who'd followed him to the backyard performed the same action but at a ground floor window.

With his night-vision goggles down, everything in the house was bright and glowed green—Gaz saw everything as if it were clear as day. He was in a bedroom. There was nothing on the walls and no one in the bed. In the corner of the room was a mattress on the floor. Next to it was a lamp—simple, sparse. Whoever lived here wasn't planning on staying for long.

"We're inside," he said to Colt.

"Anything unusual?" Colt asked.

"Only that there's nothing. This place is mostly empty."

"Keep looking."

Gaz moved to the bedroom's exit, placing his shoulder against the door's frame. He heard the footsteps of the troops on the ground floor.

Once the ground floor was clear, the SAS officers outside the house, in the front garden, were given the signal to approach the front door and were let in. Gaz met them all at the top of the stairwell on the second floor and whispered, "Anyone else in here?"

"Doesn't look like it, sir. He might already be gone."

Gaz nodded and updated Colt. He then led the rest of the team through the house. They were surgical in their approach. No stone was left unturned. With only one floor left to check, Gaz radioed Colt. "Last floor," he said. "Still no sign of the port master. Do you think he fled? This guy's a damn ghost."

"He's in there," Colt said. "I can feel it. Just watch your six and make it count. Remember, we need him alive."

"Will do."

Gaz led the team to the top floor. It was the attic, and there was only one entry point: a door at the top of a narrow, steep stairwell. He stopped when he got to the top. He heard someone talking in the attic.

"I did what you told me," the man in the attic said. He had a Lebanese accent. He sounded irate. "I didn't run. I did everything you told me to do!"

Gaz turned back to his troops and smiled. "We've got him."

The man in the room continued, "Screw you! You'll never find me... Oh really? Well, if you've found me, I'll tell the world what you plan to do. I'll tell the world where you are! I'm the one who delivered the goods! I helped them get the stuff out of the country ... What do you mean? Rot in hell!"

The port master was marching around the room. His footsteps were loud and heavy.

"Let's move," Gaz said.

His men nodded, and Gaz kicked open the door. But instead of running inside, he tossed a flashbang grenade and waited for the bright blast to ignite. The disorienting device blinded the old man.

"Get him," Gaz shouted to his men.

The port master fell to the floor. His cellphone was in his hand. His vision was still adjusting from the effects of the flashbang. "Who are you? Are you them? Are you here to kill me?"

"You're coming with us," Gaz said. "We're SAS. We're bringing you in for questioning."

"Oh, thank Allah! I'll tell you everything. Everything!"

"Come on," Gaz said. "We need to go."

He and his men handcuffed the old man and lifted him up from the floor.

Colt continued to listen in and watched the security camera from inside the van. His troops had the port master. He was about to jump up into the driver's seat and meet them all at the front of the house when he noticed a white moving truck appear on his surveillance screen. The large truck came to a stop directly in front of the house and blocked his view of the front door.

"Hold on, Gaz," Colt said.

"What is it?"

"We've got a truck outside."

"A truck?"

Colt watched the video monitor closely. The footage was grainy, and he couldn't really make out the driver. It looked like a skinny man wearing a black suit and balaclava. The thin man jumped out of the truck and ran to its trailer. He opened it, tossed something inside the trailer, and then ran off.

"Oh no," Colt said. "Gaz, you've got to move. Get out of there."

"We're making our way downstairs now, sir."

"Hurry!"

Gaz and another trooper carried the old man down the steps toward the ground floor. It was clumsy and awkward, but they did their best.

The port master sensed something was wrong. He began to cry. "They're here," he said. "They said they were here. We are all dead."

"Shut up," Gaz said. "We're getting you—"

Colt's earpiece turned to static. The video feed turned snowy.

"Gaz?" he shouted. "Gaz!"

The shockwave from an explosion one block away made the van rattle. Colt fell over and climbed into the driver's seat. He kept repeating his troops' names in his headset as he drove to the house, but there was no response. Just static.

He saw the billowing, bright red clouds of smoke emerge above the suburban treetops of his hometown as he careened the van around a tight corner. He knew what had happened before he saw the truth. The truck that had parked outside the house his men were in had exploded. The house was leveled, as were the two other houses on either side of it.

Colt jumped out of the van when he saw the flames. He walked up to the ruins. Sirens bellowed in the distance. Neighbors walked out onto the street. Colt fell to his knees. They were all gone. His men were dead.

He felt a pain in his chest. One he'd never felt before.

His left arm stiffened.

He grunted, fell on his side, and began to convulse. He felt numb.

One of the civilians who had come out of their house to investigate the blast rushed to Colt's side. Colt couldn't move. He closed his eyes, and his world went dark. He wanted to die. He wanted to be with his troops.

But that didn't happen.

FIVE

A stroke.

Colt's doctor said if not for the good Samaritan who'd rushed to his aide, he would have been dead.

The wanker, he thought.

He spent two months in the hospital and a month in rehab. He missed the funerals for his troops. He missed his chance to say goodbye to the men he'd fought alongside for years. When he was finally released, he returned to his apartment in London and found a letter on his floor.

From her Majesty's Royal Military,

This letter is an acknowledgment of your dedicated service to the Royal Air Force, the Royal Marines, and the Special Air Service. Thank you for your patriotism and commitment, and we wish that the next stage of your life, your next endeavor, is fruitful, fulfilling, and rewarding. Your hard work and dedication will ne'er be forgotten. Your commitment to Queen and Country was unparalleled.

Thank you.

God Save the Queen,

Graham Howe.

Forced retirement. Whatever you wanted to call it, Colt was now officially done with the SAS. He called Howe and complained about the letter, fighting for reinstatement, telling his commanding officer that it was bullshit. But Howe said the matter was out of his control. Colt's medical history made it impossible for him to be a captain, and the fact that the operation had gone so terribly wrong meant that London needed someone to blame. Howe said he'd keep Colt in mind for a training position, but space was limited, and Colt would need to pass several psychological assessments before being allowed back. They couldn't have him damaging the young recruits with his 'old-school' mentality, as Howe put it.

So that was it. Colt was just a citizen. He was alone.

He just had the memories of the past, which he could only escape with a diligent commitment to alcohol: six beers before dinner, six after. He'd be in bed by ten, and then he'd wake up at noon and repeat.

It'd been three months since the explosion and he was tired. His whole body felt sore. He felt like a corpse.

His alarm buzzed, and he pushed himself upright. Hungover and pissed off. He took the heart medication that rested on the table beside his bed, washed the pills down with an almost empty can of pilsner, and stumbled into his kitchen.

He sat down at his dinner table, atop of which were a pile of newspaper articles relating to the missing ammonium nitrate. No one had found it. A mystery, the papers said. Vanished into thin air. London had covered up the explosion in Edinburgh. No one knew that the explosion and the missing ammonium nitrate were connected. London told the press it was a gas line explosion, and that was it.

Colt sighed, stood up, and stretched. He needed a walk, and the cold air would sober him up enough that he'd want to drink again. He splashed his face with some water from the faucet, got dressed, grabbed his overcoat, and greeted the crisp London air outside his apartment. He made his way to his favorite pub, which was the closest pub to his apartment.

Once there, he found a spot far enough away from everyone else that he couldn't hear their conversations. He just wanted to drink.

There was a pilsner on the bar before he sat down. Colt nodded at the bartender, picked up the pint, and drank it slowly. His mind wavered between thoughts of the past and his dead troops. His little boy. Gaz. He felt like he'd lost his second child that night in Edinburgh.

The highlights of the latest soccer match played on the television, but Colt barely noticed. He rubbed his brow and tapped on the bar to signal he'd need another pint soon. He was spiraling out of control. Would he last another year? With a ticker like his, probably not.

"Long time no see, Clyde. Mind if I join you?"

It was a familiar voice. Very familiar. A voice he hadn't heard in a long time. He turned around, his eyes red from lack of sleep, his face flushed. He smiled. "I didn't think I'd ever see you again, Kate."

It was his ex-wife, the mother of his dead son.

Kate Price was American, CIA, and a real pain in the arse. She was the only woman in the world strong enough to put up with Colt's gruff nature. The last he'd heard of her was that she has become the director of a special Black Ops division called Terminus. Like him, after the death of their child, she'd thrown herself into her work. The only difference was she rose up the ranks, and he'd stayed a captain.

"You've changed," she said, gesturing to his belly.

"You look the same."

He wasn't lying. Her hair was a little grayer at the roots, her skin a little more wrinkled around the eyes, but she didn't look fifty-four. Hell, she didn't look a day over forty.

"Are you drunk?"

"I'm working on it."

"You're an idiot," she said.

"Well, I haven't changed that much then, have I?"

Price laughed and sat down on the barstool beside him. They stared straight ahead, and both sighed. Their relationship had ended bitterly. They were angry at each other, angry at the cancer that took their child away from them—angry at everything. But those old emotions were just scars on the skin now. They were fading, as all things did.

The silence was beginning to make Colt uncomfortable. "What are you doing here, Kate? Is this an intervention or something? You haven't talked to me since—"

She cut him off before he brought up their dead son. "No, this isn't an intervention. And I don't want to talk about the past. That life is over. Graham Howe, said you'd be here. I want to talk."

"The bastard is still watching me, eh?"

"He cares about you."

"Well, if the arsehole wanted an update, he should have just called."

"He told me you had a stroke."

"I did."

"You're older now," Price said. "You need to slow down. He's just trying to keep you around."

"What for? I've done what I was put on this earth to do, and now I have nothing left. I'm a dinosaur, a relic. I just want to drink."

"The Clyde Colt I knew never felt sorry for himself."

Colt shook his head and yelled out to the bartender. "A pint! I need it now. My ex-wife just showed up."

The patrons at the bar laughed.

Price shook her head and smiled. "You see me for the first time in ten years, and you just want to drink."

"You have that effect on people, love."

She pulled her stool close to his and kept her voice low. "I heard about your troops," she said. "I'm sorry. They were looking for the missing ammonium nitrate, right?"

Colt nodded. "Aye."

She tossed a brown envelope on the bar in front of him. "Read it," she said.

"What's this?"

"Just read the damn document."

The bartender placed a new pint in front of Colt. Colt reached for it, but Price stopped him. "Read it, then drink."

He grunted and opened the document. Inside was a white piece of paper.

URGENT
For Kate Price

The document was stamped with a thick red 'classified' marker.
"A communications document?" Colt asked.
"Keep reading."

Transcript from Ali Bajal (recording)
To Kate Price, an old friend:
Please send Jason Drake to these coordinates: 34.8021° N, 38.9968° E in three days at midnight to meet AK. Only Drake. Concerns the location of the ammonium nitrate. AK knows where it is.
End transmission

"Is this real?" Colt asked. He rubbed his eyes and read over the transcript once more. He couldn't believe it.

"Yes," she said. "It's genuine. Along with the transcript, there were pictures. Apparently, this AK person knows where it is. They want to tell us. Well, they want to tell Jason Drake."

"Can you trust the person who sent it?"

"Ali Bajal was a contact my Black Ops officers used in Syria. He owns a nightclub in Damascus, the Zorba House. He's an arms dealer on the side. We used him to transport weapons to the Syrian rebels when we were aiding their cause. Can we trust him? No, we can't, but we have no other lead. It's worth the shot."

"And why are you showing me this, Kate?"

"Because I need your help."

"The transcript asks for Jason Drake. Shouldn't you be talking to him?"

Price called out to the bartender. "Whiskey on the rocks," she said, turning away from Colt and drifting off into the past. She spoke as if she were talking to herself. "Terminus was shut down five years ago. We were the ones you called when you had no other option. But things went wrong when one of my officers went rogue. He killed a US senator and disappeared. The CIA have been looking for him ever since. Due to the nature of the incident, Terminus was disbanded."

"Explains why you're not CIA Director yet," Colt said. "I'd figure you'd be in charge of that place by now."

"After what happened, I knew Director was never going to be for me."

The bartender placed the whiskey in front of Price. She shot it back, winced, and took a deep breath.

"But what does your story about Terminus have to do with me?"

"Each one of my Terminus officers had been given psychological enhancement training, injections of various drugs to increase their endurance and mental faculties. We were told they were safe ... maybe they weren't."

"You still haven't told me why you need me."

Price looked at Colt and smiled. "Jason Drake was the officer who went rogue. He's the one who killed the senator and the reason why Terminus was shut down. He's a wanted man. I need you to go to him and tell him what's in the transcript."

"And where is he?"

"He's been on the run for years. The Director of the CIA, Tom Fowler—remember him?"

"Aye, the man with the big nose and the nasally voice. How could I forget? I almost punched him in that nose during our wedding night. He's Director now?"

"Yes. He's an asshole, and if I tell him about Jason, he'll end this operation before it even begins. He's too caught up in Washington politics. He's too worried about his job."

"I see," Colt said. "So Jason is on the run. He's hiding. And you can't use CIA resources to get him."

"That's right."

"And he's former Black Ops, which means he's good at hiding."

"Very good."

"And he's a murderer?"

"He had his reasons."

Colt shook his head. "So, how do we find him?"

"I already have."

"What?"

"One year ago, I read a report in a San Juan newspaper about a man the locals call El Soldado or The Soldier. He keeps to himself, stays in the shadows. He's earned a Robin Hood-like reputation down there."

"You think it's Jason? Why?"

"The locals described a scar under his left eye, and ..."

"And what?"

"His piercing blue eyes."

Colt burst out laughing. "Blue eyes and a nickname, that's all you've got?"

"Yes."

"And why don't you get him?"

"If I go down there, or if I send anyone I trust from Langley, he'll run or send them back in a bodybag. He'll sniff us out faster than a bloodhound does an injured deer."

"And what do I tell him? Hey, Mr. Jason Drake, do you want to come to help the organization that's hunting you down?"

"No," Price said. "I want you to tell him that I can clear his record if he helps with this."

"Can you?"

"I don't know, but it's worth a shot, and we need him."

Colt shook his head. "You know, this is why I never joined MI6. You spies live twisted, sordid lives."

"And you don't?" Price said. "You're trying drink yourself to an early death."

"I thought you said this wasn't an intervention?"

"Listen, I just need you to go down to San Juan. Find Jason and tell him that he's the only chance we have at finding the ammonium nitrate. That transcript I received from Ali Bajal was sent to me yesterday. That means we have two days to get Jason to Syria to meet AK."

Colt took a long swig of his beer and mulled over his options. If he stayed in London, he'd continue to drink and maybe be dead by the fall. Gaz and the rest of his troops would still be six feet under, their deaths still in vain. But if he went to Puerto Rico, if he found Jason Drake, he might be able to give his troops some peace. Hell, he might even be able to convince Howe to let him back into the SAS. "Alright," he said. "I'll see what I can do."

"I have a ticket for you. It'll take you to San Juan." She pulled out a brown envelope. "That's everything you need. The flight's at six a.m. When you get to San Juan, ask around for El Soldado. From my experience with Jason, he's probably in the seediest, most dangerous bar in town. If you look for trouble, you'll find him."

"Sounds like my kind of guy," Colt said, stuffing the envelope in his pocket. "Well, now that that's settled. Where are you staying tonight, love? It's been a while."

Price smiled, leaned in, and whispered in Colt's ear. "Not with you."

SIX

The North Atlantic Ocean loomed like a dark void out of the cab's back window. The sun dipped below the horizon, and the whole sky was painted in a deep blood red. Colt exhaled a long and heavy breath.

"You okay, *amigo?*" the cab driver asked, noticing Colt's expression in his rear-view mirror.

Colt rubbed his brow. "Yeah," he said. "Just need a pint."

The cabbie smiled and nodded. "The nectar of the Gods."

"Damn straight."

The cab driver was bringing him to the dingiest, seediest, most dangerous bar in the city: *el Concha Polvorienta,* the Dusty Clamshell. When Colt approached the cab at the San Juan airport, he'd asked where he could find fast drugs and cheap women. The cabbie turned off his radio and then smiled at Colt. "You want fun?"

"I want danger."

"I know where you can get both."

The cab rolled to a stop. Colt paid the driver and greeted the salty, humid air. The sounds of laughter, music, and the crashing waves against the shoreline gave the place a vacation-like atmosphere. This was where he should have gone three months ago. Why the hell did he choose Brighton?

The Dusty Clamshell's corrugated metal siding was rusted and warped. The neon sign that displayed its name had been drilled too close to the top of the roof so that it swayed and flickered from even the slightest of breezes. The stench of a rotting animal crept out from inside a large garbage bin. It made the whole place smell like a dump.

Colt pulled a cigar from his pocket, stuck it in his mouth, lit it up, and walked to the front door. He was about to push his way inside when a man twenty years his senior warned him in English, "You'll find only trouble in there, *padre*."

"That's what I came here for."

The older man laughed.

Colt pushed open the door and walked inside. The place was busy, loud, and smelled even worse inside than outside. Drunk tourists. Drunk locals. Drunk bartenders. After walking past a crowd of prostitutes who looked underage, he walked up to the bar, scanning every face he saw along the way. Price had given him a picture of Drake, so he knew what the guy looked like. Square-jaw and blue eyes. The only other defining feature was his height.

Colt placed his hands on the bar and waited for the bartender.

The jukebox played forty-fives in the corner, and a drunk patron had just selected Little Richard's 'Long Tall Sally (The Thing)'. As the song began to play and the record's cracks and pops reverberated throughout the tight space, Colt bobbed his head to the rhythm. The song reminded him of his youth. He used to listen to American military radio stations when he was falling asleep. His appreciation for the song was interrupted when the bartender, a young guy with a thin mustache and slicked-back hair, slammed his palm on the bar to get Colt's attention. Like everyone else in the bar, the bartender knew Colt wasn't a local so he greeted him in English. "What do you want?" His Spanish accent was thick and heavy.

"Pilsner."

"We don't have any beer, *padre*. Only spirits."

Colt shook his head and mumbled to himself, "What kind of bar doesn't have a beer?"

"What will it be? I'm busy!"

"Right, right." Colt looked at the selection of drinks on the wall behind the bartender. "Gin and tonic," he said, and then out of frustration added, "amigo."

The bartender nodded and walked off to prepare Colt's drink.

"Damnit," Colt muttered. All he wanted was a nice cold pilsner.

As the bartender placed the gin and tonic on the bar, Colt leaned in close and slid the bartender the photo Price had given him of Drake. "You know this guy?" Colt asked. "Goes by the name El Soldado, I believe."

The bartender looked at the photo, then at Colt and then back at the photo. "You should leave."

Colt's eyebrow rose. Price was right. He was here. "I want to talk to him," he said to the bartender. "Where can I find him?"

"Leave," the bartender said. He snatched the gin and tonic he'd just placed in front of Colt away. "You're not welcome here!"

Colt reached in vain for the drink, but he was too slow. "Shit," he muttered to himself as the bartender walked away.

He'd have to find Drake another way. He turned around and continued to look around the bar. Someone would tell him where *El Soldado* was. He just needed to find the right person.

There was a large brute of a man sitting in a booth. He had a sleeve of tattoos on both of his arms and up to his neck. He was chatting up one of the young prostitutes, grabbing at her waist and not letting go of her arm. She tried to push him away, but he wouldn't let her.

If Drake was attracted to trouble, then he'd have to get close to trouble. Colt walked up to the brute and said, "Excuse me, mate. I think the girl wants to be left alone."

The brute loosened his grip on the girl's wrist and cursed in Spanish as she ran into the crowd of patrons. He turned to Colt and said in broken English, "Bad move. Don't know who am? Tough guy."

Colt shook his head. "No."

"I'm a monster. I'm going to mess you up."

He pushed himself up from the table, slamming his large, thick hands down on its top, knocking over his drink in the process. The disturbance got the attention of the other patrons. The bar grew quiet. All that could be heard were the final bars of 'Long Tall Sally' and the odd burp.

"Are you scared?" the brute asked.

Colt took a long drag of his cigar. "I'll walk away if you tell me where this man is." He pulled out the picture of Drake. "El Soldado? I want to know where to find him."

The brute smirked. "Is that a threat?"

"Threat?"

The brute didn't respond; he just swung his tree-trunk-sized arms wildly at Colt. The man had no sense of purpose or direction with his swings. He relied on pure testosterone and intimidation. Each swing missed Colt by a mile. The patrons laughed at the stumbling oaf of a man.

Colt stepped back. "Listen, I just want to talk to El Soldado. I don't want to fight."

"I'm El Gallo," he said. "The Rooster! Top cock! I'm king of this bar. That man ..." The oaf spat on the floor of the bar. "El Soldado is a coward. He's scum. He thinks he's some hero, but he's a bum. A washed-up—"

One of the patrons had stepped forward and put El Gallo in a chokehold. He held him for three seconds, waiting for El Gallo to pass out. Once he felt the other man go limp, he dropped him onto the floor. El Gallo's limbs were splayed out like the limp neck of a dead chicken. The other patrons went silent again.

The lighting in the bar was dim, so Colt couldn't quite make out who the man who'd interfered with the brute was, but he looked large—tall. "Who are you?" Colt asked.

The man stepped into the light. Colt's eye widened. The man's eyes were blue, and he had a sharp, square jaw. It was him. "Jason?" Colt asked.

Drake struck Colt in the face, right on the temple. Colt fell to the ground, right next to El Gallo. His world went dark, but he'd found the man he was looking for. El Soldado.

SEVEN

Colt woke up groggy and tired. He was in desperate need of a drink. As his eyes slowly focused, he realized he was in a small trailer. There were weapon cases on the floor, maps strung by pins to the walls. He tried to move but couldn't. He was manacled. His wrists and ankles were tied to the arms and legs of a small wooden chair.

"Who are you? What were you doing at the bar?" Drake asked in a low and growly voice.

"I wanted a drink," Colt said.

"Tourists don't go to the Dusty Clamshell for drinks. They go for trouble. And they definitely don't go in there with pictures of ex-CIA officers in their pockets."

Colt chuckled.

"What do you want with me?"

"You didn't have to hit me across the face, mate. I'm an ally."

"And you didn't have to pick a fight with *El Gallo*. That's my job. The guy's been bugging girls in that bar for months now."

"Kate Price said you were drawn to trouble. I needed to find you."

Drake pulled a knife out from his pocket and stabbed it into a thick, wooden coffee table. The action took less than a second. He was quick. Accurate. "Are you CIA?"

"No," Colt said. "I'm SAS."

Drake growled and stood up. He looked like a towering beast in the small trailer. He was so tall that his head hit the ceiling. His shoulders were as broad as an Olympic swimmer's. "Do you want a beer?" Drake asked.

Colt smiled. "Yes, I do."

Drake walked to a small fridge in the corner of the trailer. He was wearing denim blue jeans and a green t-shirt that was ripped and had grease stains. He'd been working on his motorcycle all afternoon.

Aside from the fridge, the kitchen was mostly bare. A slow cooker and a coffee maker. That was it. He lived meagerly and humbly. He lived like a man who was ready to move in an instant.

Drake opened the fridge, pulled out two beers, and sat back down across from Colt. He placed the beers on the coffee table next to his knife.

"Either the blade or the beer. It's your choice."

"Is that a threat?"

"What do you think?"

"I'll take the beer."

"Then you'll tell me what Kate wants. Why are you here?"

"She needs you."

"That's what she always says."

"She needs you to go to Syria."

"She must be crazy if she thinks I'm going back to that hell hole."

"A contact of hers says he knows someone who knows where a stockpile of missing ammonium nitrate is. But they'll only talk to you."

"How inconvenient."

"Listen, if you help Kate with this, she'll wipe your slate clean. She'll make sure the CIA doesn't continue to hunt you. She told me you're a wanted man."

"I doubt she'll do that."

"I'm sure you have reasons for doubting her, but I can tell when she's telling the truth."

"How?"

"I'm her ex-husband."

Drake smiled. "That's not a very convincing argument."

Colt tried to switch gears. He had another angle to get Drake to relax. "Have you heard about the missing ammonium nitrate?"

"Yeah, I watch the news. I've heard about it."

"What wasn't in the news is that six SAS troops died looking for that stuff."

"They were your troops."

"Yes."

"My condolences, but if you think that's going to help me do whatever Kate wants me to do, you're mistaken. The CIA wants me dead. I'm a wanted man. This is probably some ploy to get me back state-side. And even if it was a mission, I'm done. The CIA is as crooked as a dog's hind leg."

"Listen, mate. Do you want to keep running your whole life?"

"I'm happy doing what I'm doing."

"Dealing with small-time criminals? Living like a bum?"

"Yes."

"Just let me tell you what Kate's plan is. This operation is off the books. It's just you, me, and her. No other CIA officers are involved. She's told the Director she's running a fact-finding mission in Iraq. She's rented a bunker in Al Asad air base. It'll serve as our operations center—you're going to be safe."

Drake cut him off. "You don't know when to call it quits, do you?"

"No, I don't."

Drake picked up the blade. "I was doing some good here. I was cleaning up this dump of a city up, but now I'll have to leave. I knew I should have been more cautious."

"Are you going to kill me?"

"No," Drake said. "I want you to give a message to Kate."

"What's that?"

"The next person who comes looking for me will die. CIA or not. Understand?"

"You sound like a real nice guy."

"I'm what they made me."

"In my back pocket, there's a copy of a transcript Kate received. If you cut my wrists and ankles free, I'll show you."

"Your testing my patience."

"Just read the damn transcript. Stop being a wanker."

Drake rubbed his brow. He cut Colt free from the wires holding him to the chair. Colt grabbed the beer Drake brought from the fridge and took a long swig. It tasted good as it slid down his throat—he downed the whole bottle in one go.

"The transcript," Drake said.

"Right," Colt said. "Here." He pulled out the transcript and handed it to Drake.

Drake read it over and then froze. Colt noticed Drake's pupil's narrow, his muscles tense. Something in the transcript had triggered him, knocked him off balance.

"You need to leave," Drake said. "There's a main road a mile north from here. Follow it east and it will take you to town. From there, you can catch a cab to the airport."

Colt sighed. "If you want to keep running, stay here," he said. "I'll be at the airport in the morning." He pulled a small envelope from his pocket and threw it on the floor of the trailer. He left and followed Drake's instructions back to town.

Drake opened the envelope. There was a passport inside. It was Canadian. He flipped it open and looked at the picture. It was his, but it wasn't his name. Wyatt Barlow. He stuffed the passport in his pocket, stood up, and walked to a small couch in his trailer.

The source in the transcript. AK. *Could it be her?* Memories of Syria flashed through his head. His final mission with the CIA. Kill the Butcher of Baghdad.

Aya Khan was his desert guide. He thought she was dead.

Was AK Aya Khan? Was she alive?

EIGHT

Drake turned on his television and tried to let it pull him away from thoughts about his past.

The news anchor, a man who looked like he had a pickle stuck up his ass, talked about the US president, Roy Clarkson. "The president's approval ratings are at an all-time low," the anchor said smugly. "With the election just months away, many in Washington believe President Clarkson's days are numbered. In response, Clarkson brought up the fact that the US economy under his watch has never been better. Aidan Stark, the man running against him, scoffed at the president's remarks, calling them an obvious deflection. Stark said that Russian and American relations are at a dangerous precipice, adding that one mistake could trigger a war. My opinion: we need assurances from our Commander-in-Chief that he is taking the threat of Russian military action seriously. Making matters worse, Clarkson still hasn't been able to locate the missing two thousand tonnes of ammonium nitrate ..."

Drake changed the channel and rubbed his brow. He didn't need the news. He flipped through channels, his mind a maze of thoughts and regrets. Was Aya Khan alive? He'd spent months after the incident looking for her.

He stopped flipping through channels at ESPN. Highlights from the night's hockey games were on. His favorite team, the Dallas Stars, were in the midst of the NHL playoffs first round. Their opponent, the San Jose Sharks, were gritty and talented. The Stars were in for one hell of a fight.

He gulped back a beer and watched the highlights, and drifted off to sleep. But his dreams betrayed him and brought him back to the past.

———————

THE BUTCHER of Baghdad was an Islamic State commander. One of the worst. He was an ex-Iraqi army general who had a penchant for ritualistic, medieval-style killings. Unlike other ISIS leaders, he wasn't dogmatic about his religious beliefs; he just wanted an excuse to kill. He'd burn people alive, behead them, feed them to wolves. The CIA believed he was impossible to kill. The man was a human cockroach, they said. No matter how many drone strikes they threw his way, he always managed to survive. Price's Terminus division was called in as last resort.

Price sent Drake to Syria to do the impossible: kill the Butcher.

The agency had little intel on the Butcher, so Drake had to track down the mass murderer himself, which he knew was going to be difficult without help. The Syrian desert was vast and complicated.

With the help of Ali Bajal, Drake struck a deal with the Syrian rebels. If the CIA gave the Syrian rebellion force weapons, they'd provide Drake their best sniper and tracker. Her name was Aya Khan.

Drake met Aya in Bajal's club, the Zorba House.

He was nursing a rum and coke when she approached his booth. At first, he thought she was one of Bajal's girls. A gift. Her hips swayed with a seductive rhythm. Her green eyes glowed like the waters of the Gulf of Mexico during sunset. He couldn't keep his eyes off her.

"Are you Jason Drake?" she asked.

"Are you here to entertain me?"

"I'm the sniper."

"You're the sniper?"

"I'm the one who's going to help you kill the Butcher. Who did you think I was?"

"You're ..."

"I'm a woman?"

"It's not that."

"Then what is it?"

"You're just not what I expected."

She blushed and then pulled out a pistol from her holster and placed it on the table, spilling some of Drake's drink in the process.

"I will help you kill the Butcher, and you will give my people weapons."

Drake smiled. She was tough. Beautiful and deadly. "We leave in the morning," he said.

She put the pistol back in its holster. "Good."

For six months, Drake and Aya hunted down the most wanted man in the world. They spent their nights camping under the stars, sleeping in caves or in the ruins of the ancient cities that dotted the Silk Road, the medieval trade route that connected the Eastern world to the West and was the central conduit of travel and trade between the two regions until the eighteenth-century. The name was given to the route because silk was the primary item traded from China to Europe during that period. Syria was a land full of history and danger.

During those months, Drake developed more than a physical attraction to Aya. The fire and passion that burned within her soul were as intoxicating as her beauty. She was fighting for something bigger than herself, and she knew it. She often spoke about how she felt the eyes of destiny were staring at her and no one else. She said she knew she had a bigger purpose. She said that once the rebels had toppled the corrupt Syrian government, she'd dedicate herself to helping those in need.

"I'll be a school teacher," she said, lying next to Drake, looking at the stars.

"How many men have you killed?" he asked her. "The only thing you could teach children is how to pull a trigger."

She punched him in the arm, rolled over, and embraced him. They were miles from anyone else. Alone in the world, save for each other and their mission.

"I could teach the girls how to spot bad men," she quipped.

"Oh, really?"

"Yes."

"And what does a bad man look like?"

"Like you."

He laughed.

They made love.

She was young and hopeful despite growing up in a world full of death and destruction. She believed something good lay at the end of her country's struggle. She believed democracy and freedom would prevail. Drake wasn't so optimistic.

The night they'd finally tracked the Butcher down was the night of the Syrian incident. The night he knew he was done with the CIA. It was the night that changed his life.

A bright moon had turned the desert sand a milky blue. Drake and Aya rested atop a small sand dune that overlooked a dip in the desert. One hundred yards away were four tents. Four of the Butcher's men were guarding the perimeter of the campsite. The Butcher knew he was being tracked. That was why he was hiding in the middle of the desert, in the middle of nowhere.

But men like him always carry an insurance policy. He knew he'd be found eventually. To mitigate the threat of a drone strike, he had his men kidnap a bunch of children from local villages. He was using them as a human shield.

The day before the incident, Drake and Aya stumbled upon the body of a dead child. The Butcher was trying to send a message to those tracking him.

The child had been tortured. Brutally. His face was frozen in a final moment of terror. Despite growing up amid a civil war, Aya had never seen anything like it. When she saw the child's body, a darkness crept into her world and made her feel less hopeful, less sure about the light at the end of the tunnel.

She leaned over to Drake, who was looking through his night-vision goggles at the campsite, and asked him, "Do you see the children? Are they still alive?"

"Yes," Drake said. "Three in each tent. I'll make sure the CIA don't send in a drone. This son of a bitch is evil. We'll have to use our rifles. Time our shots. If we miss, the Butcher's men will fire on the kids."

Aya pulled out her rifle. "If another child dies, I'll never forgive myself."

"I need to call my handler," Drake said. "Let her know the situation, let her know that the predator drone won't be necessary."

Drake tapped his headset mic on and informed Price, who was stationed at Al Asad air base in Iraq. "Calling Watcher, you read?"

"Loud and clear," Price said.

"The target is in sight, but we've got a problem."

"What is it?"

"Children. He's using them as a human shield. We'll have to use rifles."

There was a muffled sound on Price's end. She was talking to someone and covering the mic. It sounded like she was yelling. She came back on. "Confirmed, Jason. Use your rifles. Make it quick. Call me when you're done."

Drake tapped Aya on the shoulder. Together they readied their rifles.

"I've got him in my sights," Aya said.

"I've got one of his men," Drake said. "On three."

"One, two, three," Aya said.

They pulled their triggers at the same time. Thunderous roars rang out and howled through the desert valley. The head of the Butcher exploded into a mist of pink blood. Bone, flesh, and brain splattered against the side of his tent. The cockroach was squashed. Finally.

Drake and Aya dropped the rest of the Butcher's men with relative ease. It was simple.

Aya felt a sense of relief, catharsis. She stood up. "The children. Let's go! We can save them!"

Drake knelt down and called Price. "We've hit the target," he said. "We're going to the site."

"Roger that."

Drake turned off his headset and followed Aya, who was halfway down the slope of the dune, to the campsite.

He then heard something in the sky. He looked up. It sounded like a lawnmower. It was a predator drone. It flashed across the face of the moon. He knelt down and called Price again.

"Calling Watcher," he said.

"What is it?"

"That drone is awfully close to the campsite. Are you sure it's called off?"

"Yes."

"Then what is it doing here?"

"What are you talking about?"

NINE

Aya and Drake ran toward the tents. The sounds of crying children reverberated through the valley. The cries reminded her of the frozen face she'd seen in the desert. It seemed to be caught in some sort of perpetual cry of agony. She couldn't see that again. She wouldn't let it happen.

"Aya, wait up!" Drake called out. He was fifty feet behind her.

She didn't slow down. Her mind was too focused on the children and their faces. She was so close. She ran to the nearest tent and pulled open its front flap. There were three children inside. They were in a metal cage. Their faces were bruised, their skin dirty, but they were alive. "You're safe!" she said to them.

She pulled out her sidearm and shot the locks off of each cage door. She then guided the children out of the tent.

FIVE THOUSAND FEET above the desert, a General Atomics MQ-1 Predator drone flew in for the kill. Its pilot was sitting in a dimly lit, air-conditioned trailer located in Creech Air Force Base in Nevada. The pilot looked at the glowing video and data screens in front of him, toggled the joystick that controlled the drone gently, and lined up the targets. It was like a video game. Four tents. They all needed to burn. He'd just gotten word from his commander that he was clear to engage.

He didn't know any of the specifics about the target. He was just told to pull the trigger and unleash hell. Which he did.

The one-thousand-pound drone, powered by a Rotax 914F 4-cylinder air-cooled piston engine and armed with two AGM-114 Hellfire missiles, fired on the target. Both Hellfires sped up to just below Mach one. Whoever was at the campsite wouldn't have time to react.

The pilot in Nevada yawned as the screen turned bright. His job was done. His day over. He'd been in the trailer for twelve hours, a typical shift for a drone pilot in the military. His eyes glazed. He stood up, stretched, cracked his knuckles, and sipped his energy drink.

He didn't know what he'd just done. He had no idea that he'd created a monster.

DRAKE SAW the light from the Hellfire missile rockets ignite. He knew it was too late, but he couldn't stop; he wouldn't give up. He ran toward the campsite and Aya.

"Aya!" he screamed. "Aya!"

The missiles struck almost in sync, and as they hit, Drake's body was flung to the slope of the dune. Fragments of metal chewed up his arm and punctured his leg and chest. He tried to get up but couldn't.

The campsite was a crater, a burning, smoldering pit of death and destruction.

"Aya," he mumbled. His words were breathy and weak. "Aya." He couldn't see her. "Aya!" He passed out.

WHEN HE CAME TO, he was in Al Asad Air Force Base's medical bay. A doctor with a long face and pale skin was staring at a medical chart. She noticed Drake's eyes open.

"Hello," she said.

"Where am I?"

"Al Asad."

"What happened?"

"You're lucky to be alive," she said. "Your body was littered with over eighteen pieces of shrapnel. You're going to have a nasty scar on your cheek."

"Aya!" Drake said. "Where is she?"

"Aya?"

Drake took a deep and labored breath. He'd never told Price about Aya. He'd never told anyone about her. He simply referred to her as the 'guide'. He didn't want anyone at Langley to know how he felt. "Where is Aya?"

"Who?" the doctor asked.

"A woman," he said. "About twenty years old. She was with me at the campsite."

"You were the only survivor the air force pulled from the wreckage."

"And the children?"

"You were the only survivor."

Drake didn't say anything else to the doctor. He didn't say anything when he spoke to Kate Price on the phone later that day. She was back at Langley, trying to put together the pieces, trying to find out how the drone strike, which she'd believed had been called off, had, in fact, occurred.

"The doctor said you were lucky," Price said to him as they spoke on the phone.

Drake, on his medical bed, growled, "Did you order it?"

"Order what?" she said.

"The drone."

"Of course not, Jason."

"Then who did?"

"I don't know yet. I'm working on it. I'll tell you when I know."

He hung up.

Over the next few months, he found out what had happened. A US senator. Ted Glimsbey had used his influence to get the drone to fire. Glimsbey had shares in some new drone technology and pulled strings. He needed his new drone tech to take out a big target. The Butcher was as big as they got. He got the air force to launch the strike, even though the CIA had called it off. Glimsbey didn't care about the kids or Drake. He was more concerned about the message, and his wallet. If the drone technology that he'd invested in worked as well as the air force said it did, he'd make millions.

When Drake returned to the states, he found Glimsbey and killed him. Point blank while he slept.

While the CIA had no proof that Drake was connected to the murder of the senator, Drake's disappearance made him a chief suspect. And that was that. Drake stayed in the shadows and eventually found refuge in San Juan.

But if Aya was alive, if she wanted him, he'd have to find her. He'd have to find out what happened the night of the incident. He needed to know.

TEN

Drake awoke from his dream in a cold sweat. He hadn't dreamed of Aya in years. It was three a.m., and he'd been asleep for four hours. He got up from his couch, stretched, looked around his trailer at the life he'd been living for years. He felt ashamed. He'd been running for too long.

He stuffed a change of clothes, a couple books, and a water bottle into a duffel bag. He'd have to leave his weapons. He wouldn't be able to carry them across customs.

He dug a hole in his backyard and buried his weapon cases there. Once he was done, he hopped on his motorcycle and rode to the airport.

As the sun rose above the horizon, he arrived. He used the dummy passport Colt had given him at check-in and picked up his ticket. Colt was sitting at the gate, wearing a Tilley hat pulled low over his face.

"This better not be some game," Drake said, dropping his duffel bag on the floor.

Colt jumped. "Jason?" He pushed himself up from the uncomfortable plastic seat. "I knew you'd come. The way you looked at me when you read that transcript. I know that feeling, mate. Who's AK?"

"It's just you, me, and Kate?" Drake asked, not wanting to answer Colt's question.

"Yes."

"Good," Drake said.

"Who was AK?"

"Just get this straight," Drake said. "I'm not here because of your dead men. I'm here to talk to Aya and to get what Price needs, and then I'm going dark again."

"Aya?"

"Aya Khan. AK. She's a woman I knew in Syria."

Colt smiled. "It's always about a woman, isn't it?"

Drake sat down and looked out at the tarmac. The 777 that was going to fly them both to London, then to Germany, then to Iraq, was getting fueled up.

Colt kept his eyes on Drake the whole way. He was wary of the CIA officer and his abilities, but also in awe of them. While Price had warned him in London that Drake was violent, he'd never met anyone who was so quick or precise. It was as if a ghost had emerged from the patrons of the Dusty Clamshell and struck him in the head. He hadn't had a chance to react.

Their boarding passes were called at the gate, and both men grabbed their luggage and boarded the Boeing 777. They flew commercial from San Juan to London, and then London to Ramstein Air Base in Germany. After twelve hours in the back of commercial airliners, eight warm beers between, and twelve shitty meals, they boarded a C-17 at Ramstein and took off for Iraq.

Six hours later, Drake walked down the loading bay of the C-17 and took in a deep breath of dry desert air.

Al Asad air base was located in the Anbar province and was the second-largest US military air base in the country. It was home to the II Marine Expeditionary Force/Multi-National Force West, among many others. The base was big and heavily fortified. One could argue that it was the safest place in the Middle East. The US president often made visits to the air base ahead of Thanksgiving. It was located one hundred miles west of Baghdad and resided within a part of the Syrian Desert that was mostly composed of rock and gravel. The land surrounding the base was flat and desolate.

The sun felt heavy. Drake followed Colt to the hanger and wiped his brow. Neither man had talked to each other since San Juan. Both knew there would be time for chit-chat later.

Wearing civilian clothes, Drake stood out among the grunts who'd disembarked from the military transport plane. He could feel their eyes watch him as he walked toward the hangar. He found it amusing.

He'd once been a grunt, too. He knew they'd gossip and whisper to each other when they got to their sleeping quarters. They'd theorize over who that strange man with the duffel bag and the leather jacket was. It was how they'd beat the boredom. That was one thing they never told you in the recruitment flyers. Life in the army was mostly hurry-up-and-wait. Those soldiers had nothing better to do than shoot the breeze and gossip like teenage girls on prom night.

Colt held the door open in hangar 2A, and Drake walked inside. A deluge of harsh light spread into the dark space. There she was.

"I never thought I'd see you again," Price said to Drake, knowing it was his silhouette standing at the door.

"This better not be a trap."

"It's not. No one at Langley knows you're here."

"When this is done, I'm leaving."

"That's fine. I won't follow."

"Will you clear my name?"

"I'm a director at the CIA, Jason. I have connections. You help me, I help you."

"What's the plan?"

"We have coordinates where AK will be. You're going to fly to the location tonight. We don't have a lot of time, so we won't have long to go over operational details."

"Good," Drake said. "The quicker this is over, the better."

He pulled up a seat across from Price's computer station. On her monitor was a map of Syria. There was a red dot blinking on the map in the middle of the country. "Is that where I'm headed?" he asked.

"Yes," she said.

He nodded. "How many hours until I leave?"

Price turned to him and said, "We have a Black Hawk helicopter on stand-by. It's scheduled to leave in three hours."

"And weapons?"

"Whatever you want. The armory is close by. Take what you need."

Drake smiled. That was the first bit of good news he'd heard all day.

Colt walked into the hangar and sat down. "Are you going to tell her about Aya Khan?"

"Aya Khan?" Price asked. "Is that AK?"

"She was the guide I was with when I was hunting the Butcher."

"She was with you? I thought you said the guide died?" Price asked.

"That's what I thought."

"What's she like?" Colt asked.

"She's a sniper," Drake said. "Trained. Efficient. When she joined me, she was working with the Syrian Democratic Forces or the SDF."

"A Syrian rebel?" Price said.

"Yes."

"You think she's still fighting for the rebellion?" Colt asked.

"I don't know," Drake said.

"Why do you think she reached out to you?" Price said. "If AK is, in fact, Aya Khan."

"I don't know, but I want to find out."

ELEVEN

Drake boarded the Black Hawk and was flown to the AO.

A sharp breeze ran loose over the desolate terrain. Yellow, red, and brown stones jutted up from the dry, flat rock like the claws of a dying animal reaching for warmth and light.

Looking down at the terrain from inside the helicopter, Drake became aware that the civil war that had ravaged the country for ten years was far from over. Blasted out shells from exploded bombs, burned-out vehicles, and bodies littered the desert like something out of a post-apocalyptic movie. It felt like a land caught between the living and the dead.

The chopper dropped him off deep within the southwestern Syrian desert, close to the coordinates Ali Bajal had given Price.

As the Black Hawk ascended into the dark sky, Drake walked through the desert and pulled out a small GPS device to confirm his location. He scanned the horizon. He spotted a tent a mile away and walked toward it.

He was wearing generic insulated black tactical pants, standard-issue boots, pilot gloves, and a bulletproof tactical vest overtop a thick, insulated, long-sleeved compound shirt. On his shoulder was an M4 assault rifle outfitted with a quad rail system so he could add several accessories. Among those was a handle to help with close-quarter maneuvering. In front of that was a laser-light LED. On top of the rail, he'd attached a holographic reflex sight with a floating reticle. The final accessory was a collapsible stock. The gun felt light, was easy to handle, and would be powerful and accurate enough to rely on in a range of scenarios. His sidearm was a Beretta M9 9mm, the primary sidearm of the United States Armed Forces.

It was colder than he'd thought it would be. He'd forgotten just how cold Syria could get. He cursed himself for not putting on another layer.

The tent was held down at the corners by large stones as the soil was too hard to drive stakes into. Outside was a smoking fire pit.

Drake took a deep breath and was about to enter when he saw her silhouette cast from the light of a small oil lamp inside. Her figure looked as spellbinding as ever. It was her. AK was Aya Khan. He opened the front flap, allowing a gust of wind to rush inside and make the light from the lamp on the floor flicker.

A ghost. The woman he thought dead was alive.

He was attacked. Not by her, but by an old friend.

A large dog jumped up from the floor of the tent and pounced on him, making him lose his balance and fall onto his side. The animal had been chewing on a bone from a dead goat, and its breath stunk like rotten meat.

"Down boy, down," he said, pushing the dog back, gagging at its bad breath, and surprised to see that it was still alive.

The dog ignored Drake's command and kept licking his face and wagging its tail like an excited puppy. The dog, whose name was Houston, was well over ten years old, but age hadn't slowed it down one bit. And clearly, it hadn't forgotten who Drake was.

"Houston missed you," Aya Khan said from the corner of the tent, a wry smile across her face. She put her sniper rifle over her shoulder. It was a PSL-54C, corrugated and with a spring-loaded stamped steel buttplate, which helped reduce recoil.

Drake pushed the dog away and sat on the floor of the tent. He grabbed a rag from his pocket and wiped Houston's slobber from his face. "You could've helped me a bit there?"

"And what? Spoil the fun?"

He looked up at her. *Was she real? Was any of this real?*

He wanted to tell her he was sorry, that the drone strike wasn't his fault. He wanted to tell her that he'd searched for her for months after the incident, but he couldn't find the words. Instead, he said, "You still use the PSL?

She looked at her rifle. "It's my baby."

"I tried to find you ..."

"Don't," she said. "Let's not talk about the past. As far as I'm concerned, I died that night. When I woke from the wreckage and found you unconscious, I left you. I knew you were alive, and I knew the CIA would come looking for you, but after what they did to those children ... I ..."

"I understand."

"It became clear to me that night—the world was not what I thought it was. I knew you were looking for me, but I made sure to stay hidden."

"You're still as beautiful as ever."

"And you're still as handsome." She gave him a seductive look. "Come here."

He smiled and embraced her.

"I missed the way you taste," she said.

They looked into each other's eyes and stayed silent for what felt like minutes.

"Do you want to know where the ammonium nitrate is?" she asked, breaking the silence. "That's why you're here, isn't it?"

"That's why the CIA brought me here, but that's not why I'm here."

She smiled.

Houston was licking Drake's boots. He turned around and patted the dog on the head. "I missed you, too, old boy."

He'd rescued the dog shortly after arriving in Syria. It was after he met Aya for the first time. He'd found the animal lying under an abandoned truck in Damascus, emaciated and with a piece of metal sticking out of its hip. What struck him about the dog when he found it was that it wasn't whimpering or scared. Its eyes were fixated and determined. Its breaths were slow and labored. It wouldn't let go of what little life it had left. It wasn't going to just accept death. It was fighting, clawing, accepting the pain, and willing to die struggling for every last second. Drake admired the animal's will. Its breed was Canaan, also known as the Bedouin sheep dog, common in the Middle East.

Aya picked up the bone Houston had been chewing on and tossed it outside the tent. The dog ran after it.

"We should leave," she said. "We have a bit of a hike ahead of us. I'll show you where the fertilizer is."

She got up and crawled toward the tent's exit. She made sure to exaggerate her hip movements in Drake's face. He reached for her and pulled her back toward him. The two of them kissed passionately, but before he could go any further, she pushed him away.

"There will be time later," she said.

She pushed herself up, and opened the flap of the tent, and checked on Houston. The dog was looking up at the mountain that loomed above them. There was a blinking LED light flashing about halfway up.

"They are on the cliff," she said.

"They?" Drake asked.

"You know what Syria is like," she said. "It's not safe to travel alone. My brother, Ajmal, and a group of rebels are going to guide us toward the fertilizer."

He shook his head. "Your brother is an idiot," he said to Aya. "He almost got us killed in Aleppo."

"I know, but he's all I have."

Drake nodded, and the two of them left the tent. He helped her pack up her campsite and then followed her up a ridgeline toward the cliff where her brother and the other rebels were waiting. Houston stuck to his side like glue as they ascended the mountain.

It was good to be back, Drake thought. It felt like he was home.

TWELVE

Inside hangar 2A at Al Asad, Price watched a satellite feed on her computer monitor. A weather map was overlaid on the digital feed. She'd just finished reading an email from the CIA director and was feeling agitated.

Kate,

Base Commander Tusk at Al Asad air base has updated me with the status of your so-called fact-finding operation. The president is hounding me to get to the bottom of this missing ammonium nitrate. If you help me with this, I'll be sure to help you out.

Don't let me down.

-CIA Director Tom Fowler

She rolled her eyes. Typical groveling Fowler. Relying on the work of everyone else to get ahead. Taking credit when an operation went well, and deflecting blame went it went wrong. He was conniving and dishonest. It was why he was CIA director and not her.

Price was too honest. Too blunt. She'd pissed off too many people and had too few friends.

After the email, she sighed. She'd worry about office politics later. For now, all that mattered was the mission and Drake.

"Storm is moving in," she said to Colt. "Communication might be affected."

"Murphy's law," Colt said. "If it can go wrong, it will. You want some coffee?"

"Sure."

Colt sat across from Price in the middle of the mostly empty hangar. He got up and made his way to a coffee station he'd set up an hour after Drake had left. He'd stolen the coffee pot and coffee from the Al Asad cafeteria. He lied to the cooking ladies who were guarding it, saying he was a repairman. He winked at them and made them both blush. He walked out with enough coffee to last him and Price a week.

"How did you convince Jason to help?" she asked.

Colt poured coffee into two cups and smiled. "He read the transcript you gave him."

"Who do you think Aya Khan is to him?"

"I tried to ask him, but he was too defensive. I figure he loves her." He handed Price her coffee and sat back down at his station.

Price shook her head. "Jason Drake in love. I doubt that. The man had a reputation for being fast with women. He never once mentioned anything about the guide he'd hired to kill the Butcher."

"A man like him wouldn't proclaim his feelings loudly."

"Maybe."

The two of them sat in silence, sipped their coffee, and waited. It felt strange, like old times, but different. While they'd never been on an operation together, they'd spent plenty of time sitting in silence, both relieved that they didn't have to face their demons alone.

"He was a hell of a fighter," Colt said in a solemn, quiet voice.

Price knew immediately who he was talking about. She turned and looked at the picture of her son she'd placed on the desk.

"He was," she said.

"I remember the day that photo was taken," Colt said, noticing the direction of Price's gaze. He stood up and made his way to her station. He stood over her, looking at the photo. His eyes reflecting nothing but the face of his little boy. He could still hear his laughter. He could still feel the warmth of his cheeks as he hugged him on Christmas morning.

"Me, too," Price said.

"Why do you keep that photograph on your desk? How do you stay focused with the past staring at you like that?"

"Because it reminds me why I'm here," she said. "It reminds me to keep fighting. The cancer that took him was chaos. Cancer cells are a breakdown of order. My job at the CIA is to fight for order."

Colt took a big sip of his coffee and walked back to his desk. He put the empty cup on his desk and pulled out a pack of cigars. "You want one?"

"No," Price said.

As he lit up, his face glowed like a bright orange pumpkin. "Time is a bugger," he said, exhaling a deep, thick cloud of smoke from his mouth.

"When he died, I shut down," she said.

"We both did."

The place was beginning to smell like a Cuban bar. Price didn't mind that—it brought her back to their honeymoon in Paris. It brought her back to their life together, no matter how short it had been. They'd only been married for five years. They were the best years of her life.

Her headset buzzed with static and brought her to the present, away from the thoughts about her past life with Colt and the dead child they shared.

"This is Drake calling Watcher. You read?"

Price put her coffee down and picked up her mic. It was time to focus on the present. It was time to find the ammonium nitrate.

THIRTEEN

Drake, Aya, and Houston hiked for an hour up the ridgeline toward the cliff where Ajmal and the other rebels were waiting. The wind had picked up, and a light snow had started to fall—the snow covered the rock and plant life with soft frosting.

Sitting on a large rock and smoking a cigarette, Ajmal narrowed his eyes when he saw Drake. He flicked his cigarette onto the ground and jumped off the rock. "The man who betrayed my sister," he said to Drake.

"Betrayed?" Drake asked.

"The CIA almost killed her."

"They almost killed me, too."

"You're an asshole," Ajmal said. "Your people are cowards. They shoot at us from the sky, from their robotic jets!"

"Good to see you, too."

"Screw you," Ajmal spat back. "My sister helped you, and she was repaid with scorn."

Drake took an intimidating step toward Ajmal, which caused the smaller man to stumble backward and fall on his ass. The other rebels Ajmal had brought with him laughed.

"Shut up," Ajmal yelled at them. "You're all assholes. All of you!"

"Get up," Aya said to her brother. "You're an embarrassment to me and our cause."

Ajmal stood up and turned to Drake. "If you try anything funny, I'll kill you."

Drake wasn't in the mood. He stared at the stout Syrian rebel and smiled. He wanted the little asshole to know that he wasn't going to play nice.

Ajmal tensed up and flung his hands in the air in frustration. He walked away from Drake, jumped back onto the rock. "Screw you," he said. "The CIA think they're helping us, but they're not. They never helped us. Do you know that our president, the corrupt son-of-a-bitch, uses sarin gas against our people? Do you know the Russians are bombing our farming villages with drones and fighter jets? They're supporting our corrupt government! This country is a nightmare, and it's because our people don't have the help they need. If the CIA actually gave us what we needed, we'd at least have a fighting chance, but they don't. How can we combat fighter jets with rusty AK-47s? How can we survive bombs without shelter? The CIA doesn't care about us. America doesn't care about freedom."

Drake rolled his eyes and shook his head. He didn't need a lecture about the nuances of the Syrian civil war. He'd spent six months in the country. He knew it was a mess, and he knew the CIA wasn't doing enough, even though they'd promised the rebels that they would.

Ajmal sneered and grabbed another cigarette from his packet. He stuck it into his mouth in the manner of a rebellious teenager and lit up.

Drake turned to Aya and said, "What now? Where are we headed? The sooner we get this over with, the better."

Aya walked up to Drake and stared into his blue eyes. Her face was expressionless. She moved with a stillness that made her seem ethereal in the dark. "Before I tell you where it is, I want some assurances."

"Assurances?" Drake asked. "Aya, cut the bullshit. Just tell me where the damn ammonium nitrate is."

"Your people killed those children. They murdered them. They knew we'd already killed the Butcher. Yet, they still fired. Your people are not to be trusted."

"What do you want?"

"There's a reason I asked for you."

Drake grunted. "Get to the point."

"If we help you, will you help us? Will you help the rebellion?" she asked.

"The CIA?"

"No," Aya said. "You. I want you."

"Like I said in the tent, the agency will give you what you need. Weapons, shelter ... whatever you want."

"Shut up."

"Excuse me?"

"Let me explain," she said. "The rebels want your expertise. All we're asking is that you stay here. Just for a couple of months. You taught me so much during the six months we spent in the desert together. If the rebels had someone like you at their service, we might be able to put an end to this awful war or at least have a fighting chance."

Drake shook his head. "And if I refuse?"

"We won't tell you where the ammonium nitrate is. We're only asking that you stay for a couple of months."

Drake gritted his teeth. He knew Aya wasn't lying. The woman he'd known five years before didn't like to play games. There was no reason to suspect she'd changed. She'd played her hand wisely to get him there. She'd got what she wanted. "Okay," he said. "I'll stay. But when I decide to leave, I'm gone."

"I understand. It's not like it was before. I was a silly girl then."

"So then, where is the stuff?"

"It's being held in a warehouse in an oil refinery in the valley below. That's why we're up here. I figured you'd want to scout the area before we move in."

"Move in?"

"Your handlers will want photographic proof, won't they?"

Drake nodded. "You can get me that close?"

"Of course," she said. "Like I said, you help me, I help you."

"Who's holding it?" he asked.

"Arms dealers. They're ex-military. Typical bad guys. They stole the ammonium nitrate from a port in Beirut and smuggled it to Syria, looking for a buyer. They're trying to broker a deal with the remaining ISIS factions. They're holding out for the highest bidder. If that stuff falls into the wrong hands, it could spawn the rebirth of the Islamic caliphate."

"Alright," Drake said. "Let's scout out the area before we head down there. I want to know what I'm dealing with. If it's loaded with bad guys, though—we're not moving in."

"Follow me," Aya said.

She guided Drake to the other side of the mountain. Houston, Ajmal, and the other rebels followed. After the short walk, Drake joined Aya on a small cliff. "There it is," she said, pointing out to the dark valley below.

The refinery was ominous in shape. Its four fifty-foot tall smoke-stacks cut up the horizon, and its various distillation and processing centers were like a black void on the ground. It was nestled in the valley, cradled by the Euphrates river.

"How many arms dealers are down there?" Drake asked.

"Five or six. They keep their numbers low to not attract attention. It's probably why no international force has any clue about it."

"Will we be able to get close without alerting them?"

"That's why I had Ajmal bring the other rebels. If we alert them, we'll kill them. It'll be just like old times."

Drake looked back at the rebels Ajmal had recruited. They weren't an intimidating bunch. They were dressed in dirty combat gear, and their boots had holes. Their weapons looked old and rusty; M14 battle rifles, AK-47s, and MAS-36 bolt-action rifles. Worst of all, they looked tired and beat, like they'd been facing real combat daily for years and knew that there was no end to it. Before the war, they would have been civilians, not soldiers. But civil wars make soldiers out of barbers, butchers, and mechanics.

Drake turned to Aya. "Will Ajmal's men follow orders?"

"Yes."

He shrugged. "Alright," he said.

He pulled out his night-vision goggles from his backpack and scanned the refinery. His viewfinder displayed various buildings that dotted within a fence that scaled the refinery's perimeter. There were distillation and processing stations, maintenance sites. The valves and pipes that connected each station were like tendons under the skin. At the north end of the complex were four large warehouses, and two large trucks were parked outside.

"The warehouses," he said. "Is that where the ammonium nitrate is?"

"Yes."

"Were there trucks there last time you checked?"

"Yes," Aya said. "There should be two of them."

"Okay," Drake said. "I'm going to radio my handler. Let her know I'm going to give her photographic proof. She was going to send in a larger force to get this stuff. I want us to be quiet about this. This is just a fact-finding mission."

Aya nodded and turned to the rebels and her brother and began barking orders at them.

Drake put the goggles into his backpack and looked at his watch. Zero dark—12:00 a.m. "Price, you read?"

"Loud and clear," she said. "How are you?"

"Good. I think I've found it."

"Roger that," she said. "There's a storm moving in. How's the weather?"

"Cold," he said. "It's snowing."

"Damn," she said. "Where is the stuff?"

"It's in a warehouse in an oil refinery in the valley that's closest to my location," he said.

"Oil refinery?"

"Yes, in the warehouses. According to our rebel contacts, a group of arms dealers are holding onto it. They're trying to sell it to ISIS factions."

Price tried to speak, but her voice was muffled with distortion. The snow and cloud cover were interfering with their signal.

"Watcher?" Drake asked.

Price came back on. "We're going to have to keep communications to a minimum. The storm will make it difficult."

"The rebels say they can get me close enough to get photo ID on the nitrate."

"Are you going in then?"

"Yes."

Price tried to say something else, but it was static. The clouds were too low and thick.

Drake turned off his radio and stood upright. Houston moaned and rubbed up against his leg. The dog had yet to leave his side. Drake rubbed the dog's back. "What is it, boy?" he asked. "Is something bugging you?"

The dog panted and licked his gloves.

Drake sighed. It was a good night for a mission, even with the communication disruption. The dark and the cold would make any hostiles grip their weapons too tight and throw off their aim just enough that he and the rebels would have an easy time picking them off—if it came to that, which he hoped it didn't.

"Are you ready?" Drake asked Aya.

"Yes," she said. "We're ready when you are."

FOURTEEN

The inhabitants of the Syrian Desert called the valleys that sloped down from the mountains wadis. It was an Arabic term and referred to the dry riverbeds at the base of mountains that contained water only when it rained. The oil refinery was located close to the bottom of a wadi.

Drake and Aya and the rest of the rebels walked slowly down the ridgeline toward the wadi's bottom. Houston was at Drake's heels, his tail wagging, his nose close to the ground, searching for a scent.

"You're quiet," Aya said to Drake. "Aren't you happy to see I'm alive?"

Drake looked at her, his face still and expressionless. Was he happy to see her? Of course, he was. Deep down, he'd always suspected she'd survived the drone strike. But he was weary. She seemed different. There was anger behind her eyes now. "What have you been up to these past years?" he asked.

"Fighting," Aya said. "Fighting and killing."

"Is there anything left worth fighting for? This country looks like a wasteland."

Aya smiled. "Not really. The desert is dead. Many cities and towns have been leveled. If you're asking if I've thought about leaving, the answer is yes. I've thought about it a lot, but every time I get close, I get dragged back into the fray."

Drake nodded. "I know the feeling."

He was glad to see that Aya had matured, although it saddened him to know that she'd become so fatalist—cynical. She was fighting to fight.

"What have you been up to?" she asked. "Still hunting the bad guys?"

"In a way," he said.

"Are you still a CIA puppet?"

"No. I left the CIA after I thought you were dead. I killed the man responsible for the drone attack—he was a US senator. I'm a wanted man in America. I did it for you and those children."

Aya was surprised. "Really? I figured you'd never leave the CIA. How did you get my message if they want you dead?"

"Bajal reached out to my old handler. She reached out to me. She understood why I killed the senator."

Aya looked confused. It was as if she was expecting another response from Drake. Both she and Drake remained quiet for the rest of the walk to the refinery.

After another hour had passed, they arrived. They scaled the refinery's premises, using the inside of a dried-out creek to stay hidden. They came to a stop near one of the distillation tanks.

"The warehouses are just beyond the fence, past those three large buildings," Aya said.

Drake crept up to the brim of the creek and looked at his surroundings. "I'm going to cut a hole in the chain-link fence, and we'll all move in," he said. "Once we're inside, make the rebels stay in the shadows—stick to the walls. Can you guide us to the warehouses?"

"Of course," Aya said.

Drake nodded and jumped up from the ledge of the creek. He made his way to the fence and pulled some bolt cutters from his backpack. He cut a hole big enough that a linebacker could fit through. He whistled when he was done, and the rebels climbed up from the cover of the creek and ran through the hole. They made their way inside the refinery, ducking behind the first bit of cover they could find.

Aya was at the back of the pack and turned to Drake before entering.

"There are no drones in the sky?" she asked, a wry smile across her face. "I don't want to have to leave you in a smoking crater again."

"Just get moving," Drake said.

She laughed and joined the rebels inside the refinery. As had been the routine the whole night, Houston stuck to Drake like glue.

"Let's find us some ammonium nitrate," he said to the dog. "Let's get this over with."

FIFTEEN

Maneuvering inside the refinery was simple. The place was cluttered with buildings. Pipes of various shapes and sizes spread out from each building like vines in a forest, creating a canopy overhead. Drake and the rebels slowly walked under the pipes, staying within their dark shadows.

The warehouses where the ammonium nitrate was believed to be located were on the south side of the refinery, about a football field away from where Drake and the rebels had entered. It didn't take them long to get there.

Within the shadow cast from a fifty-foot tall, oblong-shaped distillation tank that sprouted out finger-like pipes from its wide frame, Drake ran up to a small building across from the warehouses and shimmied his way to its corner. The rebels mimicked his actions, staying close behind.

"Do you spot anyone?" Aya whispered to Drake. "The ammonium nitrate is in those buildings."

"No," Drake said. "But those trucks outside the warehouse, they're Russian military trucks. Are you sure they're arms dealers?"

"Yes," she said. "I'm sure. Those trucks were probably stolen. You know how Syria is."

Drake raised an eyebrow and shook his head. "I don't like this,

Aya. I'm going to move in alone. Whether they're arms dealers or not, I want to make sure that you and the rebels stay safe. All I need is a picture of the stuff. I'll upload it to my handler, and we'll get the hell out of here."

"Of course," she said.

"What's wrong?" he said, noticing her hand in her pocket. It looked like she was fumbling with something.

She blushed. "Just cold," she said, pulling her hand out. "It's freezing."

"Weren't you wearing gloves earlier?"

"I gave them to one of the rebels. He was young and was worried about frostbite. I did it before we came into the refinery."

Drake rolled his eyes and turned back to the warehouses.

Each warehouse represented the final step of the oil transformation process. Years ago, when the refinery was fully operational, those buildings would have held barrels of petroleum, gasoline, diesel fuel, or some other by-product manufactured from the crude oil the refinery processed. Each warehouse was a steel fortress, an emblem to the gas and diesel engines that made the twentieth-century one of expansive and explosive progress.

Houston made a growling noise. He'd heard something. Drake scanned the area. It was too dark to see in the narrow alleyways between each warehouse, so he pulled out his night-vision goggles and looked through the viewfinder.

"Two of them," he whispered to Aya. "They're approaching from in-between two of the warehouses. A small alley. They've got guns. MAS-49s. They look like Russian soldiers."

The MAS-49 was a semi-automatic rifle common in the Middle East. The gun had a reputation for being reliable in poor conditions and didn't need a lot of maintenance. It was an ideal weapon for the Syrian Desert, despite the fact it was slow and heavy.

The men who Drake spotted walked into the light and leaned up against the corrugated metal siding of one of the warehouses. They laughed and spoke Russian. One of the men pulled out a pack of cigarettes—the other a lighter. They were dressed in standard Russian army attire. They were grubs—low level.

Drake turned to Aya. "Those aren't arms dealers," he said. "Those are Russian soldiers. I'm going to radio Price. Let her know this situation is a little more hot than we had anticipated. We can't go in. Not like this."

Aya looked over Drake's shoulder at the Russians and sighed. "I was sure they were arms dealers," she said. "They might be Russian soldiers, but this is definitely not a Russian military site. Whatever they are doing out here, it is illegal. They might be defectors, trying to make a quick buck."

"That's a lot of supposing," Drake said.

"I guarantee the ammonium nitrate is in there. It's the same ammonium nitrate that was stolen from Beirut. I saw it with my own eyes. Trust me. I would not have brought you here if I wasn't sure about this."

Drake rubbed his chin and looked into Aya's eyes. "Okay," he said. "But this situation just went from lukewarm to burning hot. We need to be careful. We cannot, and I repeat, *cannot* engage with Russian forces. I'm going in alone, and I need you and the rebels ready to commandeer one of those trucks if we have to get out of here in a hurry."

Aya smiled and nodded. "We'll do whatever you tell us. It will be just like old times."

SIXTEEN

Drake watched the two Russian men from his cover. When they were done with their smoke break, he would make his way toward the warehouses and find out whether or not they were Russian military and whether or not they still had the ammonium nitrate on-site.

"When those Russians leave, I'm going to move in," he said to Aya, noticing that she was warming her hands up in her jacket pockets again.

She nodded.

The two Russians finished their cigarettes and disappeared back down the alleyway between the two warehouses.

"Okay," he said. "On three. One ..."

"One," Aya said.

"What? Aya, I'll take the count ..."

"Two."

"What are you doing?" he said.

"Three."

He turned to scold Aya but felt a sharp pain in his neck. With the efficiency of a well-trained assassin, Aya had pulled out a small needle from her pocket and jammed it into Drake's neck. She pressed down on the plunger, inserting the tranquilizer into a vein in his neck. Ajmal and the other rebels rushed Drake before he could fire his M4 or grab his sidearm. The rebels each held one of his limbs down so he couldn't break free. They'd have to keep him like that until the tranquilizer took effect and rendered him asleep.

Houston barked and clawed and dug his teeth into one of Ajmal's hands as Aya's brother held Drake down, ripping off bits of flesh in the process. Ajmal howled in pain and loosened his grip to smack Houston.

One of Drake's arms clawed free. He reached for his combat knife, which was attached to his vest but was whacked in the face by the butt of Aya's sniper rifle before he could do anything. His head flung back and hit the dirt. He lay motionless on the ground. The world around him was a blur. He was woozy. Barely conscious.

The storm had picked up, and the place was immersed within a flurry of snowflakes.

Ajmal pulled off his AK-47 from around his shoulder and aimed it at Houston. He pulled the trigger, but Aya pushed his arms, so he lost his balance.

"No!" she said. "Not the dog!"

The bullets from Ajmal's gun sprayed and hit the warehouses' metal siding and the cold dirt. The Russians inside the building ran out, believing they were under attack.

Houston disappeared into the shadows.

"You idiot!" Aya screamed at Ajmal. She slapped him across the face. "That dog was mine!"

"He bit me," Ajmal said, gesturing to his hand, which was bleeding badly.

"He was just defending Jason," she said. "The dog is confused."

Ajmal grabbed a cloth from his backpack and wrapped it around his hand. "That animal is a demon."

The Russians walked up to Aya. They were holding their guns. "What the hell?" one of them said. "You're early? We expected you later."

Aya turned to the leader and growled. "What the hell?" she said in a mocking voice. "You were supposed to stay in the damn warehouse. Why were two of your men outside having a smoke break? I was going to stab him in the neck with the needle when we were inside. Like I had told you I would do."

"We needed a smoke!"

"You almost cost us everything."

The Russian shrugged. He was a big, burly man with a large, round belly and a shaved head. He took a long drag from what was left of his cigarette and looked at Drake. "Is this the CIA officer? Is this the payment?"

Drake could hardly move. The tranquilizer Aya had injected in his neck was beginning to take effect. He could feel himself losing control. He was beginning to feel nothing. He tried to move, but he couldn't.

"Yes," Aya said to the Russians. "I gave him enough tranquilizer to put down a horse, but clearly, he needs a bit more."

All Drake could do was muster out a simple sentence. "What is this, Aya?" His voice was weak. "What are you doing?"

"What do you think?" she said. "It's an arms deal. I need a payment. A CIA officer can fetch a lot from the Russian military. I give them you; they give me hydrazine, which is what I need to explode the ammonium nitrate."

"What?" Drake said, even more confused. "You have the nitrate?"

"The stolen ammonium nitrate you were looking for isn't here, but the hydrazine I needed for it is. The Russian military was more than willing to bargain, but it was expensive. They wanted a CIA officer."

"But why?"

"I'm going to make your country pay for killing those children. I'm going to make your country burn. In one week, your capital buildings will be leveled. Seven days and the world will change."

Drake summoned every last bit of energy he had in him and broke free from the hands of the men holding him. He grabbed Ajmal, who was tending his injured hand, by the throat. He squeezed. He wanted to rip Ajmal's esophagus out of his neck; he wanted to kill someone, but he couldn't. His fingers grew numb and frail. His vision turned black. He lost consciousness.

Ajmal kicked Drake in the stomach. He then spat on him but

missed and hit one of the Russians inspecting Drake's equipment in the head. The Russian leered at Ajmal and snarled in anger.

"I'm sorry," Ajmal said, cowering away behind his sister like a scared child and raising his hands in the air.

Aya laughed. Her plan had worked—by the skin of its teeth, but it had worked. She'd been working on administering the needle into Drake's neck for days, practicing on goats in the desert. She needed to hit a specific vein for it to take an immediate effect. She knew she'd only get one shot at it.

The Russians finished inspecting their payment, stood up, and turned to Aya. "The hydrazine is already loaded in one of the vehicles. The keys are in the ignition."

"Good," Aya said.

"Why don't you stick around?" one of the Russians said to Aya. "We're drinking vodka all night. You are, uh ..." He looked Aya up and down. "You're welcome to join if you want? I could show you a good time." He smiled, exposing yellow teeth.

Aya rolled her eyes. Damn Russians, she thought. Always concerned about their vodka. "No, thanks," she said. "I need to get this hydrazine out of the country."

She walked away from Drake's body and looked out into the dark of the refinery where Houston had run off. "Houston?" she yelled. "Houston!"

She waited, but Houston didn't show. The dog was gone.

Ajmal put his hands on his sister's shoulder. "We should go, Aya," he said.

Aya turned around and punched her brother in the nose. He fell to the ground. "You are an idiot," she said.

"The dog bit me!" he cried.

"Man up," she said. She looked at his hand. "It's just a scratch."

She growled and walked to the truck that the Russians had pointed to and opened up the back trailer. As promised, in the back of the truck were barrels of hydrazine. Everything she needed.

"I'm sorry, sister," Ajmal said, hobbling to her side. His nose was now bleeding as badly as his hand. "I should not have shot at your dog."

Ajmal was standing far enough from her that she couldn't punch him in the face again. She took a deep breath and rubbed her brow. She'd have to move on without Houston. Time was of the essence. "Let's go," she grunted. She opened the passenger side door of the truck and got in. "You're driving."

"But my hand?"

"It's a scratch, brother. Get over it."

The group of rebels stood behind Ajmal. They waited for direction. They'd held Drake down after Aya stabbed him in the neck. They'd done what they'd been instructed to do. Ajmal turned to them. "In the back," he shouted. "Guard the goods. We can't lose one barrel."

Ajmal then hopped into the driver's seat, slammed his foot on the gas, and drove out of the refinery into the desert. The tires dug up the dirt and snow. He had the windshield wipers working overtime.

Back in the refinery, the Russians dragged Drake's unconscious body inside the warehouse.

SEVENTEEN

It'd been two hours since their last communication. Price had called him a dozen times. Her finger clicked the button of her mic so often that she could feel a blister growing. "Drake? Are you there? Do you read? Where are you?"

Static.

Every time.

Colt paced back and forth behind her. He had one cigar left in his pocket, which he was saving for after completing the operation. It would be a celebratory moment, he'd thought.

"What's his GPS tracker say?" he asked.

"It's still pinging at the oil refinery. He's there. He's just not responding."

"Something's wrong."

"No shit," she said.

Price began to check various radio channels that Drake might have accidentally switched to. Nothing. She looked at the weather map. The storm was terrible, but not so severe that communication would be impossible.

"Check with the air base's command center," Colt said. "See if anyone else around here is running into similar problems."

Price nodded and dialed the command center. She knew what

the answer would be, though. If something was wrong, they would have updated her.

"This is Command Center, you're speaking to Private Morton," a pleasant-sounding man at the command center said.

"This is Kate Price of the CIA. I'm stationed at Hangar 2A. We've lost communication with an officer out in the field in the Syrian Desert. I'm wondering if there are any communication disturbances reported in the area."

"No, ma'am. Aside from the storm, lines are clean and open. If you've lost contact, the problem most likely lies on your officer's end."

"Shit," Price said aloud. "Shit, shit, shit."

"Excuse me, ma'am?" Morton asked.

"Nothing," Price said. "Thanks for the update." She hung up and turned to Colt. "What are we going to do?"

Colt looked at the satellite map and stared at the blinking red dot in the middle of the valley close to where the helicopter had dropped Drake off. "We need to get to the refinery."

"What? That's crazy."

"Is it? Because I know why you're stressed. I know what you're thinking. If you escalate this, Langley will find out. And if Langley looks into this, if the CIA director finds out that you've been hiding Jason all these years, the ammonium nitrate will be the least of your problems. We need to solve this problem ourselves."

"So what are you going to do? Steal a US Air Force helicopter and fly to Syria?"

"I was a helicopter pilot for years. I know how to handle them."

"But they'll shoot you out of the sky before you get off the ground."

"That's why you need to speak to the base commander and get me clearance."

"What if Jason is dead?"

"What if he is? All I know is that we sent him there to find the ammonium nitrate. If it's there, I want to know. I don't care about Jason, but I do care about my troops. And as long as that fertilizer is out there, their deaths mean nothing."

Price looked at her computer monitor. "I won't be able to get you clearance."

"Just try."

She picked up her phone and rang Private Morton again. "Can you please punch me through to the base commander? This is an emergency."

"Roger that," Morton said. "Please hold."

She grew anxious, but she knew Colt was right. If she asked Langley for assistance, they'd uncover the truth about Drake. She'd be done at the agency, maybe even end up in a prison cell. She wasn't willing to go down that path, not yet at least.

"This is Base Commander Tusk. What do you quacks at the CIA want this late at night?"

"We've lost audio communication with a man in the field," Price said to Tusk. "I'm requesting a Black Hawk for a pickup."

"Why are you going through military channels? Why not go through Langley? You know the order of events, Kate. I've worked with you for years."

"I need a favor."

Tusk chuckled. "Spy shit, eh? Alright. I'll arrange a Black Hawk in the morning. But what are you going to do for me?"

"I need it now."

"You'll get it in the morning. It's three a.m. I'm sure whatever clandestine operation you're running can wait."

"It can't."

"Damnit," Tusk said. "I knew I shouldn't have agreed to this operation. You always give me a headache. I know you're hiding something from Langley. Those two men in that hangar with you ... who are they?"

"It doesn't matter."

"It does," Tusk said.

"This is an international emergency."

"No, it's not," Tusk said. "It's a Kate Price emergency, and it can wait until the morning. Good night."

He hung up.

"Damn it," Price said.

"No luck?" Colt said.

"No."

Colt closed his eyes and smiled. He pulled out his last cigar. "I was going to save this," he said. He lit it up and took a long drag. "Keep me updated." He walked to the exit of the hangar.

"Where are you going?"

"I'm saving your ass and finding out if the fertilizer is there or not," he said.

"But you'll get shot down if you try to leave," she said.

"I'll improvise." He took another puff from his cigar, winked at her, and opened the door to the hangar.

"Clyde, for Christ's sake, don't be an idiot," she said. "There's got to be another way."

"Don't say the Lord's name in vain, sweetheart. You know that bugs me."

Price shook her head. "Clyde ..."

"Love you, lassy."

He left the hangar.

Price sat back down at her station and looked at the picture of the son they'd shared. His name was Cody. He had been just like his father—stubborn and steadfast. He never stopped smiling, even after the cancer that finally took him spread throughout his entire body. Cody fought right until the end. He didn't give up.

Neither would Colt.

Exhausted, Price rubbed her brow.

A storm was brewing. She'd have to prepare to go into damage control mode. She looked at her monitor and the satellite display pinging Drake's location. She tried to reach out to Drake again, but again, there was no response.

It was chaos. Pure chaos.

EIGHTEEN

Drake was semi-conscious and still suffering from the effects of the tranquilizer. He drifted in and out of consciousness, images of the past and the present blurred together in his head. It was kind of like being drunk, but worse.

The Russian soldiers who'd purchased him from Aya dragged him into one of the warehouses. They lit a small fire inside an empty barrel to keep themselves warm. They manacled Drake to a metal beam and began drinking copious amounts of vodka. They were singing Russian folk songs. Celebrating.

Drake watched them, closed his eyes and then when he opened them again, he saw his step-father standing above him, a silhouette of darkness and anger. His hands were fisted. Drake's mother was on the floor. She was crying, and her left eye was swollen. He swung at his step-father. The two of them fought. They fought until one of them was dead.

He shook his head. He was back in the warehouse. "What the hell?" The memory had been so real, so vivid. He could feel the darkness swelling in him again. The Russians were now dancing. He tried to stay in the present, but he couldn't. He had to ride it out. The world went dark once more.

He opened his eyes. It was the day he'd returned home from the juvie center. He found his mother in the bathroom, a needle stuck in her arm. She was lying in a puddle of vomit and piss. He woke her up, gave her some water. She scolded him, threatened to kill him, said it was all his fault. She pulled out a gun and fired at him.

He ran.

The next wave passed. He was beginning to feel better, but only a little. He could finally move his feet. He felt cold, but at least he could feel.

The next wave came hard. His vision turned dark, and when he finally could see again, he was in Denver, in the back of a railroad car. There was a man in the car with him. An old US Army vet. He told Drake he'd been a CIA officer once. He told Drake about his assignments in Vietnam and Nicaragua. He told Drake that he'd been broken by experimental drugs, something called Project MKUltra.

Again, Drake was brought back to the present. His hands tingled. His heart skipped a beat. His vision went dark again.

When he came to, he was in a training center. An undisclosed location. It was during his Terminus division training. Price was in his ear.

"Drake, take the shot."

He looked down the sight of the sniper rifle he was holding, adjusted the knobs for elevation and windage. He pulled the trigger. The dummy's head snapped back and exploded in a puff of straw and glue.

"Confirmed kill," he said.

"Bingo. Atta boy," Price said.

His mind snapped back to the present.

He felt a warm feeling on his body.

He opened his eyes.

A Russian had his fly down and was pissing on him. "Hey, look, Boris!" the drunk Russian with his dick out shouted to his comrades. "The American is awake!"

The Russian soldiers all laughed.

Drake kept his eyes and mouth closed. He was now fully conscious and needed to figure out how the hell he was going to escape.

NINETEEN

Colt pushed open the door to his sleeping quarters and grabbed a plastic case from under his mattress. He opened it up by keying in his passcode—the date Cody was born. Inside the case was his HK33 assault rifle. He had the weapon outfitted with a scope, a thirty-round magazine, and an integral bipod. He swung the assault rifle over his shoulder and then grabbed his Glock 17 pistol and a combat knife. Holstering his sidearm in his belt and his knife into a small leather rivet on his shoulder, he left the room and made his way to the helipads.

It was a short, five-minute walk from his sleeping quarters. The Black Hawk helicopter that had dropped Drake off in the desert was being refueled. Its pilot stood at the chopper, yawning.

Colt walked up to him. "I need the bird," he said.

"Excuse me?" the pilot responded, turning around and looking Colt up and down. "Who are you?"

"I need your helicopter."

"Who the hell are you?"

The pilot looked like a good kid. Probably got straight As through school and had been on his varsity track and math team. Doubt he would have had imagined then that all that hard work would result in him being stationed halfway across the globe, running transport missions in Syria and Iraq. But he probably came from a poor family, and the only way he could pay for his college tuition was to join the military. In four years, he'd be out—get a job in Wall Street or at some engineering company on the West Coast, have some kids with a pretty wife, and have a happy future. All he needed to do was survive his stint in the military.

"Is it fueled up?" Colt asked, ignoring the pilot's question. "I'll be in the air for a couple hours."

"I just finished refueling it," the pilot said. "But do you mind telling me what you mean about needing it? What the hell is this? Is this some sort of joke?"

"No," Colt said. "Where are the keys?"

"In my pocket," the pilot said, getting angry. "Who are you?"

"I'm an SAS captain working on a joint-op with the CIA," Colt said. "My name is Clyde Colt. I've got a man in a vulnerable position in an oil refinery in the middle of the Syrian Desert. I need to get to him. I need your bird."

"You know this is a US Air Force base, right? There's a chain of command, a process. I haven't heard a thing about you or your mission."

Colt shrugged. He didn't want to have to do it, but he knew he had to. It was the only way. "I'm sorry about this, mate," he said.

"Sorry about what?"

Colt put the young pilot in a chokehold. He counted to three, making sure the pilot's body had gone limp before placing him next to an oil bin close to the helipad. He rummaged through the pilot's pockets and grabbed the keys and his identification. Once inside the aircraft, he radioed Price.

"I've got a bird," he said.

"Jesus," she said.

"Hey," he said, "what did I tell you about the Lord's name."

"How did you get it?"

"I knocked a pilot out."

"Goddamnit, Clyde."

"You're really testing my patience," he said. "You curse on the

Holy Father again, and I won't take this helicopter to Syria and save your sorry arse."

"Just be quick."

"I will, sweetheart. I'll be back before you know it. Just sit tight." Colt put the pilot's key in the ignition. He waited.

"Sleep tight," Price said. It was something they said nightly when they were married.

Colt started the helicopter up and checked that the controls were full and free. He turned on the Black Hawk's mains, beacons, and fuel pumps, pulling up on the collective, adding fuel to the engine. Once he was sure the oil pressure, amps, and fuel pressure were ready, he engaged the rotor blades. When they were synched and pitch was optimal, he pulled up on the cyclic and lifted the bird up into the air.

Black Hawk helicopters had been used by the US Air Force since 1979. The more modern variant was the UH-60 model. It carried up to eleven troops with equipment. It was known for its versatility, capable of tactical and transport missions.

"Um, UH-60 AR2, you aren't scheduled to fly."

It was the Air Force radio traffic controllers in the command center.

Colt chuckled and did his best to control his tone. He looked at the pilot's ID and did his best American accent. "This is ... Pilot Rivers. Requesting departure. I'm on special assignment."

A small dust storm was created in the helicopter's wake as it rose from the ground. A maintenance crew on the tarmac looked up at him in awe.

"We don't have any—"

Colt cut them off. "Just check with the base commander."

"We're a little confused."

"Understood. I'll hold."

"Thanks, Rivers. We're ..."

Colt changed direction by using the rudder pedals. He then tipped the cyclic forward slightly, causing the helicopter to move forward.

"Um, Rivers?" the traffic controller said. "You're leaving the base."

Colt was just trying to create confusion. "Check with the base commander. I'll hold."

He guided the Black Hawk over the base's walls. When he was almost a mile from the base, he lifted the bird up to a cruising altitude and relaxed.

Air traffic came back on. "Lt. Rivers, you need to come back now."

"That's a negative. Have you checked with base commander?"

"Yes."

"Um ... please hold."

"What?"

Colt switched his channel to Price's. "You might be getting a call from the base commander," he said.

"You asshole."

Colt chuckled. "Sorry, sweetheart," he said. "But I had no other choice."

"I'll be on standby," she said.

"I'll keep you updated."

He turned his attention back to flying. It'd been too damn long. He missed the rush. He checked the pulse at his neck. He wanted to make sure that he wasn't over the doctor's prescribed 120 beats per minute. Ever since his stroke, he'd been told to keep it slow and steady. He counted for ten seconds and extrapolated the results from there. His pulse was seventy. He smirked. Maybe all he'd needed was a little adrenaline, a little excitement.

He hadn't felt this good in months.

TWENTY

Empty bottles of vodka and playing cards were strewn about the floor of the warehouse. Two of the Russian soldiers had passed out from drink and were lying up against each other. That left six to deal with, but his hands and wrists were still manacled, and he was still a little groggy from the tranquilizer. His neck where Aya had stabbed him throbbed, and his eyes had difficulty focusing.

Drake's focus panned from left to right. He took as much of it in as he could.

One of the Russians approached him. He was a man with a big belly, the one Aya had spoken to. He looked like the group leader or boss—he had on special boots and wore a flashy insignia on his unbuttoned military jacket. His face was greasy with sweat, and his eyes were bloodshot. "Are you awake, American?" he said, his words slurring.

Drake looked up at him and nodded.

"I have an important message for you."

"What's that?" Drake said.

"Fuck America!"

The Russians who were still sober enough to comprehend what was going on in the warehouse burst out laughing. The fat leader turned back to his comrades. "This American smells like piss! Did you do this, Evgeni?"

That only increased the laughter of his men. Fuel to the fire.

"What's your plan with me?" Drake said. "You seem to be celebrating."

"Of course we're celebrating," the fat Russian said. "All we had to do was take some hydrazine from a warehouse close to Moscow, bring it to Syria, and give it to some bitch who wants to attack America. She came through with her promise by delivering you. You know how much money you're going to get me from the Kremlin?"

"Tensions are high between our countries. You're risking war."

"Yes," the fat Russian said. "But I don't care. If I get enough money from the Kremlin, I'll retire happy. Live my days on some resort in Spain. Drink my nights away."

Drake tensed up. "Where is she taking the hydrazine?" Drake asked.

"I don't know, and I don't care." He laughed. "Do you know she sucked my dick to convince me to help? She's crazy."

"Fuck you," Drake grunted.

The fat Russian kicked Drake in the stomach. "Don't tempt me," he said.

"I said, fuck you."

The fat Russian smiled and kicked Drake again. "You will learn your place, spy!" He kicked Drake once more. "Once you get to Moscow, they're going to cut your brain open."

There was still enough tranquilizer in Drake's bloodstream to mitigate the pain from the kicks, but not enough that he didn't feel the wind knocked out of him.

"When the sun rises," the Russian said, "we leave."

Drake caught his breath and tried to pull himself free but couldn't. The manacles on his wrists and ankles were too strong. He needed a miracle. He needed some luck.

He saw something from the corner of his eye. A small shape moved quickly in the shadows of the warehouse.

He smiled.

He knew who it was.
It was a miracle.

TWENTY-ONE

The Black Hawk whizzed through the desert like a buzzsaw through dry wood. The ground two thousand feet below seemed like a blur. Holding the helicopter steady at a max cruise speed of 159 knots, Colt knew he was getting close to the refinery. He'd been in the air for forty-five minutes. The horizon glowed with early morning light.

"Do you see it?" Price said through the radio channel.

"Not yet, but I'm slowing her down," Colt said, pulling back on the throttle and slowing the rotor spin.

"Anything?"

Colt looked out the cockpit window. He'd been following the Euphrates for most of the journey. The only time he avoided the river was when flying over known hotspots: towns, military bases, etc. "I see the smokestacks," he said. "Four miles due east. There it is. That's the refinery."

"Bring it down slowly and don't get too close," Price said. "If anyone is in there, you'll no doubt get their attention. Drake's signal is still pinging."

Colt did the opposite of what Price requested. Not to spite her, but because landing was never his strong suit—even when he was flying helicopters daily for the Royal Air Force. He brought the aircraft down too quickly. The landing gear croaked when it hit the soil, and he was sure he heard something break.

He looked out the front window and checked the gauges. Everything looked good.

"What was that noise?" Price asked. "Are you okay?"

Colt unbuckled himself and turned the helicopter's engine off. Before removing his helmet, he said, "I'm good. The bird might need a few repairs when I bring it back, though."

Price cursed.

He chuckled.

"How's the weather?" she asked. "Is it is still snowing?"

"No," Colt said. "Sky's clear. Snow's melted."

"Good," she said. "Before you leave, I got word from Tusk."

"What is it?"

"You're going to be arrested when you come back."

"I figured."

"Just find out what happened. With any luck, Jason is still alive."

"I'm going dark," he said.

He took off his helmet and jumped out of the chopper. He grabbed his weapons and checked that everything was good to go.

He jogged to the refinery's chainlink fence and made his way inside.

TWENTY-TWO

The fat Russian barked orders at his men to pack up and get ready to leave; their night of celebration was over. The hard work was about to begin.

Three Russian soldiers ran outside to their military truck and prepped the back trailer for Drake. They were going to tie him down like a rabid animal.

The rest of the soldiers walked up to Drake with their weapons drawn. An amused smile crept across Drake's face when he saw the precaution they were taking. Two of the men lifted him up and removed the manacles.

"Try anything ... get two bullets in back," one of them said in broken English.

Drake said nothing. He just stared into each of their eyes.

The Russians pushed Drake toward the exit of the warehouse. Their faces were contorted by the smell of ammonia. Drake's clothes had dried, but the stench of urine was still there. They quipped with each other back and forth that Drake smelled like the urinal at their military barracks in Crimea.

Drake moved slowly. While he felt better, there was still some tranquilizer in his system. He wasn't going to try anything.

Not yet.

Two of the soldiers pressed the barrels of their guns against his back. "Move," one of them said.

Drake hobbled toward the door.

He stopped.

They all stopped.

There was a banging on the warehouse doors. The fat Russian ordered one of the men close to Drake to investigate. The soldier, a young Russian with a shaved head, ran to the door and lifted it up.

As the metal door rose from the ground, a small object rolled underneath into the room. It stopped at the fat Russian's feet.

Drake knew what it was instantly and closed his eyes, even though it wouldn't really help.

The flashbang grenade exploded, and all the remaining Russians winced. Their world had turned into blinding white light, and a few of them dropped to their knees. The flashbang's effects were exaggerated by the dangerous amount of alcohol still circulating around each soldier's bloodstream.

Colt burst into the warehouse, his HK33 stock firmly welded to his cheek. His trigger arm was down and pulled in tight, close to his body, creating a smaller target for the Russians to shoot back at. His other arm grasped the handguard and his steps were slow and steady. He dropped every one of them, save for the fat one.

Drake felt a spray of blood hit him in the face. When he opened his eyes, he saw the damage done.

He saw Colt.

The former SAS agent nodded at Drake, his HK33 still up high in his arms. "Are there any left?" he asked Drake.

"Yes," the fat Russian said. He was holding a Nagant M1895, a seven-shot, gas-sealed revolver. The M1895 was an old weapon, more ornamental than anything, but still useful. It was known for its sturdiness and ability to withstand abuse. There was a saying about that weapon: if something was wrong with it, you could always fix it with a hammer. "Drop your weapon or die."

Colt complied. "Shit," he said. "You're fast for a fat one."

The Russian chuckled. "You just killed Russian soldiers."

"Who were holding a CIA officer hostage."

"You're not American?"

"No, I'm Scottish."

"What is this? Comedy hour?" the Russian leader said.

Colt was on his knees.

Drake was on the floor, lying down. He tried to push himself up and reach for one of the dead Russian soldiers' weapons, but the fat man kicked them away before he could get any.

The fat man placed the barrel of his gun against Colt's head. "I don't need a Scot. I just need an American. You don't realize, but you've made me a happy man. I don't have to share the bounty with any of my men now."

"You twat," Colt grunted.

Suddenly, from out of the shadows, Houston leaped and grabbed the fat Russian's wrist.

The Russian pulled the trigger of his pistol. He missed Colt's head by inches.

Houston was rabid with his attack. The dog twisted and turned the Russian's wrist, tearing tendons and breaking bones. The fat Russian howled in agony.

Colt picked up his HK33 and fired. He put a bullet straight between the fat Russian's eyes. Brain matter splattered on the floor of the warehouse.

Colt looked at Drake, then at the dog. "What the hell happened here?" Colt asked. "Where's the ammonium nitrate? Where's Aya Khan?"

"Long story," Drake said. "Let's just say I've been betrayed."

"By who?"

"By Aya."

TWENTY-THREE

It was eleven a.m. and surprisingly hot. The storm that had brought snow to the desert the night before felt like a distant memory. It now felt like midsummer in the Midwest. Another trait of the Middle East.

Price paced back and forth on the helipad's tarmac. Her skin was caked in a layer of sweat, and she knew she was knee-deep in a shit storm that she couldn't control.

Base Commander Tusk and a team of US military police were standing behind her. They were there to arrest Colt when he landed. He'd broken numerous laws when he'd commandeered the Black Hawk and rendered the US Air Force helicopter pilot unconscious.

Price had used what little influence she had to make a compromise with Tusk. He'd get Colt deported back to England, she'd leave, and he'd keep Langley out of the loop about the whole matter. The less noise made about it all, the better. Tusk didn't want the Pentagon to know that an SAS officer had commandeered a helicopter from his air base under his watch as much as Price didn't want Langley to know about her operation in the desert.

It was mutual. A fair trade.

She looked out at the horizon. "Where the hell are you?" she said under her breath.

Her last communication with Colt was thirty minutes after he'd left the refinery. All she knew was that he had Drake and that Drake was alive. She wasn't told anything else.

Her hands were shaking. For the first time in years, she craved a cigarette.

"Where are they?" Tusk asked, growing more impatient by the minute. His face had thick, deep lines, and his jawline was abnormally square. He looked like the kind of guy who laughed once a decade.

"The last transmission I received, he said they were about thirty minutes away. They should be here any minute."

Tusk sneered and talked to his military police; they didn't seem like a friendly bunch. They were carrying unmodified M4s. If Colt pushed, they wouldn't think twice to put him down.

She heard the two General Electric T700 turboshaft engines. She lifted up a pair of binoculars and saw the reflected light from the chopper's windows as it emerged from a low cloud.

Tusk squinted and scowled. The military police raised their M4s. It was showtime.

The helicopter approached the air base and landed with general ease. Colt was now fully in control of the bird. He could have performed stunts with it if he had a bit longer with it.

As the helicopter's engines died down and its rotor blades slowed to a stop, Price approached it. Her clothes danced in the swell of the turbulent wind created by the spinning rotors, her hair in her eyes. She wanted to be the first to see them both.

The door to the helicopter slid open, the metal of the door grinding against the helicopters bent chassis.

A dog jumped out and sat down at Price's feet.

"What the hell?" she said.

Next was Colt. He lifted his hands when he saw the military police and jumped from the helicopter. He let them put him in handcuffs. He'd expected it. He knew Price would have had no choice but to sell him out.

"What the hell happened at the refinery?" she asked him before he was taken away. "And what's with the dog?"

Colt gestured toward Drake, who was still in the helicopter. "He'll tell you everything," he said. "We're in trouble. This is big."

The military police dragged Colt away from the landing pad.

Commander Tusk approached Price and whispered in her ear," You keep this quiet, I'll keep this quiet. But I want you out of here by tomorrow morning. I've already arranged a flight to take you to Langley."

"Of course," she said.

Tusk nodded and followed the military police to the holding cells where Colt would be kept until his deportation.

Price walked to the helicopter. The rotors had stopped spinning. It was finally quiet. Drake was inside.

"What the hell is going on?" she said.

"You mean the trap you sent me into?"

"Trap?"

"You owe me an apology."

"Really? An apology?."

Drake chuckled and jumped down from inside the helicopter. "I need to go back to Syria," he said to Price. "I know who has the ammonium nitrate. We don't have a lot of time."

"Who?"

"Aya Khan."

"The woman we sent you to meet?"

"Yes. Like I said, it was a trap."

"Where is it? Where is she?"

"All I know is we have one week."

"I just made a deal with Commander Tusk. We need to leave tomorrow morning. We can't stick around here."

He patted Houston on the head. "Good boy," he said, ignoring Price.

"Jason, we need to leave in the morning—"

He cut her off. "We need to talk. I'm going back to Syria. This concerns American lives."

TWENTY-FOUR

They'd been traveling for ten hours. Aya stared out the front window of the Russian military URAL-4320 truck that was loaded with hydrazine and watched the desert roll past. Mountains turned to dunes, which turned to mountains again. The ancient landscape felt like an enchanted forest. Once you were in, there was no way out. It felt endless.

They still had another six hours before they reached their destination: headquarters.

The road they were driving on was mostly quiet; a few cars passed, a few military trucks. But the fact that they were driving a licensed Russian military vehicle meant no one wanted to bother them—that was all part of the deal with the Russian military soldiers they'd handed Drake to.

She expected to feel better after betraying Drake. She thought she would have found some catharsis in handing him over to the Russians, in selling him for a chemical that would cause his country to burn and would engulf the whole world in flames, but she didn't.

Ajmal concentrated on the road. He swerved in and out of pot holes and rivets. No road in Syria was smooth. His hand still ached from Houston's bite, but it was bandaged now, and the bleeding had stopped. His nose still hurt from Aya's punch, though. It felt like she'd broken it.

"We need to pull over," he said.

"We can't stop. Not until we are close to the border with Iran."

"My hand! I don't want it to get infected. It's the hand I use to paint."

"I don't give a damn about your hand. That was your own damn fault."

"But it's the hand I use to paint!"

"You're pathetic," she said to her brother. "Pull over at the next stop. You might want to change your diaper, too."

At the next stop, Ajmal pulled over, jumped out, and went about cleaning his wound. With the bandage off, he saw the actual impact of Houston's bite. The dog had taken a substantial chunk of flesh. Once it was clean, he walked to the truck's trailer and checked on the rebels. They were drinking raki and were smiling.

"Give me some of that," he said.

One of the rebels handed him the bottle.

He shot back a swig. His face winced, and he coughed. The Syrian moonshine was strong.

The rebels laughed.

He'd been laughed at too much that night. His face turned red, and he dumped the bottle onto the ground.

The rebels all moaned.

"Ah, you don't like that? Remember who is the boss here!"

"We know who the boss is," one of the rebels said. "It's not you. You're a bitch."

The rebels in the back laughed.

Ajmal cursed and left them.

He jumped back into the driver's seat of the truck and turned the engine on. "I just want to be back with my paintbrushes," he said. "This whole operation has been stressful."

"I should have killed him," Aya said, not looking at Ajmal but straight ahead at the endless desert.

"What do you mean?"

"I should have killed Drake. Maybe we should go back. I should have killed the Russians, too. I should just kill them all."

Ajmal could tell his sister was in one of her moods. She'd been suffering from them daily for some time now. He'd hoped that when the ordeal with Drake was over, she'd start to feel better. Clearly, that wasn't to be the case.

He tried to talk some sense into her. "You know very well, sister, that if you killed Drake, if he was dead, the Russians would not have agreed to the deal. They gave us clear instructions that they wanted the CIA officer *alive*. It was the only way they would give us what we wanted. The ammonium nitrate is no good without the hydrazine."

Aya shrugged. "We could have just killed them all—the Russians —everyone. We could have figured it out on our own."

"You want to kill the Russian military?"

"Yes."

"We need the Russian military to be complicit in this. This whole operation is dependent on them—you know our leader's plan. There's no point in doing any of this if they can show that we harbored ill will toward them. We need it to look like they were on our side all along. We need them to play along. We are trying to start a world war."

Aya rubbed her brow. All the political scheming was making her tired. She was a soldier, not a politician. She wanted results, not nuance.

"Aya, if you truly want revenge, you'll follow the plan. This is years in the making. Think of what you lost. Think of your daughter ..."

That stopped Aya in her tracks.

She wiped her mouth and stared down her brother with disdain. She'd told him not to mention Amira ever again. She'd warned him about it.

She felt an impulse to grab her knife and slit her brother's throat right there and then for breaking his oath.

Ajmal noticed the look in his sister's eye. He knew he shouldn't have mentioned her dead daughter. "I'm sorry," he said. "I'll shut up. I won't mention Amira again. I'm sorry."

Aya turned away from Ajmal and looked back out at the landscape she now despised.

Her phone buzzed.

It was him. Their leader.

Andrei Zadorov.

The man who'd just delivered the ammonium nitrate to the warehouse in Washington. The man who had put this whole plan in motion.

PART 2 - THE HUNT

TWENTY-FIVE

The angiocatheter dug deep into the main vein on Andrei's arm. The poison injected into his blood burrowed through his body, interfering with cell division, breaking him down. He felt fatigued, nauseous, and tired.

He'd been sitting in the medical clinic in Sochi for hours.

He looked out the window. The glare of light from the sun as it bounced off the Black Sea made him wince.

A nurse walked into the clinic's room and pulled the needle out of Andrei's arm. He rolled his sleeve down and rubbed his hand through his thin hair, noticing a large lump in his palm. He was once a vain man, but not anymore. He looked like a rotting corpse. There was nothing left of him to be vain about.

The chemo administered was to prolong his life—it wasn't to cure anything. It was merely to give him a couple more weeks or days. He was killing his body to die slower. He felt it a fitting analogy for what he was about to do to the world.

He was about to administer his own shot of chemo into the world's veins.

He left the clinic and met his driver outside. He stepped into the back of his Bentley Mulsanne and watched the mountains surrounding Sochi grow as the car approached them.

His phone rang. He didn't want to answer it, he was so lethargic, but it was one of his contacts in the Russian military—a mole whom he paid well.

"What is it?" he answered.

"Your girl delivered the CIA officer, and she got the hydrazine."

"Good."

"No, it's not good."

"What? Why not?"

"The Russian soldiers who purchased him are dead."

"Who was it? Syrian rebels? ISIS?"

"The Russian military doesn't know."

"Was the CIA officer killed, too? Because that would look very suspicious."

"The CIA officer was not found at the refinery."

Andrei rubbed his chin. His plan was delicate, had many moving parts, and relied on precision. He couldn't have one thing go wrong. It would upset everything he'd set in place. "Aya has the hydrazine," he said. "Everything is still a-go. It could be worse."

"I just wanted you to know," the contact said. "I'm sure you'll read more in the papers."

Andrei hung up and cursed.

His private compound was deep within the mountains and close to a small village, which he had his security forces protect.

When the vehicle rolled to a stop, he thought about Aya. He'd have to tell her. He couldn't keep her in the dark about this. She'd doubted the operation with the CIA officer from the get-go. She feared him, which was surprising to Andrei. She didn't fear anyone. He wanted to hear her thoughts on the matter.

As he walked up to his mansion, he dialed her number.

"What is it?" she said.

"My contact in the military says you have the hydrazine."

"I do."

"I'm back at the compound. The ammonium nitrate is in Washington. All it needs is you."

"And the hydrazine."

Andrei chuckled and then broke out in a fit of coughing. Blood stained his hands. He sat down at his dinner table. He didn't have the strength to stand and talk. "Sorry," he said.

"Everything went to plan," Aya said. "The CIA officer, Jason Drake, is with the Russian soldiers. You were right. I was wrong."

Andrei paused. "Not exactly," he said. "Turns out, the Russian soldiers who bought him are dead."

"What?" Aya screamed into the phone. Her cry sounded like the shriek of an eagle. "I should have killed him. I told you I should have killed him!"

"Stop!" Andrei said. "You were right. I was wrong. A misstep, nothing more."

"Nothing more? You don't know him like I do. He's a monster. Deranged. He'll stop at nothing to get to us. To find us."

"How will he find us?" Andrei said.

"Ali Bajal."

"The club owner?"

"Yes," Aya said. "I used him to get in contact with the CIA. Jason will find Ali, and he will get him to talk."

"Then we will get to Ali first. Kill him before he squeals."

"I should go back to Syria," Aya said. "I'll deal with this."

"No!" Andrei said. "You need to come back to Russia. This is a blip. Nothing more. My mercenaries will take care of Ali Bajal. If he's the only one we need to kill to keep this Jason Drake off our back, then it could be worse."

"I told you the deal with the Russians was a bad idea," Aya said. "I told you we should have killed Jason Drake."

"We needed the hydrazine, and you wanted revenge. You can't always get what you want."

Aya growled in frustration.

"Stop," Andrei said between winded breaths. "It's okay. You need to relax. I will get my mercenaries to kill Ali Bajal. Jason Drake will not be able to find us."

"And what if Jason gets to Ali Bajal first? If Jason finds us?"

"He won't."

Andrei hung up the phone and slammed his fist on the table, rattling the expensive cutlery his mother had purchased years ago. A plate fell on the ground and smashed into a dozen pieces.

He pushed himself up from the dinner table. "I'm sorry, Natalay," he said, apologizing to his dead mother. "I will not be so clumsy going forward."

He coughed as he picked up the pieces, his blood staining each one.

TWENTY-SIX

Drake and Price were in the hangar. It was night, and there was only one light on. Price was at her desk, the back of her head lit by her computer monitor's blue glow.

"Our flight out of the base is scheduled for five a.m.," she said.

"I'm staying."

"Jason, please. I've made the arrangements with the base commander. He's going to keep your identity a secret, but I need you to come with me. If you stay—I won't be able to protect you."

"Protect me? The way you protected me from a drone strike?"

"You know that wasn't me."

"If it was, you'd be dead."

"Listen, you've done what I asked. You came to Syria. It was a bust. Twenty-four hours ago, you wanted nothing to do with this, and now you're telling me you want to take it further."

Drake shook his head. "She said we had seven days."

"She's probably lying. Intelligence agencies around the world have been looking for that ammonium nitrate for months. She won't be able to move it across international borders without arousing suspicion. I can't see how she'll move two thousand tonnes of the stuff, let alone attack an American target."

"Aya isn't like most of the terrorists you've dealt with. She's smart. She'll find a way."

"You're crazy, Jason. You should just leave. Head back to Puerto Rico or disappear. If you honestly think that some Syrian rebel will be able to transport that much fertilizer halfway across the world, maybe—"

Drake cut her off. "I thought she was dead until twenty-four hours ago. I'm not taking it off the table. She told me she had the ammonium nitrate, and now she has hydrazine—rocket fuel. That shit will magnify the impact of the fertilizer explosion. She fooled you once by bringing me here. She can fool you again."

Houston was curled up at Drake's feet. The dog looked as peaceful as a baby, happy to be back with his proper master. In a way, Drake felt the same thing. He turned away from Price and patted the dog's head.

"Who is she," Price asked, "this Aya Khan?"

"She was the guide."

"Cut it out, Jason. What is she to you?"

"I loved her. She was the first good thing in my life. The first thing that made me feel like I was fighting for the good guys."

"You didn't feel that before?"

"No."

"Why?"

"I was a CIA assassin. You gave me a target, and I took them out. I didn't ask why. Aya always had a 'why'. She knew what she was fighting for. I was a monster. She was a saint."

"She stabbed a needle into your neck and tried to sell you to the Russians."

"And that's why I have to go back to Syria. That's why I have to find her."

"She's the monster, Jason. Not you."

"You don't know what I am."

Price was beyond frustrated. From her point of view, the mission was beyond a failure. She just wanted to clean it up as quickly as she could. She wasn't going to let this operation get her kicked out of the CIA. She needed her job. She didn't know what she would do without it. If she ended up like Colt, she'd probably resort to the same tactics as him. She'd drink a bottle of wine before lunch and a bottle before dinner. She'd try to quell the pain of her past.

"I'm telling you the truth," Drake said. "You shouldn't doubt me."

"Doubt you? You killed a senator, which resulted in my Terminus division's cancellation. You've been a pain in my ass for years. Trust? This has nothing to do with trust."

Drake's eyes narrowed. "I'm going back to Syria. I'm going to find her. It's your fault for bringing me into this mess."

"And when you find her, what will you do?"

"I don't know, but if she's telling the truth, and I believe she is, then we don't have a lot of time."

Price closed her eyes and took a deep breath. "I'm going back to Langley," she said. "I have to."

"You do what you have to do."

Outside the hangar, a C-17 approached the air base for landing. Its massive engines made the walls of the hangar shake. Houston grew scared and hid under Drake's tree-trunk-like legs.

"If you don't come with me, I won't be able to stop the CIA director from finding out about you."

"I don't care."

"And you're going in there alone?"

"Not alone."

Price's eyebrow rose. "Who are you taking with you? Are you going to recruit a grunt from the air base?"

"I'm thinking Clyde Colt," Drake said. "The man's resourceful. I wouldn't be here without him, after all."

"You can't take him. He has a heart condition. And anyway, he's in the holding cells!"

"He rescued me: now I'll rescue him."

"Rescue? You'll be taking him into a warzone."

"He'll come if I ask him."

Price rubbed her head. "Screw it," she said. "Okay. Go, find out where that ammonium nitrate is, and stop her. If you fail, I'm screwed. If you leave with me, I'm probably screwed, too."

"You're a black ops director," Drake said. "If Langley turns to shit, don't be afraid to get political."

"That's never been my strong suit," Price said.

"Well, you might have to get out of your comfort zone and challenge yourself," Drake said with a smirk. He stood up, patted Houston on the head. "You need to take the dog with you, too."

"What?" Price said.

"Take the dog. It's not negotiable."

"You're not really in a position to give orders, Jason."

"It's not negotiable."

Price looked at the dog. It moaned and rubbed up against her. She scratched its head. "Fine," she said.

Drake nodded.

"Just tell me one thing, Jason."

"What's that?"

"Why did Aya betray you? You thought she died during a drone strike? She can't blame you for that. You were almost killed, too. It took months to recover. You were lucky. But she went out of her way to bring you back."

"That's what I don't know, but it's something I plan to find out."

He opened the door to the hangar and was about to step outside but stopped. He lowered his head. "All I know is I brought her into this mess. I made her the monster she has become, and I need to stop her. She was my light, and now, she is my darkness."

He slammed the door behind him as he walked out into the darkness of the air base.

TWENTY-SEVEN

Colt was in his cell, tossing a rubber ball against the wall and cursing the stuck-up asshole who had informed him that his SAS commanding officer, Graham Howe, was scheduled to fly to Iraq to pick Colt up from the American air base.

The phone conversation he'd had with Howe had been quick.

"What the hell are you doing in Iraq?" Howe screamed. "You're supposed to be retired. You should be relaxing."

"My ex-wife came looking for me. She brought me here."

Howe moaned. He was beginning to realize this was partially his own fault. "She said she wanted to reminisce with you. When I told her where you were, I didn't think she'd bring you on a mission."

"She did," Colt said. "And, to be honest, it's exactly what I needed."

"SAS command is pissed," Howe said. "They don't want this news to leak. The last thing the *Daily Mail* needs is a story about a drunk, retired SAS captain stealing a helicopter on a US air force base. For Christ's sake, Clyde!"

"Hey!" Colt said. "Don't be an arsehole. You know how I feel about the Lord's name."

"For a man with a mouth as dirty as yours, you certainly have a weird sense of what's right and wrong to say. Listen, I'm on my way. Sit tight."

Their conversation ended when Colt called Howe a bastard. After his call, he was dragged back to his cell, and that was where he had been since.

The building where the holding cell was located was small. There were eight cells, and it was close to the sewage tanks, so it smelled like shit and piss. There was one window in Colt's cell, high up, ten feet from the floor, and barred.

He kept tossing the rubber ball and watched the moonlight as it crept along the floor. The light caused the shadows of the bars to elongate in an unusual manner.

He let out a long sigh. If Howe was right about SAS command, his chances of getting back into the SAS were doomed. Colt knew he'd be spending the rest of his life in a pub, drowning himself in beer until his heart finally gave out.

Outside, he heard laughter. Two young army grunts were sneaking through the air base with bottles of whiskey in their hands. They were searching for the darkest corners of the sprawling military installation to drink.

"What the hell are you doing?" Colt said to himself. "Did you really think this would work? You daft, old goof! You should have stayed in London. You're washed up. Useless. Your best days are long behind you."

He had a habit of talking to himself. It was one he'd developed when he was forced to go on a solo mission in Siberia in the late nineties. He'd spent three months walking through the tundra, camping under the stars, avoiding wolves and bears and men with rifles. He was there to investigate a Russian satellite station. Russian military command said it was nothing more than a telecommunications center, but the SAS believed differently. Needless to say, it was a nuclear launch site, and the months Colt spent in Siberia uncovering the truth about it changed him.

His thoughts of the past vanished when he heard a clanging noise. He looked up. "What the hell?"

He heard the clang again, but this time, the object making the noise wiggled its way through the window's bars. It was a stone. He stood up and approached the cell wall. He heard a voice.

"Colt?" a voice whispered outside.

"Who wants to know?" Colt did his best to keep his voice low. The guard watching the cell was a mere twenty feet from the cell's door. He had to be quiet.

"It's Jason."

"You here to brag? Tell me I'm an arsehole for bringing you into this mess?"

"No."

"Then what do you want?"

"We don't have a lot of time."

Colt rubbed his brow. He knew what the 'we' meant. 'We' meant he was about to get caught up in something. 'We' meant he'd be in more trouble with his superiors than he wanted to be. 'We' meant he'd be back on the field soon, back where he felt alive. 'We' gave him a reason not to drink.

"If you haven't noticed, I'm in a cell," Colt said. "There's a guard less than twenty feet away. How the hell are you going to get me out of here?"

Drake didn't respond.

All Colt heard next was the pattering of footsteps as they walked away from outside his cell window. Within minutes, Colt realized what Drake's plan was.

"What was that noise?" the guard monitoring the cell block said. "Who's there? Show yourself!"

The lights in the cellblock turned off.

Colt heard a body hit the floor with a loud thud. The lock clicked on his cell door.

Colt stood up. "Two days ago, you were about to kill me," he said with a wry smile to Drake. "Now, you're breaking me out of jail."

"Do you want to find that ammonium nitrate?" Drake said.

"Of course."

"Then we need to go to Syria."

"Syria?"

"Yes," Drake said. "We need to talk to Ali Bajal. I reckon he knows where Aya is."

"And if we find Aya ..." Colt said.

"We find the ammonium nitrate."

Colt smiled. "That's just what I needed to hear, mate. Where are we going to find this guy?"

"In Damascus, in his club, the Zorba House."

"Then what are we doing sitting around here?"

Drake nodded.

The two men carefully made their way out of the holding cells and snuck toward the air base's garage. Drake pulled out a set of keys and opened the garage doors.

"How'd you get the keys to the garage?" Colt asked.

"How'd you get the helicopter?" Drake responded.

Colt chuckled. "Then, I guess we should get going before the son-of-a-bitch in the holding cell wakes up."

"He's not the only one I've knocked out tonight. We need to get the hell out of here and quick. We'll have the US army on our tail in the morning."

TWENTY-EIGHT

Getting out of the air base was easy. Almost too easy, in fact. But that was mostly because the US military personnel on the base were in the process of withdrawing. Iraq was a lost cause. The US military had spent almost twenty years in the country. While Saddam was gone, the vacuum of power created in his wake made things worse. Washington needed to re-evaluate. They wanted a new plan for the Middle East, one that didn't involve more than a thousand troops stationed in a hostile warzone.

The Iraqis who were taking control of the air base were ill-equipped and poorly trained.

As Drake pulled the military jeep up to the air base's gates, he spotted two Iraqi soldiers. They were carrying M16s and looked nervous.

"Where are you going?" one of them asked.

"Hookers and coke," Drake said. He knew what to say.

The two Iraqi soldiers smiled and waved him through. They'd later get reprimanded by their superiors for it, but they weren't really to blame for their lapse in judgment. Drake slipped them his bottle of Jack Daniels, which he'd stolen from the base's kitchen.

Drake slammed his foot on the gas as soon as he passed the front gates and didn't hold up until he was ten miles down the road. It was only then that he eased up on the engine, not wanting it to overheat in the middle of the desert and screw them over before they crossed the border.

Plus, he didn't know how far he'd have to travel. He was still on Iraqi soil, and Syria was a big country.

Before breaking Colt out of his holding cell, Drake had made sure to grab three necessary items.

The first was a medical kit. Inside were bandages, clotting agents, an abdominal wound trauma kit, shears, scissors, splints, and alcohol pads.

The second was weapons. He brought the M4 he'd outfitted for the initial operation with Aya and the M9 pistol to act as a sidearm. Colt's HK33 was in the holding cell in a safe room, and Drake wasn't going to bugger around with trying to figure out how to bypass the code lock, so they'd had to leave Colt's equipment behind. Colt was rather pissed off about that, but Drake had a surprise for him. He'd made a quick visit to the base armory before getting the jeep and grabbed an HK416N assault rifle outfitted with an Aimpoint CompM4 sight and a vertical foregrip. It was the same kind of weapon used by Delta Force and the Navy SEALs. That put Colt's mind at relative ease.

The final items on Drake's list were rations and fuel. He grabbed a few cans of beans and a few prepackaged meals from the cafeteria. Standard stuff. Enough that they could survive a few days in the desert. And then he made sure to head to the fueling station, where he loaded up three gas cans full of diesel.

All they had to do now was get to Damascus, talk to Ali Bajal, and hope he knew something about Aya and the ammonium nitrate.

Bajal would be easy to find. His club was in the city's heart and was a popular place for soldiers, rebels, and locals to congregate. It was how, despite all odds, the club's owner/arms dealer had survived as long as he had. His club served as a no man's land of sorts—it was the eye of the storm.

AFTER TEN STRAIGHT hours of driving, Drake pulled over and tapped on Colt's shoulder. The old Scot was sleeping.

"It's your turn to drive," Drake grunted. "We're in Syria."

Colt rubbed his eyes and nodded. The two men changed positions.

Drake reclined in the passenger's seat and closed his eyes. The last time he'd got any good shut-eye was during the flight from San Paulo to Iraq.

Colt placed his hands on the steering wheel and yawned. He looked out at the horizon, which was desolate in all directions. It'd been twenty-four hours since he'd rescued Drake from the Russian soldiers, and the sky was the same light pink it had been outside the refinery the previous morning.

He started the engine and shook his head. "Which way to Damascus?" he asked.

Drake opened his eyes, looked at the long road that stretched toward infinity, then stared at Colt. "There's only one road," he said dryly. "Which way do you think?"

"But what if I come to an intersection?"

"You won't.

"How do you know?"

"Because I know."

"I spent ten years living in London, and I still don't know my way around the city."

"Syria isn't London."

"You're an asshole," Colt said.

"And you're a drunk."

Colt sneered. Drake closed his eyes, trying to give Colt a hint that he wasn't in the mood to talk.

Before pressing his foot on the gas, Colt checked his mobile phone. He hadn't checked it since falling asleep. He used an old flip phone. He was one of those guys who didn't hop on the smartphone bandwagon and wasn't going to start now. Price had messaged him. She was about to board the C-17 back to Langley.

Good luck. You boys are on your own. Once you find the
ammonium nitrate, send me everything you know.

Colt stuffed his phone into his pocket and turned the jeep's engine on. He pulled the jeep back onto the road and drove. As the wheels broke up the stones and pebbles on the road, he felt a sense of calm overwhelm him.

It'd been more than a day since his last drink. His blood hadn't been this clean in a long while. The hangover and mental fog that had plagued him for months was gone. He felt good.

The jeep was nothing special, but it did have an advanced armor kit attached to the top of its fully enclosed metal cabin. It was the perfect vehicle for traversing the harsh desert and would provide him some level of protection if shit hit the fan. The Syrian desert was loaded with landmines and IEDs. Ten years of civil war had relegated even the country's most remote landscape to one of perpetual danger.

After six hours of driving, he realized Drake was right. There was only one road to Damascus. It was long and straight. He saw the lights of the city emerge above the horizon before he ran into his first intersection. Damascus's high-rises speckled the black of the sky.

Colt hit Drake, who was still asleep, in the arm.

Drake opened his eyes, stretched, and yawned. "Good job," Drake said to Colt. "You managed to get here without getting lost."

"Screw you, mate. You know, we might just kill each other before we find the ammonium nitrate."

Drake shook his head and watched as the city enveloped them both. To be honest, he wasn't sure what to expect. It'd been five years since he'd been in Damascus. He'd hoped that the city would show some signs of improvement, develop some sense of normalcy since then, but it hadn't. In fact, the city looked worse now than before.

It was a shame, Drake thought. Aya revered Damascus. She told him that Syrians referred to Damascus as the City of Jasmine. It was the largest city in the country, with a population of just under two million. It was once one of the most flourishing cultural epicenters of the Arab world, but after the civil war started, the Economic Intelligence Unit had labeled it as the least livable city in the world.

As they drove through the outer crust of the city, Colt turned to Drake and said, "This place has seen better days." They were passing a large shantytown.

Drake nodded. This whole part of the world has seen better days, he thought. "This is one of the reasons I left the CIA. We came to this country to make it better, but we just made it worse."

"The CIA is just an intelligence agency," Colt said. "It's the people in power in this region that have made it like this. Not the CIA."

Drake shrugged. The US and Russia were using the country the same way they used Vietnam in the sixties and seventies and Afghanistan in the eighties. Syria was a playground. The people in power here didn't have as much control as they believed they did.

"Down this road," Drake said.

Colt followed Drake's instructions and drove deeper into the city, driving parallel along the Barada River. Eventually, the Four Seasons Hotel's lights gleamed along the surface of the river, and Drake knew they were close.

"The Zorba House will be on your next left," he said.

Colt nodded and spotted the large red neon sign for the Zorba House. There was a small crowd gathered outside—women in skirts stood beside men in suits. The ground around them was muddy, the pavement cracked, and the buildings across from the club were etched with bullet holes.

"Looks like a nice club," Colt said sarcastically, as he rolled the jeep into a dark alley. "You sure you'll be fine in there alone?"

"No," Drake said. "But this is the only way we'll find Aya."

"Good luck."

Drake left his M4 in the jeep, but he took his M9. He hid it under his leather jacket and stepped out of the jeep into the cool, dark night of the Syrian capital. He could feel the eyes of the patrons lined up in front of the club's front door watch him as he approached. His jacket, blue jeans, and leather boots were not going to help him blend in. He would have been more at home in a country bar in West Texas than in a posh club in Syria.

The bouncer standing guard at the entrance laughed as Drake approached.

"Is Ali Bajal inside?" Drake asked.

The bouncer's laughter stopped. He stared at Drake and pulled out his gun.

If that was the way it was, then Drake knew what he'd have to do. He didn't waste time.

He punched the bouncer in the side of the head, knocking him out.

The crowd of patrons outside gasped. One of the girls fainted.

Drake winked at one of the cute girls in the line. She blushed.

He made his way inside the club. It was time to talk to an old friend.

TWENTY-NINE

The George Bush Center for Intelligence was the headquarters of the CIA. It was a short twenty-minute ride from downtown Washington and buried within a swath of trees close to the Potomac River. It was the epicenter of United States intelligence and was the heart of the deep state.

In a large office on the top floor, CIA Director Tom Fowler sat behind his imported black wood desk. His fingers delicately tapped its expensive surface. He was careful with his nails, though; he'd just had them manicured.

His assistant sat across from him. Sierra White looked good. Real good. As she droned on about his upcoming schedule, he watched her lips and thought about what kind of underwear she was wearing under that short skirt of hers. She kept droning on, and he kept thinking about that underwear.

He was at the top. He'd worked years to get to where he was. He'd kissed ass, he'd manipulated—he'd done what he had to do. He deserved a beautiful assistant like Sierra. She was a prize for all that hard work. A trophy.

"And you have a meeting with the president tomorrow evening in the Oval Office," she said. "He wants to go over the missing ammonium nitrate. It's a top priority."

Fowler nodded in a daze, lost in his dirty thoughts, not listening to one word she said. Sierra was everything he desired in a woman. Luscious, red-haired, smart, and most important of all, subservient. She did what she was told.

"Sir, the meeting—do you remember?" she said again, realizing her boss wasn't listening.

"What was that?" he said, shaking his head. "That last bit ... something about an evening thing?"

"You have a meeting with President Clarkson tomorrow evening at the White House. He wants an update on the missing ammonium nitrate."

"What? Did I agree to that?"

"Yes," Sierra said. She licked her lips.

Did she do that on purpose? Fowler thought. Was she flirting with him? He couldn't be sure. He felt hot, so he loosened his tie. He couldn't stop thinking about her. She was the best and worst part of his day.

"Sir," Sierra said, "what is your plan?"

Fowler shook his head. "I believe Kate Price is in Iraq looking at air force satellites—some sort of fact-finding operation. See what she's dug up. I'll use whatever she's found. Just get her on the phone. That should keep the president more than satisfied."

"Of course, Director."

Sierra winked at him as she left.

Fowler giggled. He watched her as she opened the door and left his office. He admired each and every one of her footsteps. She was new to the agency, but if she played ball, she'd rise quickly. And Fowler wanted her to play ball.

He adjusted his pants and cleaned up his desk. He was fastidious and needed every item to sit perfectly straight. Once he was settled, once the image of Sierra had left his mind, his phone rang.

It was Sierra again. She wasn't going to let his mind rest.

"What is it?" he said. "Did you forget something? You can always come into my office. The door is open to you."

Sierra laughed. "I have a call for you, sir. It's from the Al Asad air base base commander."

"And?"

"He will only speak to you."

"Put him on."

Fowler waited for Sierra to punch the base commander through.

"You better have a damn good reason for sending that bitch over here!" Tusk growled through the phone. "Kate Price is a nightmare. Always has been!"

"Excuse me?" Fowler said.

"You're the CIA director?" Tusk said.

"Yes."

"Well, that black ops bitch, Kate Price ... she's going to be the reason why you're fired."

"Can you elaborate?" Fowler asked. "Deputy Director Price went to Al Asad to look at air force satellite imagery. What are you talking about?"

"Talking about? Are you dense? She had my air force pilots fly those two men of hers in and out of the desert. Hell, one of those men attacked a US Air Force pilot. And the other, well, he stole US military property. I've got a military jeep, weapons, rations, medkits—all missing."

Fowler's neck became strained. His veins bulged from the surface of the skin. "Repeat that?"

"You heard me. Kate Price wasn't running a fact-finding mission. And the fact the CIA director doesn't know any of this is pretty damn embarrassing. When I tell the joint-chiefs ..."

Fowler took a deep breath. "Don't do that."

He'd worked too hard to fail now. He'd sacrificed too much. He cursed himself for agreeing to Price's silly mission. "Just tell me everything you know. I'll clean this up."

"You better," Tusk said. "You better."

THIRTY

Price was thirty-five thousand feet above the Atlantic. She'd escaped the air base before Tusk knew that Drake had busted Colt out of the holding cell and that the two men had stolen a US army military jeep and left the air base.

After putting Houston in a dog crate and placing him in the C-17's storage hold, Price made her way to the fuselage and strapped herself into her seat. She felt terrible about putting the dog down there, but she didn't have a choice.

She pulled out her thermos full of coffee and sighed.

The Boeing C-17 Globemaster III transport aircraft flew through some turbulence, and the coffee in her thermos spilled on her leg. She cursed and tried to soak it up with her sleeve but was distracted when her phone buzzed. She put the thermos on the floor and held it between her boots. "This is Kate Price."

"You sound chipper." It was the CIA director. Shit, she thought. She composed herself and got ready for the onslaught. She'd have to play dumb until she knew what Fowler knew.

"I just spoke to Base Commander Tusk. What the hell is going on over there?" he said.

"What do you mean?"

"What were you doing in Syria? I thought you were looking at military satellites?"

"Can you be more specific?"

"Don't play dumb with me. You were running an operation over there, something off the books. I want to know."

"I'm a Black Ops Director," Price said. "Everything I do is off the books."

"And I'm your boss. I should know what you're doing. Who did you have out there? Tusk said something about an old guy and a young guy. He said that the old guy commandeered a US Air Force helicopter and knocked out a pilot. Tusk said the young guy busted the old guy out of a holding cell ... and that the two of them stole a US Army jeep. What the hell is going on, Kate?"

Fowler had played his cards. He'd revealed what he knew. That was always his weakness. He was vulnerable to exploitation. The only reason he was director was that he was a good ass-kisser. He was a 'yes-man.'

"Tusk isn't lying," Price said. She'd have to be strategic, careful. "There were two men with me. They were investigating the whereabouts of the missing ammonium nitrate."

"And who were they?"

"I'll tell you when I get back to Langley."

"You better," Fowler said. "You know, many people around here think that you should've been director and not me. But you're prone to mistakes. Your missions backfire. I don't need to bring up your Terminus division, do I?"

"No, sir. You don't."

"One of your officers went rogue and killed a senator."

"I thought we weren't going to talk about it."

"I won't, but when you come back to Langley, I want answers. I want to know what's going on. No more spy shit."

Price rolled her eyes. He was the Director of the CIA, and he didn't want 'spy-shit.' He was in the wrong line of work.

"Of course, sir," she said.

"I don't want this affecting my position. The president is already down my neck."

"There's no need to worry, Tom," Price said.

"I'm willing to let this slide if you share what you have with me. I have a meeting with the president tomorrow evening. I'd like to provide him with some solid intel. Will you do that for me?"

"Of course."

Fowler hung up, and Price smiled. The director's weakness was his job and his paranoia that everyone at Langley was after it.

The last job on earth she wanted was that of CIA director. And now that she knew what Fowler's real worry was, she could exploit it and buy Drake time—at least a day or two. That may be all he needed.

Price forgot her thermos full of coffee. It rolled away from her feet toward a group of soldiers playing video games on their phones. They didn't notice her thermos. It rolled under their feet, spilling what was left of her coffee along the way.

She sighted and pulled out her laptop from her travel bag. She'd need to send some emails, read the news, and make sure that she knew the lay of the land before she met Fowler in the morning. She'd have to get ready to play some political games. The very thing she hated the most about the agency.

THIRTY-ONE

Ali Bajal was a family man first, night club owner second, an arms dealer third. At least, that was the order he put it in. Everything he'd ever done, he did for his family. He did it so they had a future away from the war and far from Syria. Some people in Damascus called him a traitor; some called him a saint. He knew he was somewhere in between. He liked it that way. He played all sides.

The Zorba House had been open for ten years. He envisioned it as an escape from the terror on the streets. He wanted to create a refuge, a place where people could meet and talk freely without worry of condemnation or death.

He modeled the club after one he'd visited in Greece, decorating the walls with paintings of Athens and velvet drapes that hung low from the ceiling. The club had two floors with tables for poker, lounges, and space for plenty of scantily clad women. The women would crisscross the main floor and strategically bend over in front of the *right* patrons.

In a rigid society like the one in Syria, Bajal had to pay off the Syrian National Army soldiers who regularly frequented his club. They were more than happy to accept the small bribe and just as thrilled to enjoy the delights and sights within: nice drinks, nice women.

Bajal's office was large and had a wide one-sided window that overlooked the club's ground floor lounge. From his vantage point, he could see almost everything that happened inside. He could see the soldiers looking at his waitresses, the rebels mingling at the bar. It was a microcosm of the country: chaotic, violent, and bursting with life. He loved it.

He was sat at his desk, nursing a rum and Coke, when his phone rang. It was the bouncer who manned the front door.

"What is it?"

"A man. An American. He just knocked me out. He's in the club. He's looking for you."

"What did he look like?"

"He was American. Leather jacket. Blue jeans. He had these strange blue eyes."

Bajal shook his head and hung up. He'd made a bad gamble, one that he knew he was about to pay for.

The door to his office was flung open.

Bajal burst out laughing. "I knew it was a stupid idea getting you to come back here," he said. "I didn't know what the hell she was thinking."

"Hello, Ali. Your club looks as busy as ever."

"Jason Drake, it's been too long."

"I should put a bullet between your eyes."

Bajal shot back the rest of his rum and Coke. "And why would you do something stupid like that? I know where she is. I know where you can find her. You need me alive."

Drake laughed sarcastically. Typical Bajal. He played everything defensively and always had an answer to every question.

Drake walked into the office, sat across from Bajal, and put his feet up on the club owner's desk. "Where is she?" Drake asked.

"She's not in Syria."

"Really?"

"She's not who she was."

"No shit. She stabbed a needle full of tranquilizer into my neck and tried to sell me out to some Russian soldiers for hydrazine."

Bajal laughed. "Yet here you are."

"Here I am."

"Aya is damaged," Bajal said. "She's broken. She's no longer a rebel. She's been manipulated and has entangled herself in a conspiracy which I do not fully understand."

Drake pulled out his sidearm and aimed it at Bajal's head. "Tell me what you know."

"You won't kill me. I have the power here, Jason. I have the information. You know how it works. You kill me, you know nothing."

"You're cocky for someone in danger."

"Danger? From who?"

"Who do you think?"

Bajal waved his hands dismissively, and picked up his phone and called the bar. "What's your choice of drink, Jason?"

"An old fashioned."

"Farid, can you please bring me another rum and Coke and an old fashioned for my dear old friend."

Drake shook his head. "You don't get it, do you?" he said. "You think you're smarter than everyone. You think that being a useful tool will keep you alive."

"It's worked up until now. I work with the CIA, the Syrian National Army, the rebels, the Russians. Everyone needs me. I'm oxygen. Without me, their fires wouldn't burn."

"You have a blindspot," Drake said.

"And what's that?"

"Aya made a mistake in handing me to the Russians, and she knows you know where she is. She knows I know that. Your life is in danger."

"I did what she asked. I'll weasel my way out of it. I always do."

"I thought you were smarter than this."

"I'll tell you where she is for immunity and protection for my wife and daughter."

"You don't get it," Drake said.

"Get what?"

"You'll find out soon."

The door to Bajal's office opened. Farid, the bartender, walked inside and handed both men their drinks.

"Cheers," Bajal said to Drake, lifting up his drink.

"Cheers."

Their glasses clinked, and Bajal was about to down his drink but stopped when his phone rang. It was his wife's number. His brow furrowed, and he put his glass down on the desk.

"Ali, my beloved—the house, there are men inside,"□ she said.

"What is going on, Nayla?"

"Men with guns," she said. "They burst into our house. You need to come home."

"Stay hidden. Stay in the shadows. Keep Hamila safe." Hamila was their daughter.

"I'm scared, Ali," Nayla said. "Oh no, they heard me."

Shots echoed through the receiver, followed by faint breaths and sounds of moaning. He heard voices. Men. They sounded Russian.

Bajal's skin turned white. He looked at Drake and lowered his cellphone from his ear. He dropped it onto the floor of his office and began to shake. Tremors moved through his body. He wanted to scream. He opened his mouth, but no words would come out. All he could muster was, "They're dead."

"They were looking for you."

"They're dead."

"I told you Aya would consider you a loose end. She doesn't need you."

"But ... I did what she asked. She still needs ..."

"We need to get you out of here,"□ Drake said. "If they're at your house, they'll be here, too."

"Why would she do this?"

"Because of me."

Shots burst out on the ground floor. Armed men carrying AK-47s ran inside the club and fired at random.

Drake finished his drink and ran to the one-way window in the office.

Bajal slumped to the floor in the fetal position. Everything he'd fought for, his reasons for living, were wiped out, pruned from existence because he'd become too confident.

"We need to go," Drake said.

Bajal groaned.

Drake picked the club owner up from the floor. "We need to go."

"My family is dead. Just let me die."

"You created this mess. You thought you were in the clear, but your luck has finally run out."

"My ... daughter!" Bajal sobbed.

"Follow me,"□ Drake said. "I'm getting you out of here, and you're going to tell me everything you know. Understand?"

Bajal didn't say anything. He just continued to moan.

Drake pulled out his sidearm and dragged the chubby man out of the office. He needed to keep Bajal alive. He needed to get him somewhere safe.

He needed to find out where Aya was hiding.

THIRTY-TWO

The men who'd stormed the club were engaged in a shootout with some of the patrons. The club wasn't just a microcosm of the civil war at that moment; it was a living re-enactment of it. Rebels fought Syrian soldiers, who fought gangsters and Russians.

The war had finally crept into the Zorba House, and it was a blood bath.

The assailants who'd stormed in were wearing tactical equipment—helmets, body armor, boots, and gloves. They looked like special forces. Whoever they were, they had little regard for life and were well equipped. It was clear that they wanted Bajal dead at any cost.

Drake and Bajal were at the bottom of the stairwell that led down from the club owner's office. Drake peered through the door's window. Bullet holes peppered the walls of the club, and blood pooled on the floor.

"What are we going to do?" Bajal asked.

"Calm down."

"Fuck you, Jason! Calm down? My wife and daughter are dead!"

"You reap what you sow," Drake grunted. He had little sympathy for the man who'd sold him out. "What's the fastest way out of your club?"

Breathing heavily and using the wall of the stairwell to keep himself steady, Bajal turned to Drake and said, "The kitchen, but it's across from the main floor. We'll have to make our way across the gunfire. There's no way we'll make it with all that shooting."

Drake cursed and slid the door open ever so slightly to get a better lay of the land. He counted six shooters. They were carrying AK-12s modded with extended magazines. They were also wearing bulletproof armor. It wouldn't be long before they cut through the drunk rebels and Syrian national army soldiers who were slowing their advance.

Drake wouldn't be able to take them all out. He'd have to sneak out of the club and hope they didn't notice him and Bajal in the process.

He pulled out his phone and dialed Colt.

"What the hell is going on in there?" Colt said. "People are running out of the place. Some are covered in blood. Do you need help?"

"I've got Bajal, and he knows where the ammonium nitrate is."

"Do you need help?"

"No," Drake said. "But we're trapped inside."

"What?" Colt said.

"We're going out the back door. You'll have to leave. There's a Four Seasons Hotel along the Shoukry Al-Qouwatly highway. We passed it on the way here. We'll meet you at the bar in the hotel."

"Okay," Colt said. "I'll meet you there."

Drake hung up and turned to Bajal. "Stick to me like glue! If you don't, we're both dead."

Bajal nodded.

Drake grabbed Bajal by the collar and pulled him from the stairwell to a nearby poker table that had been flipped over. From their vantage point, it was clear the rebels and Syrian soldiers were about to be overtaken by the shooters. The rebels were hiding in a booth at the far end of the club, and the Syrian army soldiers were hiding by a stage in the middle of the room. Both the rebels and soldiers were shooting Makarov and TT-33 pistols.

The infiltrators were hiding behind the bar and were strategic with every burst of fire they unloaded. One of them threw a grenade toward the soldiers by the stage. When it exploded, the soldiers all dropped.

That seemed to be the straw that broke the camel's back for the rebels. There were three of them left, and it was clear that they'd all determined their best chance at survival was to run. They made a break for it and fired blindly at the shooters.

The shooters were patient. They'd been trained well. They knew what they were doing.

The rebels ran out of ammo before they made it to the exit. The shooters heard the silence and popped up from behind their cover, littering the fleeing rebels with lead.

There was an eerie silence, momentarily interrupted by the moans of the dying.

"What now?" Bajal whispered to Drake. "The shooting has stopped. Shouldn't we run?"

Drake gestured for Bajal to keep quiet and waited for the infiltrators inside the club to make the first move. Every battle was different. Patience would be the key to surviving this one.

The infiltrators took slow and cautious steps toward the stairwell. Cracked glass, heavy breaths. Drake focused on every sound.

Bajal was about to speak again, but Drake drew his pistol and aimed it at Bajal's temple. He held it there until the club owner got the hint. Now wasn't the time to speak.

The infiltrators walked up the stairwell. Their footsteps grew faint.

"Now," Drake said to Bajal. "Run!"

He pulled the fat club owner, and they ran toward the kitchen. They would have made it out of the club, too, had it not been for one of the rebels, who was still alive. His body littered with holes, he didn't know what was going on. He just didn't want to go out without a fight. He aimed his Makarov at Drake and fired. He missed Drake by three feet, but the sound of gunfire alerted the infiltrators that the action on the ground floor wasn't yet complete.

Bajal froze at the kitchen's entrance. Drake pushed him inside and dove after him.

The infiltrators were inside Bajal's office but spotted Drake and Bajal as they disappeared into the kitchen.

"Don't stop running," Drake said. "Not until I say so."

THIRTY-THREE

Drake and Bajal crept through the alleyways of Damascus and made their way toward the Four Seasons. They were in the rich part of the city. BMWs, Mercedes-Benzes, and Porsches were parked in every driveway. The houses were big and had tall iron fences.

Drake periodically checked for any shadows or signs that he and Bajal were being followed by the men who'd stormed the club, but he didn't see anything. They were in the clear.

For now.

Police sirens echoed throughout the dark. The city sounded like it was moaning, screaming into the darkness that it wanted to be put out of its misery.

"Just let me die," Bajal moaned. "I'll tell you where she is, but just let me die."

"We're headed to the Four Seasons. You'll tell me there."

"My poor daughter," Bajal sobbed. He could hardly move. He was overwhelmed with anguish and regret. His feet slid across the cobblestoned streets.

"Come on," Drake said. He pulled Bajal and was rude about it. Ali Bajal was the scum of the earth. A cockroach. He stunk and lived in dark, shadowy, moist areas. He had a wife and a child, but that didn't mean he was a nice guy.

"She's in Russia," Bajal said, falling to his knees in the middle of
the street and pushing Drake's hands away. "She's with a—"

Drake picked him up. "You'll tell me at the bar. You can drink
yourself to death there."

Bajal nodded and followed Drake. The club owner seemed to get
the hint. There was no point in fighting.

It took thirty minutes to get to the hotel, and when the two men
walked through the entrance, the hotel staff looked at them suspi-
ciously. Drake's clothes were dirty and torn, and Bajal's face was
bright red.

Colt was sitting alone in a booth in the corner of the bar. There
was a pint of beer in front of him—a pint that he was looking at
nervously and hadn't yet touched. It was his first in days, and he was
wondering if he needed it. He felt strange asking himself the question. Beer had always been like water to him, something his body
needed, but maybe he'd been compensating for something. Perhaps
he'd been drinking too much?

He was about to take his first sip when he saw Drake and Bajal.

"Took you chaps long enough," Colt said.

Bajal sat down at the booth, grabbed Colt's beer, and gulped it
back like a thirsty fish. Colt's eyes widened in protest, and he was
about to punch Bajal, but Drake stopped him from interfering.

"He just found out his wife and daughter are dead," Drake said to
Colt. "Let him drink."

Colt nodded and pulled his hand back.

Drake sat down across from Colt.

"Were you followed?" Colt asked. "That club was crawling with
dangerous men."

"I don't know. Were you?"

"I don't think so."

"Let's hope not."

"I need another drink," Bajal said, slamming Colt's empty pint
glass on the table. "I am going to tell you everything, but I want to be
drunk."

Colt lifted his hand and waved the bartender over. The
bartender walked up to the three men and looked at them suspi-

ciously. It was clear they weren't foreign businessmen or politicians. They were soldiers. Trouble. "How can I help you?" he said.

"I need another pint," Colt barked. "And get this chap here whatever he wants." He gestured to Bajal. "Man's had a rough night."

The bartender nodded and then looked at Drake. "And you?"

"I'll take a beer," Drake said.

Bajal pulled out his wallet and a roll of Syrian pounds. Here's five thousand," he said. "I want all your rum."

The bartender snatched the money and stuffed it in his pocket before Bajal could change his mind. He then walked back to the bar and got to work on the orders.

"You're going to kill yourself if you drink that much rum, mate," Colt said to Bajal.

"That's the point," Bajal responded.

"I know how that feels, mate. I lost a—"

Bajal cut Colt off. "You know nothing. What are you? Scottish? You don't know anything about Syria. I did what I did to provide for my family." He slammed his fist on the table. "No one can escape this war. It's a mess ... it's a fucking mess ..."

"I'm sorry," Colt said.

"Don't apologize," Drake said to Colt. "He did this to himself. He's a coward, and he knows it."

"Fuck you," Bajal said to Drake.

"That's a little cold, mate," Colt said to Drake. "He just lost his family."

"This guy didn't think twice about Aya selling me to the Russians," Drake said. "He's a piece of shit. He supplied weapons, transportation, women to whoever he saw fit. He did what he did because he wanted to survive."

Bajal's head rested on the table. "I'll tell you what I know, but then you both need to leave. I want to drink alone."

"Then tell me where she is," Drake said. "Who is she working with? You said she's being manipulated."

Bajal's sleeves were covered in snot and damp with tears. He lifted his head up from his arms and looked at Drake. "She's in Russia," he said. "She's being manipulated by an oligarch's son. His name is Andrei Zadorov. I don't know much about him, only that he has money."

The bartender reappeared. Both his arms were wrapped around six bottles of rum. He placed them on the table and said he'd be back with the beer.

"Before we get started, I need a drink," Bajal said. He opened a bottle of rum and took a long swig. "Andrei convinced Aya a few years ago to join his cause. He was in Aleppo looking for people."

"And what's his cause?"

"He wants to start a war between the US and Russia. He wants to start World War Three."

THIRTY-FOUR

The three men talked for over an hour. The bar had mostly emptied out. Most of the lights had been turned off. The bartender was putting chairs on top of tables, closing up. Aside from Drake, Colt, and Bajal, the only other patrons were a young woman in a red dress who was eyeing up Drake from the bar and a European businessman who had his head on his table and a bottle of scotch in his hand.

"World War Three?" Colt said with a laugh. "How's this Andrei fella going to do that?"

"I don't know," Bajal said, "but Andrei has contacts in the Russian military and intelligence services. He's well connected."

"Sounds like Russian SVR," Drake said. "I bet he was a spy."

"I don't know if he was SVR or not," Bajal said. "He made sure to keep his circle small. He was in Syria, and then he left. He got what he needed, I guess."

"Do you know why he wants to start a war?" Drake asked. "What's in it for him?"

"Like I said, I don't know much about him," Bajal said. "All I know is that Aya is helping him."

"And where are they?" Drake asked.

"Golovinka. Close to Sochi."

"And how do you know that?" Colt asked.

"Because I helped Aya smuggle the ammonium nitrate to their compound. It's massive and protected by security. Like I said, Andrei is rich. He has a mercenary army patrolling the town. If you want to know why no one has found the fertilizer, it's because of that."

"So we've got to go to Golovinka then," Colt said. He slammed his palm on the table.

Drake nodded and stared into Bajal's drunken eyes. "Thank you," he said.

"I'm not a good man," Bajal said. "You were right about me. I've done bad things. Many lives have been lost because of me, but my wife and daughter ... they were innocent. They were pure. You need to stop her. I was wrong to help her get you here. I was blinded by money and ignorance."

"I'll stop her," Drake said. He stood up from the table and tapped Colt on the shoulder. "Let's go."

Colt nodded and followed Drake out of the bar.

The US Army jeep was in the parking garage below the hotel.

Bajal watched them as they left and then turned to his collection of rum on the table. With any luck, he'd be dead by sunrise.

THIRTY-FIVE

The US Army jeep was between a Jaguar and a Lexus in the Four Seasons' parking garage. It stood out like a sore thumb.

"We need another vehicle," Drake said to Colt. "Its US military license badge will attract too much attention."

"How do you expect to get another vehicle?"

Drake looked around the parking garage and walked up to an old, beat-up red Toyota truck. He smashed open the driver's side window with his elbow, unlocked the door, and hopped inside. He hot-wired the vehicle and started the engine.

"Where'd you learn how to do that?" Colt asked.

"When I was a teenager, I used to hot-wire cars," Drake said.

"You're a weird guy," Colt said. "Coudn't you have picked one of the Porsches?"

"Those vehicles have too many security systems to bypass, and we don't have the time. We just need to get to Russia or close to it. We now know where the ammonium nitrate is. We need to get to Golovinka."

The two men grabbed the weapons and gear from the jeep and threw them into the red truck's cargo bed.

Drake sat on the driver's side of the truck and pulled out of the garage. He drove it back onto the streets of Damascus. A couple of military trucks, two police vehicles, and an ambulance drove past them as he cautiously rolled down the street.

"We won't be able to drive to Russia," Drake said to Colt. "It'll take too long."

"And we can't go back to the US Air Force base, I presume," Colt said.

"No," Drake said. "We'll need help."

"There's a Royal Air Service base in Turkey," Colt said. "It'd be about an eight-hour drive north from here. I can make a few calls. I might be able to convince them to help."

"If that's our best chance, that's what we have to do."

"I'll get on it."

Drake drove the truck down a busy street in the middle of the city. He kept looking at the rear-view mirror. Two pairs of headlights had caught his attention. Two black SUVs with tinted windows. They'd been on his tail for a while. He wanted to see if they were following him.

Colt opened his phone and found a message from Price.

"Price is in Washington," he said to Drake. "She just landed at Dulles. She's meeting the CIA director soon."

"Good," Drake said. "When we get clear of this, tell her we know the ammonium nitrate is in Russia. Tell her it's in a town called Golovinka."

Colt nodded. "I'll text my contact at the SAS first," he said.

Drake rolled the truck to a stop at an intersection.

Colt texted Graham Howe to get access to the air base in Turkey. Howe was going to have questions about it, but he'd deal with that later. He hit send on the message, and was about to update Drake when he noticed the CIA officer looked tense. "What is it?" he asked.

"Those two SUVs are following us."

Colt looked out the back window of the truck. "Fucking hell!"

"Get your weapons ready," Drake said, his attention solely on the road ahead. "They'll fire on us soon."

Colt pulled out his assault rifle from his backpack. He readied it and aimed down the sights toward the SUVs.

"If they fire, fire back," Drake said.

They fired.

The back window of the truck's cab exploded. Glass shattered in every direction.

"Damnit!" Drake grunted. The street was log-jammed, tail to tail. Traffic wasn't moving at all. It was probably why they'd decided to fire. Her slammed his foot on the gas and sped off between a row of traffic.

"Are you hit?" Colt asked.

Drake patted his body. "No. I'm good."

"Good," Colt said. He pulled down on the trigger of his rifle and fired back at the SUVs.

Getting out of Damascus was going to be difficult.

THIRTY-SIX

Colt continued to exchange fire with the two SUVs while Drake navigated the truck through the narrow gap between traffic. The two SUVs on their tail wouldn't let up. They followed the truck down every road, street, and alleyway.

"These boys are packing some serious gear," Colt yelled to Drake. "I'm running short on ammo. We need to figure out how the hell we're going to get out of this. What's the end game?"

"Stop firing blindly," Drake said.

"I can't get a good shot with you swerving like a mad man," Colt said, doing his best to hold his HK33 steady.

"Goddamnit!" Drake barked.

"Screw you!" Colt said. "Stop cursing the Lord's name!"

Drake hadn't eased up on the pedal in minutes, he deftly guided the truck between the cars and trucks in his way. He only let up when he had to make a sudden turn, pulling on the handbrake and turning the steel wheel violently toward the direction he knew they needed to go. The truck was chewing up bits and pieces of the streets; stalls, trash cans, phone booths. No civilians. Drake was careful about that.

"This problem could become a very big one if we keep this up any longer," Colt said. "We're tearing up the city. The Syrian army are going to notice this."

Colt had made a valid point. One that was racing through Drake's head. He knew he needed to resolve the situation. He needed to find a quick solution. He pulled the truck up onto the sidewalk. The truck screeched as it hit the street's curb. Pedestrians ran in all directions.

"You think this is better?" Colt asked. "What the hell are you doing?"

"Just keep firing back at the SUVs!" Drake shouted.

Despite its age, the truck was somehow holding together. Whoever had owned it had taken good care of it. Drake felt bad about stealing it. The vehicle most likely belonged to one of the Four Seasons' workers and not one of their rich, elite guests. A blue-collar layman loved this truck and labored over its internals, and treated it right. And now Drake was laying waste to it, using it to survive. The poor bastard who owned it would see it on the front page of the papers in the morning. Drake wondered what he'd think as he kept driving down a sidewalk. He had a plan, but it was going to be risky.

He turned down a narrow alley.

"How much ammo do you have left?" Drake yelled at Colt.

"One magazine!"

"I'll keep it steady. Just keep firing."

"What are you doing?"

"Just trust me."

Colt looked out the back window. He cursed himself for drinking that beer at the hotel and took a deep breath, trying to steady his hand. He couldn't waste any more ammo. It was do or die.

One of the SUVs on their tail had followed them down the alleyway. The other had chosen another route.

Colt unleashed an entire magazine into the engine of the SUV that followed them down the alley. The SUV slowed down, its engine smoking. It crashed into the wall of the alleyway and came to a stop.

"Haha!" Colt shouted. "Got him!"

"Get ready for the other one."

"The other one?"

"The other SUV! Jesus!"

"Hey! What did I say? Don't say the Lord's name in vain! The other SUV is either stuck behind the one I shot, or it's ..."

"There they are!" Drake said.

"What?" Colt asked.

At the exit of the alleyway, the other SUV appeared. It rolled to a stop, and the men inside were lining up their rifles, poking their barrels through the opened backseat windows.

"Get down!" Drake shouted.

Both he and Colt ducked below the dash. Bullets peppered the truck's front, rendering its metal hood into swiss cheese and leaving nothing of its windshield.

Drake didn't pull his foot off the gas. The truck sped up.

"Brace yourself!" he yelled.

"Ah, fuck," Colt grunted. He made the sign of the cross and closed his eyes. "This was your strategy? Suicide?"

The truck was a tank. Even though all its tires were flat, its engine smoking and leaking oil, it managed to hold its momentum long enough to ram into the side of the SUV at the end of the alley.

It hit the SUV with enough force to send it sliding into the middle of the street. The men inside it were tossed about like clothes in a washing machine.

Civilians ran in all directions, panicking, calling for help. Vehicles that weren't impacted drove off in all directions.

"We need to hurry," Drake said, gathering himself and shaking his head. "It won't be long before we have the army on top of us." He grabbed his M4 and kicked the driver's side door open with his foot. "Watch your six," he yelled to Colt, who was opening the passenger side door, slowly.

The crash had severely impacted Colt. He was injured. He had a big cut on his head, and blood was splattered on the dash. He lifted his rifle and checked the alleyway behind them. He ducked behind a trash bin and avoided fire from two men running down the alley from the other SUV—the one stuck in the alley. When the bullets stopped, he stood up and dropped both the hostiles.

Drake cautiously approached the SUV in the middle of the street. He pushed past fleeing civilians and hopped over an abandoned cab. He aimed down the sights of his M4 and examined the inside of the SUV.

The men inside were groggy. They were wearing ski masks and looked like the same men who'd attacked Ali Bajal's club. He put a bullet in each of them. He was merciless about it. Cold. He had the advantage, and he took it.

A thick stream of blood crept out of the bullet holes in each one of their heads as sirens sounded in the distance. It wouldn't be long before the police and Syrian Army were at the scene.

"Come on," Drake yelled to Colt, who was still hiding behind the trash can.

Colt got up and ran to Drake.

Meanwhile, Drake inspected the back of the SUV. He found a rocket launcher. He checked that it was loaded and lifted it up over his shoulder. The sirens grew louder. The police and army were moving in.

"What the hell are you doing?" Colt asked, running to Drake's side. "We're in a shit tonne of trouble now. You think you're going to take on an army?"

"I'm going to buy us time."

"Time?"

Down the street, two Syrian Army vehicles approached. They were military trucks, loaded with twenty men in each. Drake turned to Colt and said, "You need to find a vehicle. Once I fire this thing, we'll have to disappear. We'll need to be back on the road."

"Are you serious? Back on the road? Are you a crazy?"

"Just do it. If you don't, we'll end up dead."

Colt shook his head and ran off toward a group of civilians who were hiding behind a grocery stall. There were three of them. One looked like the shop clerk, the other two looked like farmers.

"Do any of you have a vehicle?" Colt asked in English, hoping one of them would understand. To ease the tension, he'd put his gun over his shoulder, letting them know he didn't intend to kill them.

The civilians lifted their hands up, covering their faces and whimpering.

"If you don't give me your keys, I'll take 'em from you. I don't have time for this," Colt said.

One of the farmers stood up. He pulled the keys out of his pocket. He spoke in broken English. "I am ... with ... boy. Take ... keys. Truck ... behind ... building. Take."

Colt grunted. "No," he said. "I don't want your keys. You're a farmer. I want his keys." He stared at the grocer and exposed his teeth like a growling dog. "Give me your keys."

The shopkeep stood up. His pants were wet at the crotch. He reached into his back pocket and pulled out the keys to his vehicle.

Colt snatched them from his hands. "I hope you have insurance, mate."

The shopkeep shook his head.

"Where's the vehicle?"

"In the back ... behind this building. It's black," the grocer said. The asshole spoke good English. He'd been playing dumb, hoping that Colt would take advantage of the farmers and not him.

Colt ran behind the stall and got in the vehicle.

OUT ON THE STREET, Drake lined up the two approaching military trucks. He held the rocket launcher firm in his hands. He waited until they got close. The street was mostly empty by that point. The gunfire had scattered most of the pedestrians. He felt comfortable with what he was about to do. There would be little collateral damage.

He fired the rocket so it hit the ground between the trucks. It was a two-birds-one-stone maneuver, one he'd been taught while in the military. The trucks embraced the shock of the explosion and toppled over, each on the opposite side of the street. On their sides, they skidded to a stop.

At the same time, Colt pulled up beside Drake in a Porsche Cayenne SUV. Drake shook his head when he saw the vehicle. He jumped inside and said to Colt, "You couldn't have picked a vehicle less conspicuous?"

"Just get in, ya arsehole!"

Colt slammed on the gas and disappeared into the dark.

THIRTY-SEVEN

Price joined the CIA when she was twenty-three. It was the late eighties, and the Soviet Empire had just collapsed. A ten-year war in Afghanistan and a CIA-backed mujahideen ended the Cold War, although one could argue it created another.

Young, smart, and driven, Price was a patriot first and foremost. She admired her country. No other country had a legal document like the Constitution. Since 1789, when it first came into force, it was the United States's spine and the country's moral compass. With it, the principles of freedom, democracy, and justice had been upheld and preserved. Price's goal had always been to honor the Constitution's mission and protect it at all costs.

But it didn't take her long to find that the Constitution was always under attack in Washington, DC.

The Central Intelligence Agency was created in 1947 after Harry S. Truman signed into law the National Security Act, which was a direct response to the growing tensions between the USSR and the US following the end of World War II. But it quickly turned into a political wing of power in the United States. Its directors, deputies, and executives used Machiavellian-like moves to establish their worldview and assert their influence on the government.

Hidden from the burdens of international law, free from blame, a rot grew within the CIA; it was like a cancer. Too many directors and too many executives had become compromised by either their personal desire for power or by foreign agents with big pockets.

As Price rose in the ranks, led various clandestine missions, and spearheaded her Terminus division, she learned the true scale of the rot.

Freedom.

Democracy.

Justice.

All were compromised and vulnerable.

Clifton Taggart was the Director of the CIA when Price started Terminus. He was old school, one of those guys who understood the world's realities and didn't presume to know the answer to every question he was asked. He relied on his team, demanded the truth, and never shied away from danger or conflict—and didn't care if he was wrong.

After landing at Dulles, Price thought about Taggart and one of the first conversations she had with her former director. She was a young officer. Green to the realities of the world. They two of them were in his office.

"Whenever you're in doubt," he said. "Remember the unofficial motto of the agency ... 'and ye shall know the truth, and the truth shall make you free.'"

"That's John chapter 8, verse 32, isn't it?"

"Have you read the Bible?" Taggart smiled.

"Yes."

"Are you a believer?"

"No."

Taggart chuckled. "There's still time to be saved, my dear."

"Our officers deal in lies, exist in shadows," Price said. "The motto seems counter to what we are."

"Ah," Taggart said. "But the truth lives in the shadows. The easiest thing a spy can do is lie. Lies live out in the open. Lies are cheap. The hardest thing to find is the truth. We spend all our time at the agency trying to uncover it because we know it is the one thing people try to hide the most."

He was probably Price's only true ally in the agency. He understood her the way no one else seemed to.

After he died, she had no one she could trust.

Thinking about the past made her confident. She knew what she was about to do was the right thing. Once off the plane, she purchased a dog leash for Houston from an airport shop. She'd been using a rope she'd taken from the hangar at the air base up until that point. She hailed a yellow cab and jumped into the backseat. The cabbie was pissed about the dog, but Price promised a good tip if he kept his mouth shut. The cabbie shrugged and drove her to Langley.

She led Houston into the main building of the CIA. Security, analysts, officers, and executives all gave her weird looks. She bought a coffee and made her way up to Fowler's office.

"Thanks for holding the door for me, Sierra," Price said to Fowler's assistant. "It's good to see you again."

"Of course, ma'am," Sierra said, nodding to Price and looking at the dog with an odd expression. "Anything for the woman who helped me land this job."

Price smiled. Sierra was one of the few people she had on her side. An essential ally at the CIA. Sierra was Price's way of keeping an eye on the director.

Price sat down and told Houston to sit, which the dog surprisingly obeyed.

She sipped the coffee she'd bought from the Starbucks in the lobby.

She looked at the wall of pictures in Fowler's office. The man had turned ass-kissing into an art form. He was everything she despised about the agency—power-hungry, corrupt, and he didn't give a rat's ass about the Constitution.

Fowler pushed open the door and marched inside like a petulant child. Houston growled as soon as he saw the director. Fowler nearly jumped when he saw the dog.

Price smiled. "You don't like dogs?"

"What the hell is that thing doing in here?" Fowler said. "It stinks!"

"I thought I'd need some extra security. You sounded a little upset on the phone."

"For Christ's sake," Fowler said. "Doesn't this building have a no-animal policy?"

"Probably," Price said. "Do you think I care?"

Fowler shook his head and sat at his desk, readjusting his pens as he did so. "If that thing shits or pisses on my floor, the clean up bill is coming out of your salary."

"That's fine."

"You have a lot to explain."

"What do you want to know?"

"What do you know about the ammonium nitrate? Why didn't you tell me that you were running an operation? Who were the men with you at the air base? You know I don't like messes."

"The truth is messy."

"Get to the point."

"Two weeks ago, I received contact from an old ally in Syria," she said. "He said he had word that a young woman, a rebel fighter, knew where the ammonium nitrate was, but she would only talk to one person."

"And who was that?"

Price closed her eyes and thought once more about her conversation with Taggart. She was about to make a calculated gamble, but she knew to always trust in the truth when in doubt.

"Jason Drake," she said.

Fowler clenched his jaw. His face went red. "The CIA officer who we believe murdered a US senator."

"He had his reasons."

"We've been looking for him for years."

"And I found him—"

Fowler cut her off. "Then where is he? I want him in here. I want him arrested. If it ever gets out that a former CIA officer killed a US senator, I'll be fired, and I'll be sure to take you down with me."

"Jason is in Syria."

"You stupid bitch. Was he one of the men you had out there?"

"Yes. The other one was my ex-husband."

"I should send every resource I have after Jason. That man is a walking time bomb."

"You won't do that," Price said. "If you want to find the ammonium nitrate, you won't do that."

"So, I have to rely on a wanted man?"

"Yes."

Fowler shook his head. "If any of this leaves this office, if any of this gets out—you're done with the CIA. Hell, you should have been done after that Terminus debacle. I never knew what Taggart saw in you."

"Jason will find the ammonium nitrate."

"You're dismissed," Fowler said. "I want a report about this. I have a meeting with the president tonight, and he wants an update about the fertilizer. When this is all done, we'll discuss what we do with Jason. How we bring him in."

"Of course," Price said.

She left Fowler's office and was about to leave the building when her phone buzzed. It was a message from Colt.

His text was simple, to the point.

'You might be hearing about us in the news. We ran into a bit of a problem in Damascus. There's more dead Russians and maybe a few dead Syrian soldiers—but we know where the ammonium nitrate is. It's in Russia. A town Golovinka. Some Russian named Andrei Zadorov is behind it all.'

Price gritted her teeth. She called a cab and fumed. If Drake or Colt were seen on any security cameras or if Fowler suspected that Drake was behind the mess in Damascus, then she'd have to come up with a new plan. Fowler didn't care about the ammonium nitrate as much as he did his own job. An international incident involving the CIA would be enough for the president to fire him. Fowler would go down swinging. Shit would hit the fan.

THIRTY-EIGHT

They drove for days, from Syria to Iraq, through Iran, Armenia, Georgia, and then finally into Russia. They had to take a long route to get to Golovinka. The straight path wouldn't work. It was far too dangerous.

When they finally crossed the border into Russia, the sun was setting. Ajmal was no longer driving the truck. Aya had grown tired of him and ordered him to the back. She felt bad about it at first, but he kept bringing up the past, and she didn't want to look back. All that mattered was the mission and her revenge.

The driver who replaced her brother was quiet and kept his eyes on the road. She liked that about him.

Golovinka appeared amid a valley between two tall mountains. It was a small town. A dozen or so buildings dotted either side of the main road, which cut through the town like an artery. The road was serpentine and went up and down like the temperature in the fall or spring.

Andrei's compound was just north of the town, in the thick woods. It was the perfect place to hide in. The forests in the area were heavily protected by Russian military surface to air missile sites, and the locals who resided in the town had all been paid off and told to keep quiet. They turned a blind eye to the mercenaries that Andrei had hired to protect his presence.

The Russian military truck rolled past the front gates of Andrei's compound and pulled into the long driveway. It came to a stop just outside the main building, a large mansion with Greek-inspired pillars.

Aya jumped out of the vehicle when it came to a stop. She wanted to talk to Andrei. She needed to know about the status of Ali Bajal, wanted to know whether his mercenaries had succeeded in getting to him before Drake. If Drake got to the arms dealer first, then everything would have to change.

Andrei stood atop the front steps of the mansion. He was using a cane to keep himself upright. His sickness was beginning to take over.

Aya paused when she saw him. He looked at least twenty pounds thinner, and his skin was ghost white. It had been three months since they'd last met, and those months had been bad for Andrei.

"We killed Ali Bajal," Andrei said. "The loose end is taken care of."

"Was he alone? Was Jason there?" Aya asked.

Andrei closed his eyes and shrugged. "The men I sent to kill Bajal are dead. I have good reason to assume that it was Jason who killed them. So ... it's not good, but it's not bad."

"Piece of shit," Aya said. She knew if Drake was in Damascus, he had spoken to Bajal. "Then that means ..."

"Don't worry," Andrei said. "I've made the appropriate arrangements. Nothing will be affected. We will make America burn, as we planned. The date of the art exhibit has been moved forward."

"To when?"

"Three days from now."

"Two days ahead of schedule? How will I get there? How will the hydrazine get there?"

"I've made plans."

"And I'm to trust you? Even after you didn't listen to me about Jason? I told you he was a threat."

"And I told you that you were right. I was wrong."

Ajmal approached from the back of the truck. He put his arm

around Aya and looked up at Andrei. "She was right," he said. "We should have listened."

"Shut up," Aya said to her brother. "You are a nuisance and a pest."

"It will be okay," Andrei said to the two siblings. "The complication with the CIA officer, Jason Drake, was unforeseen but manageable. I have made sure that we will be safe. He will not stop us."

Aya pushed away from her brother's arm and made her way up the mansion steps toward Andrei. She sneered at him as she passed.

She made her way inside and walked to her sleeping quarters. She wished she had Houston with her. The dog provided her comfort and assurance.

Ajmal ran after her, but Andrei stopped him, extending his arm and turning to Ajmal. "Don't," Andrei said.

"She needs to be consoled."

"Everything is fine," Andrei said. "She just needs to accept it. She'll learn."

Ajmal nodded. "I just want what's best for her."

"I know you do."

"Then what should we do?" Ajmal asked.

"It's already been done," Andrei said. "Things have been moved. This will be the last night Aya is in Russia. She's scheduled to leave the country tomorrow."

"Okay," Ajmal said. "I trust you."

"I know."

Once inside her quarters, Aya laid on her bed and screamed into her pillow. She should have killed him. She should have ended his life when she had the chance. She should have stuck the needle into his heart and laughed. She'd made a mistake. She'd warned Ajmal and Andrei about him, but she ... she was the one who wanted to see him again. She cursed herself.

After an hour of venting, she fell asleep. She woke up to a knocking at her door in the middle of the night. It was Andrei.

"Are you ready?" he said.

"Ready?"

"You need to leave now."

"I'll be traveling with the hydrazine?"

"Yes. You're going to take it to America," he said. "You're going to go with it to ensure its safe delivery. You'll be executing the final stage of our plan alone."

"And I will be met by your team in America?"

"Yes."

"And if Jason comes there? If he comes to find me?"

"He will come here first, and I will stop him."

Aya shook her head. "You won't be able to stop him."

Andrei laughed. "No, probably not. But I will be able to slow him down. And that is all we need."

Andrei left her room, and Aya began to pack her things. She wouldn't need much. It was going to be a one-way trip. As she stuffed a change of clothes into a suitcase, her thoughts drifted back to the past.

They drifted to the moment she woke up in the rubble of the Butcher's campsite. Before she knew what her purpose was.

Before her whole world had changed.

THIRTY-NINE

Four years earlier

Aya awoke in the dark rubble of the Butcher's campsite and knew that she'd been lucky. Everything around her was fire and death. She pushed herself up and ran toward what was left of the tents, looking for survivors, looking for the children.

They were all dead.

All she found were frozen faces, locked in their deathly stares.

She saw Drake. He was fifty feet from the campsite. Unconscious. His body sprawled out on a sand dune. She thought of waking him up but chose against it. She needed to get away.

He'd either die or be found by his handlers. She was confident of that. After all, the CIA had been watching everything. They were always watching, listening.

She stumbled from the top of the sand dune and walked until she found herself in the nearest town. It was a quiet little place called Qu'ri. From there, she called her brother.

"What is it, Aya?" Ajmal asked. He was in Aleppo, busy with the rebellion. "Are you done with the CIA assassin?"

"I need help."

"Help?"

"I'm in a small town called Qu'ri. I need you to pick me up. I need you to get me out of here."

"Where is the American?"

"He's either dead or ... I want nothing to do with him."

"What happened?"

"I'll tell you when you're here."

She hung up and waited for Ajmal to arrive at Qu'ri. It took him six hours to show up.

"Aya!" he said, noticing her fatigue, noticing the cuts and bruises on her face. "Are you okay?"

"No."

He drove her from Qu'ri to the room where he was staying at in Aleppo. For two months, she kept a low profile and stayed there. Healed.

Three months after the drone strike, she woke up feeling sick, tired, and nauseous. She ran to the toilet, unleashed from her mouth what was in her belly, and knew something was wrong.

"What is it?" Ajmal asked.

"I don't know," she said. "I need to go to the doctor."

FORTY

Aya was pregnant.

When she heard the doctor's confirmation, she felt she was cursed.

She thought of every option. Would it be merciful to end the pregnancy and not bring a life into a world of chaos and destruction?

But when she heard the heartbeat on the ultrasound, she knew she had no choice.

"What do you mean you're going to keep it?" her brother asked her. "Kill it! It's not alive! Not yet, at least!"

The two of them were still in the room he was renting in Aleppo. It was small and only had one bed. For months Ajmal had slept on the floor.

"It's alive. I can't kill it. I've seen too much death in this war. I won't be responsible for the death of another child."

"Who is the father?"

"Does it matter?"

"Who is it?"

"Shut up," she said.

"It was him, wasn't it?" Ajmal said. "That CIA spy who you were parading around the desert with. You whore. You couldn't keep your legs closed."

Despite how sick she felt, she kicked her brother in the balls so hard she felt a crack. Ajmal fell to the floor, his face red, tears streaming from his eyes. It hurt so bad he thought he was going to die.

"I'm keeping the child," she said. "And you're going to help me keep it."

Ajmal pushed himself up and fought through the pain. "The rebellion needs you, sister. Our cause, our struggle. We need all we can get. If you bring this child into your life, you'll be pulling yourself away from the war."

"The rebellion?" she said. "I don't care about the rebellion. I'm done fighting. I need to protect this child. It's all that matters to me. I won't let this child freeze."

"Freeze?"

"I won't let it die. I won't let its face be frozen."

"And our country? Our cause?"

Aya closed her eyes. "I thought I was meant for more, but I now realize the truth. There is no light at the end of the tunnel. I need you to find me a place to hide. A safe place. Far from the violence, far from the rebellion and the war. If I am going to give birth, I want it to be safe. I don't care if it's in Syria or out of the country. Just find me somewhere safe."

"I'll do my best," he said. "I'll do it for you, sister."

FORTY-ONE

While Aya remained cooped up in a tiny Aleppo room, Ajmal did his best to find a place for her to hide outside the city. He searched everywhere; asked everyone. But trying to find help in the war torn country wasn't easy.

One night, while drunk at a bar, his head in between his arms, his thoughts full of sorrow and regret, Ajmal felt a hand on his back.

"You don't look good."

Ajmal looked up. The man speaking to him was Russian and dressed in an expensive suit. The man took off his Gucci sunglasses and smiled.

Ajmal first thought was to rob the man, kill him even; steal his wallet and take what he could back to his sister. But whether it was the booze or the way the man looked at him, he stayed on his barstool and nodded. "My life is over," he said. "Of course, I don't look good."

"You're life is over?"

"Yes," Ajmal said. "I've spent years fighting for something that I don't believe in. I fought for it only because my sister told me to. I fought for it because I believed in her, but now she wants to give up. This country is cursed if our best fighters will no longer fight. We will lose and every dream, every hope we've had will fade into memory."

"Why did your sister give up?" the man asked.

"Because she's pregnant."

"Interesting."

Ajmal soured. "Who are you anyway?"

"I'm a man looking for people with nothing to lose."

"Nothing to lose?" Ajmal shook his head. "This is Syria. Nobody here has anything left to lose."

"If you could have anything right now, what would ask for?"

"I need a place for my sister. Like I said, she's pregnant. I've been searching for months for a place where she can stay, but ..."

"But what?"

"But you Russians, you've turned the tide of the war. There is hardly a rebel left in Aleppo I can trust. I honestly don't know what to do. No one will help us."

"My name is Andrei Zadorov."

"I don't care," Ajmal said. "Please, leave me alone. I just want to drink."

Ajmal turned away from Andrei and asked the barkeep for another glass of arak, a traditional alcoholic spirit in the Middle East. It was comprised of grapes and aniseed. The aniseed gave the drink a licorice taste.

"I can help you," Andrei said. "I can help you and your sister."

"Screw you."

"Are you like this with everyone you meet?"

"I'm a Syrian Democratic Forces rebel fighter."

"I don't care."

"You're Russian," Ajmal said. "And you're in Syria, which means that you're here to kill rebels on behalf of the Syrian president."

"I'm not here to kill rebels."

"Then why are you here?"

"I'm here to find help," Andrei said. "I need the right kind of people for a special operation."

The bartender placed the milky white arak in front of Ajmal. He grabbed the drink and shot it back. He then looked at Andrei. He studied the Russian's face. Had he said too much? Should he trust this man?

"Your sister was a rebel fighter, too?" Andrei said.

"She was one of our best. She was an excellent sniper and even worked with the CIA. She's ..." He stopped himself. "I shouldn't say anything more."

Andrei rubbed his chin. "I see."

Ajmal was about to call the bartender for another drink when Andrei stopped him. "I'll get this," Andrei said. "Let's sit and talk. I want to help you and your sister. I want to give you exactly what you want."

FORTY-TWO

At first, Aya didn't trust Andrei. He was Russian, and he was a spy.

When they met in a small cafe, one mile from the Aleppo Citadel, one of the oldest and largest castles in the world, Andrei explained who he was. He didn't hold anything back.

Aya stared at the Aleppo Citadel as Andrei spoke. She tried to focus on what he was saying, but it was difficult. She hadn't been sleeping well, and she was exhausted. Instead, she stared at the citadel. It had been occupied by the Greeks, Byzantines, Ayyubids, Mamluks, and Ottomans. Her country had seemingly been at war with itself since the beginning of time.

"I'm not spying on the rebellion," Andrei said, noticing Aya's gaze had drifted back to the ancient fortress. "My mission is to get the Russian military out of Syria as quickly as possible. I believe my country is wasting their time here. I want Syria to be at peace."

"He can help us," Ajmal said to his sister. "As long as I help him, he'll help you. He's trying to build an army."

"I don't just trust the Russians," Aya said. "Their bombs are killing our people on behalf of our corrupt government."

"You shouldn't trust me," Andrei said. "You're a Syrian rebel. The Russian military has gassed, bombed, ripped your forces to shreds. But remember this: your struggle is made more difficult because the

Americans abandoned you. They supported you with half-assed measures. The weapons and rations they sent to your rebels were never enough. This is modern warfare. Syria is a playground for new technologies, for the military-industrial complex to make their quarterly goals. Syria is a wasteland of the past being torn up by the present."

Aya turned from the citadel and stared into Andrei's eyes. They were blue, like Drake's. "So what? My brother helps you, and you help me find a place outside of this country where I can raise my child?"

"Yes, but I don't have the connections to transport you out of the country just yet. With your brother's help, by the time your baby is born, I should be able to get you and your child out of here."

"And you'll do this, Ajmal?" Aya asked her brother. "You'll help this man? You'll leave the rebellion to help him?"

"Yes," Ajmal said. "I'll do whatever I can for you, my sister. And, anyway, he wants a Syria that is peaceful. Isn't that what we are all fighting for? But I told him I'd only do it if you thought it was a good idea. That's why I wanted you to meet."

"Okay," Aya said. She turned to Andrei. "I have many connections in this country. If you betray my brother or me, I will kill you."

Andrei laughed. "I won't betray you, Aya. I am here to help."

Aya agreed to the arrangement, not because she was comfortable with it, but because she had no choice—she needed a place to stay hidden from Syrian armed forces, and she needed it quick.

Andrei had a large house in the middle of Aleppo that was surrounded by a thick stone wall. He told Aya she could stay there as long as she needed to. He had staff that took care of meals and provided a semblance of security. He was wealthy like no one she'd ever met and provided for her like no one ever had.

She stayed there for months, and her stomach grew large. For the first time in her life, she felt at peace.

Every now and then, thoughts of the past swelled in her head like a turbulent wave. Images of the dead children in the desert. Flashes of Drake's smirk. They all crashed into one another. She'd wake up drenched in sweat from time to time. She screamed his name.

"Jason!"

She was alone in her room, save for the child growing inside her. Should she have left him there? Was he alive? Was he dead?

The night before she gave birth, Ajmal and Andrei left for Russia. The two of them were going to Russia to set up a compound. Her brother had done everything Andrei had asked of him. He'd found enough men to help Andrei's cause, which both Aya and Ajmal were still unclear about.

"We're leaving in the morning," Ajmal said to Aya as she lay on the bed in her room.

The sun was not yet above the horizon. It was dark and eerie.

"Where are you going?" Aya asked. "My child could come any minute."

"We're going to Russia," Ajmal said. "The next stage of Andrei's plan."

"And what is his plan?"

"He says he needs a hub," Ajmal said. "There are too many eyes in Syria. He needs a place where no one will look."

"And will he help me leave Syria? Will he help me take the baby away from here?"

"Of course," Ajmal said. "He is a man of his word. We have no reason to doubt him. He's done so much for us already. He's provided a safe place for you to stay, and he's put me to work. We have never lived better."

Aya smiled. Her brother was right. Had they stayed with the rebellion, she'd be spending her nights in tents or dilapidated buildings.

Ajmal and Andrei left. And mere hours later, Aya gave birth to Amira. The most beautiful thing she'd ever created. Something born of her violent past, yet alive and perfect in the present.

Three weeks after the birth, Ajmal returned from Russia.

"Are you ready to leave?" he asked. "Andrei has arranged for Amira's transportation out of the country."

"Amira's?" Aya asked.

"I need to take you across the border into Turkey one at a time. It's the safest way. As soon as I get to Turkey, I'll call you. You'll stay in Aleppo until I return. You'll only be apart for one or two days. This is the only way."

"And why can't I go with you to Russia?"

"It's dangerous there," Ajmal said. "I've learned more about Andrei's plan. He wants to attack America. You would not be safe in Russia."

Aya gathered her supplies. She knew it would be like this. Nothing in Syria was ever easy.

Once she was done, she handed Amira to Andrei and turned away. She couldn't bear watching her brother leave.

She collapsed on the floor and cried as she heard Andrei's vehicle drive away. She could feel her heart grow thin as the sound of his vehicle's engine dissipated in the distance. She'd given Ajmal her heart. She'd given him the only thing keeping her sane.

FORTY-THREE

Two days passed.

Aya had heard nothing from Ajmal. She'd tried calling his cell-phone a dozen times, but he never answered.

Panicked, she called Andrei, who she believed was still in Russia.

"Hello?" he said. "Aya?"

"Yes," Aya said. "My brother. My child. Where are they?"

"I am on my way from Russia. I am almost in Aleppo."

Aya's tone changed. She screamed. It was violent and fierce. "Where are they?"

"I will be at the house in Aleppo shortly. Within the next couple of hours."

"Hours? You're already in the country?"

"Yes," Andrei said. "I will be with you shortly."

Aya hung up and walked frantically around the house she'd been cooped up in for months. She paced back and forth through every room. She wanted out. She hadn't been outside the walls of the house for months. She'd trapped herself. She felt like a caged animal.

It felt like there were hands around her neck, squeezing every last bit of air out of her lungs—killing her. Her vision went dark in the corners, and she began to shake. Her hands wouldn't keep still.

She tried to close her eyes and talk herself down from the panic, but when she did, she saw the eyes of the dead children in the desert; she saw Drake's body lying on the sand.

"No!" she screamed. "No!"

She kept screaming until Andrei burst into the house. He put his arms around her.

"Aya, it's okay," he said. "I'm here."

Aya's eyes were glazed with tears. Her breaths were heavy and long. "Where are they?" she said.

Andrei closed his eyes. "I don't know," he said. "I've sent a team to investigate."

Aya's mind snapped at that moment. It felt like there was a fire burning at the back of her head. She could almost hear the crackling sound of the flames. A wave of anger and rage swelled through each of her muscles.

Andrei held her tightly. "It's okay," he said. "I am sure they are fine."

Aya pushed Andrei away and stood up. She walked to the kitchen and poured herself a glass of water.

Andrei walked into the kitchen and approached Aya but stopped when he noticed she had a steak knife in her hand.

Aya looked at the wealthy Russian and smiled. She wanted to dismember anything that stood in her way. If someone had harmed Amira, she would tear the flesh off their bones and boil them alive.

"I warned you," she said.

"You have every reason to be mad," Andrei said.

"If anything has happened to her, I will cut your heart out."

"Ever since that morning, when we first met, I knew you were a force to be reckoned with. I knew you would follow through."

"Enough talking," Aya said. "All you do is talk. What do you know?" She slammed the steak knife down into a wooden cutting board.

"Please, sit," he said, gesturing toward the dining table.

Aya took cautious steps and sat down. Andrei walked to a liquor cabinet and poured himself a glass of vodka.

"I got word from your brother a day ago."

She tensed up. "Where is he?"

"He's alive. He's on his way back."

"Where is she?"

"Aya ... I ..."

Aya lunged from her seat at Andrei with the quickness of a feline. She held the steak knife to his throat. "Where is she?"

"Everything went to plan. Your brother handed over Amira to the smugglers, but they were attacked. Ajmal saw it all from a distance."

The blade of the steak knife pressed against Andrei's throat. It was about to break the skin. "Listen, I know you're upset, but—"

"But what? I should cut your head off!"

"We know who did it."

"*You* did it. You arranged this plan. I should have gone with her."

A streak of blood dripped from Andrei's neck.

"It was an American drone," Andrei said. His voice was frantic and scared. "An American drone!"

"What?"

Aya felt the breath leave her lungs. She felt weak. The world spun around her like she'd drunk a dozen shots of whiskey. She pulled the blade away from Andrei's neck.

"Your daughter died because of an American drone strike," Andrei said. "Ajmal tried to rescue her, but he suffered burn wounds."

Aya fell to the floor of the kitchen. She slipped away. Time stopped moving.

Andrei stayed with her and tried to console her.

She didn't even realize he was still in the room with her. She stayed on the floor of the kitchen for the entire night.

The next morning, Ajmal returned. He was bloody. Aya embraced her brother and then went to her room to pack up her belongings.

If she couldn't have a future, then no one should.

She was going to help Andrei.

She was going to go to Russia.

FORTY-FOUR

President Roy Clarkson's approval ratings were the lowest they'd been since he'd been elected.

He needed a kick, a win.

It had been too long since anything had gone well for him. He'd been elected on the promise that he would keep America out of foreign wars and focus strictly on the economy, but that was becoming tricky.

Russian aggression in the Middle East and in Eastern Europe, along with an intelligence community that resented him, had made it difficult for Clarkson to get control of his foreign agenda.

A businessman first, he believed America's exceptionalism was built upon the backs of its workers and innovators. Stuffy, bureaucratic nonsense, an infestation of legalese, and corruption at almost every level of government had stifled what had made America great. He wanted people to do what they did best. He didn't want them bogged down by internal political strife and paperwork.

He took a long drag from his Cuban cigar as he looked over the south lawn from inside the Oval Office. As he exhaled, he shook his head. It was the final year of his first term, and he felt like he was in over his head.

It was night, and the stars were beginning to shine outside.

Twilight loomed. The sky was faint and purple and black. The Washington Monument shot up from the edge of the horizon and cut through the dark like an obelisk of freedom and hope.

On his desk was the latest copy of the President's Daily Brief. The PDB was a top-secret document produced each morning for the president. It contained highly classified intelligence analysis, information about covert ops that the CIA was running, and reports from sensitive US sources or allied intelligence agencies.

Clarkson had read every word twice.

Aside from Russian military aggression, the report mostly focused on the missing ammonium nitrate. It had baffled the intelligence community for months. Two thousand tonnes of fertilizer had vanished. Clarkson wanted answers, but all he'd gotten from his Director of National Intelligence and the CIA Director were bullshit.

"We're working on it, sir."

"On it, Mr. President."

Assholes, Clarkson thought. Sycophants.

His phone rang, and he answered. "What is it?" the president asked.

"CIA Director Tom Fowler, Mr. President," his secretary said. "He's here for his meeting."

"Nancy, you know I hate that *Mr. President* bullshit. Just call me Roy."

"Yes, Mr. ... I'm sorry. Yes, Roy."

"You'll get it eventually," he said. "If I get re-elected, that is."

She chuckled. "I'm sending him in."

Clarkson hung up and sat at his desk. He rubbed his hands through his thick hair that was turning salt and pepper. The first term did a number on you.

Fowler walked into the Oval Office, holding a file. Clarkson rolled his eyes and took another drag of his cigar. More paperwork, more bullshit.

"Mr. President, I hope you're well," Fowler said.

"Cut the crap. Have a seat and tell me what you know about the ammonium nitrate."

"Right, right," Fowler said. "I don't want to waste your time."

Fowler put the file he was holding on the President's desk.

"I read the PDB this morning," Clarkson said. "This better not reiterate what I already know."

"It doesn't."

Clarkson grabbed the file and flipped through it.

It was new information. He was surprised.

He looked up at Fowler and smiled. "There was an operation in Syria?"

Fowler nodded. "Yes, sir. My Deputy Director of Black Operations, Kate Price, received word from a source that we had insight into the location of the ammonium nitrate."

"And we have an officer in Damascus working on it?"

"Yes, sir. The officer is in Damascus as we speak. Just like the report says. Once he uncovers the location, we'll make a move. It will be a big win for you, sir. A huge win."

Clarkson rolled his eyes. He wasn't convinced just yet. He'd believe it when he saw it. He continued to look at the report when his phone rang. Fowler's rang at the same time.

Both men answered their phones in unison, listened to what the person calling them said, and then looked at each other awkwardly.

"Damnit," Fowler said.

Clarkson closed his eyes and took a long drag from his cigar. Too good to be true. His grandfather always referred to that refrain when things were looking up and then unexpectedly took a left turn. If it looked too good to be true, that meant it probably was.

Both men hung up at the same time.

"You were just told about the attack in Damascus, I presume," Clarkson said to the CIA director.

Fowler nodded. "You need to understand, Mr. President, that this is nothing to be concerned about. What happened in Damascus is not out of the realm of control. The officer in question ... there's got to be an explanation. Details are still coming in."

Clarkson slammed his fist on his desk. "I'm at my wit's end, Director," he said. "Your agency has caused my government so much grief over the past few years that I don't know who to trust. I've got four months until re-election. Four months. But, the truth is, I don't care about that as much as I care about the American people. If you can't do your job, I will find someone who can."

"Absolutely," Fowler said. "The fate of the American people is why I do my job. I will figure this out."

"I'm sure you will," Clarkson said, unconvinced.

"I'll make this work in our favor," Fowler said.

Clarkson shook his head. "Just find the ammonium nitrate. Find out where it is. Re-election ..." He tailed off. "Listen, at the end of the day, if I can say that I did my best, then that's all that matters. So do your best."

"I'll clean this up."

Fowler left the president's office and messaged Sierra. His heart pounded in his chest. He'd never been so angry in all his life.

"I want Price apprehended," his text read. "And I want you to organize a task force. Get Trent Freeman to spearhead it. This is a red alert. My job is on the line."

He left the White House and raced down the road in his Lexus toward Langley. He was going to make the bitch pay.

FORTY-FIVE

Colt drove across the Turkish border. It'd been almost twenty-four hours since the shootout in Damascus. No one had followed them out of the capital, though. They were in the clear, finally.

A moment of peace?

Colt hadn't known a day of peace since his child passed away. It was a gnawing feeling. Like teeth biting down on his flesh but never tearing away the pain—just pulling, causing pain, hurt.

He avoided all the main roads as he drove the SUV out of Syria. Drake had instructed him to drive down the old paths that Bedouin herders had used for centuries. They weren't paved, but the sand had been so packed down from hundreds of years of use that they were practically as good as any paved road in Britain. The main benefit of those paths was that they weren't monitored by Syrian soldiers.

The two men didn't talk much on the drive. There wasn't much to say. They now knew where they were headed: Golovinka. Russia. Aya. The ammonium nitrate. That was all that mattered.

As the sun pierced the horizon, Colt rubbed his brow and thought of his past, of the moment he'd learned his life was over.

"He's got cancer," Price said to him over the phone. She was in Langley.

He was in a hotel in Berlin, on assignment. It was 1997. The two of them were trying to make their long-distance marriage work.

"What? No," he said. He remembered the sick feeling he'd had. It felt like his breath was leaving his lungs.

"It's true," she said.

"How bad is it?"

She didn't respond, but her silence said more than words ever could.

"What now?" he asked.

"Can you come home? I need you."

Home? The idea of a place that was permanent, settled, and forever seemed odd to Colt. In their five-year marriage, Colt and Price had barely shared their home at the same time for more than three months. 'Home' was simply an idea, a place they both agreed they would end up one day—but not today. A promise they'd told themselves would become real when they were done with their work and were ready to focus on each other and their family.

"I'll do what I can," he said.

He called Graham Howe for dismissal from his Berlin assignment. Howe granted it without question, saying to Colt, "Stay strong, old friend."

"Ah, shut up," Colt said.

When he was back in Langley, Colt found Cody lying on his bed in his room, barely breathing. His son's skin was pale. His body was shaking. The young boy could hardly open his eyes.

Between raspy breaths, he asked, "Papa?"

Colt broke down at the bedside. He held onto his son's pale frame, feeling the tenderness of his boy's fragile warmth against his rough, unshaven face. "I'm sorry, Cody," he said. "I'm so sorry."

Colt drank himself to sleep every night as he waited for the inevitable. It was the only way he could shield himself from the pain and worry. His world was wrought with anguish. It was terrible. He barely talked to Price. The two of them knew the future would not be what they wanted it to be.

Months passed. Colt was assigned new missions. Price busied

herself in her work. Cody did his best to fight the terrible disease eating away him. Then one day the future arrived.

Price told Colt that Cody's condition worsened. He came back home.

He stayed in Langley until it was settled, until the priest said his final words at the funeral, until the dirt was tossed onto the grave. Colt left a rosary atop Cody's grave and then headed back to Britain for a new assignment.

It was uncontrollable. Perhaps that was why he felt the way he did. There was no stopping it. Drake's experience in Syria, the ammonium nitrate ... they all seemed like events that were pre-planned, pre-determined even.

As he drove through the endless desert in Syria toward the Turkish border, he wondered why his mind had taken him back to such dark thoughts, to memories that he'd thought he'd squashed with years of destructive drinking and bad habits. He shook his head and focused on the horizon. The sun was climbing above the lip of the desert's edge. Those memories needed to die, he thought. He needed to move on.

"You okay?" Drake asked, noticing Colt's sullen and strained expression. He was in the passenger seat watching the dry, endless desert pass.

"Yeah, mate. I'm fine," Colt said, shaking his head. "Just tired."

Drake nodded and stared out the passenger's side window.

"Ah, what the hell?" Colt said. "I'll tell you what's bothering me. It's the past. It sneaks up on you and tries to pull you back. The horizon is all that matters, where you'll be when the sunsets. The sunrise is only a memory. Nothing more. It's the sunset, the eventual end ..." He trailed off.

"That's almost poetic," Drake said.

"Aye," Colt said. "Almost."

The two men said nothing to each other for the rest of the ride. Once Colt had taken them comfortably across the Turkish border, he guided the SUV toward a small town. The vehicle needed some attention, and he needed a break. The rear left tire was flat, there was something wrong with the rear differential, and the engine was smoking.

The town he drove to was called Gurney. Turkish soldiers were sporadically stationed throughout, but they didn't seem too bothered by Drake or Colt's presence. It was either that or they were good at hiding their suspicions. It wasn't every day two foreigners rolled into a town like Gurney in a broken-down jeep.

Colt pulled the SUV to a stop outside of a restaurant. Both men got out and stretched.

"Are you sure the British military will be able to help us?" Drake asked.

"Yes," Colt said. "My superior at the SAS, he told me he'd help if I ever asked. There's a Royal Air Force airfield close to here. All I have to do is make the call."

"How close is it?" Drake asked.

"To the west, maybe fifteen miles."

Drake looked at the smoking engine of the SUV. "I'll look for a mechanic. Someone who can help us get this thing back in working order."

Colt nodded. "I spoke to Kate while you slept. She's back in Langley. The president is meeting with the CIA director. She said it's only a matter of time before everyone knows about the shootout in Damascus. She hasn't texted me in a while, so I imagine things aren't good. They might already know. We need to get out of this town before word spreads."

Drake nodded. "Sounds good."

"While you find a mechanic, I'm going to get a drink, call my commanding officer and ask for his help. I'll tell him we know where the missing ammonium nitrate is and that the only way the SAS will get credit for finding it is if they help us," Colt said. "That should speed everything up. The sooner we get to Golovinka, the better."

Drake nodded and looked around the town. The place was sparse. The villagers were staring at him and Colt like they were aliens from another planet. The sooner they got out, the better.

Unlike the dilapidated villages in Syria, most of Gurney's buildings were still standing, and there was an odd sense of normalcy to the place. Kids wore designer shoes, a woman held bags full of food, and the men carried tools instead of rifles.

Drake left Colt in the street and wandered out into the town. All he needed was a good mechanic.

Colt called Howe. The last time they'd spoken, the SAS commanding officer was on his way to Al Asad to get Colt out of the holding cell. Colt knew it was going to be an awkward conversation.

"Where the bloody hell are you?" Howe yelled into the phone. "SAS command is properly upset! I flew to Iraq and was rightfully embarrassed by the United States base commander there. I just got back to London last night. I feel like a fool!"

"I'm in Turkey," Colt said. "I couldn't stick around Al Asad."

"First a helicopter, then a damn jeep! What the hell is going on, Clyde? What have you got yourself embroiled in?"

"I need help," Colt said.

"You're damn right, you need help!"

"Just relax," Colt said. "Keep your knickers on."

Howe screamed into the phone. He shouted expletive after expletive. He'd finally snapped.

Colt chuckled.

When he finally cooled down, Howe said, "What is this about?"

"I know where it is."

"Where what is?"

"The ammonium nitrate. I know where it is."

"And where is it?"

"It's in Russia. A small town named Golovinka."

"How do you know?"

"Because I'm with a CIA officer who knows. You need to help us. I'm in a town called Gurney. It's close—"

"I know where it's close to."

"Can you pick us up?"

Howe remained silent. He was mulling over his options. When he finally spoke again, he said, "I want a full debriefing when you come back to London."

"Of course."

"Stay put," Howe said. "I'll send a team to get you in the morning.

And Clyde, you'd better not be lying. I could have you institutionalized for something like this."

"I'm not."

Colt hung up. At least he and Drake would have a way out of Turkey. That was all they needed for now. Convincing Howe to get them to Russia would be another matter. One step at a time, though.

He noticed Drake talking to a gas station attendant a quarter mile down Gurney's main strip. He checked his watch and then spotted a bathhouse. He had the time, and he needed to relax. It was either the bathhouse or the bar, and frankly, the days he'd spent with Drake not drinking were some of the best days he'd had in months.

He pushed open the front doors of the bathhouse. He'd never been in one before. Unlike the Roman bathhouses he'd visited while on assignment in Italy, Turkish bathhouses reversed things. Instead of starting with dunking yourself in cold water and then proceeding to the warmer, more relaxing waters, it was the opposite. It was warm then cold. Architecturally, the layout was very similar: three basic, interconnected rooms, one hot, one warm, one cold.

He walked inside and, for the first time in days, felt a sense of peace. He dunked himself into the hot water, took a deep breath, and forgot about his past.

All that mattered was the horizon.

FORTY-SIX

Price woke up. Her phone was ringing non-stop. It was the middle of the night, and she'd had a terrible sleep.

Houston was a very affectionate dog. He'd kept licking her face. She couldn't close her eyes.

Hearing her phone ring gave her a chance to get up from her bed. It was Sierra.

"What is it?" she asked.

"You're in trouble," Sierra said. "You need to leave. They're coming for you."

"What do you mean? Who's coming for me?"

"Fowler's gone apeshit. He's unleashed every agency officer at his disposal to bring you in. He's sent a team after your guy in Syria, too. He thinks you're trying to embarrass him, go after his job."

"That asshole."

Price knew this was about the shootout in Damascus. She'd hoped she would have a bit more time before Fowler found out, but she didn't. She needed to think of a contingency plan. Quick.

"What should we do?" Sierra asked.

"We? You need to keep quiet, Sierra. You shouldn't even be calling me."

"You're the only honest person in this whole agency," Sierra said. "You're the only one I trust."

Price smiled. It was nice to know she still had some allies in Langley. "Just look after yourself," Price said. "I'll be fine."

"Are you going to let the director's men pull you in?"

"No," Price said. "I'm going to go into hiding. Wait for word from me. And if you find out anything regarding what the director plans to do, let me know."

She said goodbye to Sierra, got out of her nightwear, and put on some clothes. Houston had jumped off the bed and frantically paced around the room.

"It's okay," Price said to the dog, trying to calm him down.

She grabbed the backpack she always had prepared for an emergency like this. Inside was a burner phone, five thousand dollars cash, a pistol, and a fake ID.

Once she had everything, she ran to a window, opened it, and saw a white van pull up in front.

"For Christ's sake," she said.

She grabbed an overcoat and a fedora and was about to leave when she heard Houston moan. She looked at the dog and shook her head. "Come on," she said, tapping her leg and rolling her eyes. Evasion was going to be more difficult with the dog, but she couldn't leave it behind.

Houston ran to her side, and she attached the leash she'd bought from the airport to his collar. She opened the door to her apartment and looked left and right down the hallway. When she was sure it was clear, she and Houston ran to the stairwell.

As she opened the door to the stairwell, she heard footsteps coming up from the lower levels. Heavy steps. They were wearing boots and equipment that rattled with each step.

"She's up here."

"Sixth floor."

"Hurry!"

They were CIA officers. She yanked on Houston's leash and guided the dog up the stairwell toward the seventh floor. She made her way to unit 706, the unit directly above hers. She knocked on the door.

An old woman named Olga Vensk answered. "What is it, Katy? It's very late. Would you like tea?"

"Not today, Olga. Can I come inside?"

"Well, I was just about to go to bed ..."

Price pushed her way into Olga's apartment and made her way toward the elderly woman's balcony.

"I'm sorry, Mrs. Vensk," Price said. "I just need to hang out for a second."

"Oh, dear ..."

"It will only be a couple of minutes. "

"Okay ..." The elderly woman was wearing a pink dress and held a romance novel in her hand.

Price and Houston walked out onto the balcony and knelt down. She did her best to keep quiet and listen to the voices coming from inside her unit.

"Where is she?"

"I don't know."

"Her phone pinged that she was here."

"She's spooked. She must have jumped. These spies have allies. Someone warned her. She's probably miles away by now."

"What does she look like?"

"About five-seven, good body. She's older, though ... so ..."

Both men chuckled.

"We'll set up a watch outside the building. If she comes back or if she's here and hiding, we'll find her."

Price cursed under her breath.

Olga was looking at Price from inside her apartment. Her hands trembled.

Price made her way back inside Olga's apartment. "I need to borrow your car."

"Excuse me?"

"Your car," Price said. "I need it."

"But ..."

Price grabbed the keys from a small counter close to the exit. She turned and looked at Olga. "Do you mind looking after the dog?"

"I'm allergic, sweetheart."

"Damnit," Price said. She'd have to take Houston with her. "I'll pay you back for any troubles, Mrs. Vensk. If anyone comes looking for me, just tell them the truth."

"Who is looking for you, Katy?"

"The government."

Price and Houston left.

"Oh dear," Olga said.

FORTY-SEVEN

In his office, Fowler learned of Price's evasion from the officers he'd sent after her.

"They didn't find her," Sierra said.

"She ran? How'd she know?"

"I don't know, sir."

Fowler stared at Sierra and clenched his jaw. The blinds in his office were open just enough that the light from the setting sun oozed into his office, covering everything in its blood-like glow.

"The bitch," he said, gritting his teeth. "The president wants me to throw everything at the ammonium nitrate. But this is a whole new can of worms. Kate is up to something. Going behind my back like this ..." Fowler's voice trailed off, his mind a confluence of paranoia.

"Sir?" Sierra asked.

"I want her detained. I want her handcuffed and in a cell, do you understand?"

Sierra nodded. "And what about Price's operative in Syria?"

"I have a wet team in Syria. They're tracking him down. He left Damascus in an SUV. They're on the hunt."

"A wet team?"

"I want him dead. The longer he's alive, the more trouble he'll create for me."

"And the ammonium nitrate?"

"One problem at a time, Sierra. I know Kate wants my job. We need to put out that fire first."

Sierra smiled. She knew Price well enough to know that being director was the last thing Price wanted.

"Why are you smiling?" Fowler said. "You don't believe me?"

"It just seems out of character," Sierra said. "Kate Price is a recluse here at the agency."

"She's wanted my job for years," Fowler said. "I know it. She was just waiting for the perfect time. She's trying to screw me over."

He looked at his computer monitor. He was waiting for an update from his wet team. Once they killed Drake and apprehended his companion, they'd get to work tracking down the ammonium nitrate—but only after they killed Drake.

The wet team were like chess pieces on a board. They'd eventually find Drake. He knew they would.

Sierra watched her boss with an odd curiosity. He seemed to go in and out of the present. He'd shift between fits of anger and silence. A vein on his head bulged and pulsated with the rhythm of his heart.

An encrypted email popped up in Fowler's inbox. His eyes narrowed. "You are dismissed, Sierra."

"Of course, sir."

She got up and left the director's office.

Fowler's eyes were transfixed on her, watching her like an eagle studies its prey. How did Price find out about the feds? It couldn't be. No, but maybe. He'd have to keep an eye on Sierra White.

He opened the email, unencrypted it, and read its contents.

We found him in Damascus. A contact in the Turkish army spotted him. We're moving in.

Fowler deleted the message and smiled. One problem at a time, he thought. One problem at a time.

FORTY-EIGHT

Price pulled down her fedora and undid her overcoat as she walked into Washington, DC's, Willard Hotel. Located at 1401 Pennsylvania Avenue NW, the Willard was one of the most beautiful and important buildings in the country. Constructed in 1816, the hotel was host to the Peace Congress of 1861, a last-ditch effort between the thirty-four states to avoid a civil war. It didn't work, of course. At one point during the Civil War, President Lincoln had to be smuggled into the hotel to avoid an assassination attempt. American author Nathaniel Hawthorne wrote that 'the Willard Hotel more justly could be called the center of Washington than either the Capitol or the White House or the State Department.'

The Willard was where Sierra told Price to meet.

Outside it was raining, and Price's overcoat was drenched. The weather in Washington during April was strange. Unpredictable. It could snow in the morning and be hot enough to put shorts on in the afternoon. Like the politicians who controlled the country, not much made sense.

Price stomped her feet on the freshly cleaned lobby rug and made her way to the hotel bar. She was alone. Houston was back in the motel room. He was safe.

At the bar, she sat down, kept her head low, and ordered a drink.

"Not a nice day out there, is it, ma'am?" the bartender said.

"Rum and Coke."

The bartender rolled his eyes, walked to the liquor cabinet, and got to work. Just another uptight DC asshole, he thought. No one in Washington liked small talk.

Two women about Price's age were in a booth, drunkenly laughing and rattling their jewelry like buffoons. Price wagered they were the wives of some lobbyists, spending their afternoons blissfully unaware of the world around them, of the machine that was Washington's politic. Their faces flushed with drink, and their words vapid and meaningless. But at least they lived in peace.

Ignorance was bliss, Price thought.

The bartender placed the drink in front of her and made his way to another patron. She sipped the Coke and felt the soda crackle in the back of her mouth. She took a deep breath. The alcohol would calm her nerves.

She felt a tap on her shoulder and nearly jumped off the stool.

"The director has gone insane," Sierra said.

She sat next to Price.

"He's a paranoid lunatic," Price said to Sierra, "As long as he doesn't find my operative, we should be okay."

"That's why I've called you here."

"What?"

"He's found your operative. He sent a wet team."

"Shit." Price finished her drink. She'd need another soon.

"The director is convinced you want his job," Sierra said. "He's pulled all resources from investigating the ammonium nitrate. He wants you and your operative out of the picture."

"Of course, he does."

"Everyone at Langley is confused. Just hours ago, our primary objective was finding that fertilizer, and now ...."

"And now Tom feels threatened," Price said. "I didn't know what to expect, but he's always been like this. Afraid of someone else getting credit. Assuming everyone's objective is selfish."

"I just wanted you to know," Sierra said.

"I'll contact my operative and let him know that the director's wet team is moving in. Do you know what the president said to Tom? I know they met."

"All President Clarkson said was that he wanted Fowler to focus on the ammonium nitrate."

"Interesting," Price said. "So Fowler's gone against the president's orders."

"Like I said, he thinks you're trying to undermine him."

Price froze. Fowler was making a mistake. He was leaving himself vulnerable. A plan quickly formulated in her head. A plan that she knew she'd later regret but would help her tip the scales in her favor. A plan that would help Drake find the ammonium nitrate.

The bartender noticed her empty drink, but he also saw Sierra White. "Can I get you a refill?" he said to Price. "And can I get you anything?" He winked at the young CIA assistant.

Sierra blushed.

Price rolled her eyes. That was why she'd put Sierra in front of Fowler. Sierra knew how to use her good looks to her advantage. She was your typical honeypot—she made the men and sometimes women around her weak. She appealed to their base nature. She got the men around her thinking with their dicks and not their brains. She made the women envious.

"I'll take another rum and Coke," Price said.

"Surprise me," Sierra said to the bartender, adding a slight giggle at the end of it.

The bartender's voice cracked. "Yes, ma'am."

When he was gone, Price turned back to Sierra. "This could work out to our advantage."

"How so? Honestly, Kate, you don't have many allies left in the agency. With Fowler going nuclear like this, you need to be careful. I don't think I'll be able to meet you again."

"I don't want to be the director."

"I know you don't."

"But I need to become the director."

"What are you planning?"

"I'm going to get Tom fired. You're going to embarrass him. Leak everything to the press. Everything."

"And how will that make you director?"

The bartender reappeared with two drinks. He placed them in front of Price and Sierra. "Um ... I got you ..." The bartender's face went red. He shook his head and took a deep breath. He turned to Sierra, flashed a toothy smile, and said, "Your drink is one ounce of vodka, one ounce of tequila, one of gin, and one of rum."

"Mmm," Sierra said. "What's it called?"

"The Leg Spreader."

Price gave the bartender a look that said, 'are you serious?' Sierra winked at the bartender. He giggled and walked away.

"How do you put up with that all day?" Price said.

"It's power," Sierra said. "I have the power. He'll do anything I ask him after this."

"You'll be a damn good spy one day," Price said.

"So, what's the plan?" Sierra said while sipping her Leg Spreader. It was so strong her face winced when the alcohol touched her lips.

"My operative's name is Jason Drake. He was in the Terminus division."

"What's that?"

"An old program I ran. It went bad. It had to be shut down."

"Why?

"Jason killed a senator."

"What?" Sierra said.

"Don't worry," Price said. "The senator deserved it."

Sierra nodded, but she looked nervously at Price.

Price continued, "When the president finds out about Tom's shift in strategy, you'll need to convince one of his advisors or senators to meet with me. Tell his staff that I know where the ammonium nitrate is, and if the president wants a success story before the election, he'll have to meet with me."

"And you'll be the director?"

"If I am the director, nothing will stop us from doing our job."

"Tom has a lot of power. He has connections all over the world," Sierra said. "And he cares only about power—he won't let you take it from him easily."

"This is about protecting Americans," Price said. "Jason said that the woman who has the ammonium nitrate is planning on using it against an American target. I believe him. And in order for Jason to get to the ammonium nitrate, I need to become director. Just make sure you leak everything to the press when I tell you to and get me a meeting with the president. I'll do the rest."

Sierra finished her Leg Spreader. "Okay," she said. She got up from her stool and winked at the bartender as she left.

Price tapped on the bar. One more drink wouldn't hurt.

She pulled out her phone and messaged Colt.

She was about to fight fire with fire, chaos with more chaos. She wanted to make sure that Drake and Colt knew they'd have to walk through hell to make it work.

FORTY-NINE

A controlled burn or a burn-off is a fire intentionally set for the purposes of forest management. Fire is a natural part of a forest's ecology, and, as such, a controlled burn can be a tool foresters use to maintain the health of a forest. In other words, a burn-off can be a useful tool to mitigate a disastrous fire. A small fire to put out a bigger one.

Colt and Drake were gathering their belongings, getting ready to leave Gurney. Colt said the SAS officers picking them up would be in the small town in a couple of hours.

They were inside a hotel room and felt refreshed, relaxed, and ready for the next step. Once they were with the SAS, they'd be able to focus on Russia and getting to Aya.

As Colt put on his backpack, his phone buzzed. It was a message from Price.

He read it, and his heart sank.

Things were about to get messy.

"We're in trouble, mate," he said to Drake.

"What is it?"

"The shootout in Damascus has caused quite a little stir in Washington. The CIA is after Kate and you. They've sent a wet team.

Apparently, the director doesn't give a rat's ass about the fertilizer. Price is in hiding. She says we won't have a lot of time."

Drake let out a long sigh. "I figured this would happen," he grunted.

"Kate says she has a plan, but she needs us to make some noise. We can't just run. We need to take out those bastards who are after us."

"A burn-off," Drake grunted.

"A what?"

"It's an agency tactic. Kate is trying to create a fire to put out a larger one. She's making some noise for the papers."

"Isn't that what we did in Damascus?"

"A shootout in Syria is one thing. One in Turkey is something else entirely."

"So, what do we do?"

"We make some noise, light some fires."

"How do you expect to do that?"

"Creating a fire."

"A literal fire?"

"Yes."

Colt went silent. He didn't want to hear it. He called Price. There had to be another way. They had been lucky to escape Damascus. Eventually, their luck would run out.

Price answered immediately.

"What the hell are you suggesting?" Colt asked her.

"I'm at a bar in Washington. I can't talk."

"Jason thinks you want to start a fire. A literal fire."

"He's right."

"What the hell, Kate! This is crazy!"

Drake snatched the phone from Colt's hand. "Are you sure this will work?"

"We need to get ahead of this, Jason. The director is exposed. I can get him out. I can get him fired."

"And then what?"

"I'll have to become director."

Drake chuckled. "You'll finally get what you always wanted."

"You know I never wanted this."

"We have SAS service members on their way to pick us up—what about them?"

"Figure it out. Like I said, if you don't do this, I can't get Tom Fowler fired. I need you to make sure this is newsworthy. Make it flashy."

Drake took a deep breath and said, "Okay."

He hung up and tossed Colt back his phone.

"What are we doing?" Colt asked.

Drake walked to his duffel bag and put it over his shoulder. "When are your SAS contacts arriving?"

"An hour ..."

"Tell them to meet us on the outskirts of town. This whole village is about to light up."

"Jason, what the hell is going on?"

"Just follow my lead."

Drake and Colt left the hotel. They walked out onto the busy Gurney streets. It was early morning. The sun was rising, and the sky was light pink. Shop owners were busy setting up their stalls, and traffic was light. The Turkish Army soldiers stationed at almost every intersection watched Drake and Colt with suspicious glares.

"Jason, there's got to be another way."

"There's a gas station up ahead," Drake said.

"What about it?"

"Just follow me."

"That's a bad idea, mate," Colt said.

Drake stopped walking and confronted Colt. "Listen, I only brought you along because I thought you wanted to give your men, your troops, some peace in the afterlife. I need to find Aya. She has the ammonium nitrate. The only way we can both get what we want is if we trust Kate and do what she asks."

"So what? You're going to blow up a gas station? How does that help."

"It will attract a lot of attention. I'm going to make sure that the wet team gets caught up in the fire. With any luck, they'll be apprehended by the Turkish military. It will be an international scandal. CIA officers engaging in a shootout in the middle of Turkey?"

"And we'll escape?"

"Yes."

Colt huffed. "You better know what you're doing."

Drake led Colt to the gas station, pulled out one of the pumps, and began pouring gasoline onto the ground.

"Get the attendants out of the booths and make sure this place is clear," he shouted at Colt. "Use your weapon if you have to. Do whatever it takes. If you don't, innocent civilians will die."

Colt cursed and grabbed his sidearm. He ran up to the attendant booth. There were two teenagers inside. When they saw Colt's gun, they raised their hands.

"Get out of here!" Colt screamed at them.

The two attendants cried and ran away from the gas station in a panic.

Drake looked around and made sure that no one else was close. He lit a match. Colt approached him but then had to duck for cover from incoming gunfire. Bullets ricocheted off the pumps and metal surfaces around the station.

"Is that them?" Colt shouted to Drake.

Drake joined Colt. The two men were using the body of a Subaru Impreza for cover. "That's them."

"Just in the nick of time," Colt said.

"Yes."

"And what now?"

Drake dropped the match on the ground. Colt's eyes widened.

"Run," Drake said.

The dropped match lit a fire that crawled quickly along the gasoline which Drake had coated the entire station. The little town of Gurney was about to become a war zone.

As they ran from the gas station, bullets whizzed past them.

Drake looked back and saw an SUV with four men inside. That was where the shots were coming from. He kept running until the gas station exploded. A fiery shockwave knocked both Colt and Drake to their knees.

Drake pulled out his M4 and looked back at the gas station. A cloud of thick black smoke rose from its remains. He waited, making sure they weren't being followed.

"Come on," Colt yelled.

When Drake was sure they were in the clear, he ran after Colt.

Firetrucks and the Turkish military arrived on the scene almost as quickly as the fire started.

Drake and Colt ran to a small clearing nearby and watched the chaos unfold.

Drake pulled up his rifle again. The wet team's van tried to leave the scene, but Drake made sure they didn't get far. He put three bullets in the engine, making their escape impossible.

He watched as the entire team was apprehended by the Turkish military. He knew they wouldn't be in custody long, but the scale of the explosion and the intensity of the fire would certainly help slow their pursuit and give Price time to do what she had to do.

Colt smiled as he saw the CIA wet team members get pulled out of the van. "Serves them arseholes right," he said.

It was a mess.

A controlled mess.

When the insanity died down, Drake and Colt wandered down the road leading out of Gurney. Sirens, police, and ambulances echoed in the distance.

"The SAS officers will meet us up the road," Colt said.

"Perfect," Drake grunted.

FIFTY

They wandered through the desert for hours. The sun was setting, but the smoke from the fire Drake had started in Gurney could still be seen on the horizon.

The two men looked like vagabonds, travelers from the West who were backpacking from town to town. Their dirty clothes and large backpacks helped support the aesthetic. Thankfully, none of the military or emergency vehicles that drove past them on the highway stopped to investigate what was inside those backpacks.

While they wandered through the desert, Colt texted Price about what had just happened. He then called Howe.

News about Gurney had already spread to the West.

"I hope that shootout in the Turkish town isn't your fault," Howe said.

"It's not."

Howe scoffed. Although, technically speaking, Colt was telling Howe the truth. He hadn't lit the fire; Drake had.

"Let me know when you're at the air base," Howe said. "I want to know where you are every step of the way."

"Where are the SAS officers picking us up?"

"I've expedited the matter."

"What does that mean?" Colt barked.

"You'll find out."

Thirty seconds after the exchange, an SA330 Puma helicopter landed close to their location.

"That dickhead," Colt muttered.

Drake and Colt boarded the chopper and were flown to the Royal Air Force base nearby.

Once there, Colt updated Howe about his status. Howe told him that he'd arranged a private jet to fly them from Turkey to England. They'd leave in the morning. Before they could go to Russia, Howe wanted to speak to both men in person. He wanted to be fully onboard.

In the air base's cafeteria, Colt sipped his earl grey tea and watched the news. There was a small thirteen-inch screen hung up behind the counter in the kitchen.

He was waiting to see if Price's controlled-burn strategy had worked; if the events in Gurney had gotten the CIA director fired.

He wondered what she was planning. Drake had mentioned something about her becoming director, but Colt laughed at the idea. Price hated politics. She didn't like to play games. She would be a terrible director.

As he sat sipping his tea, listening to the monotone BBC news anchor drone on about US and Russian relations, his phone buzzed. It was the woman on his mind.

"Did you call to apologize?" Colt said.

"Apologize for what?" Price asked.

"You had your officer blow up a gas station. We could've been killed."

"I needed to escalate the situation."

"Right."

"Hey! You're the one that punched a helicopter pilot out and stole a US Air Force helicopter," Price said. "I'm in the middle of a political upheaval over here. I had no choice."

"I see," Colt said, rubbing the hairs on his mustache. "What's your plan now? Set off a bomb in London? Blow up the Eiffel Tower?"

"Screw you," she said. "I needed Jason to set a fire. It was the only way I could save your asses. The Director of the CIA had it out for me, and if I didn't put him to an end, then, well, he would have had it out for the both of you."

"Did you tell your director about the ammonium nitrate? Did you tell him why we're here?"

"Of course, I did. But this is Langley, and everyone looks out for themselves. He's more concerned about power than the truth. You know how it is at the top."

"So, what now?"

"We wait for the news about Gurney to spread."

"I hate waiting."

"I know," Price said. "How's Jason?"

Colt looked at Drake. The son-of-a-bitch was asleep on a small chair in the corner of the large room. How he managed to fall asleep with such ease shocked him. He wished he had that ability. "He's good."

"When will you arrive in London?"

"Tomorrow afternoon."

"And from there?"

"Hopefully, Russia. Hopefully, to put an end to all of this. I'll need to see what the SAS has to say about that. Graham's being a bit of a dick about all of this."

"He arranged to pick you up in the middle of Turkey."

"He's still a dick."

Price laughed. "I'll talk to you later."

"I'm glad you're safe," he said to Price.

"Same here."

Colt hung up, reclined back in his seat, and closed his eyes, still listening to the news. He felt a sense of relief, knowing that Price was going to be okay in Washington. But he knew that the hard work was just about to start. Drake would need to get to Russia. The ammonium nitrate and Aya were still out there, and the clock was ticking.

FIFTY-ONE

News about the explosion at the gas station in Gurney spread like wild fire through the various media channels around the world. Three dead Turkish civilians, two dead Turkish soldiers, and four CIA officers in custody.

It was a mess—more signs of trouble in the Middle East, more evidence that the CIA couldn't control their own.

Price was sitting at a patio outside a cafe in Washington. Houston was at her feet. She was contemplating the events of the last several days. She knew how it would look at Langley. She knew the move she was about to make would look like she'd planned it all along —would perhaps lend some sense of credibility to Fowler's paranoia.

She'd been fighting rumors that she was envious of Fowler for years. She called it agency gossip and dismissed it the same way a teenager at high school dismisses rumors about who they're going to take to prom.

She wasn't power-hungry.

She'd promised herself that if she ever got that kind of power, she'd use it only to set the house straight. The director's job was too boring. She was more a boots-on-the-ground kind of gal.

Thinking about it all made her upset. Was she lying to herself? Did she not tell Fowler about Drake's involvement earlier in the operation because deep-down she knew it would piss him off and leave him vulnerable? Or did she do it because she had the power and not him?

She sipped her coffee, watched the traffic on Constitution Avenue, and waited for the text message from Sierra to arrive.

The sun was out, and the clouds were thick and white. Dozens of tourists walked past. Houston watched them all. The dog had a keen sense of anticipation. It read people better than most spies. Its antics gave Price some light entertainment. Drake seemed to have trained the dog well.

"Where are you?" Price said, talking to herself.

Sierra's last message to Price stated that she was at the Washington Post's headquarters. Her ex-boyfriend worked there and had an in with the editor-in-chief. Sierra was going to leak that the CIA director, Tom Fowler, sent a wet team in Turkey to assassinate a SAS officer who was on the hunt for the missing ammonium nitrate.

Price made sure that Jason Drake's name was left out of the report.

Sierra had enough receipts to corroborate the report. She was Fowler's assistant. She saved everything he'd sent her.

Fowler wouldn't survive the storm. He'd be blacklisted. Fired. His career would be over. He may even end up in Prison.

Price's phone buzzed.

'Check the Washington Post,' Sierra's message read. 'It's done.'

Price loaded the page for the Post, and a smile crept across her face.

Attack in Turkey! CIA director Fowler to blame?

The headline was perfect—a nuclear bomb burning up Fowler's career and future. Fowler's paranoia and stupidity had finally gotten the best of him. Had he just focused on the ammonium nitrate and trusted Price, he would still be in power.

But that wasn't his specialty.

Sierra sent one more message.

I have a meeting booked with you and the president tonight. Get
ready. It's showtime.

Price smiled.

She'd need to get ready for her meeting. With Fowler out of the
picture, she could finally get to work.

FIFTY-TWO

"Hello, Mr. President," Price said, shaking his hand and feeling slightly nervous.

She'd never been to the Oval Office before. It felt a little unreal. She'd been a Director of Black Ops for years at the CIA, but she'd never been invited. She was more used to hanging out in empty warehouses and hangars or safe houses the CIA had all over the world. She liked her khakis and her boots. She didn't like having to wear a suit and expensive shoes.

It didn't feel right.

"Please, cut that 'Mr. President' bullshit out," Clarkson said. He sounded tired and fed up. "All I want is the truth. Nothing more."

"That's what I want to give you, sir," Price said.

"Then tell me what the hell is going on." He walked to his desk and pulled out a bottle of whiskey from below his desk. "I don't usually drink on the job, but I can't really help myself now. My wife says I've aged fifteen years in four."

Price remembered how Clarkson looked during his inauguration. His young, powerful, and stoic manner had become stifled by four years in Washington. The swamp creatures in the House and Senate had finally got to him. Washington had a habit of chewing up good men and making them weak.

"I want to start by thanking you for taking the time—"

Clarkson shot back a glass. "You had someone leak that informa-tion about the former director to the press. I know how it works. You knew I would take the bait. Well, here you are. You want Director Fowler's job? Convince me why you deserve it."

"Sir—"

"Don't lie to me," he said.

Price stared in admiration at the president. She'd never met him in person. Based off what she'd seen in the papers or on the nightly news, he seemed simple and out of touch, like a man who decided to campaign as president for publicity alone. The media hated him. Although, it was obvious to see why. He was too much of an outsider. He didn't play the game the way you were supposed to play it. "I'm sorry," she said. "I told you I would tell the truth. Yes, I did the leak the story about Tom to the press."

Clarkson shook his head. He poured himself another glass of whiskey, shot it back, and looked at Price with steely eyes. "Don't lie to me again."

"I won't," she said.

"I've got less than seven months before the American public choose their next leader. My polling numbers look awful. The people are dissatisfied. Angry. I don't blame them. All of this in-fighting. All of this nonsense. Every time they turn on the news it's one politician going after another politicians throat. No one is working together and the world is falling apart. There are threats against this great country, threats that can't be seen if we keep aiming our weapons at each other. Do you understand?"

Price nodded. "I think so."

"Tom Fowler's only concern was his job. You didn't need to leak any story to the press for me to see that. He was a fool."

"I needed your attention. I needed—"

"You want his job?"

"No, sir."

"You're lying to me."

"I'm not," Price said. "I don't want his job. If you think I want to be Director of the CIA you are mistaken. I leaked that story to the press because I want to save American lives. The ammonium nitrate ... I think it's headed our way. I think something bad is about to happen and I know the only person who can stop it."

"I didn't want to be president," Clarkson said. "I didn't want any of this. But I couldn't sit back and watch my country eat itself to death. The last few years have been hard on us all. Endless war after endless war, tragedy after tragedy. All of which are made worse by a media that seeks to enflame our differences."

"I didn't know you felt that way," Price said.

"Why would you? I stopped talking to the press a year ago after I noticed they were twisting every word I said."

Price nodded. Clarkson poured Price a shot. She slammed the glass on the presidential desk when she was done. "All I want is to save American lives, to uphold the Constitution," she said. "There's a thin line between chaos and order, sir. I've spent years in the shadows. Years fighting to control that balance."

"I'm going to name you the new CIA director," Clarkson said. "But I need you to promise me that you can find that ammonium nitrate."

"I can."

"Good."

"I've got two men. They're with the SAS in London. I'm going to meet them. They have good reason to believe the fertilizer is in Russia."

"And what are the Russian's planning on doing with it?"

"My operative in Syria almost died getting this information. He said that those with the ammonium nitrate are planning on using it against a US target. The Kremlin isn't involved. This is all the work of a lone individual with immense power and influence."

Clarkson shook his head. "Russia? President Sergei Makarov is looking for any reason he can to make it look like we are the aggressors. If you are going to head into Russia, you need to keep it quiet."

"With the help of the SAS, we should be able to get to it without the Russia knowing."

"And what will you do when you find it?"

"We'll destroy it. Remove it as an option."

President Clarkson stared deeply into Price's eyes. There was a moment of silence between the two of them. He saw a kinship in her. Like him, she was doing what she did because she believed in the promise of America.

"Director Fowler doesn't yet know he's fired," Clarkson said. "I'll make the call."

Price didn't smile. She didn't do anything. She just nodded. She was about to throw herself into the fire, the lion's den. As long as the ammonium nitrate was still out there, she couldn't pat herself on the back.

The president stood up from his desk and looked out his window. "I might only be a one-term president. In and out. But if that Russian ammonium nitrate gets detonated on US soil, the American public will want blood. They'll want revenge. They'll want war. I need you to restore order. Our country cannot get embroiled in another conflict, especially one with cataclysmic consequences."

"I will not let you down."

"Good," President Clarkson said. "You're dismissed. Do what you need to do to save American lives. Do what needs to be done."

FIFTY-THREE

The Phenom 100 private jet landed in London in the early evening. The flight from the Royal Air Force base in Turkey was rocky. The small aircraft was at the mercy of turbulent winds.

When Drake and Colt stepped out of the aircraft, they were met with some proper English weather. It was raining and cold.

"You ready?" Drake asked Colt.

"I'm ready."

Howe was standing on the tarmac. He was wearing a long overcoat, a top hat, and was smoking an old wooden pipe. He exhausted a long, thick plume of smoke from his mouth and looked at Colt the same way a father looks at a son who's been nothing but trouble.

"I should arrest you," Howe said to Colt. "You know how many laws you broke in Iraq?"

Colt chuckled. "Shut up, ya bastard."

"Of course," Howe said, unamused by Colt's vulgarity but happy to see that his old colleague was alive and well. "And you must be the infamous Jason Drake? Nice to meet you."

Drake shrugged. He wasn't in London to make friends. He had one thing on his mind and one thing only: finding Aya.

"Is he always like this?" Howe asked Colt.

"Get used to it, mate. He's almost as much of an arsehole as you are."

"Come with me," Howe said. "I don't know why I'm doing this ... I suppose I'm glad to see you not buried in a bottle, Clyde. And, well, I guess I want to find the buggers who killed our men in Edinburgh."

"Damn straight," Colt said.

"Then let's get to it for Christ's sake," Howe said.

"Hey!" Colt shouted. "You know I don't like it when people take the Lord's name in vain."

Howe smiled and said, "You know, you're a bloody nuisance. Now, are you going to tell me what you know?"

"We were in Syria trying to find the missing ammonium nitrate that every intelligence community in the world can't seem to find," Drake said to Howe. "And the longer we spend talking about it on a tarmac in London, the less time we have."

Howe eyed Drake up and down. It was obvious to see why he was a threat. The man was intimidating. His shoulders seemed too broad to be real, his frame too sleek. His body resembled a blade.

"Right," Howe said. "Then we should get going."

There was a black Rolls Royce parked on the tarmac behind Howe. A security officer standing behind the SAS executive opened one of the back doors.

Price walked out of the Rolls Royce. "You boys made it out of Turkey in one piece. I'm impressed."

"Kate?" Drake said, surprised to see her.

"Hello," she said.

Drake stared into her eyes. "Where's Houston?"

"I thought you'd ask first how things were in Washington?" Price asked.

"Where's the dog?"

"He's with my assistant. He's safe."

Drake nodded. "Good."

"Why are you here?" Colt asked Price.

"Because I'm going to help you boys get to Russia."

Colt smiled. "Are you the CIA director now?"

Price nodded.

"Well, now that we're all acquainted," Howe said, "should we?" He gestured his head toward the car. "I've booked you all hotel rooms close to an airfield near Central London. You're to leave tomorrow afternoon."

"I thought I was retired," Colt said to Howe.

"This is your mess, Clyde. I expect you to help clean it up."

Colt smiled. "You bastard."

Drake and Colt got into the car with Price and Howe.

Howe didn't waste much time explaining to Colt and Drake the plan he'd cooked up with Price was. "We're going to fly Drake and another SAS officer, who I will introduce you to tomorrow, to Russia via a C-17 aircraft. Flying a helicopter in there would be too risky. You'll have to airdrop. Can you do that?"

Drake nodded.

"I thought you said I was going with him?" Colt asked.

"You are," Howe said. "The C-17 will be flying at forty thousand feet and circling the area of operation. If they need back-up, you're going to drop a supply crate from the loading bay."

"I see," Colt said. "I'm tagging along to cut the rope."

"I know it's not ideal," Howe said. "But if that place is loaded with Russian military, we have to be careful."

The Rolls Royce drove through the dense and dark London streets. Not many words were spoken between them once they all knew what they had to do. Not much needed to be said. Each one of their worlds had changed significantly over the last couple of days. And if each one of them was honest, they'd tell you they were uncertain as to what came next.

Drake and Colt were dropped off at a hotel on the west side of the city. As they stepped out of the Rolls Royce, Howe said to Colt, "Don't have too much fun tonight."

"Ah, screw you," Colt said.

Howe laughed. "I'll see you both at the airfield in the morning."

Price and Howe drove off.

Standing outside in the fog, Colt turned to Drake and said, "I know this part of the city. How about we grab a good pint? I know a great place. It's called the Hound's Tits."

Drake nodded. "I could use some food."

Colt smiled. "Finally," he said, "we get to have some fun."

FIFTY-FOUR

"You've poured yourself another perfect lager," Colt said to the bartender of the Hound's Tits. He admired the work of art he'd just been handed. He watched as the yellowy bubbles rose to the white foam at the top of the glass. The glass's sweat glistened in the dark of the pub. He took a long swig and closed his eyes, cherishing every second. He hadn't realized how much he missed England or beer.

Drake sat next to him and had just finished a pound of hot wings. He was doing his best to ignore Colt's overzealous ramblings about what made a good pilsner.

"A pilsner is just a pale lager that originated in Pilsen in the Czech Republic. A proper pilsner should be aromatic, delicate, and crisp ..." Colt rambled while holding up his glass of beer like it was a rare diamond. "This is good. Really good."

Drake liked beer, but preferred his whiskey. A British Premier League game was on the television behind the bar, but Drake wasn't watching the soccer match. His eyes followed the scroll of sports stats and scores at the bottom of the screen. It was the middle of the second round of the NHL playoffs. When he saw the score of the Dallas Stars game, his mood soured. "Damnit," he grunted.

The Stars were down 3-1 in their series with the Anaheim

Ducks. It wasn't good. Such high hopes, almost completely burned out. One more loss and they'd be sent back to Dallas.

He stood up from the bar and was about to head to the hotel Howe had set them up in when Colt grabbed his arm. "Stay, mate. Have another pint. We should be celebrating. We're going to find the ammonium nitrate, and you're going to get some revenge. You're finally going to get a chance to kill that bitch that stabbed you in the neck with the needle."

"I'm not doing this for revenge," Drake said. "And don't call her a 'bitch.'"

"She stabbed you in the neck and sold you out to the Russians."

"I don't care."

"Listen, take it from an old-timer like me, have another pint. Let's celebrate."

Drake rubbed his brow. There was an earnestness in Colt's eyes. The older man looked like he knew his days were numbered. He'd worked too hard for too long, and he'd lost too much. He didn't want to be alone. "I'll stay for one more."

"Hah, that's a good lad," Colt said, slapping Drake on the back. "Tomorrow, you're going to drop from thirty thousand feet in the sky. You don't want to regret what may be the last night of your life."

Colt called out for two more pints. "Oy!" he said to the bartender. "One more round over here."

The bartender nodded.

The Hound's Tits was busy. Shoulder to shoulder, patrons were jammed inside like sardines. The place was popular with young men with stylish haircuts and young women in short dresses. Drake felt out of place. It wasn't that he felt old. It was more that he never really felt comfortable in public places, especially ones as busy as the Tits. He looked left and right, planning an escape route if necessary, keeping watch for any potential problems. It was a habit. One he'd tried to kick long ago.

There was a big drunk guy in the corner of the bar. He was six pints deep and had the eyes of a man looking to pick a fight.

Another man with slicked-back hair was watching two young

women at the bar. His eyes were on the drinks in their hands. He was fumbling something in his pocket. Date rape drugs, most likely.

The pub was full of danger.

Drake felt tense. Angry. The world was a ticking time bomb. Ready to explode at any minute.

The bartender placed the new round of drinks in front of them. Colt tapped him on the shoulder. "You know you're allowed to relax," he said.

"I will when I can disappear again."

"Kate will help you with that."

"I doubt that."

"Why's that?" Colt asked.

"She'll let the power get to her head. They all do."

Colt sighed. "You might be right."

"I am right."

"So what, you're going to find Aya and then vanish?"

Drake took a long swig of his beer. "Yes."

"You can't keep running from your past."

"I'm not," Drake said. "I'm trying to put it to rest."

"Is that what you're going to do to Aya when you find her? Kill her?"

"I'll do what needs to be done."

"You loved her, didn't you?"

"I don't want to talk about it," Drake said.

"No way, mate. You owe me the truth. We're about to go to battle together. I traveled with you through Iraq, Syria, and Turkey. You haven't told me the whole truth. Who is she? She wasn't just some girl. I can see it in your eyes."

"Shut up," Drake said.

"Will you be able to kill her?"

"I said, shut up."

"She stabbed you in the neck, and you can't answer the question."

Drake turned to Colt slowly. "Aya was pure. She was fighting for something. She needed to be protected."

"And you blame yourself?" Colt said. "You blame yourself for what she became."

"I know what I am," Drake said. "I'm a monster. When I was in the Terminus division, I was injected me with so many chemicals. Advanced stuff, she said. Gene-editing. They cut my genetic code up to help me focus, increase my endurance, enhance my body's ability to heal."

"Yeah," Colt said. "She said all the Terminus operatives went through that shit."

"They did, but the side-effects were terrible. Those enhancements left me feeling empty. I couldn't feel. At least, not until I met her."

"Aya?"

"Yes."

"And now you have to kill her?"

Drake clenched his jaw. "I'll stop her."

"Will your heart get in the way? Will you be able to do what needs to be done?"

"I thought we were going to have a nice relaxing conversation," Drake said.

"Aye," Colt said. He finished his pint and tapped on the bar for another. He closed his eyes and took a deep breath. "I'm sorry. Maybe it's my age ... I don't really know, but I think too much these days about what-ifs. Like you, my past weighs heavy on my life. I have a lot of regrets." A tear fell from one of Colt's eyes. "Kate and I were ready to focus on family life. We both knew we couldn't keep doing what we were doing. We were ready to slow down, but then that choice was taken from us."

Drake finished his beer and wiped his mouth on his sleeve. "I'm sorry for your loss."

Colt nodded. "Life makes monsters of men," he said.

"And women."

"Aye," Colt said, nodding. "And women."

Suddenly, on the sportscast, highlights from the Dallas Stars' game began to play. Drake watched them and felt a hint of normalcy return. He felt himself relax.

"Do you like that game?" Colt asked, looking up at the television.

"What?" Drake said.

"Ice hockey?" Colt said. "These crazy buffoons who put blades on their feet and slide around at breakneck speeds into each other."

"I like it," Drake said. "Hockey is violence, speed, and momentum. It's not a soft game. It's hard. Chaotic. It's a game that doesn't reward patience. It's a game that exists on impulse alone."

"What's a soft game?" Colt's eyebrows perked up. "You better not be talking about soccer, mate?"

"If I am?"

Colt chuckled. "You know, when you knocked me out in Puerto Rico, I thought we were going to spend this entire time hating each other, but you're not that bad for a Yank."

Drake stood up from the bar. "That's it for me," he said. He left Colt in the bar and made his way to the hotel. He walked through the cold, foggy, rainy streets of London. It felt like a scene from a Dickens novel. Despite the modern high rises that decorated the skyline, there was something ancient about the city, something ethereal and mystic.

After spending an hour walking around the grey and quiet streets, he made his way to his hotel. It was called the London Guard. The lobby was ornate. Inside was a red carpet, a gold chandelier, and that musky smell that you found in really old buildings.

"Hello, sir," the man at the hotel desk said. He was your typical Brit: a stout old man with a thick mustache and heavy accent. He wasn't from London. His accent was Northern.

"I'm here to check in," Drake said. "There should be a reservation under my name."

"Your name?"

"Drake. Jason Drake."

"Ah, yes," the old man said. "Here you are." He grabbed a pair of keys that were strung up behind the counter. "Room 18."

Drake grabbed the keys and left the lobby. He went to his room, collapsed on his bed, and was about to fall asleep when he heard something. He wasn't alone.

He pushed himself upright and saw a darkened silhouette in front of the window.

It was Price.

FIFTY-FIVE

"Hello, Director," Drake said with a wry smile. "Did you come here to spy on me?"

"I'm sorry to bug you. I know you have an early morning. Were you at the pub with Clyde?"

"Yes."

"Is he still there? Drinking himself silly?"

"What do you think?"

"He's an idiot."

"And you married him."

Price sighed. Drake got up and flipped the light switch in the room. He sat down on an old wooden chair in the corner of the room. "Why are you here? Aren't I meeting you at the airfield tomorrow?"

"I'm here to apologize."

"For what?"

"For bringing you into this. For ordering you to risk your life in Turkey. For pulling you out of San Juan."

"Shut up, Kate. You're not a good liar. You're not sorry for any of that."

Price shook her head. "I didn't want to be the director, Jason."

"Well, sometimes you get what you don't want."

"Once you're done in Russia, I'll clean your slate. You'll be able to travel freely in the States. You'll be free. Your history with the agency will be wiped clean. Everything you did. Every crime you committed."

"I thought you already offered me that."

"I came here also because I felt it only fair if I gave you one last option to walk away."

"Don't be stupid."

"If you find the ammonium nitrate there, I need you to destroy it. You've already sacrificed so much."

"I'll do what I have to do."

"Civilians may die."

"I'll do what I have to do."

"You don't have to do this, Jason. Graham Howe told me he can get a team together, one that could do what we need them to do."

"Do you really think I'll let you do that? Do you really think that I'll just sit back and let a bunch of assholes try to finish this? I'm too deep into it now. This is my mission."

"The SAS team Graham has put together is experienced. I'm trying to be nice, Jason. I feel awful for what I've done to you." |

"Graham's team will get to Golovinka and then they'll panic. Shit will hit the fan. It will get messy. They don't know the desperation they're up against. Aya isn't just some terrorist."

"What is she? Why did she turn? Why is she working with some Russian?"

"You think I know that?"

"You want to know. That's why you want to push forward. You know there's more to this and you won't stop."

"You know what I am, Kate. You know what you did to me. You fucked me up—you fucked all of us Terminus division operatives up. You changed our DNA and then you discarded us."

"You killed a senator," Price said. "After you did that, the division had to end."

"I'm going to see this through. I'm going to finish this."

"And like I said, once it's done, you're free. Why are you smiling?"

"Isn't it funny? This whole operation ... everything. It all comes back to the reason why I hunted down that senator. Terminus ended not because of me, but because of him. I killed that son-of-a-bitch because he killed those children and I thought he killed Aya."

"Collateral was cleared for that operation, but I see your point."

"Is that what you call a dozen dead kids? Collateral?"

Price closed her eyes and took a deep breath. When she spoke again, it was clear to Drake that she was holding something back. There was a pain inside her, a regret. But her new role within the agency made it impossible for her to speak candidly.

"Just be careful," she said. "You don't want to start a world war by trying to stop it."

"Of course."

"Thanks," Price said, her voice quivering. She stood up and walked to the door of the room.

Drake wondered if the role of the director was already getting to her or if it was something else. Was there something about Terminus' end that she was holding back? Before she left the room, he asked her. "What happened to the old director? Is Tom Fowler playing nice?"

"No."

"He was a powerful man, Kate," Drake said. "You should be careful. He might have eyes on us, even now."

"He was a better politician than I was," Price said. "But I'll sniff out his moles. I'll stop him."

"I doubt that."

"I will."

"You should check on Clyde when you're done here," Drake said. "He might need you tonight."

"I'll meet him. I just wanted to tell you I was sorry."

"I need to sleep," Drake said. "Goodnight."

"Goodnight."

Price left the room and waited for Colt in the lobby. An hour after her chat with Drake, Colt hobbled into the hotel. He was a wreck. Falling apart. He smiled when he saw her.

"Well, isn't this a sight for sore eyes?" he said.

She grabbed hold of him and helped him check in to the hotel. She brought him up to his room and spent the night with him.

FIFTY-SIX

The next day was one of those rare sunny and warm days in England. The air smelled thick and humid. Summer was on the horizon, and Drake noticed that the city locals seemed more pleasant than usual. The hotel concierge held the door open for him in the lobby,

Drake had been to London a dozen times as an operative. Each time, he'd learn that Paris, in general, got the short end of the stick when it came to its reputation between the two cities. London was by far the rudest city in the world. His first time in London, he asked a sensible-looking man in a suit where he could buy a coffee, and the man told him to, "Fuck off!" And that was the nicest person he ran into that day.

Although, maybe that was what Drake liked about the UK. The people there didn't beat around the bush. They weren't stuck-up like the French. They weren't trying to act like they were better than anyone else. They were hostile and aggressive. Bulldogs.

Colt waited for him in the hotel lobby. The old Scot's eyes were red, and his face was white, but he was smiling.

"I expected you to be a little more hungover," Drake said.

Colt laughed. "I had a special visitor last night."

"Good for you," Drake said dryly.

The two men got into the back of a black BMW SUV that was waiting for them on the street, and they were driven to the airfield.

Fifteen minutes later, they met Howe and Price on the tarmac, just beside a large hangar. The C-17 was getting fueled up. The giant aircraft looked like a beached whale. It felt unnatural seeing it out of the sky.

"Are you boys ready?" Howe asked Drake.

"Yes," Colt said.

Drake nodded.

"Good," Howe said. He then turned to Drake. "Kate said you were exceptional, but Americans tend to exaggerate everything."

Price smiled. "Jason is beyond exceptional, Graham. Jason did numerous airdrops as an operative. He knows what he's doing."

"Who's the other SAS operative joining me?" Drake asked.

A tall man dressed in a flight suit walked out from inside the hangar. He had broad shoulders and a thick dark mustache. He approached Drake slowly. "My name is Flynt Wicker," the man said. "Nice to meet you."

"Likewise," Drake said.

"Private Wicker will be joining you on the operation," Howe said. "The two of you will drop from the C-17 and sneak into Golovinka. You'll find out where the ammonium nitrate is and then get the hell out of there. We need to be careful not to ruffle too many feathers. If there is Russian military on-site or if you run into any trouble, we need to make sure we don't escalate current geopolitical rifts."

"We're going to drop you in close to the town," Price added. "You'll be in a forest close to a compound we've identified via satellite imagery. The compound is surrounded by a large stone wall and has about four buildings inside. With any luck, that's our AO."

"So, you're guessing?" Drake said. "All I told you was that Ali Bajal said Andrei Zadorov had a compound in Golovinka."

"You didn't tell us much, Jason," Price said. "I had our team at Langley make a logical guess based off of our most recent satellite fly-by. If we were wrong, then you can scout the town."

"We'll explain more inside the hangar," Howe said.

Inside the hangar, they went over more details; the flight speed of the C-17 before the drop, the altitude, the area of the forest in the mountains that they were to drop into. Drake knew the information was only useful as long as the operation ran without a hitch, which he didn't expect to happen.

They spent four hours running over the operation, analyzing maps, and getting their gear ready. When they were done, Drake, Colt, Flynt, and two C-17 pilots, John Major and Ben Offstaff, boarded the aircraft.

Before boarding the C-17, Drake made sure to take full advantage of his equipment and weapon selection. He grabbed an M4 assault rifle with a mounted advanced combat optical gunsight on its rail. It was a TA31RCO model, designed to the specifications of the United States Marine Corps. The reticle pattern provided quick target acquisition at close combat ranges, enhanced target identification, and an eight hundred meter bullet drop compensator. As a sidearm, he grabbed a SIG Sauer P226.

He attached four magazines to his combat vest and put on a black hoodie. Underneath the hoodie was an insulated black sweater. Alongside the sweater were insulated pants and thick, rugged combat boots.

"You ready to put your past to rest?" Colt said to Drake before walking up the landing ramp of the C-17.

Drake grunted.

The two of them walked to the C-17. The four Pratt and Whitney F117-PW-100 turbofan engines fired up. Each engine had more than forty thousand pounds of thrust. The C-17 was massive, about half the length of an American football field.

Drake and Colt joined Wicker, who was already strapped to his seat inside the fuselage.

Drake hadn't talked to Wicker much, but he trusted that the kid knew what he was doing. He was SAS, after all. He had a rugby player's body shape and didn't like to chat—both good signs to Drake.

Howe and Price were speaking to the pilots when they saw Colt and Drake enter the fuselage.

Howe walked up to them and said, "This is it, gentlemen. This is where we find out if I'm a complete idiot for putting my faith in the CIA."

Price spoke to Drake. "If the ammonium nitrate is there, destroy it. We need to end this."

Drake nodded.

"If you can't destroy it, let us know. We'll send in some bombers, whatever you need."

Howe spoke to Colt. "Be careful, old chum. The last official mission you ran with us, you ended up in the hospital."

"I'll be thirty thousand feet in the air," Colt said. "There's nothing to worry about, mate."

"Good, good."

Howe and Price left, and Colt and Drake strapped themselves to their seats.

Wicker turned to Drake and said, "I'll take the lead. I'll drop first. I always drop first."

"Do whatever the hell suits you," Drake said.

Wicker smiled. "Good."

It was the first time Drake had felt a bit nervous about flying with Wicker. The kid seemed a little too aggressive, too hostile.

He didn't have long to dwell on his feelings, however. The C-17 engines fired up, and before long, it was at a cruising altitude.

FIFTY-SEVEN

Fowler looked at his laptop and smiled. It was a brief respite from the anguish he'd been living through for the past couple of days. He picked up the glass of expensive scotch he was drinking and shot it back. The malty alcohol burned as it slid down his throat.

He was in his home office. His office's window, slightly open to dampen the smell of the cigar he'd just smoked, overlooked a quiet suburb. The sounds of the neighborhood children playing in their front yards crept inside. He looked out the window. The sky was a dark purple, and the American flags attached to each house waved gently. Boys were playing catch with their fathers. Daughters skip-roped down the street.

It was an idyllic scene, a portrait of American freedom and serenity.

He sneered.

Fuck America, he thought.

He'd kissed ass all his life. He'd dotted the I's, crossed the T's. He'd done what he'd had to do. But he'd been sabotaged by that bitch.

Kate Price.

His paranoia, his conspiracy theory-laden thoughts, all confirmed it. He was fired and now under investigation. Price had turned the media against him, and a president, who was more concerned about his polling numbers than the truth, had taken action.

There was a map of Russia on his laptop. The southwestern part of the country was demarcated with a large red blotch.

If the world that he'd trusted, put his stock into, had turned on him so suddenly and so easily, then he had no choice but to set it aflame, to burn it all up.

He opened up a private and encrypted email account. Outside his window, a young child began to cry. A boy had fallen off his bike. The droning, tearful pleas for help made Fowler feel sick. He hated weakness. He closed the window and turned back to his laptop.

Price's allies at the agency and in the media had screwed him.

It was time he screwed her.

He had allies, too. And they'd told him through the grapevine that there was an operation going on in Russia with the SAS. Fowler made a couple of quick calls and knew what he was going to do.

Pay the right man the right amount of money, and anything can be done.

He was about to send all his dogs out. He knew one would return with the prey.

If Price thought her goody-two-shoes act was going to help her restore order, then she was an idiot.

He was going to sabotage Price.

He was going to make sure that her stint as director was short-lived.

FIFTY-EIGHT

They were flying at a cruising altitude of thirty-five thousand feet. It was a turbulent flight. The giant aircraft was at the mercy of massive air pressure pockets that made the wings bend and the metal chassis of the aircraft croak.

Drake, Colt, and Wicker had their headsets on. It was the only way they could communicate with each other and hear updates from the pilots.

"We're entering Russian airspace," one of the pilots radioed to them all from the cockpit. "Once we fly over Golovinka, we're going to dip down to thirty thousand feet, but only for five minutes. The loading bay doors will open, and you guys will be good for the drop."

"Roger that," Drake said.

Russian airspace was sensitive, and the C-17 wouldn't be able to go any lower for an extended period without setting off every alarm in the country. Still, five minutes would be more than enough.

Drake put on his parachute, closed his helmet, and checked his oxygen levels. A drop from thirty thousand feet meant he and Wicker would need oxygen for a good portion of the drop.

Wicker followed suit and began to put on his gear.

"Once we drop in, we should be close to the town of Golovinka,"

Drake said to Wicker. "The compound should just be a three kilometer walk from there."

"I know what the mission is," Wicker snapped. "Just worry about yourself."

Drake shrugged. Typical hot head. He walked over to Colt, who was inspecting the supply crate.

Colt nodded at him. "If you boys need ammo, I'll drop this close to where you land."

"We'll only need ammo if everything goes wrong, and we have the Russian army on our trail."

Colt looked at Drake, his expression flat. "That's exactly what I expect to happen, mate. I've been with you for almost a week now, and nothing has gone right."

Drake smiled.

The pilot radioed again. "We're descending into Russian airspace. Are you boys ready? Loading bay doors will open in sixty seconds."

Colt tapped Drake on the shoulder. "Good luck, mate."

Drake nodded, walked to the loading bay doors, and waited for them to open. Wicker was rifling through his backpack. "You joining me, Private Wicker?" Drake shouted.

"Yes, sir," Wicker grunted.

The kid seemed pissed off. Tense. Drake kept his eyes on him.

Wicker walked up to Drake and stood beside him as the loading bay's thick metal doors revealed the dark and black world thirty thousand feet below. A gush of cold wind rushed inside the fuselage.

Drake and Wicker walked to the edge of the loading bay.

"On my count," Drake said. "One ..."

Wicker snapped. "Fuck you," he said.

"What?" Drake said.

Wicker grabbed Drake by the arm and elbowed him in the stomach. Drake hobbled backward and fell to his knees. Wicker kneed Drake in the head, causing Drake to fall to the ground.

From his periphery, Colt saw the struggle. He'd just finished getting the supply crate loosened up from the belts that had it tied to the plane's floor. He ran to Drake, hoping to help.

Wicker was about to hit Drake again, to **render him uncon-scious**, but Colt dove into the younger SAS officer. The two men rolled on the ground.

Drake was woozy. The kid had caught him off guard.

"Burn in hell, old man," Wicker said to Colt. He pulled out his sidearm and fired a point-blank shot into Colt's thigh.

Colt grimaced and released his grip on the young SAS officer.

Wicker stood up and checked his watch. He didn't have much time. He tossed an object from his backpack into the hull of the aircraft. "Enjoy the afterlife," he said. He ran to the loading bay and jumped out.

As Wicker dropped toward the surface of the Earth, he pulled out a trigger from inside his jacket.

Drake had pushed himself upright. He walked to Colt. "Colt, are you alive?"

Colt moaned. "I'm alright," he said. "A flesh wound." He chuck-led. "That little piece of shit leave us?"

"Yes," Drake said.

Before Drake could treat Colt's wound, a bomb detonated on the aircraft. It created a six-foot hole in the fuselage.

"What the hell?" one of the pilots screamed over the radio. "We're losing altitude. What's going ... Jesus!"

The C-17 rolled onto its side. Drake and Colt tumbled against the wall of the fuselage, doing their best to keep their balance.

Colt suffered the worst of the tumble. He hit his head against a metal beam as the aircraft violently rotated 180 degrees. The old Scot was knocked unconscious.

The plane began to break apart. The air pressure and speed at which it was traveling were just too much.

Drake held onto the corrugated metal flooring of the aircraft with his fingers. As the aircraft rolled, the g-force caused the flesh on his face to bend. He fought through it and maintained his consciousness. Colt was close by, tumbling like a rag doll. Drake pulled himself to Colt and grabbed him.

With Colt in one arm, Drake let go of his grip on the corrugated floor. He and Colt slid along the floor of the aircraft toward the loading bay.

Drake held Colt tightly and readied himself for the free fall. The two men fell from the aircraft, dropping at twelve thousand feet per minute. They'd be on the surface in less than 120 seconds.

Drake felt the force of the passing air compress his suit. He did his best to shield Colt from the effects of the change in pressure and wind speed, as Colt was not dressed for the conditions. Thanks to how far the C-17 had fallen, oxygen was not a problem.

The two men dropped through a dense, thick cloud. Drake checked the altimeter on his wrist. He was at nineteen thousand feet. Then eighteen. Falling quick. Shit. They were lower than he'd expected.

When they got to eight thousand feet, Drake knew he'd have to pull the chute. He straightened his body and got ready to pull the line.

Three thousand feet.

He pulled the string at the point of no return and saw the ground approach.

He was closer than three thousand feet. Way closer.

His altimeter was wrong.

He did his best to slow the descent, tilting the chute back and forth, but it was made difficult with Colt in his arms.

A thick brush of trees rapidly approached, and he tried to evade a puncture as they crashed into them.

He fought through a few big branches, Colt still in his grip, but he couldn't hold on. He let Colt go, who dropped thirty feet, hit a couple of branches on the way down, and then landed on the hard ground.

Drake's descent finally stopped.

In the distance, he heard the sounds of a massive explosion. The C-17 had just hit the ground. The ball of flame from the engines shot up into the sky and could be seen through the web of branches above him.

Drake was stuck in a tree, the lines from his parachute caught.

He pulled out his combat blade and cut himself down. He dropped twenty feet but didn't break anything.

He checked the compass on his watch to figure out his position. He walked back to where he'd dropped Colt.

He was in Russia and close to Golovinka. That was all that mattered.

FIFTY-NINE

Back in London, Howe and Price got word about the status of the C-17 from the air traffic controllers in the airfield. They both already knew something was wrong, having lost communication with Colt and the pilots, but they'd held out hope it was just a blip, a matter of interference.

"What are you telling me?" Howe said into his phone.

Price watched the color of Howe's skin turn white. She rubbed her head. Her first operation as director was a shit show.

Howe paced back and forth, hung up, sat down across from Price, and sighed. The two of them were in a hangar at the airfield set up for SAS field operations. Maps were on the walls, computers on desks showing GPS and weather information.

"What happened?" Price asked.

"Air traffic received a mayday call from the pilots. They went down."

"Were they shot down?"

"I don't know. We can check Russian comms, but ... I doubt they were shot down. If they were shot down, we'd have heard something."

"What happened?"

"I don't know," Howe said.

Price walked over to the radio and checked the channels. She began to scan through the various channels she knew Drake would use.

"Jason, this is Watcher. Do you read?"

She repeated the same sentence a dozen times. Nothing. It was like Syria and the refinery all over again.

"We need to plan for the worst," Howe said. "They're most likely dead."

"What are you suggesting?" Price asked.

"There's a C-17 aircraft on Russian ground. That aircraft is loaded with sensitive material. We need to send a team to blow up anything the Russians could use against us. We can't let them get a hold of our technology."

Price tried Drake again. "Jason! Jason!"

She kept hailing him. Minutes past. Howe watched her and took a long breath. He placed his hand on her shoulder. "We need to work on a plan B," he said. "We need to send a team to sift through the wreckage. Find the black box and burn anything that ties this to the SAS or the CIA."

Price dropped the mic and nodded. "Okay," she said.

SIXTY

"Calling Watcher," Drake said into his headset mic. "Watcher, you read?"

Colt rested up against the base of a wide tree. He had his hand on his leg. Drake had just taken care of the wound, albeit with an aggressive and barely-FDA approved measure.

When Drake found Colt, he injected him with an XSTAT-30 GEN 2 device. The device injected more than 108 tiny sponges into the bullet hole on Colt's leg. The sponges would absorb the blood and quell the bleeding. Once inside, they rapidly expanded. The device would extend Colt's life by hours. Hopefully more.

"Watcher, do you read?" Drake said.

"It's no use, mate," Colt said. "Your headset is damaged. Hell, I'm surprised we're alive."

"Damnit," Drake grunted.

Every breath hurt. Colt felt lightning bolts of pain flow through each muscle and bone. He looked out into the dark forest. A thick fog permeated the space.

"We should just wait here," Colt said. "Graham will send a team in to clean up the C-17 wreckage, destroy any sensitive materials. We'll head back to London and reassess."

Drake was in the shadows. His body was immersed in the thick and cool fog. He stood up, looked in the direction of Golovinka, and shook his head. "We're too close to turn back."

"Don't be an idiot," Colt said.

"You stay here," Drake said. "Wait for the SAS to arrive. You're too injured. I'll go."

Colt clenched his jaw and pushed himself up. He gritted through the pain. "You know, I thought my drinking was going to kill me ... but now I see that it's you."

"Don't be dumb," Drake said. "You should stay here. You'll only hold me back. You're injured."

"Shut up," Colt said. "If you're going to act like a hero, then I want some of the credit."

Drake let out a quiet laugh. "First, we need to head to the C-17 wreckage. We need to check for the supply crate you were working on. There'll be some medical supplies in there—painkillers, drugs. Once we've grabbed what we can, we move to Golovinka."

Colt hobbled to Drake, his left shoulder dipping with each step in an awkward, uncomfortable way. "Sounds good. The quicker we get those drugs, the better."

SIXTY-ONE

The forest was dense and thick. The voluminous clouds that had caused them so much trouble during the flight had cleared and revealed a bed of stars and a bright moon. The light from the moon cut through the rough brush, casting slivers of milky light that Drake and Colt made sure to avoid as they made their way toward the C-17 wreckage.

"We need to be cautious," Drake said to Colt. "That son of a bitch Wicker might be down here somewhere. Watch your blind spots."

"Aye," Colt said.

For over an hour, they pushed through the bush. The forest floor dipped and rose with the geological formations of the mountain range. The fact that they were always walking on a forty-five-degree slant only exacerbated Colt's pain. He wasn't going to last long. If they ran into some heavy fire, he'd be more of a hindrance than anything else. He could feel his heart pound in his chest, and for the first time since meeting Drake in Puerto Rico, he felt incapable of keeping up.

They made their way over fallen trees, stones, and through small creeks. The sound of birds chirping and the howls of wolves echoed throughout the woods. There was a beauty to its eeriness and, if not for the threat of Wicker they would have felt calm.

Drake moved like a shadow. His steps barely made a sound. Colt wondered if the CIA assassin was even breathing at times. Colt knew he sounded like a tank as he moved through the bush. He couldn't help it. He'd bandaged up the wound on his leg as best as he could, but that didn't mean much. He felt sore all over.

After thirty minutes of walking through the forest, both men approached the fallen C-17.

The giant fallen engines of the aircraft created a whizzing sound in the forest. Black columns of smoke rose from its remains. There was the sound of a howl as if an immense animal was fighting to survive in the blackened dark.

The heavy dark blue of the bush turned to a thick red light.

The cold turned hot.

The air seemed solid.

Fragments of the aircraft laid scattered among the trees. Bits of fuselage, metal, and electrical components littered the forest floor.

"We'll be lucky if the storage crate is in good condition," Colt said.

"Some supplies are better than nothing," Drake said. "We need ammo, and you need meds."

They continued to follow the trail of debris. After five minutes of searching the remains, they found the supply crate. It was mostly in one piece. A bit of luck. Finally.

"Approach it slowly," Drake said. "Private Wicker could be watching us."

The fires that surrounded them created horrifying, baroque shadows. The two men moved through the forest. Drake's eyes scanned every darkened corner, monitoring for any slight disturbance, any flutter of the unexpected.

A shot echoed in the dark. There was a blast of light from a muzzle.

Colt dropped to the ground. He howled in pain. Another bullet had got him.

Drake turned to the origin of the flash and was liberal with his clip. He heard his bullets chop chunks of wood, but he also heard the moans of a man.

He ran toward the gunfire. Wicker was on the ground, bleeding out. Drake had put at least four bullets inside him.

Wicker tried to raise his rifle at Drake, but Drake kicked it out of his hands.

"You should be dead," Wicker said. He coughed up some blood. "How the hell did you survive?"

"Who hired you to kill us?"

"I'll never tell!"

Drake slammed his boot down on Wicker's ankle, putting enough force on it that he felt the bone bend and crack.

Wicker yelped.

"Who hired you?"

Wicker kept crying.

Drake slammed down on Wicker's other ankle. He made sure the broken bone pierced the skin this time. He made sure the pain was worse than before.

"You son of a bitch!" Wicker said. "I'll never tell you." Tears streamed from his eyes.

Drake wasn't in the mood for negotiation. He looked at Colt, who was slumped over. Breathing, but not in good shape. Two bullets had cut him down. The old man needed a break.

"You have a choice," Drake grunted.

"Choice?" Wicker said.

Drake pulled out a knife. "Slow or fast. Now, who hired you?"

Wicker's eyes widened. He knew Drake was serious. "I'm ... I ... Was ..."

Drake wasn't going to let him get away with it that easily. He cut Wicker's ear off. Slowly. He made sure to yank the final bit off with his hand. The knife had done enough work.

Wicker did his best to fight through the pain, but he couldn't. He howled, raged, and convulsed in unnatural shapes.

Drake didn't want to admit it, but he took some pleasure in it. He hated that fact about himself, but Wicker was the evil he knew he was made to eradicate. Wicker was the scourge.

"I'll tell you, oh God, please ... I'll tell you!"

"I'll cut the other ear off if you don't," Draske grunted.

"It was a guy ... Tom Fowler ... The CIA director ..."

Drake sighed, took out his pistol, and put a bullet through Wicker's head. He was quick and efficient about it.

He'd expected to hear Fowler's name. He just wanted to be sure.

When he got back to America, Drake would make sure that Fowler received a special visit.

Once he was sure Wicker was down, Drake made his way to Colt to check on him.

Colt was face-first in the mud. Drake rolled the old Scot's body over.

Colt was smiling. "I don't think I'm going to make it out of this alive," he said. "Another bullet in the leg."

"Are you okay?"

"It didn't penetrate," Colt said. "The bullet scraped me. Help me up."

Drake helped Colt, and the two of them made their way to the supply crate. They grabbed from it everything they could, everything that was still in working condition—bandages, magazines, a pair of night-vision goggles that had miraculously survived the thirty thousand foot drop.

Drake used one of the medical kits from the crate to treat Colt's wounds.

Once Colt felt better, the two of them made their way deeper into the forest, toward Golovinka and the ammonium nitrate.

SIXTY-TWO

Colt winced with each step. The pain from the bullet was relentless and overbearing. He knew he wouldn't be able to go on much farther. He needed relief. He needed some drugs.

"Hold up!" he yelled to Drake.

Colt dropped to his knees and rummaged through the medical supplies he'd pulled from the supply crate. He grabbed a morphine sulfate autoinjector needle and stabbed himself in the thigh. The painkiller helped offset the pain in his leg. It was like a jolt of confidence. He instantly felt better.

"I thought you were saving that until we got to the compound?" Drake asked.

"I'm in bad shape, mate. I don't know if I'll make that far."

"You should head back to the crash site. If a cleanup crew arrives to take care of the C-17, you can go with them. I may not be able to get you out of there."

"But, you'll need another set of eyes in the town and at the compound. You can't do this alone."

"I've made it through worse."

"Shut up," Colt said. "Enough of that American, Yankee doo-da, superhero crap. You'll need the help."

"And what about Kate? What if you die? She'll be distraught."

"She'll be better off without me. Hell, I didn't even know she knew I was alive until a week ago."

"You're willing to die for this?" Drake asked.

"I've been killing myself for years, mate. This is as good a night as any to burn out, and, to be honest, I can't think of a better reason. This is for my men who died in Scotland."

"You should head back," Drake said. "You're going to be a distraction."

"Fuck you! If you keep talking like that, I'll put a bullet in your belly."

Drake sighed. He knew the old Scot wasn't going to budge. There was a look in Colt's eyes—a desperation. The bastard was as stubborn as a mule. "Did the painkiller work?"

"Just keep moving," Colt said. "If I keep up, then you'll get your answer."

The two men pushed through the woods until they saw the glimmer of lights from Golovinka emerge through the brush. The town was in a valley between two massive mountains. A wide river cut through the middle of the town, and there were two main roads on either side. The town was comprised of about fifty buildings. The compound that the SAS had spotted with their satellite imagery was on the other side of the river, across from Colt and Drake's position.

"What now?" Colt said, looking down toward the light of the town, breathing slow and heavy but feeling better.

"We make our way to the town, cross the river, get into the compound, and put an end to this."

"The town might be crawling with men paid off by this Andrei Zadorov fellow. If your friend Ali Bajal was correct, he has enough money for an army. The only way he's kept this fertilizer a secret from the world is his deep pockets. I bet he has the whole town on his side—and maybe a dozen or so mercenaries, like the ones who tracked us down in Damascus."

"Probably."

Colt shook his head, wiped a thick glob of sweat from his brow, and followed Drake down the mountain's slope toward the town.

Once they made it to the floor of the valley, Drake turned to Colt and said, "You should check your equipment. We'll only get one shot at this."

Colt was relieved to take a break. He flopped to his knees, pulled out his HK-33, and checked that things were in order. He'd attached a silencer and magnification scope along with a red dot laser sight to his assault rifle. Everything looked good. He was ready.

The M4 Drake was carrying was slightly modified. Attached to it were two sights that could be interchanged depending on the scenario. One of the sights was a night vision scope; the other was a laser sight. He screwed on the silencer and then checked his combat gear.

"Do you need another shot of morphine?" Drake asked Colt. "Will you be able to keep up?"

"I'll be fine," Colt said. "The bleeding isn't as bad as it was. I should be able to make it."

The two men were in a small ravine close to the first road they'd have to cross. The road was empty. Black. Not many people traveled at night around these parts of the world. When they were sure it was clear, they crossed and hid behind a small building that looked like an auto shop on the other side.

They heard voices.

Drake signaled to Colt to duck and peered around the edge of the building.

Colt's suspicions had been correct. Two mercenaries stood smoking cigarettes under a street lamp. They were fifteen yards away, close to a cluster of townhouses, and on the main road. They held AK-47s with laser sight attachments. They were dressed like the assholes who'd attacked Ali Bajal's club in Damascus.

Drake turned to Colt. "Two men, fifteen yards. They've got AK-47s."

"If there's two, then there's probably thirty more."

Drake nodded. "I have an idea," he said. He pulled off his backpack and grabbed C4 charges.

"A distraction?"

"Yes," Drake said. "We're going to need to make a lot of noise when we want to get out of here. We light these things up, they won't know what to do. They won't be able to chase us."

"Sounds like a plan."

Drake handed Colt five C4 charges. "We'll have to be quick. When I move, you move. Stick to the walls and stay in the shadows."

"Just stop yer yapping and keep moving," Colt snapped.

They moved from building to building. Colt made sure not to let too large of a gap grow between him and Drake. He didn't want Drake to ask him how he felt again. The son-of-a-bitch was getting on his nerves.

They placed the C4 plastic explosives in strategic positions all throughout the town. One under a truck, one in a trash can, one on an oil barrel. When they were done at the compound, the town would light up like the fourth of July. All Drake would have to do is hit the trigger in his pocket.

As they crisscrossed the town, setting C4 traps everywhere, Drake recognized that Golovinka was not dissimilar from any small mining town in the middle of Indiana or Pennsylvania. It was just one of those places where people went about their lives, separate and apart from the chaos of the larger world; people who were happy to exist and live without feeling the need to be part of anything more significant. Everyone in the town would know each other, be friends with one another—exist in their own peace.

He didn't want to disturb that quaintness, but he knew he wouldn't have a choice. If shit hit the fan, he'd light up the C4, and the whole place would burn.

When they were done laying charges, they made their way across the second main road and waded through the river, holding their equipment above their heads, making sure not to get it wet. Once on the other side, Drake guided Colt up toward the compound.

Colt gritted his teeth and let the blood from his wound dampen the soil as he followed Drake up the slope.

In the distance, wolves howled. The moon serenaded the thick branches and pines with its milky light. Within this nature, within this peace, lay the rot of the world, the anger, the torment that would need to be culled, cut out, and vaporized.

Andrei and Aya were about to meet their end.

Drake's eyes were focused and narrow. He could feel his heart pound in his chest. Would he be able to do it? Would he be able to kill Aya?

SIXTY-THREE

"We're going to send a helicopter team in from a Royal Air Force base in Georgia. They should get there in forty-five minutes," Howe said to Price. "That is assuming they don't run into any bad weather or surface-to-air missile sites. Once they get to the crash site, they'll destroy all sensitive materials and rescue whoever may be alive."

"But I thought we couldn't send a helicopter team in? That's why we had Drake and Wicker drop in from the C-17?"

"The hornets' nest is rattled," Howe said. "It's more important we destroy the burning remains of the C-17 than anything else at the moment. We have to take the risk. I wanted this operation to be discrete, but you can't always get what you want."

"Have you informed SAS command about our operation?" Price asked.

"Yes," Howe said. "They're rightfully pissed, but I don't mind. Clyde's been right about me for years. The bureaucratic bullshit was starting to really bother me. I figured it was time I did what was 'right.'"

Price smiled. "You'll have to tell that to him when he comes back. He'll be shocked to hear you say that."

"Ah," Howe said. "I don't want to give him another stroke. I'll just tell him I'm upset with him. That should keep him calm."

Price chuckled and then stopped. She thought of Colt. He was a good man being dragged through a torturous life and doing his best to fight his demons and keep them at bay.

"I need a coffee," she said. "You want one?"

"A tea would be nice," Howe said.

"Of course," Price said. She stood up and walked to the coffee pot in the hangar. It was along the wall, next to the equipment Colt and Drake had sifted through before the operation. Next to the coffee maker was a pile of ammunition.

She prepared a coffee and put an electric kettle on for Howe's tea. As she waited, her mind drifted back to the night she and Colt had decided to call it quits, end their marriage.

It was March. Cold and rainy. Miserable.

"It's been a cold winter," the bereavement officer said to them both. He was an old, thin guy with a goatee and dark eyes. He looked like the living embodiment of the grim reaper. "The ground is still too frozen. We can't bury him yet."

"I just want to bury my child," Colt said. "Put him to rest." His face was red with drink, and there were tears in his eyes. "How long do we have to wait?"

"We just want to give our little Cody a place to rest," Price said. "Are you sure we have to wait for another month?"

"I'm not a weatherman," the officer said. "It might be two months. This year has been unnaturally cold."

"Ah, fuck this," Colt snapped. "I should—"

Price stopped her husband before he swung at the bereavement officer. "Stop it, Clyde!"

Colt looked into her eyes and wanted to scream. The light of his life had just been taken away from him. Did he have a reason to live anymore? He didn't know. He wondered if he cared. He wanted to tear the world apart.

"Just breathe," Price said. "Just breathe."

Colt pushed away from Price and left the office, slamming the door and making his way out into the frigid air outside. He looked at the graveyard grounds where he was hoping to bury his son. The grass was yellow and spotted with dirty snow.

"Is there anything you can do?" Price said to the officer.

"No," the officer said. "I'm sorry. The ground needs to thaw. It's still too cold."

She left the office, met Colt outside, and the two of them stood in the negative thirty-degree air for at least twenty minutes. Her face felt numb when they finally decided to go to their car.

"So, what now?" Colt said.

"I need to go to work," she said.

"Aye."

"And what are you going to do?"

"I'm not on assignment. I'll head to the pub."

"And drink yourself dead?"

"Why not?"

"You're a coward," Price said.

"I don't care. My life is over. My boy is dead. Taken away by a monster."

"I'll call Graham," Price said. "I'll get you on assignment. You need it."

"If I go, I'll be gone for a while."

"I know."

And that was it. Price saved Colt from drinking himself to an early grave by calling Howe, and before long, they'd grown so far apart that there was no point in reliving their painful past.

The coffee pot began to drip. The tea kettle was boiling. Price brought a cup of coffee and tea to the station Howe had set up for them.

She handed Howe his tea. He smiled and nodded at her. "Thanks," he said. "Let's just pray our boys are alive out there."

"If I know Clyde, he's not out of this fight yet," she said.

"The helicopter team just left the air base," Howe said. "They should be in Golovinka within the hour to clean up the mess. They're going to tell me what they find."

SIXTY-FOUR

Drake and Colt approached the stone wall of the compound. It appeared as if by magic in the dark of the forest. It was thick, six feet tall, and had vines growing alongside it.

"What now?" Colt asked.

"We finish this."

"About fucking time."

Colt rummaged through his medical gear and injected the last morphine injection he had in his leg. He'd been saving it. The climb up toward the compound was torturous. The gauze he'd injected into his bullet hole had grown damp, and the blood was seeping through his pants. He needed relief. As the morphine flooded his system, he felt a wave of euphoria. He felt better.

The two men navigated their way around the wall until they found a concealed section in a shadow cast from a large tree.

Drake pulled himself to the top of the wall and helped Colt climb over. Once on the other side, the two men hid behind a small wooden shed. Drake peered out and examined the terrain.

Inside the compound were four large buildings: a mansion, a greenhouse, a garage, and a guest house. There were spotlights, and at least twenty heavily armed men. Mercenaries. They were carrying AK-47s, shotguns, and submachine guns.

"Looks like we've hit pay dirt," Colt said. "The SAS satellite intel was right to suspect this place."

"Yes," Drake said. "And that truck over there is the Russian military truck that was in the refinery."

"Then we've found her!"

"Looks like it."

"So this is it, eh? I'll finally be able to put my troops' souls to rest."

At the center of the compound was the large mansion. It was built from red brick and had four massive white pillars at its entrance. It was ornate, lavish.

"You check the garage," Drake said. "We'll need a way out of here. If you can get us a vehicle, we'll be better off."

"Where are you going?"

"The mansion."

"Alone?"

"When shit hits the fan, make sure you have a vehicle."

"And how will I know if shit hits the fan?"

Drake winked. "You'll know."

"And you're sure you won't need my help in there?"

"Not in your shape," Drake said. "You're out of morphine. You need to rest. Your body won't be able to take much more of this."

Colt begrudgingly nodded.

"When I sprint for the mansion, you need to sneak into the garage. Be silent. We can't raise any alarm bells. Not yet, at least."

"Got it."

Drake waited for a patrol of five mercenaries to pass. When they were all out of the way, he sprinted toward the mansion and slid into a garden. He went prone and crawled into a thick evergreen shrub. From his position, he saw Colt slowly creep from the shed and make his way toward the garage.

"Hold it together, Clyde," Drake said to himself.

Drake turned back to the mansion and crept through the garden, hugging the redbrick of the mansion's wall so tightly that the contours of the brick rubbed against the fabric of his gear. Periodically, he remained still to avoid detection. The mercenaries patrolling the mansion walked around its perimeter every couple of minutes.

Clearly, they'd either seen the C-17 go down or heard the explosion. The entire place was on high alert.

Drake made his way to the rear of the mansion. He was crawling under an open window when he smelled roast beef stew. He was outside the kitchen.

A man's voice came through the window. "I need a smoke," he said.

"You heard what Andrei told us," another man responded. "We're to stay inside. Something about a downed airplane: they don't know what it is. Ajmal is going to investigate."

"You also know what Andrei says about smoking inside. He says it hurts his lungs."

"Andrei won't last long."

"No, he won't."

"Just be quiet about it then and come back in. We need to clean up. I'm tired."

The outside door to the kitchen opened shortly after. A man walked out. He was large and wore a white apron and a chef's hat. Drake popped up from the garden. He made his way to the man, grabbed him by the neck, and counted to three. The cigarette in the man's mouth dropped, his body went limp. He then dragged the body behind the evergreen bush and made his way inside the mansion.

The lights were off.

"Alex?" a man in the kitchen said. "Are you back? I thought I heard a struggle."

Drake stayed in the shadows of the kitchen, hiding behind an island counter.

"Alex? Where are you?"

Drake maneuvered around the island and then put the second man in the same hold. Once he was sure the man was unconscious, he stuffed him into the pantry closet.

Drake made his way deeper inside the mansion. He took out his pistol.

He walked by an ornate grandfather clock, a dinner table that could seat over twenty people, and then through a large foyer with a circular staircase that led to the second floor.

Voices reverberated through the open foyer from upstairs. Two men. They sounded upset at one another.

Drake made his way up the circular staircase to the second floor. The whole place reeked of rich decadence. Ali Bajal was right. Andrei Zadorov was wealthy.

On the second floor, there was a large doorway. The voices were coming from that room. They were louder now. Angrier.

Drake walked up to the door, leaned against it, and listened to the conversation from inside.

"We need to get out of here! An aircraft just went down, you know it's him!"

Drake's eyebrow rose. It was Ajmal.

"We're fine. I have the men on high alert. And anyway, if the downed aircraft is connected to this Jason Drake fellow, then something went terribly wrong. He could be dead. If he's alive, we'll kill him."

"You don't know him like I do. It's probably already too late. We should get out of here."

The man Ajmal spoke to was Russian. He sounded young but seemed very tired and out of breath.

"I am not leaving," the Russian man said. "I am staying here. If Jason Drake is on his way, if it's too late, then I'd like to meet him. He is the one, after all, who trained your sister, who made her what she is."

The Russian man broke out in a fit of coughing.

"I am going to head to the crash site and investigate. I can only pray that he is dead," Ajmal said. "If he isn't, then it's too late for us all."

"Do whatever you want."

Ajmal grunted and stormed out of the room. He walked past Drake, who was hiding in the shadows just outside the room. Ajmal didn't notice a thing.

Drake waited for Ajmal to reach the ground floor and then pushed open the door into the large room. He went inside.

Andrei Zadorov was standing at an alcohol cabinet, pouring himself another shot of vodka. He swung back the shot and sighed.

He looked out a window. He was frail and thin. Not the man Drake was expecting.

Drake pulled up his sidearm, aimed it at Andrei, and walked toward him slowly. "Where is Aya Khan? Where is the ammonium nitrate?"

Andrei didn't flinch when he heard the voice. He turned around. There was a smile on his face. "Jason Drake, I presume? What took you so long?"

SIXTY-FIVE

Colt hobbled to the garage windows. His wound was leaking blood onto the muddy ground. "Shit," he grunted to himself. "Come on, Clyde. You can do this. Just hold on for a little bit longer."

He looked through a window into the garage. There were two men inside. They were holding AK-47s and had on radio headsets to communicate with the others in the compound. He'd have to take them out at the same time.

He pulled out his combat knife and walked along the garage wall until he found an open door. He went inside, staying in the dark and hiding behind a large truck.

The two guards spoke to each other in Russian.

"Ajmal seems paranoid."

The other guard chuckled. "He's a weakling. Who knows what kind of aircraft went down in the forest? Let the Russian military investigate. It's not our problem. Why do we have to go?"

"When will he be here?"

"He said he needed to speak with Andrei first."

"Did you bring vodka?"

"Of course, I did. I'm not spending a night in the woods with Ajmal without a drink."

The two men laughed.

Colt seized the moment of levity. He didn't know what they were saying, he didn't speak Russian, but he knew they weren't expecting him. He hit one of the Russians in the temple with the butt of his blade and then slit the other's throat. It was grisly, but it had to be done. As the man with the slit throat grabbed hold of his neck to stop the flow of blood, Colt cut the other man's throat. When he was sure they were both dead, he rummaged through their pockets for keys to the truck.

Once he found a set of keys, he slid both the bodies into a darkened corner of the room.

He was about to check out the truck when the main door to the garage opened.

"Are you assholes ready?"

"Fuck," Colt said. He ducked behind the truck and disappeared into the shadow.

Ajmal walked into the garage. He didn't see the pool of blood on the floor, but he felt it. He knelt down on the ground, touched the blood, and knew right away that it wasn't oil.

"What the hell?" Ajmal said. He lifted up his rifle. "Ilya? Pavel? Are you here?"

Colt's face soured. Shit. He should have waited a bit longer. He was about to grab his assault rifle but decided against it. If he fired any shots, he'd alert the entire hornets' nest. His and Drake's chances of escape would be spoiled before they even began.

"Who is in here?" Ajmal asked.

Colt stayed quiet. He'd have to wait the asshole out. He watched as Ajmal took a few cautious steps around the truck.

"Who the hell is in here!? Is it you?!"

Colt wondered who the hell the guy was talking about. Unlike the two men he'd killed, the guy wasn't Russian. He had a Syrian accent.

"Is it you, Jason?" Ajmal said in English.

Hearing Drake's name caused Colt to freeze. Whoever was in the garage with him had most likely been with Drake at the refinery. He felt a wave of anger swell through his body. Whoever was with him was close to the top. He took a deep breath, ignored the pain in his leg, and slowly crept toward the source of the voice.

Ajmal was shaking. He knew the downed aircraft was related to Drake. Of course, it was. Every terrible thing in his life was associated with Drake. He'd light the dick head up, he thought. He'd unleash an entire clip into his body.

"Fuck you!" Ajmal shouted. "I'll kill you!"

Colt rolled his eyes. A tough guy. They were always tough guys.

From underneath the truck's body, Colt saw the legs of the man in the garage with him.

Ajmal was nervous. He stopped walking when he noticed something on the ground that would tip the scales in his favor. Whoever was in the garage with him was injured. There were tiny droplets of blood on the cement floor. He followed the droplets.

Colt noticed the change in demeanor in the Syrian man. He looked for another place to hide, but it was too late.

"Show yourself!"

Ajmal fired a few warning shots.

And that was it. As the bullets bounced and reflected off the ground, as the thunderous sound echoed in the garage and out into the courtyard of the compound, Colt stumbled to the ground. The pain in his leg was too much. He reached for his assault rifle, but Ajmal kicked it away.

Colt wanted to fight, but he'd lost too much blood. He tried to keep going, but he couldn't. He was finally near his end. Ajmal kicked him in the belly, which made the pain even worse.

Colt closed his eyes and accepted his fate.

"Who are you?" Ajmal asked.

"My name is Clyde Colt."

"Are you here with Jason Drake?"

"What do you think?"

Ajmal's screamed. He kicked Colt once more. "You're going to tell me everything! You hear me? Everything!"

"Fuck you," Colt said.

Ajmal whacked Colt in the head with his rifle. He wasn't going to the crash site now, he thought. He'd head back to Andrei and show him what he'd found. Maybe Drake was dead, but probably not. In any case, his only chance at finding out where he was, was by talking to Clyde Colt, and he wanted Andrei to hear it himself.

SIXTY-SIX

"Where the hell is Aya?" Drake asked Andrei.

He was close enough to the wealthy Russian that his pistol's barrel was almost pressed against Andrei's forehead.

Andrei stood by the same window he was looking through earlier. He had a smile on his face and didn't seem bothered by Drake. "She's not here."

"And where is she?"

Andrei laughed. "You must know by now. If she's not here, she's in America."

"She's in the US?"

Andrei chuckled and coughed. "Mind if I take a seat?" he said. "I'm not feeling my best today. Cancer is a bitch."

Drake cocked his gun. "Tell me exactly where she is or pay the price."

"I don't care what you do to me. I'm already dead. My body decided that I couldn't go on. And anyway, I know you won't shoot me."

Drake clenched his pistol and grunted. He whacked Andrei in the temple, causing the Russian to fall to the floor.

"You're right, I won't shoot you. But I can make the last few moments of your life miserable."

Andrei's nose bled. Tiny droplets of blood splattered on his expensive Persian carpet. He looked up at Drake, the menacing and physically dominating figure in his office. "You can't hurt me. Like I said, I'm dying. I have no reason to tell you a thing. You'll have to put a bullet in my head to find out what's inside."

Drake holstered his gun and pulled out his combat knife. "I will cut you open. I'll skin you alive. Tell me where she is."

The threat caused Andrei to burst out into maniacal laughter. "Do it!" he screamed. "I've been putting radiation into my body for months. Every breath is pain. Every movement is pain. What is one or two more hours of pain? I welcome death. Bring it on."

Drake grunted in frustration.

Andrei pulled himself up onto the chair. He sat and grabbed a bottle of vodka from inside one of his desk drawers, and emptied half of it into his belly. "It's too late for me," he said. "And it's too late for you and your country. You lost."

"What the hell are you talking about?"

Andrei chuckled. "What? Did you really think you'd save the day by coming here? You've saved nothing. Aya is not here, and neither is the ammonium nitrate. In fact, that stuff has been gone for days."

"Where is it?"

"Like I said, she's in America," Andrei said.

"And why are you still here?"

"Because I wanted to be a distraction, and ..." Andrei took another long swig of vodka. "And maybe because I knew you were looking for us, and I wanted to meet you. After I heard that the Russian soldiers I bought the hydrazine from were dead, after I learned that you beat my mercenaries to Ali Bajal, I was impressed. I wanted to see the man himself. The man who made even Aya scared. I turned her into a demon, you know?"

"What do you mean she's a 'demon'?

Andrei coughed. "She's my demon," he said. "I molded her. I shaped her. It took years, but I did it. While you gave her the skills and provided her the tools, I gave her direction—purpose. She's the living embodiment of my cancer. And yet, she was most scared of you."

"Then why did she bring me back and try to sell me to the Russians?"

"Because she wanted you dead," Andrei said. "She blamed you for everything. She didn't want to sell you to the Russians. She just wanted to put a bullet in your brain. I was the one that forced the transaction to take place."

"You're lying."

"Aya talked a lot about you. But now, I can see why. You're a fierce creature—a work of art, even. Hell, if I could put you on display, I would. Were you engineered? Crafted? You don't look like a typical spy. As a former spy myself, I can tell you that you lack a spy's most important attribute. You stand out. You don't blend in."

"Where is Aya?"

"You don't want to talk about art? Fine. But you need to realize your role in this. You have nothing. I have everything. I'm the one asking the questions. It's men like you that made me like this: your arrogance, your self-assuredness. I want you destroyed. I want the world you're trying to protect destroyed. Why do you fight for it? The CIA, the SVR, Russian, American—they are all the same. Self-interested assholes. I want the world to burn."

Outside the mansion, Drake heard shots. He tensed as he saw through the window blasts of light coming from inside the garage.

Colt!

He wanted to run to Colt's aid. He looked out the window. A panicked expression gripped his face. He needed to hurry.

"You weren't alone, I presume?" Andrei said, noticing Drake's expression.

"Shut the hell up," Drake said. "Tell me where she is, or I skin you alive. I don't care about you or your plan."

"Oh, you're that kind of sociopath, eh?" Andrei said. "You'll flay my corpse just for the fun of it?" He sighed. "Typical CIA. And to think you call us the bad guys. I was hoping you were different. I thought maybe we would find a middle ground. But alas, that is not the case. Go ahead. Skin me. I welcome it. I welcome the pain."

Drake gripped the knife in his hand tightly and approached Andrei.

Andrei burst into maniacal laughter once again. "For decades, our countries have butted heads. We've fought proxy war after proxy war. Vietnam, Afghanistan, Syria. Our leaders were too afraid to get to the point. Our intelligence agencies were too caught up in the dance. Everyone seemed to be enjoying themselves. The status-quo. How boring. When I was diagnosed with cancer, I realized what I was put on this earth to do. I was meant to finally get our two countries to wage battle: head-to-head. To get things to the point. To cut through the bullshit."

Drake punched Andrei in the head, which only made Andrei's laughter increase.

"I'm not going to tell you where she is. You can hurt me all you want. You can strip every layer of flesh from my body. You'll never find her."

Drake placed the blade of his knife against Andrei's scalp.

"I spent five years building an army," Andrei said. "I spent five years finding the most desperate people on the planet. That was why I went to Syria. I needed people who had lost everything. Who hated Russia as much as they hated America. What better place for that than Syria? I was a spy for Russia! A spy! I did what I could for my country, but it wasn't enough. Once Aya detonates the stolen Russian ammonium nitrate on US soil, the Russian military will be tied to the explosion, and when—" Andrei stopped himself. "I guess I shouldn't disclose everything. I doubt you'll make it out of my compound alive, but if you do, I want you to be surprised."

"I'm going to give you one more chance," Drake said. "Where is she?"

Andrei shook his head. "You don't get it, do you?"

Drake was about to cut his throat when Ajmal burst into the room. Colt was with him. The SAS captain was in bad shape. Blood oozed from the wound in his leg like a river, his face smashed up by Ajmal's gun. Colt fell to the floor.

When Ajmal saw Drake, he froze. His skin turned white.

Drake aimed his pistol at Ajmal. Ajmal aimed his gun at Drake.

Andrei's face turned red, and he crawled away from Drake back to his desk, where he pulled out a pistol and aimed it at Drake.

"For the first time since I've met you, Ajmal, you finally showed some use," Andrei said, laughing and coughing. Blood splattered from his mouth.

"I told you he was here," Ajmal said to Andrei. "I told you we should have been more careful. I told you we should have left!" He was screaming, shaking.

"Why are you so scared?" Andrei said.

"Are you drunk?" Ajmal asked Andrei.

"Yes."

Colt was lying face-down on the ground. Blood pooled on the floor below him. He moaned and was trying to push himself up, but he hardly had the strength to breathe. He'd lost too much blood.

"Who is he?" Andrei asked Ajmal, gesturing to Colt.

"I thought we could question him."

Andrei rolled his eyes. "Just kill him and Jason. We have the upper hand."

"Don't," Colt said. The word came out like an exhausted breath. He was beyond the point of feeling pain. His attempts to push himself up had failed, but he kept fighting. His hands dug deep into the fibers of the Persian rug, which was now soaked in his blood. "Don't!"

"Stay down," Drake said to Colt. "I've got this."

When Andrei heard Drake's confident statement, he giggled. He looked up at Drake. "I can see what Aya learned from you," he said to Drake. "Her confidence. Her fearlessness. She got that from you."

"Shut up," Drake said.

"Yes," Ajmal said to them both. "Enough talk." He pulled down on his trigger and fired at Drake, but Colt kicked Ajmal with the last bit of strength he had. The bullets from Ajmal's gun splayed across the room and hit the portrait of Andrei's mother and father that hung on the wall. They seemed to hit everything but Drake.

In anger, Andrei fired his pistol at Drake.

Drake ducked, rolled toward the liquor cabinet, and let the thick, rich wooden panels of the cabinet absorb the bullets from Andrei's pistol.

Andrei screamed when he saw his parents' faces splintered and frayed from the bullets. "Natalay!" he shouted. "Mother! You asshole!" Andrei turned toward Ajmal. "You are a fucking nuisance. I knew I should have killed you when you handed the child over to the Russians. You've always held your sister back. I should have killed you instead!"

Ajmal froze and looked at Andrei. He lowered his pistol. "What are you talking about?"

Drake's eyes widened. He was still behind the liquor cabinet but listening to the conversation closely.

For the first time in a long while, Andrei felt out of control. His anger had caused him to say too much. He needed to shut down a loose end. He needed to keep quiet the only man in the room who knew as much as he did. He aimed his pistol at Ajmal and fired. He put three bullets into Ajmal's chest.

Drake saw the moment of weakness. He shot up from the liquor cabinet and fired at the exposed Andrei. He hit the Russian spy in the hand and leg.

Andrei howled and fell from his chair back onto the floor. He writhed in pain.

Drake emerged from his cover and approached Andrei. He loomed over his contorting body, his pistol aimed at Andrei's head. "Where is Aya?"

"Just kill me!" Andrei spat out. "I am finally going to be set free, and you will not be able to stop her. I die knowing I won. The world will burn. I made her a monster. A monster that you will not be able to kill."

Drake put one bullet in Andrei's head. The Russian spy was never going to talk. He was going to keep spouting the same bullshit over and over. If anyone would talk, it was the weakest man in the room. It was Ajmal.

Ajmal coughed and moaned. "Did he kill Amira?" he said. His breaths were labored and long. "Did he kill her? I thought it was the CIA. I thought it was America."

Drake walked to Ajmal and knelt beside the dying man.

Ajmal looked up at Drake and sighed. He'd made so many mistakes. And now, he had to accept his fate.

SIXTY-SEVEN

Four years ago

Ajmal was nervous. He held onto Amira tightly. He held on to her the way he thought a father would. She howled and screamed in his arms, and he tried to console her, but it was useless. She wanted Aya. She wanted her mother.

Andrei had instructed him that a Russian family would meet him at the Turkish border, by a small creek. It was in the middle of the desert, and it was a hot afternoon. He felt terrible for the child. He kept blowing on her face, doing whatever he could to cool her down.

He used the shade from a cypress tree to keep cool.

He saw the vehicle's approach.

The sand tore up under their tires, the wind carrying the sand into the air. Nothing could be hidden in the desert. It was ruthless that way.

He looked into Amira's green eyes and smiled. This was what Aya wanted. She wanted her daughter to be safe. It pained him to know that Aya wanted the same fate, but at least, for now, Amira was taken care of.

Amira's cries grew louder. They echoed in the distance.

Ajmal wasn't bothered by the screams. When he looked into the young child's eyes, he felt sympathy. Such an angel, he thought. Aya was right about her. She was the hope for the future. She was the reason to keep going, to keep fighting. She was going to help inspire them both to keep fighting for Syria and democracy.

"It's okay," he said to Amira. "It's okay. Look at me, little one." He made a funny face by sticking out his tongue.

Amira giggled.

"Hah, you see?" he said. "It's okay. It's Uncle Ajmal. I am here for you. Do not worry."

He felt a lump grow in his throat as he said it.

He'd only known Andrei for weeks, but he was putting a lot of faith in the man. He wondered why. Because he had money? He shook his head. He couldn't worry about such possibilities. Unlike everything else in his life, Andrei had actually come through with what he'd promised.

The vehicles far out in the desert came closer. The wall of sand created in their wake grew larger. When they were close enough, they all came to a stop.

Ajmal held Amira and waited for the people inside the vehicles to get out. He shielded the child's eyes from the sand.

As Andrei had promised, they were Russian. They were going to take Amira to Istanbul and wait in a mansion for Aya's arrival. That was what he had been told.

The sun was setting, and the last strands of daylight had turned dark. The stars began to pierce through the black of the endless sky.

Ajmal handed them Amira. He handed them the future.

"Thank you," they said.

"Be safe with her," Ajmal said. "She's the daughter of Aya Khan. If anything happens to her—"

The Russian woman holding Amira interrupted him. "There's no need to worry," she said. "Everything will be okay. We will take her to Istanbul and wait for her mother."

And that was that. Ajmal let Amira go. He watched as they disappeared into the desert, fading away in the sandstorm they'd created. They vanished. He cried.

He drove back to Aleppo, back to Andrei's house in the city. He was eager to tell Aya the news. For so many years, he'd felt like a useless tool in the war. He wasn't as talented as his sister. He was better suited for other things. Perhaps, he had found his purpose.

He arrived in Aleppo, where Andrei's men informed him that things had not gone as planned. He was told not to answer the calls from his sister. He was told Andrei would speak to her first.

When he'd learned the news, Ajmal broke down and cried.

A drone strike? American? How was he going to tell his sister? What was he going to do?

"I'll take care of it," Andrei said. "I'll tell her."

SIXTY-EIGHT

Ajmal, with what little breath he had left in his lungs, told Drake everything he knew. Which, as much as he wanted to deny it, wasn't much.

He told Drake that Aya had been recruited into Andrei's army because she blamed America for her child's death. He told Drake that her dead child, Amira, was also Drake's daughter. He explained that Aya had hidden Amira from Drake because she was angry at him and the CIA; that he and Aya had been brainwashed by Andrei.

Drake closed his eyes and let the truth linger like a strong alcoholic drink.

He'd had a daughter?

"Where is Aya?" Drake asked.

"She's in Washington, DC," Ajmal said. "In two days, she's going to explode the ammonium nitrate. It's scheduled to go off close to midnight. It's a suicide mission."

"How did she get two thousand tonnes of ammonium nitrate across the border?" Drake asked.

"I don't know. All I know for certain is that she is going to attack the city in two days. Andrei and her never let me in on the important details."

"Why are you telling me this?"

Ajmal smirked. The pool of blood around his body had grown so vast he couldn't feel anything but blood. "He lied to me. He hated me, though I loved him. I tried so hard, but I could never get him to come close to me. I tried. Oh, I tried, but he led me on. He knew how to fool men like me. But he just wanted Aya ... and he knew that the only way to do that was to kill Amira. I was so stupid. I thought that one day, he'd come close. I thought one day he and I ... It doesn't matter."

Colt had pushed himself up against Andrei's desk. He was holding his HK-33. "I can't feel my legs, mate. I'm done."

"I'll carry you," Drake said. "We need to leave."

"Like hell, you will," Colt said. He readied his HK-33. "You're going to get out of here, and you're going to stop her. You know where she is. You know where the ammonium nitrate is. It's up to you now. I'm about to meet my mates in the afterlife. I'm about to meet my son. I've been waiting for this moment for too long."

He tossed Drake the keys he'd procured from the men he'd killed in the garage. Drake caught them and said, "What the hell are you talking about?"

"This place is loaded with security. You can hear them outside and downstairs. They're going to be here any minute now. When they storm in here, I'll give 'em hell. It might buy you enough time to escape. Take the truck in the garage and get the hell back to the crash site."

"No," Drake said to Colt.

"Stop being a dick head," Colt said. "You need to leave. You need to stop a world war."

"I'll help," Ajmal said. "This is all my fault anyway. I brought Aya into Andrei's tangled web. If not for me, Amira would be alive. You need to tell her the truth. You need to tell her that Andrei killed Amira. Only then, and only maybe, will that bring her to her senses."

Drake grunted in frustration.

Shouts and footsteps echoed from the lower floors of the mansion. Andrei's mercenaries were about to make their move.

"Go!" Colt said to Drake. "Stop Aya! Save the world, ya daft idiot."

Drake stood up and walked to the alcohol cabinet. He grabbed a bottle of whiskey, took a swig, and then opened the window. Before leaving, he tossed Colt the bottle and said, "Give them hell."

"Aye! Oh, and Drake? Tell Kate I love her."

Drake nodded. "Will do, ya bastard."

Colt smiled, picked up the bottle, took a long swig, and thought about Gaz and the rest of his troops and Cody. He put the bottle down and readied his weapon.

Ajmal couldn't move his body, but he grabbed his pistol and aimed it at the doorway.

Drake climbed out of the window silently. He made his way toward the garage. As he started up the truck, he heard the sounds of gunfire ring out from inside the office.

SIXTY-NINE

Drake slammed his foot on the gas, and the truck burst through the garage door. Bits and pieces of wood and glass flew everywhere. The truck's tires tore up the mud in front of the mansion, and Drake steered onto the driveway that would take him away from the compound.

The entire compound security force was inside the mansion. The shooting inside Andrei's office had stopped, and while they heard the rev of the truck's engine, they couldn't stop Drake from getting away.

The truck burst through the front gate and down a long serpentine road. Drake didn't relent on the gas pedal. He swerved around corners like a professional rally driver. His only thought was getting to the crash site.

He made it to Golovinka and then slowed down.

The mercenaries patrolling the town were looking for him. He saw their flashlight beams and the red dots from their laser sights. They'd been radioed by the security at the compound.

A group of four mercenaries fired on him as he drove toward a small bridge. Bullets chewed up the truck's engine, peppering it with holes. Drake opened the driver's side door and jumped into the creek while the truck rolled across the small bridge toward the mercenaries.

Drake pushed himself up from the water, lifted up his M4, and waited. The mercenaries revealed themselves from atop the bridge.

Drake lit them up. As their bodies splashed into the water below and were carried downstream, he made his way to the shore.

He changed the magazine in his gun and hid in the shadows.

He was more than pissed off. Colt was a good man. Better than ninety percent of the people Drake had met in his life. He didn't deserve to go out like that.

After climbing up a small cliff, Drake ran through the town without being detected, each step precise and quiet. His mind was overwhelmed by a litany of thoughts.

A daughter?

Why hadn't he known?

Why had Aya kept that from him?

What was he going to tell Price?

His anger at the CIA, for everything, increased with each step he took. If he'd known Aya was pregnant on the mission to kill the Butcher, he would have never let her join him. He would have let her rest. He would have done it alone.

He could feel his heart pound and his pulse push blood throughout his whole body, into each muscle and organ.

He cautiously moved between each building of the town, carefully maneuvering his way in the dark. He thought he'd made it to the edge of the town without detection—he thought he wouldn't have to ignite the C4 he and Colt had meticulously laid out, but he was wrong.

One of the mercenaries patrolling the town spotted him. He pulled out his rifle and fired.

Bullets ripped up the dirt below Drake's feet.

Diving behind a small townhouse, Drake waited for the gunfire to die down. The hornets' nest was awoken. He could hear the whole town call out to each other as he crouched behind cover.

He pulled out the trigger and set off the C4.

The town shook. Buildings crumbled, and the red glow of fire emanated into the black sky. Villagers screamed. Mercenaries ran in all directions.

Drake was in the clear.

He disappeared into the fields leading up to the crash site.

He wasn't followed.

He climbed up the hillside and made his way toward the smoke of the fallen C-17.

When he got close enough, he saw the SAS cleanup crew. They were dressed in black, wore night-vision goggles, and left their own explosive devices on all the materials and debris that mattered—the black box, the electronic equipment that carried vital information like hard drives and memory sticks. They were just finishing up when they spotted Drake.

He walked toward them, his arms raised. "I'm American," he shouted. "I was here with Clyde Colt."

"Who are you?"

"My name is Jason Drake."

The SAS officer he was speaking to radioed someone on his headset. After a few nervous seconds, a quick back and forth with central command, they all lowered their weapons. Drake lowered his hands.

"Why is Private Wicker dead?" one of the SAS officers asked Drake, gesturing to Wicker's body.

"He's why the C-17 is on the ground," Drake grunted. "He was working for an ex-CIA director. He tried to kill Clyde and me."

"Impossible!" the SAS officer said.

"I'm telling you the truth."

"And where is Clyde?"

"He's dead."

"Two dead SAS officers? I should put a bullet in you."

Drake dropped to his knees, his hands back in the air. "If you want to arrest me, arrest me. But I'm telling you the truth. Just take me with you."

The SAS officers looked at each other and then nodded. They approached Drake slowly.

"We don't have a lot of time," Drake said. "I just set off a shit tonne of explosives in the town at the base of the valley. We need to leave."

"So, you're the one who lit that town up."

"Yes," Drake said.

The lead SAS officer nodded at the rest of his team. "We could just put a bullet in you and say we fired by accident."

"If that's what you want, then do it," Drake said. "But in twenty-four hours hours, when Washington, DC, goes up in flames, you'll have to live with yourself. You'll be responsible for all those deaths."

The SAS officers went silent. Shouts and gunfire echoed in the distance. Mercenaries from Golovinka were approaching.

"It sounds like they're less than a couple miles away," Drake said. "Are you boys done cleaning up this mess?"

The SAS officers nodded.

"Well, if you want to kill me, how about you do it in London?"

The lead officer approached Drake and said, "If you try anything, we will put a bullet in your head."

"I won't try anything. I just want to get back to London."

Two officers pulled Drake up by the arms and handcuffed him. They brought him to a clearing in the forest. He boarded their helicopter and watched the forest disappear as they took off. The trees danced in all directions. Drake saw the damage he'd done to Golovinka. The whole town looked like it was on fire.

He felt bad for the locals. But it had to be done. A small explosion to prevent a larger one. A burn-off.

The SAS helicopter disappeared into a low cloud and flew back to Georgia. While Drake now knew the intended target was Washington, he felt farther than ever from his goal of stopping Aya. Andrei had played them all perfectly. Andrei's plan felt impossible to stop.

Drake had less than forty-eight hours, and he was down an ally.

SEVENTY

A light rain pattered the tarmac at the Royal Air Force base in London. There was a gloom in the air. During the night, a fog had settled over the whole place. The evergreen trees that scaled the perimeter of the airfield could faintly be seen from inside the hangar.

Price nervously waited for an update from the cleanup crew in Georgia. All she knew for certain was that Drake, and only Drake, had been picked up from the outskirts of Golovinka.

When the Gulfstream G550 private jet carrying Drake dipped through the thick clouds and pulled to a stop on the runway, Price walked out from the hangar and into the rain. She didn't care about her clothes getting wet. She just wanted to find out what had happened in Russia. She wanted to know where Colt was.

The G550's doors opened, and Drake walked out. His steps were slow. He had a duffel bag in his hand and looked at Price with an emotionless expression.

Price stormed up to Drake.

He stared her into the eyes as he walked up to her, not turning away. He could sense her anguish and grief. He knew what he was about to tell her would hurt. He wouldn't be a coward about it.

"Where is he?" she said. "Where is Clyde!?"

Drake dropped his duffel bag and put his arms around her, holding her tight.

"You son-of-a-bitch!" she said. She punched Drake in the chest. "What the hell happened? Where is he?"

"He's gone."

"How?"

"He died saving me."

She punched Drake's chest again. He let her punch him. He knew she just needed to let her anger out. Her fists pounded against him. She wailed in a cry of absolute pain.

"He wanted you to know that he loved you."

Price wiped the tears from her eyes. "You should have saved him. You could have. What the hell happened?"

"We had no option."

Price's hair was flattened by the rain, and what little makeup she wore was smeared. She looked into Drake's blue eyes and tried to find some reassurance, but he didn't give it to her. He just stared back and held on to her.

"I'm sorry," she said. "It's not your fault."

"We need to leave. We need to get back to Washington."

"You're an asshole," she said. "Won't you let me grieve?"

"The attack is in twenty-four hours."

"What?"

"The capital is under threat. The ammonium nitrate is on American soil."

Price went quiet. She pushed herself from Drake's arms and walked back to the hangar.

Drake picked up his duffel bag and followed her. Howe was watching them from inside. He had put down the cup of tea he was drinking and waited for the two CIA personnel to join him. He knew what Drake had told Price wasn't good.

"Captain Colt was one of the SAS's finest," Howe said to Drake. "He was a real pain in the arse, but he was a damn good soldier."

"We don't have time for platitudes and reflection," Drake barked. "I don't want to be blunt, but I need to get to Washington. We're running out of time."

Price sat down at her station, still overwhelmed with emotion, her eyes glazed with tears. "How do you know this?"

"Aya Khan is in Washington, DC. She has the ammonium nitrate and the stolen hydrazine," Drake said. "She was working with the Russian, Andrei Zadorov. The man who owned the compound and the mercenary army protecting Golovinka."

"What?" Howe asked. "I thought you said the ammonium nitrate would be in Russia."

"We were wrong," Drake said. "Or ... late."

"How did she get it into the city?" Price asked. "How did she ship two thousand tonnes of ammonium nitrate across the ocean without setting off any alarms."

"I don't know," Drake said. "But Ajmal, Aya's brother, died telling me what he knew."

"So, we need to go to Washington and find her?" Price asked.

"Yes."

Price slammed her fist on the table. "Do you know how big Washington is? How the hell are we going to find her?"

"I know it's there," Drake said. "I'll find her."

"And why do you trust her brother?" Price asked. "Maybe he's lying to you, trying to throw you off."

"He's not."

"How are you so sure?"

"Because Andrei Zadorov tried to kill him before he told me the truth," Drake said.

"And where is Andrei?"

"I put a bullet in his head," Drake said. "He's no longer our concern."

"You didn't think to bring him in for questioning?" Price asked.

Drake's eyes narrowed, and he became still. "Are you going to ask me about the C-17? Are you going to ask me about Private Wickers? Because everything that could have gone wrong went wrong. Clyde died helping me get this intel. I'm telling you the truth."

Howe's eyebrow perked up. "The troopers who picked you up said that you accused Private Wickers of sabotaging the C-17. They found his body in the forest."

"Yes," Drake said. "I killed him."

Howe pushed himself up from his seat. "Are you confessing to killing a SAS officer?"

Drake nodded. "Yes."

Howe turned to Price. "Your officer is reckless. If I find out that Private Wickers had nothing—"

Price raised her hand and silenced Howe. "Why did Wickers do it?"

"He was a mole for Tom Fowler," Drake said. "He was trying to sabotage the mission. We are being attacked from both ends. Inside and outside."

"Damnit," Price muttered. Her head fell into her hands. "I should have known. I'll have Tom arrested when I get back to Washington."

Howe pulled out his pistol. It was a Browning High Power, a highly reliable and accurate 9mm handgun, and was the British military's standard sidearm from World War Two up until recent years. "I can't have you leave until after the investigation into Private Wicker's death," he said to Drake.

Drake stared at Howe and then turned to Price.

Price rolled her eyes, walked up to Howe, and said, "Don't be such an *arsehole.*"

It was what Colt would have said.

A look of shock spread across Howe's face. Price punched him in the gut, pulled the gun from his hand, and then dislodged the clip.

"Clyde died for this information," she said. "If you want to help, you'll arrange a flight for us to get to Washington."

Howe took a deep breath. His stomach hurt, but maybe he'd deserved that, he thought. "I'll help," he said.

"Thank you," Price said. She then turned to Drake. "Did you learn anything else?"

"Only that Andrei was a billionaire," Drake said. "And he was dying of cancer. He didn't seem scared of death. He welcomed it."

"His reasons for wanting to attack America?" Price asked.

"He's tired of the proxy wars," Drake said. "He wants the United States and Russia to fight—one on one. Nuclear power versus nuclear power."

"So he's trying to pin this attack on the Russian military?" Price asked. "On the Russian government."

"The ammonium nitrate is Russian military, as is the hydrazine. How do you think the American press will report the attack? If that bomb goes off and it kills US politicians, our countries will be at war in six months."

Price closed her eyes and tried to organize her thoughts. A week ago, when this had all started, she'd thought it was just another run-of-the-mill assignment, perhaps one of her last in the agency. She was thinking about leaving afterward, settling down, working as an intelligence consultant for a private security firm—but things were different now. Very different. She was CIA director, her ex-husband was dead, and the world was on the precipice of chaos. She looked at Drake and said, "Do you think you can find her?"

"Yes."

Howe was on the phone arranging their flight from London to Washington. He put the phone down and turned to them. "I've got you a flight," he said. "You leave Gatwick Airport in thirty minutes. God speed."

PART 3 - THE SWAMP

SEVENTY-ONE

Three days earlier

There was a light on the horizon despite the dark. The final crate of hydrazine was boarded onto the truck at Newark Airport as the light from the rising sun grew vivid and strong. Red and pink swells of color reflected off the clouds and hung in the upper atmosphere. A cluster of birds danced in the sky. Aya saw the buildings of New York City glisten on the edge of the horizon. She was in awe. American might and power were on full display.

She wanted to level the whole place.

She wanted to see it turn to rubble.

A crater in the dirt.

Ashes.

Blood.

Bone.

She was dressed in a red Gucci dress. It was expensive, something a Hollywood starlet might wear to a movie premiere. She had on makeup, high heels and wore a gold bracelet on her wrist. She felt ridiculous dressed the way she was, but she couldn't be marching about the American East Coast dressed like a Syrian rebel. She was playing a part now. Andrei had instructed her that she needed to do what she was told.

She was good at following orders.

She'd adopted the name Olga Venechenko. An art critic and presenter who worked with Dimitri Nabakov—Andrei's false name when he was a spy for the SVR.

Her mission: take the hydrazine from Newark to the basement of the warehouse in Washington. Andrei had delivered the ammonium nitrate there a week prior.

Once at the warehouse, Aya would spend the next few days making sure that the bomb would work. She'd spend the rest of her time training Andrei's security forces. And when the time was right, she'd ignite the bomb and send the world into war.

Andrei had invited numerous guests to the exhibit. Some White House officials, members of congress, and even the First Lady.

He was going to make them all pay.

As the last case of hydrazine was loaded onto the truck, Aya said to Andrei's workers, "Good job, boys."

The workers were all from Little Odessa in Brooklyn. They were good men, Russian, ex-pats. They did their job, and they didn't ask many questions. Andrei kept them on payroll while he was sick and seeking treatment in Russia, using his dead father's billions to keep them satisfied and quiet.

Aya got into the Mercedes-Benz S-Class Coupe Andrei had rented for her and followed the truck to Washington, DC. She was uncomfortable driving down the American freeways, but she took it slow. She didn't panic. When she got scared, she said her daughter's name. Amira was her purpose. Her catharsis.

She'd been rehearsing, practicing every step of the plan for months. She just needed to get to Washington. She just needed to get to the capital. Once there, she'd feel comfortable. She'd feel in control.

It took three hours to get to Washington. At the warehouse, she went to a small storage closet and took off her red dress. She put on something more comfortable: a pair of khaki pants and a green shirt. She then got to work, helping the workers unload the hydrazine.

When they were done, she handed each one a roll of American bills. Five thousand dollars each. Enough for them to keep quiet and not ask questions.

Once they were all done, she put her red dress back on and went to the hotel that Andrei had booked for her. It was close to the warehouse but not so close as to draw suspicion from any of the authorities.

The hotel lobby was lavish. There was a gold chandelier and marble walls. It was the kind of place Aya never thought she'd step foot in.

"My name is Olga Venechenko," she said to the check-in clerk.

The clerk looked her up and down. "You seem a little sweaty, ma'am."

Aya clenched her jaw and instinctively reached for her belt buckle and the blade she had sheathed to it. It wasn't there. Of course, it wasn't there. Her blade was back in Russia. She sneered, paused, closed her eyes, smiled, and said, "I've been busy."

"We have a spa on-site. I recommend you use before going out," the clerk said. "It will make you feel refreshed."

Aya nodded, grabbed her keys, thanked the clerk, and went to her room.

Her room was just as ornate as the lobby. Andrei had told her that it had been primarily reserved for European diplomats—presidents, prime ministers, CEOs.

There was a grand piano in the room and a beautiful view of the city. Art pieces were hung on all the walls.

The first thing Aya did was strip and shower. As the warm water caressed her naked body, she felt a calm roll over her. There were three days until the art exhibit. Three days until she would light the world aflame and turn America into Syria.

She washed herself and headed to the hotel spa. She received a massage and spent some time in the Swedish sauna. When it was all done, she went back to her room and fell asleep.

When she awoke, she went back to the warehouse, where she proceeded to set up the bomb. It was going to take time, and she'd have to run some tests first. If she did everything correctly, the two thousand tonnes of ammonium nitrate would blow up one block of the city, and it being as close as it was to the White House, might even damage the Oval Office and kill the president.

She could only hope.

She took joy in the process. She knew that the next day, Andrei's workers would arrive with statues and art pieces he'd sent from Russia. They'd set the pieces up on the main floor of the warehouse and then work as security for the exhibit. Andrei had pulled art from all over his country. They'd go up in flames. Russian history. Destroyed.

But all in an effort to destroy America.

So he wasn't bothered.

As she thought about history exploding, she remembered what Drake had told her about American history. The Constitution documents were nearby. He said they were located in the capital, held in a building called the National Archives Museum.

When she was confident that the bomb she had crafted would work, she left the warehouse and made her way to the museum. She wanted to see in person the Constitution—the document that enshrined American democracy—or what she called American hypocrisy.

It didn't take her long to get there. In fact, it was close enough to her hotel that she could walk.

The museum building was large and official-looking. It was located along Washington's Constitution Avenue, which was home to some of the most important buildings in the country: the United States Capitol building, the National Mall, the Washington Monument, and the Lincoln Memorial, just to name a few. Each one was a symbol of American power and exceptionalism.

There were three American flags perched high at the entrance of the building. They fluttered in the early evening wind.

She walked up the steps toward the entrance. There was a poster detailing what was inside: the original copies of the United States' three main formative documents, the Declaration of Independence, the Constitution, and the Bill of Rights. Each was displayed to the public in the main chamber, aptly called the Rotunda for the Charters of Freedom.

After purchasing a ticket and passing through the main gate, she walked up to the security checkpoint. It was busy, crowded. She handed her ticket to the attendant. The attendant, a man with a large, round belly, glanced at it and then at her. She smiled at him. He looked her up and down and smiled back. He waved her through.

She made her way inside the building toward the Rotunda for the Charters of Freedom, passing dozens of tourists, a janitor, and two security guards on the way.

The Rotunda was magnificent. The room's ceiling was a large white dome, and it gave the place a sacred feeling. Each of the country's foundational documents was held behind thick layers of glass in stoic fashion. The idealism, the hope, and the bedrock beliefs that made the nation exceptional were treated like holy scripture.

It was a place of order.

A great country like the United States of America could have only been established by documents of serene and strict reason. But like the universe's origins during the Big Bang, that order, that reason, was turning to chaos and corruption. She passed each document, admiring the words and their meaning. Her fingers traced over the display glass.

The Declaration of Independence: "We hold these truths to be self-evident ..." The Constitution: "We the People of the United States ..." And the Bill of Rights' stout protections of freedom of speech, press, religion, and assembly.

Aya left the Rotunda. She'd once been a fighter for democracy. Seeing those documents made her feel ill.

She left the museum and made her way back to the hotel.

She'd had enough of history.

SEVENTY-TWO

In a small bar, on the outskirts of Langley, Tom Fowler was working on his third beer. He belched and felt woozy. He wasn't a heavy drinker. Two was always his limit.

He'd just read a text message on his cellphone from his contact at the SAS. The C-17 Jason Drake was in had gone down, but the SAS officer who set the bomb off on the aircraft had died, and Drake was still alive.

Fowler was depressed.

Price was still in control.

He was mumbling to himself, and the bartender noticed.

"You okay, buddy?" the bartender asked.

"Screw you," Fowler spat back.

"Hey, pal, I'm just asking how you're feeling. How many drinks have you had today? You look a little sick."

"This is my third beer!"

The bartender gave Fowler a strange look and shook his head. "I'm cutting you off at three."

"Then I'm leaving."

"Good."

Fowler got up from his stool. He undid his tie and clumsily walked to the bar's exit. He pushed past a group of bikers, one of whom didn't take kindly to Fowler's rude shove.

"Hey, shit stain," the biker said to Fowler. "Come back here and apologize."

Fowler turned around and stared at the three-hundred-pound biker with the beard down to his bellybutton. "Go fuck yourself."

"Apologize or hit the dirt."

Fowler looked at the biker and his group. He smirked. "Are you threatening me?"

"Yes."

"I'd advise against that."

"Then I'd advise you to call your doctor because you're about to feel some pain."

Fowler lifted up his fists, but it was too late. The biker elbowed Fowler in the face, and he fell to the ground. He then ensured that the rich snob with the expensive shoes understood that he wasn't allowed to talk like that. He kicked Fowler in the belly, which caused Fowler to spit up some of the beer in his stomach.

"Hey, cut that out!" the bartender shouted, noticing the pool of bile on the floor.

"Sorry, Mikey," the biker said. "I'm just taking out the trash."

The biker grabbed Fowler by the collar of his jacket and pulled him out of the bar.

Fowler was so disoriented he didn't know what was going on. When he felt the gravel rub against his pants and face, he understood he was outside.

The biker loomed over him and pointed his finger in Fowler's face. "If you ever come back to this bar, I will cut you open. You asshole! I will skin you alive!"

Fowler breathed heavily and waited for the biker to leave before pushing himself up. He dusted off his pants and walked to his Lexus. He unlocked it, got inside, and cried. Wiping tears from his eyes, he screamed out in frustration and slammed his fists against the steering wheel, pushing the horn. The bartender peered out the window, and Fowler started up his Lexus and peeled out of the parking lot. He didn't want any more trouble.

As he drove down the highway, back to his house, his cellphone buzzed.

"What is it?" he asked.

It was one of his contacts in Langley, an analyst named Guy Freeman. A young man who was as mischievous and as much of an ass kisser as he was. "Price and Drake are coming back to Washington. The entire agency is getting ready for their return."

"And why are you telling me this?"

"Because I think we can take advantage of this."

"How so?"

"Director Price believes there will be an attack on US soil in the next twenty-four hours. If you want to embarrass her, you could just let the attack happen. Let Kate take the fall. She did the same thing to you."

Dark thoughts swirled through Fowler's head. Could he really let an attack occur on US soil? Would it be worth it?

He decided that it was. Freeman was right in reaching out to him.

"Hold steady," Fowler said. "Where are you?"

"I'm downtown," Freeman said. "I'll wait for you."

SEVENTY-THREE

"I have a straightforward instruction for you," President Clarkson said into the phone.

Price listened carefully. Drake was busy gathering his belongings and getting ready to leave London for Washington aboard the Gulfstream G550 SAS jet.

Price's mind was still a mess of emotions. She just wished she could see Colt once more. He always knew what to say.

"What is it?" she said to the president.

"When you come back, I need you to make sure this stays under wraps."

"Under wraps, sir?

"This isn't my idea, Director. This is the idea of my campaign advisors. They think the country has already been through enough emotional turmoil and has enough egg on its face. The only way they believe I can shift the polls in my favor is if I resolve this situation without breaking too many eggs."

"Sir ..."

"I know," Clarkson said. "It sounds stupid, but you have to realize I'm in a very tight spot. This kind of thing has never been my specialty, but the economy and the market are ..." He trailed off. "I want to win the next election. I need you to do this for me."

Price gritted her teeth. She looked at Drake, and he read her face like a book. He knew what she was going to tell him was going to upset him.

"Okay, Mr. President. I'll do my best, but I can't make any promises."

"Just do your best," Clarkson said.

Price hung up and approached Drake. "This is why I never wanted to be director," she said.

Drake had just finished packing up his weapons. He stood up, walked to the coffee station, and poured himself a cup.

"Are you giving me the silent treatment?" Price asked.

Drake sipped the coffee. It had grown cold, but he didn't care. He needed the caffeine, the kick.

"Jason, I want you to be in on this. I'm going to need your help."

Drake placed the cup down on the wooden table in the hangar and looked out the window. A C-17 was coming in. Its engines were loud and aggressive.

"You need my help, but do I need yours?"

"I deserve that," Price said. "But I've got as much in this game as you do now. Clyde—"

"Was your ex-husband," Drake said, interrupting. "Your ex-husband, who you let almost drink himself to death. I'd say his death was merciful. At least he went out the way all soldiers dream: guns-a-blazing."

"Colt's drinking was his problem, not mine."

"And whatever you're going to tell me is your problem, not mine."

Howe walked into the hangar and noticed the tension between Price and Drake. He was holding their flight documents. "Am I interrupting something?" he asked.

"No," Drake said. "Nothing."

Price shook her head. "This is why you were a pariah in Langley," she said to Drake. "You're too damn stubborn. I want to work with you. I can help you."

"I work best alone," Drake barked.

"The president wants—"

"I don't give a rat's ass what the president wants," Drake said.

"I can come back," Howe said, feeling nervous in the tension. "Seriously, if you two have something to work out."

"It's alright," Drake said. "I was just about to leave."

Drake walked up to Howe, grabbed his boarding papers, and left the hangar.

Price ran after him.

Howe stayed in the hangar.

Drake was halfway to the fueled-up G550 when Price grabbed his arm. "Why won't you listen to me?" she asked.

Drake looked at her hand on his bicep and then at her. "Why do you think? The last time I helped the CIA officially, they sent a drone strike after me. And you telling me that we need to play along with some strange ask from the president isn't settling my nerves."

"He wants us to keep this quiet," Price said. "It could help us. That should ease your fears. He doesn't want us to make a lot of noise when we're in the city."

"You do realize that when this is all over, I'm gone."

"Yes," Price said.

"So why won't you let me work alone?"

"Because we have an entire agency of resources. Analysts and officers—"

Drake cut her off. "We don't have an entire agency. Fowler will still have sway, pull. You need to be careful when you're back in Washington. You've already let power get to your head."

Price laughed.

Drake's eyebrow rose. "What is it?"

"You think I'm stupid."

"I don't," Drake said. "I just know the reason why you never wanted to be director is that political scheming isn't your forte."

"I got Tom fired. I'm not as bad a schemer as you think."

"He was overconfident. He was an easy target."

"My team in Langley is small but loyal," Price said.

"You can't trust anyone in Langley."

"Stop being so damn stubborn."

Drake grunted. He stared into Price's eyes. He needed her. She was his ride to Aya. "I guess it could work," he said. "We don't know what Aya will do when she finds out that Andrei and Ajmal are dead. We have to assume the worst. The less noise, probably the better."

"We can do this, Jason," Price said. "I promise you, the first thing I'll do when I get back to Langley is wipe your records. You'll be a blank slate."

"I don't care about my slate. I just want to stop Aya," Drake said.

SEVENTY-FOUR

Aya finished putting on her red dress and looked at herself in the mirror in her hotel room. The mirror was pristine. Smooth. Almost every mirror in Syria had been cracked. But this one was perfect. Yet, the reflection wasn't.

She stared at herself.

How was she? What had she become? Why didn't she recognize herself anymore? There was a strain in her face. She saw it in her cheekbones, her neck, and her eyes. The mere act of living had become so unbearable that each and every waking day felt like war, like she had to battle her way to nightfall.

Going to the National Archives Museum hadn't helped. She felt like she was looking at herself in the past—there was so much optimism in those documents, so much hope for a better tomorrow.

The mirror reflected none of that optimism. There was a darkness in her eyes that she could recognize. She'd spent too many years hating the world, too many nights crying herself to sleep. Her green eyes almost seemed black. A single tear dropped from her eye. She turned away from the mirror ashamed.

"Amira," she said. "I am doing this for you. I hate what this world has made me become. I hate everything and everyon—"

Her phone rang.

It was Andrei's number, and she answered, frustrated, thinking that he wasn't supposed to speak to her after she left Russia. She needed to keep going, regardless of what had happened in Golovinka. What did he want?

"We weren't supposed to talk," Aya said, wiping the tear from her cheek. "What is it?"

"It's not Andrei," the man said in a gruff and breathless voice. It was clear he'd just seen action. "I am Alex. One of his security staff at the compound. I was told to call you in case ..." His voice trailed off.

"What is it?"

"He's dead. Andrei is dead."

Aya froze and dropped to her knees. She thought she heard her dress rip, and she wanted to howl in rage. She opened her mouth to scream, but nothing came out. She'd warned him, she thought. She slammed her fist against the floor. She felt her whole body convulse in rage. After she calmed down, she asked, "How?"

"An attack on the compound. Two men. We got one of them. The other, though ... he escaped."

"What did he look like?"

"He was tall. Longish hair. He had a scar on his face."

Aya had known this would happen. She'd expected it. Drake was coming for her. But then she remembered her brother. Her hand trembled. "And Ajmal?"

"He's dead, too. Our men had to put him down. He'd turned on us."

"He what?"

"He shot at the guards? It was like—"

"He must have been drunk. Our men must have been drunk."

"I'm not lying."

"Why are you calling me?"

"Because Andrei ordered me to. He said if he was to die while you were gone, I was to call you and remind you that your child died from an American drone strike. He wanted to make sure that you finished the mission."

"Did he really doubt that? I've come this far. I'm not turning back. Not now. Not ever. I know what the Americans took from me. I know that Andrei felt the same about the Kremlin. I am going to make sure that this ends the way he'd planned. I won't turn back."

"Thank you," Alex said. He hung up.

Tears swelled in Aya's eyes. Ajmal had only ever tried to protect her. He'd only ever wanted to make her proud. She thought of the last time they spoke to each other.

For years as a rebel, Aya lived off of what little rations she could get. There was one point when for three months, she had lived off of nothing but canned vegetables and dirty water. During that time, she'd lost so much weight, every breath hurt. Every night she'd felt as if her heart was going to break through her chest and explode, simply to get away from herself and the torment inside.

Yet, despite all that pain, she'd retained hope. She was stubborn that way. Her worst and best trait, according to her brother. Once she set her mind on something, she knew she would stop at nothing to make it come true. It was that way when she met Drake at Ali Bajal's club. She knew she would be with him, knew that their lives were to be connected.

Ajmal's final words to her before she left for Washington were ominous. She'd just finished packing her gear and equipment for the plane ride from Sochi to New York.

"You know this will be a one-way trip?" Ajmal asked.

The two of them were in the garden at the base of Andrei's office. The Russian billionaire was busy self-medicating with vodka and a cocktail of other drugs.

"I know," Aya said to her brother.

"Why don't you let me go? I can do it."

"Because I know you can't do what needs to be done," she said. "Because I want to die."

Ajmal shook his head. He looked like a man who was ashamed of himself, embarrassed of the air he breathed. He'd tried to protect Aya, but instead, he'd brought her to her end. He looked like a man who hated himself. "Aya, I can't let you go. I brought you into this mess. It should be me."

"It's not a mess, and I've spent years with Andrei planning this, making it come to fruition."

"It is a mess, sister," Ajmal said. "You were right about Jason. We should have killed him in Syria. I should have convinced Andrei about that. And now, because we didn't, he is on the run. It will be days before he gets here, maybe less. He's as determined as you are."

"You finally understand," Aya said. "But that is why I must go. You are not sharp enough to get this job done, brother. If Jason does come here, I will be the only one I trust to get the job done."

"I am sorry, Aya."

"Don't be."

"I have shamed our family," Ajmal said. "I should never have handed Amira over to that family in Turkey ..."

"Don't," Aya said. "Don't talk about her. When you mention her name, I see her face."

"I was young when mother and father passed," Ajmal said. "But I remember enough. When I close my eyes, I see their smiles, but I can't see their faces. It's only when I talk about them that their faces become clear."

"That is what time does to our memories," Aya said. "It cuts them down and makes them foggy. It makes us numb to pain. The act of living is already so painful—time makes it better. Each day, just struggling to get to the end. A sunrise to a sunset and everything in between. Time blesses us with numbness. That is all I want."

"What do you mean?"

"I mean that you will one day forget me as I am. You will remember perhaps only the smile on my lips or the anger in my eyes, but I will be gone, and all you will have is a feeling. That's all I want to be. I am done with living. After Amira's death, my present life became like a distant memory. I want to exist only in a dreamlike fog."

Ajmal nodded. He didn't know why he had cold feet. He'd brought Aya into this. He was scared about everything. Always had been. He hugged his sister, and she let him. She thought of how silly it would have looked to Andrei and to his mercenary army at the compound, but she didn't really care. She knew it would be the last time she and Ajmal would hug. Her brother had always been so sensitive. She couldn't be mean to him, not now. She'd been so cruel to him already.

"I love you, brother," she said. "I know, despite your weaknesses, you always did what was best for me. I know you tried."

"I wanted to be a painter," he said. "I was never cut out for this world. I was born in the wrong place at the wrong time."

"You can still be a painter."

"I doubt that."

There was a sadness in his eyes—an emptiness. A sensitive boy like him was easily abused in a world of bullets and brawn.

Aya took a deep breath, stood up from the floor of the hotel room, and checked her face in the mirror. She left the room and made her way down to the busy Washington streets.

She pushed through the dense American capital. Expensive cars, expensive clothes, a wealth of an unimaginable variety. It was precisely as Andrei had told her it would be. He'd told her all about the disgusting decadence of American life. The things they took for granted. The silly worries they had.

But now he was gone, too. Taken by him, the man who had blessed and cursed her. Jason.

She recalled when she'd first learned of Andrei's plan. He seemed nervous to tell her. It made him almost too excited. His voice cracked at moments. Aya wasn't sure if that was caused by the medicine he was on or whether it was because he was younger than he let on.

It was one week after Amira's passing. Aya was still fighting off the urge to slit her wrists. She walked into Andrei's office in Aleppo, her face red with rage. Her eyes were raw, and her heart shattered.

"I am deeply sorry for what happened," Andrei said to her. He sounded like he meant it. He was always good at that.

"There is nothing to be sorry for," Aya said.

"Your country has been through so much. You've been through so much."

"My parents died when I was young. I was recruited into the rebellion before my thirteenth birthday, where they taught me how to shoot a sniper rifle. This sense of loss has been with me forever."

She was lying. She'd never known loss like this.

"I was told the rebellion used teenage girls as snipers during those days."

"We were more patient than the boys. Our hands were steadier."

Andrei smiled and then coughed. "And you fought for your rebels valiantly," he said. "Or so your brother says."

"My brother doesn't know what a good soldier is."

"But you do?"

"I knew a good soldier."

"And what happened to him?"

"I left him to die."

Andrei smiled. He wasn't expecting that answer. "You did?"

"He had shrapnel in his stomach from a drone strike."

"Who was he?"

"He was a CIA officer. An assassin, of sorts. He was sent to Syria to kill an ISIS commander. He needed a desert tracker. I spent months with him."

"And he was a good soldier?"

"He was one of the first true men I'd ever met in my life."

"You loved him?"

"He was the father of my child."

"I see," Andrei said. "And he's dead."

"No," Aya said. "He pulled through. The CIA picked him up from the bomb site. They cleaned him up. Saved him."

"How do you know this?"

"Because he came looking for me."

"And you didn't go to him?"

"I was done with fighting," Aya said. "If I went to him, I'd get pulled back into the same bullshit, into the same life. I wanted peace. I wanted out of the war. And he ... he was a monster—he told me that himself. He knew what he was." She stopped. "But now that Amira is dead ... I realize there was no way out. I am a soldier. I am meant to burn in the flames of war. I'm glad I didn't go to him, but I now know there is no such thing as peace. Only war."

Andrei stood up from his desk and approached Aya. He embraced her.

"You should come with me," he said. "Come with your brother and me to Russia. I will show you what I am planning. I think you will be interested."

"What is it you want to do?"

"I want to make the people who killed your daughter pay. I want to make the people who did this to your country pay."

She spent the next several months learning about Andrei's plan. He explained that he wanted to light the match that would start a war across the world. He wanted Russia and the West to finally fight.

The pain she'd felt all her life, the suffering ... he had the solution; he had the treatment. She was going to make the world feel her pain. She was going to make the world suffer.

She walked into the warehouse where the art exhibit was going to take place. She sighed.

She walked down to the basement and met the security detail Andrei had sent over from Russia. Like her, they were all men or women there to die for their mission.

She wanted to speak with a small group of them before they opened the doors and began preparation for the night.

In twelve hours, she'd light the match that would start a war.

SEVENTY-FIVE

Drake and Price were in the G550 jet. The pilot had just informed them they were about to land, and as he skillfully guided the jet through a massive grey cloud, American soil materialized below.

As he looked out the window, the world below the aircraft seemed strange to Drake. He hadn't stepped foot in the homeland in five years—not since he'd put a bullet between the eyes of a US senator and fled to Puerto Rico. The highways and roads that etched the landscape were like the scars on his face, dug deep and marred in a way that was permanent, damaged, and would never heal.

"Who is meeting us?" he asked.

"A small team. I've let the FBI know about the possibility of an attack, but I don't trust them. That said, we have to keep the operation quiet," Price said. She was across from Drake, but wasn't looking at him. Her eyes fixated on the computer on her lap. "After we land, we're going to head to Langley. We'll meet with a small task force. After that, we track her down. We get the ammonium nitrate and stop the attack."

"We don't have time to think too much," Drake said. "Is your team secure? Are they good? Trustworthy?"

"They'll be good," Price said.

"We'll only get one chance at this."

"I know."

Drake shook his head. The old Price, the one who was his handler for years, didn't have many friends in Langley. But he couldn't really overthink it. He had to go along with the plan. He need whatever resources he could get. He shrugged his head and turned from the window. He closed his eyes and tried not to think of the past. He hadn't even touched US soil yet, but he could feel memories of the past bubbling up in his head like gasoline in an engine, ready to explode at any moment. He was a wanted man. Why had he come back? For years, he stayed hidden. He trusted no one but himself.

Drake and Price remained silent until the aircraft's tires screeched along the tarmac and the aircraft came to a stop. Grabbing his duffel bag from below his seat, Drake made his way to the exit. He opened the door, took a deep breath, and went down the stairs. He was home. He felt anxious.

There was a phalanx of CIA officers on the tarmac. They all looked the same. Dark blue jackets, sunglasses, denim jeans, and running shoes. Behind the entourage were four black Cadillac Escalades.

Drake waited for Price to join him on the tarmac before moving forward. Would she order his arrest at the last minute? He was unsure.

An officer approached him. A kid. It looked like he could barely grow a beard, let alone a moustache. He voice squeaked when he spoke. His name was Guy Freeman. "What's the in the duffel bag? We need to inspect it."

Drake turned to Price and rolled his eyes. "You want me to trust you? Your officers don't even trust that you'll travel with someone secure."

Price was about to respond, but Drake thought it'd be better if he did. He turned to Freeman and said, "You want to know what's in the bag? Fine. I've got an M4 carbine and Beretta 92FS. I picked them up from an SAS armoury."

"Do you have a permit ..." the kid was nervous and his voice trailed off at the end when he saw the scar on Drake's face. The kid began to sweat. "Do you have authorization to carry?"

"No," Drake said. "I don't."

"He doesn't need it," Price said, interrupting the exchange. "I'm the damn CIA director. Why are you questioning him? He's with me."

"It's just protocol, madam director."

"Oh, for fucks sake," Price moaned. "Don't ever call me that again, you understand?"

"Yes, ma'am."

Drake chuckled. The frustration in Price's voice calmed him down. Maybe she wasn't just doing this for the power trip, he thought. Maybe he could trust her? He looked out at the other officers who stood awkwardly in front of the SUVs and wondered if he'd have to deal with anymore 'protocol', but then he saw an old friend. His heart sank and he smiled like he hadn't in days. He knelt down and embraced a flurry of kisses.

Sierra White couldn't hold Houston any longer. The dog spotted Drake immediately and yanked himself free from her grip. He ran up to Drake and leaped into his arms.

"It's good to see you, too," Drake said to Houston as the animal licked furiously at his face and knocked him back onto the concrete.

Sierra ran after Houston, but stopped a couple feet from Price and Drake. "I'm sorry," she said.

"Sierra," Price said, her eyebrow raised. "Why are we getting questioned on the tarmac?" She glared at Freeman and then back at Sierra. "We don't have time for this? Didn't you inform every one about our special guest?"

"Protocol is protocol," Sierra said. "They know about our guest, but I can't get everyone up to speed that quick. We just changed director's."

"Are we ready to head to Langley?" Price said, obviously annoyed.

"Yes," Sierra said.

Drake pushed himself up and looked at Sierra. He then turned to Price. "Is this your assistant?"

"Yes," Price said.

Sierra extended her hand. "Pleasure to meet you," she said.

Drake shook her hand. "Pleasure's mine." He winked at Sierra, she smiled back, and blushed.

It was clear to Drake why Price had picked the girl to work for the agency's old director. She was gorgeous. A honeypot if there ever was one. She carried with her the midwest innocence and ignorance that was almost impossible not to fall prey too. He'd have to be careful around her.

Houston moaned. The dog wasn't getting enough attention. Drake patted him on the back.

"He likes you," Sierra said. "He must be yours?"

Drake nodded and wiped Houston's slobber onto his jeans. "He's an old friend."

"Are we ready to go?" Price said.

Sierra nodded. "Yes, but before we go. I heard what happened to Clyde. I'm sorry. Are you okay?"

"I'm fine. He died a soldier. He died fighting for the honor of his men and his country, and he died to give us a chance to do what is right. I find solace in that," Price said. "I don't want to talk about it anymore until we're done with this mission. Do you understand?"

Sierra nodded. "Of course," she said.

Drake turned to Sierra. "I assume one of these SUVs are for us?"

"Yes," Sierra said. "Follow me."

SEVENTY-SIX

After a quick twenty-minute ride, Drake was back on the campus grounds he'd sworn he would never step foot on again. His first impressions didn't surprise him. Langley hadn't changed much. He saw the same kinds of faces marching about as he saw when he was a Terminus member. Thanks to the change in director everyone looked worried about their job and their paycheck.

"The task force I've assembled will meet us on the top floor of the building," Price said to Drake as they walked through the front doors of the main building and into the atrium. "You remember Mission Control, right? It'll be just like old times."

Drake rolled his eyes. *Old times?* Same old shit was more like it. He followed Price through the atrium toward the elevators. Sierra and the rest of the CIA officers who'd met them at the airport were on either side of him and Houston. He still didn't feel safe. His nerves were heightened. He didn't like feeling cornered. The only thing keeping him calm was Houston. The dog was right at his heel, sticking to him like glue.

Drake and Houston joined Sierra, Price and a couple other officers in the first elevator and rode it to Mission Control. Twenty seconds later, they all walked into a wide and mostly empty room.

Computer monitors and desks cluttered the space, and there was a large map of the city on a screen on the front wall. Price was right about keeping the operation a secret. Drake had run dozens of missions while an officer and had never seen the place so bare.

Aside from Drake, Sierra and Price there were five other officers. They were all huddled on the other side of the room, talking to each other, discussing what the hell was going on.

"You said the team was small, I didn't think you meant this small," Drake said to Price in a hushed voice. "We'll need more than five officers."

"Tom had many spies in the agency. I don't know who too trust. I'm relying on Sierra's judgment. This is the best we can do."

"She's the secretary."

"Hey, I want to be a field officer one day," Sierra said, hearing everything Drake and Price were saying to each other. "I took that secretary job with Tom at Kate's behest."

"Oh, really?" Drake said turning to Sierra. "Other than your looks, what makes you think you'd be a good officer?"

"That's sexist," Sierra said.

"It's called reality, sweetheart," Drake said. "I know why Kate brought you here. Don't let her kind words fool you. She'll use you like she once used me."

"Are you done, Jason?" Price said, interrupting the two of them. "Sierra is an ally and a friend. If not for her, the wet team in Turkey would have killed you. She's earned my trust in more than one way. She protected you and the mission."

"Fine," Drake said. "I just want to find Aya. The less time we spend here, the better. Get to it."

Price shook her head, rubbed her brow, took a deep breath and nodded. She walked toward the front monitors at the front of the room. Drake, Houston and Sierra stood along the wall.

Standing in front of the dozens or so monitors, Price closed her eyes and cleared her throat to get everyone's attention.

"I've called you all here today because this is a matter of great importance," she said. "We don't have much time. If you are here, it is because I believe I can trust you, and right now, I need your trust."

From the back of the room, Drake eyed up the five officers Sierra and Price had brought in. He carefully watched their faces as Price spoke. They were young, maybe too young. The asshole, Guy Freeman, who'd questioned him on tarmac about his weapons was there.

Price continued, "According to intel gathered from Russia, we believe there is a stockpile of two thousand tonnes of ammonium nitrate in the city. We don't know where it is. We believe we only have a few hours to find it before it is ignited. If that happens, half the city will be destroyed."

There was an audible gasp from the officers. Even Sierra seemed shocked. The officers Price had assembled whispered to each other. Freeman raised his hand.

"What is it, Officer Freeman?" Price asked. "More *protocol?*"

"How did two thousand tonnes of highly explosive fertilizer go undetected across the border? I take it you believe it's the same fertilizer that was reported missing in Damascus? The same fertilizer the whole world's been looking for?"

"Yes," Price said. "It's the same. We're going to split you up in teams. If our intel is correct, and the ammonium nitrate is here, then it's probably being held in a warehouse or some storage facility—somewhere big. We have to assume that whoever has it is somewhere close to the capital. They'll most likely want to take out our major buildings. We have search radius of two miles with the White House being at the center. We need to discretely check every facility, warehouse, and building in that area. Two of you will stay in Langley, checking receipts, communications, and security footage. The others half will be out on the streets, waiting for intel from our officers back here."

"Who's plotting the attack?" Freeman asked. "Al Queda? ISIS? Why have none of us heard about this until now?"

"She's a Syrian rebel. She worked with us on a mission in the past. If we find anything, we have to assume the worst. Her name is Aya Khan."

"Do we have jurisdiction to act on US soil in this fashion?" Freeman asked. "The CIA usually keeps its hands off American soil."

Drake shook his head. There it was. The little prick was going to undermine the operation with his pedantic by-the-book antics.

"This is mission critical," Price said. "American lives are at stake. We have to move carefully and quickly. I've notified the FBI about the threat but you know how they are. We don't know how much time we have. The explosion could happen at any second. You'll get any resource you need. You just need to ask. The president knows about our operation. That's all you need to know. And in an effort not to alarm any citizens or the terrorists themselves that we're coming for them, he's asked us to keep this quiet."

Freeman looked left and right and shook his head. Drake didn't like the look of the kid.

Price assigned roles to each of the officers in the task force and then dismissed them. She waited until they'd all left and turned to Drake and Sierra.

"You two will head to the National Mall," Price said. "As far as I'm concerned, that is going to be ground zero. If anyone wants to hurt us, that's as good a place as any to start. I'll update you with directions. We will find her."

"We have to find her," Drake said. "If we don't, we're dead."

He whistled and Houston followed him out of the room. Sierra nodded at Price and caught up with Drake in the hall.

SEVENTY-SEVEN

Drake and Sierra walked down a quiet street close to the National Mall. It was five p.m. and the sky was turning orange. They'd just checked four locations—a warehouse beside the United States Postal Service building, two storage facilities on 10th Street NW, and a garage located close to the FBIs headquarters. They'd found nothing.

Drake held Houston's leash tightly. The dog had picked up a scent, and while Drake wanted to let the dog go after it, Houston was used to the desert, not the city.

"Does Kate have any more intel?" Drake asked Sierra.

"Kate is pushing her team," she said. "They're checking shipping data of nearby ports. Do you know how many shipments come in and out of this country per day? It's a lot. We're trying to filter it down by looking at transport truck data coming into and out of the DC region but that's an even bigger data pile. W're doing our best. She's trying to get them to pick only likely targets. She assures us that we're narrowing down the possible locations. This is like looking for a needle in a haystack. There are hundreds of buildings in this area that could house that ammonium nitrate."

Drake shook his head. They needed a break. They needed something.

They continued to walk down the street. As they made their way east, he noticed a small plaque on the facade of a cafe. The place had opened its doors on November 8th, 1963—a mere two weeks before JFK was assassinated in Texas by Lee Harvey Oswald.

He imagined what the place was like back then. It would have been the Golden Age of the American Empire. The country was at the precipice of great change and great turmoil.

After Oswald pulled the trigger three times in five seconds on that Italian Carcano M91/38 bolt-action rifle with its telescopic sight, America's sense of idealism faded. As Jackie Kennedy desperately tried to hold on to what was left of America's hope, the insides of which were leaking onto her pink dress, she cried out and said she loved her husband. And during that entire incident, America took on a new shape, a new form.

Regardless of the conspiracy theories surrounding the assassination, the numerous investigations by various panels of different bodies in the US government, the conflicting information, the contradictory statements, the world after that moment was essentially different.

While the Vietnam war had already begun by 1963, many historians believed that, had Kennedy lived, he would have pulled the troops out after re-election.

A decade-long war, tens of thousands of US soldiers killed, continued because of Oswald. One moment changed the course of human history. Did it matter why? Did it matter who?

If Aya Khan set off the ammonium nitrate in the city, how much would the world change? Drake wondered. There would certainly be an investigation into the events. Still, like after Kennedy's assassination, or after the events of 9/11, conspiracy theories would reign supreme—information would become vulnerable to interpretation, become tangled in a web of nuance and fog. Would the who and why even matter? he thought.

It wouldn't be long before US intelligence connected the explosion to the Russian army. After all, why wouldn't they? It was Russian military ammonium nitrate and hydrazine, and it had all been orchestrated by a Russian SVR spy. The Russians would be blamed, and Andrei would get precisely what he wanted.

War.

He shook his head and continued to make his way. Drake was hoping Houston would either pick up Aya's scent or he'd seen something.

Drake then felt the air leave his lungs. He gasped and felt vulnerable for the first time in a while. He got the break he was looking for. A name of an art exhibit printed on a poster attached to a wall of nearby building was the answer. The name of the exhibit was a name he'd had heard in Golovinka. He stopped walking. Houston sat at his heel.

"What is it?" Sierra asked. "What's wrong?"

Drake pointed to the poster. "We've found it. We've found her. Call Kate."

"What?"

"The ammonium nitrate," he said. "It's going to be at Natalay's Wish."

Sierra looked up at the poster. It was an invitation only event, reserved only for the upper crest of the elite. Old Russian artifacts. A celebration. An olive branch. The door's opened in four hours.

"How do you know?" she asked.

"Andrei Zadorov—the man whose compound I raided in Russia— he said the name Natalay before he died. He was referring to his mother. Her portrait had just got etched up with bullets."

Sierra picked up her phone. "I'm going to call the director," she said.

"Good," Drake said. He went to pat Houston on the head but noticed the dog was growling. "What is it, buddy?"

Traffic on the street came to a standstill.

Drake tensed up. Something was wrong. From his periphery, he spotted three men with assault rifles step out of a black SUV.

"Get down!" Drake shouted to Sierra.

As she looked up from her phone and saw the men, gunfire rang out on the street. She ducked behind the body of a red Toyota Corolla.

Drake and Houston were using a grey BMW for cover.

"Who are they?" Sierra shouted to Drake.

Drake looked through the windows of the BMW. The men were dressed in civilian clothes, but they were carrying M4s. They looked American. CIA, most likely.

He had to duck down as one of them spotted him. Bullets chewed up the glass of the BMW and the concrete of the building behind him. Screams rang out from inside nearby shops.

"Are they Russians?"

"No," Drake said. He pulled out his sidearm and guided Sierra toward an alleyway. Houston stayed low and followed. "You need to leave," he said. "Take the dog and get to Kate. She's going to need your help. The old Director isn't done messing with us yet."

"Help?" Sierra panicked. She closed her eyes. "Jason! What is going on?"

"You know my operation in Russia was sabotaged by the former director. Well, he's trying to sabotage us again."

"You think he's trying to stop us?"

"Yes."

Police sirens blared along with the bursts of gunfire. Fowler had found the messiest guys on the market to do the job.

"You need to go," Drake said to Sierra.

Sierra nodded, grabbed Houston's leash, and ran off down the alley.

Drake turned back to the main street. He ran back to the BMW he had used for cover.

At the far end of the street, blue and red lights flashed. The MPDC were on the scene. Two of their police cruisers pulled in front of the cafe. Both officers inside jumped out and aimed their handguns at the shooters.

The shooters took aim at the cops. They sprayed fire at the cruisers, peppering the front end of each vehicle with a dozen bullets each. Thankfully, the boys in blue avoided getting hit.

Drake popped above the trunk of the BMW and fired two shots at the shooters. He wanted to get their attention on him. He wasn't going to let two cops get shot because he was behind cover.

The shooters all ducked behind vehicles on the opposite side of the street when Drake fired.

The MPDC officers seized the break in the action to radio for backup.

The shooters sprinted toward the cops. They seemed to disregard the threat from Drake. They seemed not to care.

"What the hell?" Drake muttered to himself. "Why are they going after the cops?"

He stood up to pursue the shooters but stopped when he heard a click.

"Jason Drake," Fowler said. His gun was drawn—a P226.

Drake raised his hands. "What the hell is this, Tom?"

"A political play," Fowler said. "Kate screwed with me. I'm returning the favor."

"You do realize that half the city is about to explode."

"Too bad. She'll take the fall, so will that dip shit, goody-two-shoes president."

"This is evil."

Fowler whacked Drake in the back of the head, rendering him unconscious.

His men killed the two cops. Point blank. They were merciless about it. Fowler smirked when he saw the bodies of the cops hit the ground. He was going to make sure that Price took the fall for all this. For everything.

When his men returned to him, they carried Drake's body into the black SUV.

Fowler spoke to his men as he got into the passenger-side seat. "That should keep the city busy and on edge," he said. "That should make Kate's attempts at finding the ammonium nitrate, if it's even here, impossible. Now let's head to the farm and make sure our guest stays alive. I need Jason Drake alive for this to work."

SEVENTY-EIGHT

Drake's unconscious body rolled from left to right in the back of the black SUV. His wrists and ankles were cuffed.

As he lay there, he dreamed of the final night he and Aya had shared in the desert. The night before the drone strike, before they killed the Butcher, before everything changed. From Drake's point of view, it was the last peaceful night of his life.

"What were you like as a young boy? Where did you come from?" Aya asked.

The two of them were sitting around a small fire that glowed orange. The desert sands beyond the light of the fire glistened blue from the darkened sky above. There was a chill in the air and a whistle in the wind.

"I come from Texas."

"Is that a city?"

"No," Drake said. "It's a state. I came from a city there. Dallas."

"And you stayed there your whole life?"

"No," Drake said. "I stayed there until I killed my step-father."

He had never told Aya the truth about his past. He hadn't wanted to. It was shameful, something he didn't like sharing.

She looked at him and didn't turn away. "I wanted to kill my father," she said. "I dreamed of it."

"Why?"

"Because he raped me."

"That's a good reason," Drake said.

The two of them stared into the fire, lost in their fiery pasts, lost in painful memories.

"How did you do it?" Aya asked.

"I shot him twice in the belly."

"Was he a bad man?"

"He got my mother addicted to painkillers and alcohol. He beat me and my brother. He tried to kill me ... I didn't let him."

"You were how old?"

"Fifteen."

"Did you take pleasure in it?"

Drake looked up at her. He saw something in her eyes that he hadn't seen in all the months they'd spent together searching for the Butcher—an anger, a rage, something dark and sinister.

Maybe he should have known then that she had her own dark streak—no one on this planet is a perfect saint. Still, it upset him. That said, he wasn't going to shy away from the truth. He didn't like to butter things up.

"Yes," he said. "I took pleasure in it."

"It's one of the things I regret the most," Aya said. "Not killing my father."

Drake remained quiet and let the crackle of the fire soothe his mind. "I try not to think of those days," he said. "And, to be honest, if you did kill your father, you'd end up like me. And you don't want that."

"You think that you're a bad person because of what you've done?"

"I know what I am."

"You killed a bad man. You made the world a better place."

"I'm a killer," Drake said. "After I killed my step-father, I was sent to a foster home. When I was old enough, I joined the army, then the CIA, where I let them inject me with chemicals. I let them do things to my body ..." He shrugged. "I think I'm less human now than before.

You don't want this. I live in the dark. You should live in the light. You have a country to fight for."

"I wish I was like you."

"Don't say that," he said. "There is nothing good about me. I kill who they tell me to kill. You fight for a reason."

"Sometimes, all I want is blood."

The dream faded away. Physical pain interrupted the emotional turmoil of the past.

Drake howled and grunted as he felt a stinging sensation in his arm. He tried to fight it off, but he couldn't. He was tied to a chair in what looked like a garage. There were car tires, oil cans, and tools atop work benches.

Fowler had just injected him with a needle.

Drake squinted. Fowler was shining a flashlight in his face.

All Drake could see was the dark blue sky through the open garage door. The sun had set. He was running out of time.

"Were you dreaming?" Fowler asked.

"Fuck you."

"Who is Aya Khan?"

"I said: fuck you."

Fowler chuckled, as did the five men with him. "You've got a dirty mouth."

"You're making a mistake!" Drake grunted between his clenched jaw. "What time is it?"

"Eight p.m.," Fowler said.

"I don't care what you do to me," Drake said. "Just get someone to the art exhibit downtown. It's called Natalay's Wish. That is where the ammonium nitrate is. You can kill me. You can do whatever you want. Take credit for saving the world. Just stop her."

Fowler giggled like a nervous school girl. "I don't think so," he said. "If the bomb goes off, then you and Kate get to take the blame—I'll be in the clear. The next president will re-instate me. I'll make sure of it. And if the bomb doesn't go off, then those dead police officers should suffice —you'll take the fall for their deaths. You did kill a senator, after all. Either way, I'm going to make sure that you and Kate learn your lesson."

"You power-hungry asshole. If I get out of here, I'm going to kill you. I'll tear you to shreds."

"You'll do what you're told," Fowler said. "I'll do what Kate never could with you. I'll get you to keep still, to follow orders. That relaxant my men just injected into your bloodstream should help. It should offset whatever Kate did to your body during Terminus training. It'll make you more human, more prone to mistakes. It should calm you down."

"You're really going to let thousands die," Drake said.

"I'll do whatever puts me at an advantage."

Drake tried to break free from his rope bindings. He thought about what he would do if he got free. Along with Fowler, there were five men—the same the men who'd killed the cops. They were carrying M4s and had sidearms holstered. As he struggled to break free, he began to feel dizzy. The drugs.

The chemicals were already interfering with his body. If he was going to get out of this, he'd need help. He'd need backup. His only hope was Price and Sierra.

"We're going to stay until the morning," Fowler said to Drake. "But we should have some guests before then."

Outside, a Mercedes-Benz sedan rolled to a stop in front of the garage door. When the headlights turned off, a man got out of the driver's seat and walked to the back. He pulled someone out from the backseat. He was rough with her. He dragged her from the backseat into the garage.

It was Kate.

"Hey, Jason," Price said. Her face was bruised, and she had a cut under her eye. "Long time no see. You were right about my team. I should have been more careful."

"No need to worry about that now," Drake said. He looked up at the man who'd brought Price into the garage. It was Officer Guy Freeman, the tight-assed dickhead who'd asked all the questions at the task force meeting hours earlier.

"Thank you, Officer Freeman," Fowler said with a grin. "I couldn't have done this without your help."

"The others are taken care of," Freeman said. He looked at Drake and then around the room. His face soured. "Where's the girl?"

"Girl?" Fowler asked.

"Yes," Freeman said. "Jason wasn't alone. There was a girl and a dog with him. Sierra White."

Price was lying face-first on the floor of the garage. She looked up at Drake and winked.

SEVENTY-NINE

Sierra swerved in and out of traffic. She'd been on the phone with Price when she'd heard the exchange with Freeman.

The asshole.

The sky was blood red, and thick black clouds had formed—a storm was moving in. It was six p.m. They had only hours before the doors opened at the art exhibit.

"We know where it is!" Sierra exclaimed to Price over the Bluetooth receiver in the car. "We've found it!"

"Where is it?"

"An art exhibit. Something called Natalay's Wish."

Price gasped. She'd seen the posters.

"What the hell are you doing here?" Price asked suddenly.

"What are you talking about?" Sierra said.

She then realized that Price wasn't talking to her.

"Your time is up," Freeman said.

"I thought I could trust you."

Freeman laughed.

Sierra heard the sounds of a struggle and then nothing.

"Kate!" Sierra screamed into the Bluetooth audio receiver in the car. "Kate, do you hear me?"

Houston was sprawled out on the backseat of the car, doing his best to keep his balance as Sierra drove maniacally down the freeway.

She slammed her foot on the gas and drove to the CIA buildings. That was where Price was. If she got there in time, she might be able to stop Freeman.

She pulled into the parking lot and turned the engine off. She was about to get out when she saw Price and Freeman walk out of the George Bush Sr. building. Freeman was walking close to Price. It looked like he had something to her back.

"Shit," Sierra muttered.

Houston growled.

Sierra waited for Freeman and Price to get into a Mercedes-Benz sedan and then followed them.

She didn't know what she was going to do.

For two years, she'd been a secretary. She'd always wanted to be more. Now was her chance to prove that she was ready.

She followed Freeman down the freeways and out of the city. She followed his sedan to a road that led to a farm. She pulled into the farm with the lights of her SUV turned off. She pulled to a stop.

She had a pistol in her jacket. She pulled it out. Houston jumped to her side in the passenger's seat.

"Are you ready?" she said to the dog. "It's time to find out if I'm officer material."

EIGHTY

The CIA had purchased the property in the fifties, at the height of the Cold War. It was used for their top-secret mind control program: MK-Ultra. A program whose aim was intended to identify and develop drugs and procedures to be used in interrogations. In some scenarios, participants—some of them willing, some of them not—would be given high doses of LSD and other chemicals. They would then be interrogated. In other, more controversial tests, techniques studied included electroshocks, hypnosis, sensory deprivation, and, in one extreme case, sexual abuse. In 1973, all the MK-Ultra files were destroyed. The program wasn't declassified until 2001, but the only information about what had transpired relied on direct participants' sworn testimonies.

Price had been to the property once before when scouting for facilities to use for Terminus training. She'd opted to perform the training farther away from Langley—the property was forty minutes north of headquarters.

Before the CIA had purchased the property, it was just a farmhouse. On the property was a dilapidated barn, its wood rotting and covered in thick moss. It looked like it could fall over any second. Those driving down the country road adjacent to it would assume the house had been abandoned long ago.

The house had boarded-up windows, a hole in the roof. The garage was different, though. It was maintained, preserved. The corrugated metal siding was clean.

"What is your plan?" Price asked Fowler. His men had just finished tying her to a chair beside Drake.

Fowler laughed. "You used my secretary against me," Fowler said. "You had Sierra spy on me. You ratted me out to the president. You thought you were so clever."

"You were more worried about your job than saving American lives. I did what I had to do," Price said.

"You're a bitch."

"You're an idiot," Price said.

Fowler shook his head. "You are not in a position to talk, Kate. Your little task force members are either dead or under my control. You tried to play a political game, you tried to seize power from me, but you lost."

Price snarled and tried to pull herself free from the ropes Fowler's men had tied her in.

Freeman turned to Fowler and asked, "The woman with Jason— Sierra White. I should go look for her."

Fowler raised his hand and stopped Freeman from leaving the garage. "She's a scared little girl. She shouldn't be a problem."

Freeman nodded.

Drake took it all in. His eyes slowly moved from one man to the next. Patience and calm would be the key to getting out of this situation.

Fowler walked to a workbench and pulled out his phone. He checked the news, looking for updates. All he saw were news reports about the shooting of the two police officers. They were both in their thirties. Upstanding young men. He smirked.

He didn't care about two working-class cops. They were in his way. The fact that they'd responded so quickly to the shootout surprised him. Their presence allowed him to seize the advantage. Their dead bodies were an insurance policy.

After reading the report, he did a quick search to see if any news outlets were reporting on the art exhibit Drake had mentioned. All he found was a story about some art dealer named Dimitri Nabakov, who seemed like a nice guy. According to the paper, the First Lady and a dozen or so senators were supposed to attend the exhibit.

Fowler turned to Drake. "How are you feeling?"

Drake didn't respond. He just stared into Fowler's eyes.

"I guess the drugs worked," Fowler said. "Are you sure about the ammonium nitrate? Are you sure that it's at this art exhibit? Natalay's Wish, is it?"

Again, Drake didn't respond.

"Good," Fowler said. "I wonder how they got all of that here. It came from Lebanon, didn't it?"

"Shut the hell up, Tom," Price said. "You're a creep. You're what's wrong with this damned city—this country, even!"

"Cry me a river," Fowler said. "You tried to play the game, but you failed. You didn't realize I had someone in your inner circle of trust, too. Officer Freeman fucked you the same way you tried to fuck me with—"

Two shots blasted from outside the garage. Two of Fowler's men dropped. Blood splattered from their heads.

"What the hell?" Fowler said. He turned to Freeman. "What's going on?"

Freeman and the three other men ran to the inside wall of the garage. Fowler ran for cover.

Drake smiled. He saw a small black figure out in the dark—an animal.

"Who is it?" Fowler shouted to Freeman.

Freeman and the other three officers crept to the edge of the garage doorway. "It's probably that bitch, Sierra," Freeman said to Fowler. "She must've have followed me."

"What was that?" one of Fowler's men said, noticing a strange sound.

"A dog?" another asked.

Fowler's men looked at each other with frightened expressions. Two more shots rang from outside the garage. Bright flashes emanated from behind a tree.

Two more men dropped, blood leaking from the holes in their heads. The cement floor inside the garage was now painted red.

"Get control of the situation," Fowler shouted to Freeman.

Freeman shook his head and ordered the remaining man in the garage with him to run outside. "She's at the tree," he said. "Go get her. I'll cover you."

The man ran toward the tree. Houston picked him off. The dog leaped from the shadows and bit the man in the neck. Freeman ran toward Sierra.

Sierra rolled from behind the bush, but Freeman expected her fire and dodged out of the way. Bullets sparked off the metal siding of the garage.

Freeman got up and aimed his gun at her. Sierra raised her hands and emerged from behind the tree. There was nothing else she could do. Her best option was to stay alive, and that meant giving herself up.

The corrupt CIA officer smacked Sierra across the face, and she fell to her knees. As her body lay on the ground, he patted her down. He spent an extra bit of time on her breasts. She moaned and tried to push his hands away, but he smacked her again.

He lifted her upright and put his gun against her head.

"Hurry up," Fowler said. "There's still the damn dog out there."

Drake and Price watched it all from their seats. They watched as Sierra was ordered into the garage.

"Ms. White, I expected more from you. I expected you to be a better assistant," Fowler said.

Houston sprang back into action. The dog jumped up at Freeman, biting his wrist. The animal twisted and ripped bits of flesh, making him drop his gun.

Sierra dropped to the ground. Freeman scrambled to his feet and ran into the shadows. Fowler blindly fired from inside the garage. All his bullets missed.

Sierra stood up, her pistol aimed at Fowler, who was frozen with fear. He stood up and raised his arms. Houston ran up to him, growling.

"You should not have betrayed me, Ms. White," Fowler said.

Drake whistled, and Houston came to his aid.

Sierra grabbed a knife from a workbench and cut Drake and Price free from their bonds. She didn't lower the gun aimed at Fowler once.

"Officer Freeman!" Fowler shouted. "Help! Where are you?"

Drake stood up. Stretched. He walked up to one of the men Sierra had shot. He picked up his pistol and aimed it at Fowler.

"Don't kill him," Price said. "We need to question him. Find out how deep his influence in the agency goes."

Drake pulled the trigger and splattered Fowler's brains across the wall of the garage. Fowler dropped to the ground.

Price was about to condemn Drake when she heard the sound of a Mercedes-Benz start up outside the garage. It peeled out of the parking lot. Freeman was on the run.

"You shouldn't have killed Tom," Price said to Drake. Her face was sour and angry.

"I'm not a CIA officer. I don't take orders from you."

"You're going to make this difficult," Price said. "He was better alive than dead."

"I don't care. The CIA will always be full of rot. All that matters is that I get back to the city. We might still have time."

"I'll drive," Sierra said to Drake. "We can take the SUV. It's just up the road."

Drake turned to Price. "You stay here and call for backup. Houston will stand watch."

Drake whistled and ordered Houston to his side. He then commanded the dog to stay with Price. Once he was sure the dog understood, he followed Sierra to the black SUV.

"Jason, where are you going?" Price shouted to him.

"I'm going to end this."

EIGHTY-ONE

Aya stared at the barrels of ammonium nitrate. A kaleidoscope of emotion that she couldn't entirely control or define rushed through her body.

Andrei's security were letting people into the exhibit early. The warehouse was jam packed. Everything was ready. All she had to do was hit the trigger, and one square block of Washington would explode. Everyone inside the exhibit would vaporize, and the world would be sent into war.

Above her, on the ground floor of the warehouse, there were hundreds of people. The rich, the connected, the powerful. Precisely as Andrei had told her they would be. They'd showed up at the exhibit as soon as security had opened the doors.

Aya heard someone walk down the steps of the stairwell toward the basement.

"Ms. Khan?" one of Andrei's security officers said. "Everything upstairs is clear. You can set this city ablaze whenever you're ready."

"I'm waiting for the president's wife, the First Lady," Aya said. "Is she here?"

"Not yet."

"Let me know when she is."

"Of course, ma'am."

The young man left the room. Aya turned around to catch a look at him as he left. He was so young. Why did he want to die? What was motivating him in all of this? Had he lost a loved one? Or was he just angry at the world? Did he feel he would never get what he truly believed he deserved?

Andrei had told her he'd spent years looking for desperate people to join his mission. He wanted people who not only wanted to die but also wanted the West to burn.

Aya walked up to the main floor of the exhibit. If this would be her last night on the planet, she figured she deserved a drink. Plus, she wanted to see what all the fuss was about. Andrei had spent more than thirty million American dollars putting the exhibit on. He said it was the last of his father's money. He said it was his work of art.

Upstairs, the warehouse was filled with the rich. Andrei had obviously made many friends during his time as a spy in Washington. One could almost say he was a borderline celebrity in the city—everyone in the room looked like they were worth millions of dollars. They wore expensive suits, dresses, and the women all had on excessive amounts of jewelry.

Aya pushed past them all, walked up to the bar, and ordered herself a shot of whiskey.

The bartender, a young woman with a pleasant face and thick blonde hair, handed Aya a shot. The bartender wore an engagement ring and seemed incredibly happy. She had her whole life ahead of her. Her smile made Aya feel unwell.

If only she knew that in five minutes, she'd be incinerated. She'd be turned to ash and fire.

"Are you enjoying the exhibit, ma'am?" the bartender said. She knew that Aya was the one in control. "Will Mr. Nabakov be joining us tonight? Numerous guests are asking about him."

Aya thought of what she should say. The young woman was simply trying to make light conversation, trying to make her feel more comfortable. She clearly noticed the strain painted across Aya's face and could feel the coldness emanating from Aya's eyes.

"You should leave," Aya said.

"Excuse me?" the bartender said. "You'll have to speak up."

Aya bent over the bar and leaned toward the young woman. "You should leave. You're fired. I hate you."

The bartender's eye's widened and then turned red. Tears streamed down her face. "I'm getting married in six months. You can't do this!"

"A waste of time for filth like you," Aya snapped. "Get out of here. Leave. If you're not out of here in five minutes, I'll have security escort you out."

The bartender shook her head, knelt down, and grabbed her purse. She ran from behind the bar and disappeared into the crowd. She walked out of the lobby and out onto the street.

Aya took long and heavy breaths. She felt herself in a daze. She didn't know what was going on. She wanted to scream but couldn't.

What was wrong with her? she thought.

She shot back the glass of whiskey and made her way to the office. It was located on the upper floor of the warehouse. It had a large window that overlooked the art pieces

Aya walked up to the office, pushing past the dignitaries and American nobles whom she despised. She made her way to the office and looked out the large window.

Below her was a web of power. She was finally in control.

Why was she stalling? What was she waiting for? She didn't really care about the First Lady, did she? She could start the war now. All she had to do was press the button on her remote trigger.

She felt a tingling at the back of her head, along with a crackling sound. She flopped down onto a seat and rubbed her temple. The frozen faces of those children she'd spotted in the Syrian desert flashed across her mind.

She shrieked. A ghost.

She'd kept those visions at bay for so long. Why now?

One of the security officers ran into the office. "Are you okay?"

"I'm fine," Aya shouted. "Leave me."

"You should ignite the explosion. We are all ready to die."

"Come here," Aya said.

The young man Andrei had recruited walked toward Aya. She stood up from her chair, pulled out a blade from inside her purse, kissed him, and then, when the smile spread across his face, stabbed him in the neck.

She wasn't going to take orders from him.

She would ignite the ammonium nitrate when the time was right. She would ignite it when she knew she was ready.

EIGHTY-TWO

The freeway back to Washington was jam-packed with traffic. Bumper to bumper. Sierra turned on the radio in the SUV to find out why.

"And tonight is the first game of the third round of the Stanley Cup Playoffs," the radio commentator said. "The matchup between the Washington Capitals and the Toronto Maple Leafs."

"This is bullshit!" Sierra said. "Who even watches hockey?"

"I do," Drake said, annoyed.

"What? How can you watch that shit? How do you follow the puck?"

"Just focus on the road and keep quiet. I'll explain hockey to you another day."

Sierra smiled and swerved in front of a transport truck and raced down the George Washington Parkway. She took the exit for Interstate 66, which took her toward the downtown core. In a mile or two, she'd take the exit toward Constitution Avenue.

On an average day, they would have been ten minutes from the art exhibit. But with the hockey game, things were different.

As Sierra pulled onto Constitution Avenue, she slowed down, easing up on the gas and applying pressure to the brakes.

"What are you doing?" he asked.

"I can't swerve in and out of traffic on Constitution," Sierra said. "The road is too clogged with hockey fans and tourists. And the cops are on high alert after the shooting this afternoon."

Drake grunted. "We might not have that long," Drake said. "Keep your foot on the pedal. I'll deal with the cops. Be careful, but not too careful."

Sierra looked at Drake nervously but nodded.

It was eight p.m. Time was ticking.

She pulled onto 10th Street NW. In the rear-view mirror, she watched as the Smithsonian National Museum of Natural History grew smaller and smaller. She looked at the building and felt a pang of regret. She'd been in the agency for three years, having moved to Langley from Pennsylvania. She'd been so busy as the director's assistant that she'd never found the time to go to the Smithsonian— something she'd promised herself she would do. As a child, she'd dreamed of walking through the hallowed halls of the massive building. She'd always been a bit of a history nut and knew that the Smithsonian had over 145 million specimens and artifacts within its walls. As she sped down the road toward Pennsylvania Avenue, she wondered if she'd get a chance to see it again.

She pulled to a stop at the intersection before Pennsylvania Avenue. Her hands rested on the steering wheel, her breaths heavy and quick.

"Are you nervous?" Drake asked.

"Yes."

"Don't be."

"Why not? If you're right about the ammonium nitrate, and you fail. I'm dead."

"You're death will be instant. If we fail, thousands will die today, but millions will die tomorrow. The president, if he's still alive, will have no choice but to respond and blame Russia. We'll be among the lucky ones. The world after tonight will be one of nuclear calamity."

"And you're trying to get me to relax?" Sierra said.

The light turned green across the street, and Sierra pulled into the intersection. She was driving in between a red van and a taxi cab.

When she was about halfway between the intersection, the van in front of her slammed on its brakes.

"What the hell?" Drake said.

Sierra shook her head. "These damn hockey fans."

Drake tried to peer around the traffic in front of them.

"You're not so bad, you know," Sierra said.

"You don't know me," Drake said while sticking his head out the open passenger's side window.

"You want to save the world."

"I want to stop the woman I love from destroying it."

Sierra turned to him, her mouth open in shock. "You love her? Didn't she stab you in the neck with the needle?" Sierra said. "I read the report."

Drake looked at Sierra. The beautiful young assistant who'd betrayed her former boss to help Price. He was about to respond when he noticed a pair of headlights approaching the SUV's driver's side.

"Sierra!" he shouted.

It was too late.

Before Sierra could react, a small, grey sedan slammed into the driver's side of the SUV, causing it to spin 180 degrees into the middle of the intersection.

The SUV came to a stop. Sierra was huddled over the steering wheel. Drake was dizzy. He felt drunk. Vulnerable.

Freeman stepped out of the grey vehicle. He seemed a little unsteady, as well. He stumbled up to the SUV and pulled out his pistol. Two men walked out of the van in front of them. There was a crazy look on Freeman's face. Suicidal. Dangerous. He'd bet on the wrong horse and was trying to make sure that no one won the game.

Drake shook his head and kicked open the passenger's side door. He crouched down, using the body of the SUV as cover.

"He got out of the vehicle!" Freeman shouted to the two men from the van.

Drake peered under the SUV's body. He watched as the two men from the van approached from the front. A nauseous, gross feeling rushed through his body. "Fuck," he muttered. He wanted to vomit. He felt sick to his stomach. The drugs in his system that Fowler had given him were going to make this difficult.

The moment of weakness allowed the two men to rush Drake. They pulled up their pistols.

Drake had his pistol holstered underneath his leather jacket.

As Freeman's men approached, Drake lifted his hands into the air.

The men walked up to him slowly. "You move, we shoot you."

"Keep him there. I want to kill him myself," Freeman howled from the other side of the SUV.

He didn't realize that his men had made a tactical error. An easy mistake to make. They'd moved too close to Drake. They were over-confident.

As Freeman began to walk around the SUV, Drake knocked the gun of the man closest to him out of the way. He then knelt on the ground, pulled out his pistol from his holster, and took two shots at the other man. One of them missed. The other hit him in the chest. Drake stood up and shot the man close to him in the head and turned around. He'd taken out two of them. He just needed to get Freeman.

As he twisted his body around toward the back of the SUV and Freeman, he heard the crackling thunder of gunfire.

He'd been too slow. Had he not missed the first shot, he might have had a chance at Freeman, but the drugs were moving through his body—nausea, drowsiness.

The bullet cut into Drake's lower back. A pink cloud of blood sprayed into the air—a vapor of pain. He dropped to his knees, his palms on the ground. His pistol loosened from his hand and slid along the concrete. He went to grab for it, but couldn't reach.

"You're going to die," Freeman said.

"Why are you doing this?" Drake asked. Pain swelled through his body in turbulent bursts.

"You killed my mentor. You ended his life."

"He was going to let ..." Drake stopped and took a deep breath. "Millions of lives are at stake. War. Death."

"Shut up!" Freeman said. "Shut up about your conspiracies! Tom was convinced you and Kate were lying about the ammonium nitrate.

He figured Kate brought you back to unsettle him, get him to make a mistake."

Drake reached again for his pistol. Freeman kicked it away.

"I'm going to enjoy this," Freeman said. "First you, then the bitch."

"Who are you calling a bitch!?"

It was Sierra. She was bleeding badly from a cut on her forehead. She pulled down on her pistol's trigger five times, lodging five bullets in Freeman's torso. The asshole dropped to the ground like a slab of meat on a butcher's cutting board.

Drake pushed himself up from the concrete and checked his wound. It wasn't good, but it wasn't as bad as it could've been. The bullet had gone clean through, and based on how he felt, it hadn't hit anything vital. Only guts. His only concern would be bleeding out.

"Are you okay?" He asked Sierra.

"No," she said. "Something is broken. I can't get out of the vehicle. I'm hurt bad."

Drake peered into the SUV. Her leg was twisted up in a bad way. "Stay here," he grunted and turned back to the street.

"Where are you going?" she asked.

"I'm going to stop her. I'm going to put an end to this."

"But you're shot!?"

"We can't fail."

Drake hobbled down Pennsylvania toward the side street where the art exhibit was taking place. Each step hurt; each breath felt like it could be his last.

It was the end-game.

At long last.

EIGHTY-THREE

Drake had just killed the security staff outside the art exhibit and was inside. He bled badly from the bullet he'd caught in his back but pushed through the pain. He used marble statues of Russian historical figures to keep his balance. Ivan the Terrible, Yuri Gagarin, Leo Tolstoy, and Joseph Stalin, to name a few.

The place was littered with senators and congressmen. It was a who's-who. A mess of wealth, power, and, worst of all, corruption. He was in the midst of the worst of the swamp. Whether or not those in attendance knew about Andrei's ties to the Russian government didn't matter. They'd been compromised, either too stupid or too power-hungry to realize it.

Drake hobbled from a statue of Catherine the Great and made his way toward the bar.

A bartender looked at him, not noticing the coat soaked in blood that Drake was wearing. "Are you okay, sir?"

"Hand me a drink."

"What kind?"

"Anything!"

The bartender had been instructed not to upset the guests by the security personnel. He was told to keep them all happy and do whatever they told him to do. The guests needed to stay at the exhibit. They couldn't leave. It was important.

Drake waited as the bartender poured a large glass of whiskey. Jack Daniels.

Drake shot it back, and his eyes narrowed. He felt better.

At the entrance of the large, dimly lit room were four security guards. Their guns were drawn, and they looked paranoid. He knew who they were looking for. He also knew they were trying to keep it cool. They didn't want to cause a stir.

Drake knew what he had to do.

It was time to cause a stir.

It was going to be impossible not to draw attention to himself, so he pulled out his pistol, fired it into the air, and caused every diplomat, senator, and politician in the room to scatter like leaves in the wind.

One last controlled burn. One last bit of chaos.

As dust crept down from the bullet holes Drake had etched in the ceiling, he pushed through the panicked denizens—the screaming fools. He pushed past the assholes who'd ignored him over for years. The bureaucratic oligarchy, who cared only about themselves and nothing else. He waded through the swamp.

Two of the security officers who'd stormed into the room spotted him and, now that there was no need to be inconspicuous about their presence, fired their pistols at him. Drake ducked. Two senators dropped dead in the crossfire, bullets drilled into their heads. The shots and dead bodies only increased the level of panic in the room.

Russian paintings, statues, and other art pieces either toppled over from the fleeing guests or were ripped up by stray bullets.

Drake ran through the room—wincing, pushing through the pain. Where was she? In his periphery, he spotted her. She was upstairs in a room with a large window. He knew it was her. He recognized her silhouette. Her shape. She was monitoring the situation down below.

He ran to a stairwell. More bullets chewed up fleeing senators, art pieces, or bits of wall.

Drake slammed shut the door in the stairwell and ran up toward her.

Two security guards busted through the closed door. Drake turned around and made sure that both of the security guards stayed down.

He pushed open the door of the room where Aya was, his gun raised, his steps slow on account of the loss of blood and the drugs he'd been given.

"Why haven't you set the bombs off?" Drake asked. "What are you waiting for?"

Aya's head hung over a small table that rested along the window's edge. She looked distraught. Her eyes were red. She turned to him and smiled. "I was waiting for you."

Drake stumbled up to her but then stopped. She lifted the remote trigger she was holding up in the air. "Don't come any closer," she said. "If I press this button, I'll kill us all. I'll start the war you're trying to stop. I'll end the war you started."

"The longer you wait, the fewer politicians you'll kill," Drake said. "What are you waiting for?"

"Are you challenging me?"

"Maybe."

"Screw you!"

"I know why you're angry," Drake said.

"And why is that?" Aya asked.

"Bbecause of our daughter."

Aya froze. She stared at Drake. Tears swelled down her cheeks. Her hand trembled. "Did Ajmal tell you before you killed him?"

"Your brother died protecting me. He told me about Amira. He would have told me more, but your pal Andrei killed him."

"Liar!"

"I'm not lying."

Aya shook her head and rubbed her brow. "Ajmal hated you."

"Do you blame him for hating me all those years?"

"No."

"You were all he had, and I stole you away from him."

"He was pathetic." Aya, still holding the trigger, walked to a small fridge in the room. She pulled out a bottle of water with her free hand. "I'm thirsty," she said. "I've drunk too much alcohol."

"You have cold feet. You don't want to do this."

"Fuck you!" she screamed. "You can't save me."

Drake had been holding it together as long as he could. He'd lost so much blood that he could hardly stand. He fell to his knees.

Aya noticed the blood around him. "Are you shot?"

"Yes."

"By who?"

"By the people I used to work for."

"The CIA?"

Drake nodded. "Seems there's a faction in the CIA who wants this attack to happen. More political games. More bullshit. It's just like the drone strike. If you set off that bomb, you won't get what you want."

Aya walked up to Drake. He had his hand on his pistol. As soon as he knew she wouldn't press down on the trigger, he'd end her. He'd have to.

"I see your hand on your pistol," she said.

"It doesn't have to be like this," he said.

"Your country took everything from me. Everything. They took away my daughter. They took away my innocence—my passion to fight for a better tomorrow. When I saw those dead children at that campsite ... I felt my soul leave my body. I thought my child, my sweet, sweet Amira, would lead me away from war. But alas, Amira was not long for this earth. She disappeared, and I realized I was made for war."

"Andrei took her away," Drake said. "Andrei's the one who killed Amira. Don't you see? You've been misled!"

"He was trying to help. Andrei gave me a way out. When he told me his plan, when he explained to me what he was doing, I knew I would be of great service to him."

Drake pushed himself up and rested his body against a cabinet in the office. He looked at Aya. She was still holding the trigger. There was a stone-like horror chiseled on her face—one of dread and pain. She seemed locked in a stare of sorrow and fear.

"It's only a matter of time before the men downstairs find you up here," Aya said. "They'll kill us both. I know Andrei instructed them to pull the trigger if I can't."

"And you can't?" Drake asked. He pulled out his pistol.

"I am torn," she said.

One of Andrei's security forces ran into the room. Drake quickly twisted his body back toward the door and put two bullets in the man's chest. Voices of other security personnel echoed from down the stairwell. They were loud and clear.

"Well, I guess I should just get to it," she said.

"Aya, don't!"

She turned to him. "I hate the world. I hate everything about it. The CIA never helped the rebellion the way they promised they would. They abandoned our people. They gave us just enough to keep us in a perpetual conflict with the Syrian National Army. They never cared about our struggle."

"You once fought for something real. You once fought for democracy. Don't let the world destroy you."

Two more of Andrei's men ran into the room. This time, both Drake and Aya fired on them. She'd grabbed a pistol that was resting on a table next to her. When they were done with the two security forces, Aya looked out over the art exhibit. The ground floor was mostly empty.

It'd been at least five minutes since Drake stormed into her office. If the senators and people she'd been sent to kill were now outside the building and running down the street, they'd almost be out of the death radius of the explosion. Time was running out.

Drake ran up to her and embraced her.

"Why don't you kill me?" she asked. "You could have shot me just then."

"Because I can't extinguish the only light I've known in my life."

"Screw you, Jason."

"I thought I'd be able to kill you, but I can't."

"I'm already dead," she said. "I died when our daughter died."

He looked up at her, wincing and fighting for every breath. "Give me the trigger."

"No."

He reached for it. She pulled away.

"Aya, please!"

"I love you, Jason."

"What?"

She grabbed his hand, the one holding the gun, and pulled it toward her chest. "You were never a monster," she said. "I was the monster."

"Aya, no."

Drake felt so weak; he couldn't stop her from pressing down the trigger of his pistol. She wasn't going to start a war.

She was going to end the war inside her head.

As the crackle of fire blew out from his pistol, as the bullet burst through her chest and splayed her blood across the window overlooking the exhibit, Aya fell to the ground. She dropped the trigger.

Drake, no longer having the strength to keep himself up, fell to the floor with her. More of Andrei's men stormed into the room. He reached for his gun. He needed to keep it from them. He needed to try, at least.

Andrei's security forces ran up to him, but they didn't make it. A blast of fire from a FBI agents machine gun burst through the window from the ground floor. Andrei's forces were chewed up like confetti. They dropped to the ground.

On the ground floor of the exhibit, a team of FBI agents scrambled toward the office.

Drake closed his eyes.

It was over.

It was finally over.

EIGHTY-FOUR

One week later

The damage was done. Life in the capital continued as it always had —nary a difference. Politicians arrived at Congress; citizens went about their day.

The headlines of the papers all read:

"Two Police Officers Dead. Senators Shot at Art Exhibit. Islamic Terrorists to Blame?"

Noise, Drake thought. Static. Lies. All fed by a media controlled by massive corporations who cared little for the truth and only about the ad revenue they'd generate from sensationalist headlines—from stoking emotions like they were kindle in a fire.

The civilians of the country would never know what was won or lost at Andrei's art exhibit. They would never understand that the world they had always known had almost ended.

Drake and Price were sat in the Oval Office. They were waiting for President Clarkson. Drake sighed and grimaced. His stomach felt like shit. There was a big white bandage wrapped around his lower torso, and it hurt to sit, breathe, and laugh. The doctor said he'd have to keep the bandage there for at least three weeks—the bastard. Drake wouldn't be able to leave the capital until then.

"What is it?" Price asked Drake, noticing the look on his face. "You're going to be commended for a job well done. You might even get a medal."

Drake scoffed. "A job well done? This whole structure is too fragile. The foundation of this whole place, this country—it's built on a bedrock of mud, sand, and filth. It will crumble. It will fall. We just held off its end for the time being."

Price shook her head. "No," she said. "You re-established order. You did what you were trained to do. As long as this country has people like you, we will be alright."

Drake rolled his eyes. "Cut it out with that crap. That's the same BS you told me when you were training me to be a Terminus officer. I don't care about order. I don't care about what I was trained to do. Don't you see? Terminus created Aya. The CIA created a monster. You need to re-evaluate."

"I don't believe that," Price said.

"Then you're ignorant."

"Screw you, Jason."

Drake shook his head.

The door to the Oval Office swung open. President Clarkson walked into the room. He wasn't smiling. He sat down across from Drake and Price. "Two dead police officers, a dozen or so dead private security personnel, a bunch of dead CIA officers on a farm, and four dead senators. What the hell happened?" he asked.

"Sir, I can—" Price said before Drake cut her off.

"We stopped a world war, sir."

"World war?" Clarkson said, sitting behind his desk.

"Yes," Drake said. "We found the ammonium nitrate."

"What he's trying to say, sir," Price said, "is that we prevented an international conflict between Russia and the United States. It turns out that an ex-SVR spy, someone who'd established numerous connections here in the capital under the alias Dimitri Nabakov, was holding an art exhibit. He'd smuggled the ammonium nitrate from Russia to Washington under the guise of Russian art pieces. He was using a Syrian rebel fighter he'd recruited to complete the final stage of the mission. Her name was Aya Khan."

President Clarkson nodded and rubbed his chin. "The Kremlin will most certainly deny any involvement."

"My suggestion, sir," Price said. "Let the papers think it was an ISIS attack. Don't let the Kremlin know that one of their former spies was working behind their back, trying to pull their strings. Let them figure that out on their own."

Clarkson nodded. "That's good. I like that. And we have the ammonium nitrate?"

"The FBI is cleaning it up," Price said. "This is their jurisdiction, after all." She said it with a wry smile, knowing full well that Clarkson knew Drake was responsible for some of the deaths in the city that night and that the CIA had operated in the capital without clearance.

Drake sat across from them in silence. He felt angry. He hated political machinations. The gears and cogs of the political and intelligence body were hard at work, finding new ways to keep the American public out of the loop, to hide the truth.

Clarkson turned to Drake. "And Director Price tells me you're the one to thank for all of this," he said. "Your country owes you a great deal, young man."

Drake stared into Clarkson's eyes, trying to get a read on him. All he'd seen of the president was clips from the nightly news or photos on news websites. Clarkson seemed like a good guy, albeit in over his head.

"Don't thank me," Drake said. "I cleaned up the mess we created. We're lucky this wasn't another 9/11."

"Absolutely," Clarkson said.

Price turned to Drake. "And that leads us to our next topic of discussion," she said. "Jason, what would it take for you to stay? What would it take for you to continue the fight? The medical staff at George Washington University Hospital said no one could have survived that much blood loss. They said it was a miracle—one in a million. We need you. You're an asset. All that time we spent making you. You can't leave us. You need to stay."

Drake turned to Price and smiled. She had the eyes of a director. She'd bought in. She'd become what she'd feared, and she didn't even know it.

He smiled and gave her his answer.

* * *

Sierra met Drake outside the White House. She winked at Drake as he hobbled into the back of the SUV. Houston met him in the back and licked his face. Drake scratched the head of the dog. The plucky little animal deserved as many accolades as him.

"Where to?" Sierra asked.

"The Riggs," Drake said, referring to the hotel the CIA had booked for him.

"Absolutely."

Sierra told the driver where they needed to go. Her leg was still in bad condition. Thankfully, it wasn't broken, only bruised. Still, the doctor said it would take anywhere between two to four weeks to heal. She wouldn't be able to drive a vehicle for a month.

As the driver pulled out of the White House's long parking lot and drove down Constitution Avenue toward the Riggs, Sierra turned to Drake. "What did you tell her?"

"I told her there was no way I was coming back to the agency."

"What did she say?"

"She said what any director would say," he said. "She said I was a fool."

"And how did you respond?"

"I told her what her ex-husband would have told her."

"And what was that?"

"That she was being an arsehole."

Sierra blushed. "That's crude."

Drake smiled. "Clyde was one in a million. Maybe even one in seven billion."

"You want to watch the hockey game tonight?" Sierra asked. "You can explain it to me."

A wide smile spread across Drake's face. "That sounds nice. My team is playing."

"Who are they?"

"The Dallas Stars."

Once at the hotel, the two of them, along with Houston, got out of the SUV and made their way to Drake's room.

"You didn't have to come up," Drake said.

"I know," Sierra said. "But I want to."

She walked slowly toward the window and looked out over the city. "So, if you're not going to stay here, where will you go?"

"Some place quiet."

"Where's that?"

Drake walked up behind Sierra. He inhaled the scent of her sweet perfume and studied the nape of her neck. She was beyond beautiful. There was a warmness to her.

Sierra looked up at him. His eyes seemed a million miles away. She grabbed his wrist. "Hold me," she said.

He kissed her, embraced her fullness, her youthful form.

"I won't be leaving the capital for a couple weeks," he said. "But when I do go, you need to keep an eye on Kate. She's a good person, but like all of us ... she's going to make mistakes."

Sierra nodded.

The two of them stumbled into the bedroom.

Drake kicked the door shut before Houston could follow.

EIGHTY-FIVE

One month later

The population of Deadwood, South Dakota, was about 1,500. Everyone knew everyone else. There was a hockey rink, a bar, one barbershop, and a sawmill. It was a salt of the earth kind of place. Rural, and far enough from DC that Drake knew he'd find some peace.

Deadwood was nestled along the banks of the Flatwater River in a low valley between two Black Hill mountains. A thick brush of pine and evergreens rose along the slopes. There was only one paved road in the whole place—the downtown strip.

Drake pulled his black Dodge truck into the police station parking lot. He was looking for work.

The sheriff's name was Elliot Kilroy. He was a man in his seventies and had a thick, stringy mustache that curled up at the ends.

"What brings you into town, stranger?" Kilroy said. He had a weird drawl in his voice. "You best not be bringing any trouble to these parts. Deadwood's a quiet town."

"I'm not looking for trouble."

"And what are you looking for, boy?"

"Work."

"Work? You some kind of law enforcement officer?" Kilroy looked Drake up and down. "You certainly have the frame and the presence, but I can tell you lack a certain constitution about yourself. You're missing pieces."

Drake gave the strange old man a confused look. "Listen, I'm not here to help you get cats out of trees or wash graffiti off of walls. I'm here to hunt. I came here because I heard there was some wild game causing trouble on the walking trails. Cougars, wolves and bears."

"You know how to use a rifle?"

"Yes."

Kilroy wiped his dry lips with his tongue. Drake heard the old sheriff's whiskers crackle as the man's tongue rolled past each fiber. Kilroy swallowed and stood up, adjusting his belt buckle. "You kill me the cat that's been terrorizing our neighborhood dogs, and I'll give you a hundred dollars. When it's done, come back for more work."

Drake shook the sheriff's hand and walked back to his truck. He opened the door and met Houston, who was sitting on the passenger seat. "Looks like we've found a home, buddy."

Houston's yawned and wagged his tail. Drake pulled out of the parking lot and drove out of town and into the woods.

EPILOGUE

Months later...

It was dark. Too dark.

They dragged him along cobbled, damp stones and tossed him into a small, cold cell. His body ached all over. His stomach, especially. How could it not? After all those surgeries.

The aresholes.

He was surprised to be alive.

Lucky? No.

They'd kept him alive to torture him. To squeeze him like an orange, believing there was still some juice inside. The scurvy-tongued dickheads, desperate for intelligence.

Colt was alive, though he was damned sure that everyone he knew believed he was dead.

After the shootout in the mansion, where he'd inhaled six bullets in the belly, he was dragged to a medical office in Sochi. He remembered his vision going dark as he was pulled along the expensive Persian rug in that office. Cody's face appeared. He'd thought he was finally going to find his peace. He saw the light. He heard Cody's laugh. He was almost there.

But then he awoke on an operating table.

The doctor took bullet after bullet out of him and stitched him up. They even fixed his heart valves, said they'd spotted a couple of blockages. He'd tried to break free but couldn't. His hands were strapped down with leather bracelets. He was administered a sleeping agent and passed out.

The mercenaries Andrei Zadorov had hired had brought him to Moscow. They were hoping the KGB would give them something of value for the SAS captain. Ten million rubles, maybe twenty.

Colt was taken in.

Andrei's men settled for five million.

And for three weeks, Russian intelligence tried to break Colt. They wanted to know what the hell was going on.

They had questions about the ammonium nitrate, about Andrei, and about the C-17 that had crash-landed on Russian soil.

Colt refused to talk. He didn't bend. He was trying to die.

But that bastard doctor in Sochi had done a bang-up job. His ticker was working better than ever.

Eventually, they came to terms with the fact that Colt wasn't going to talk. They figured he'd need a stint in the Gulag. They thought a month or two in Siberia would be enough to get him to squeal.

"Siberia will break you," the KGB interrogator said to him. "It will crush your soul. It will bury your will to live."

"I doubt that," Colt said. "I've been trying to bury my will to live for years now."

Colt was injected with another sleep agent.

When he opened his eyes again, he was being dragged through the damp, cold cells of the Gulag.

They tossed him into his cell, where his body brushed up against a grimy stone wall. He felt a draft and heard laughter.

"Who's there?" he asked.

"You're Scottish?" the person in the cell with Colt said in English but with a thick Russian accent. The bastard was educated.

"And you're a damn Ruskie."

The Russian man laughed. "I'm from a city called Gerdansk," the voice said. "I'm a doctor. I was betrayed."

"By who?"

"Someone you won't know."

"The world's a small place," Colt said. "And by the looks of it, we'll be here a little while."

"I was betrayed by a man named Elias Spector."

Colt's eyebrow perked. "Jesus, Mary, and Joseph," he said. He didn't like cursing, but there was always a time and a place. "Spector?"

"Yes," the Russian said. "He has my wife."

"And why are you here?"

"Because I wouldn't experiment on children."

"Children?"

"Yes," the doctor said. "The Russian military wanted me to perform medical experiments on children from Syria. They'd purchased them a man named Andrei Zadorov."

Colt took a deep breath. "Name is Clyde Colt, former SAS."

"I see," the Russian man said. "My name is Alexander Kruschev."

"I'm going to get you out of here, mate."

"I've been here for years. I doubt that."

"I will. Elias Spector worked with my ex-wife and I just helped kill Andrei Zadorov. You're going to tell me everything you know."

DON'T MISS WHAT HAPPENS NEXT

BUY BOOK 2 NOW

AUTHOR'S NOTE

To sign up for my mailing list, please visit: www.creatorcontact.com/
auston-king/
The mailing list will only be used to update you about upcoming
releases.

You made it to the end!

Thank you.

It means a lot.

Seriously.

I spent many nights slaving away, pulling my hair out, trying to find the best way to bring this story to life. This was my first thriller novel, and I wasn't quite sure how to tackle it.

My aim was to put together a story that was fun and easy to read. If you made it this far, I can only hope that I accomplished that goal.

If you spotted any errors or slight grammatical mistakes along the way, please feel free to reach me at austonking@creatorcontact.com

Even if you'd like to chat about the story, I'd love to hear your thoughts.

There is not a big corporation behind this book. I don't have a dozen editors who spot every missing word or a misplaced comma. All I have is you.

The reader.
Thank you.
On to the next one,
Auston King

ACKNOWLEDGMENTS

There were a series of people who helped make this book possible.

In order of no importance:
Meghan
Jack
Nick
Lawrence
Denise
Karen
Steve
Chuck
Brian
Sherrie
Linda
Frank
Olga
Pat
Max
Kia
Dolores
Thank you.

ABOUT THE AUTHOR

Auston King is an author based in the United States. The Assassin's Betrayal is his first full-length thriller. He lives with his wife, Meghan, his daughter, Leighton, and their pet chihuahua, Mya. His beloved four-legged friend Vinny died during the writing of this novel.

This one's for you, bokah.

If you would like to reach out to Auston, please feel free to email him at austonking@creatorcontact.com or visit his Facebook page.

 facebook.com/AustonKingAuthor

Made in United States
North Haven, CT
18 June 2023

37929102R00202